Marcia Willett's early life was devoted to the ballet, but her dreams of becoming a ballerina ended when she grew out of the classical proportions required. She had always loved books, and a family crisis made her take up a new career as a novelist – a decision she has never regretted. She lives in a beautiful and wild part of Devon where she loves to be visited by her son and his young family.

For more information on Marcia Willett and her books, see her website at www.marciawillett.co.uk

www.transworldbooks.co.uk

D0230647

*Also by Marcia Willett*

FORGOTTEN LAUGHTER
A WEEK IN WINTER
WINNING THROUGH
HOLDING ON
LOOKING FORWARD
SECOND TIME AROUND
STARTING OVER
HATTIE'S MILL
THE COURTYARD
THEA'S PARROT
THOSE WHO SERVE
THE DIPPER
THE BIRDCAGE
THE CHILDREN'S HOUR
THE GOLDEN CUP
ECHOES OF THE DANCE
MEMORIES OF THE STORM
THE WAY WE WERE

# THE PRODIGAL WIFE

## MARCIA WILLETT

**CORGI BOOKS**

TRANSWORLD PUBLISHERS
61–63 Uxbridge Road, London W5 5SA
A Random House Group Company
www.transworldbooks.co.uk

**THE PRODIGAL WIFE**
**A CORGI BOOK: 9780552158473**

First published in Great Britain
in 2009 by Bantam Press
an imprint of Transworld Publishers
Corgi edition published 2010

Copyright © Marcia Willett 2009

Marcia Willett has asserted her right under the Copyright, Designs
and Patents Act 1988 to be identified as the author of this work.

This book is a work of fiction and, except in the case
of historical fact, any resemblance to actual persons,
living or dead, is purely coincidental.

A CIP catalogue record for this book
is available from the British Library.

This book is sold subject to the condition that it shall not,
by way of trade or otherwise, be lent, resold, hired out,
or otherwise circulated without the publisher's prior
consent in any form of binding or cover other than that
in which it is published and without a similar condition,
including this condition, being imposed on the
subsequent purchaser.

Addresses for Random House Group Ltd companies outside the UK
can be found at: www.randomhouse.co.uk
The Random House Group Ltd Reg. No. 954009

The Random House Group Limited supports The Forest Stewardship
Council (FSC®), the leading international forest certification organisation.
Our books carrying the FSC label are printed on FSC® certified paper. FSC is
the only forest certification scheme endorsed by the leading environmental
organisations, including Greenpeace. Our paper procurement policy can be
found at www.randomhouse.co.uk/environment

Typeset in 11½/15½pt Garamond Book by
Kestrel Data, Exeter, Devon
Printed and bound by
CPI Group (UK) Ltd, Croydon, CR0 4YY

6 8 10 9 7 5

MIX
Paper from
responsible sources
FSC® C016897

**To my sisters' children
and their children**

# THE CHADWICK FAMILY TREE

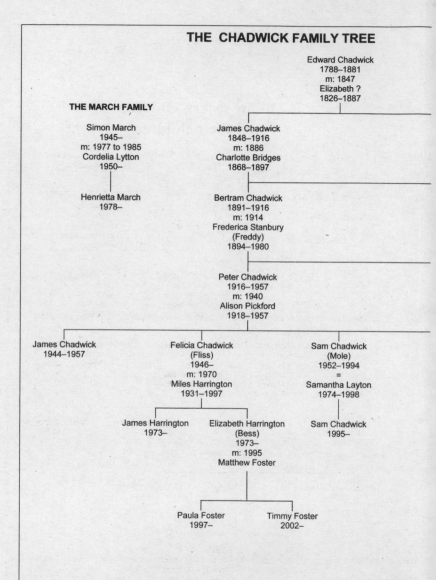

Edward Chadwick
1788–1881
m: 1847
Elizabeth ?
1826–1887

**THE MARCH FAMILY**

Simon March
1945–
m: 1977 to 1985
Cordelia Lytton
1950–

James Chadwick
1848–1916
m: 1886
Charlotte Bridges
1868–1897

Henrietta March
1978–

Bertram Chadwick
1891–1916
m: 1914
Frederica Stanbury
(Freddy)
1894–1980

Peter Chadwick
1916–1957
m: 1940
Alison Pickford
1918–1957

James Chadwick
1944–1957

Felicia Chadwick
(Fliss)
1946–
m: 1970
Miles Harrington
1931–1997

Sam Chadwick
(Mole)
1952–1994
=
Samantha Layton
1974–1998

James Harrington
1973–

Elizabeth Harrington
(Bess)
1973–
m: 1995
Matthew Foster

Sam Chadwick
1995–

Paula Foster
1997–

Timmy Foster
2002–

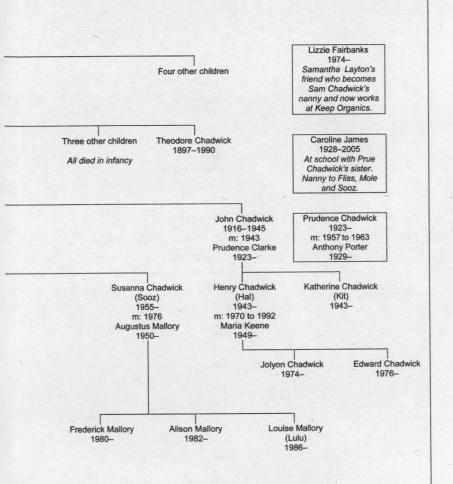

Four other children

Lizzie Fairbanks
1974–
*Samantha Layton's
friend who becomes
Sam Chadwick's
nanny and now works
at Keep Organics.*

Three other children

*All died in infancy*

Theodore Chadwick
1897–1990

Caroline James
1928–2005
*At school with Prue
Chadwick's sister.
Nanny to Fliss, Mole
and Sooz.*

John Chadwick
1916–1945
m: 1943
Prudence Clarke
1923–

Prudence Chadwick
1923–
m: 1957 to 1963
Anthony Porter
1929–

Susanna Chadwick
(Sooz)
1955–
m: 1970 to 1992
Augustus Mallory
1950–

Henry Chadwick
(Hal)
1943–
m: 1970 to 1992
Maria Keene
1949–

Katherine Chadwick
(Kit)
1943–

Jolyon Chadwick
1974–

Edward Chadwick
1976–

Frederick Mallory
1980–

Alison Mallory
1982–

Louise Mallory
(Lulu)
1986–

**NOTES:**
Maria Chadwick marries Adam Wishart (1948 – 2006) in 1995 following her divorce from Henry Chadwick.
Henry Chadwick and Felicia Harrington marry in 1998.
Full details may be found in The Chadwick Trilogy: *Looking Forward, Holding On* and *Winning Through.*

# PART ONE

# CHAPTER ONE

The wind was rising; it plucked restlessly at the storm-weathered stone walls and breathed in the chimney. It stroked the sea's glittering moonlit surface to little peaks and rustled drily amongst the stiff broken bracken on the cliff. The row of coastguard cottages turned blank eyes to the long rollers that creamed over the sand, sinking away to a delicate salty froth at the tide's reach. A cloud slid across the moon's round bright face. On the steep, slippery, gorse-plucking cliff path, a yellow light flickered and danced and disappeared.

Drifting between uneasy sleep and wakefulness, Cordelia startled wide awake, eyes straining in the darkness. As she slipped out of bed and crossed to the window the moon rose free of the cloud, laying silver and black patterns across the floor. Out at sea, the brilliance of its shining path, fractured with light like splintered glass, cast the water on each side of it into an oily blackness. Once she would have pulled on some clothes and climbed down the steep granite staircase to the tiny cove below the cottage; now, common sense prevailed: she had a long journey to make in the morning. Yet she lingered, bewitched as she always was by the unearthly magic; watching the black swirl of the tide round the shining rocks.

Was that a figure on the path below or clouds crossing on the moon? Alert, she stared downwards into the shifting, shadowy darkness where shapes thickened and dislimned as vaporous mist drifted and clung along the cliff edge. Behind her the bedroom door swung silently open and a large pale shape loomed. Sensing a presence, glancing backwards, she muffled a tiny scream.

'McGregor, you wretch. I wish you wouldn't do that.'

The tall, gaunt deerhound padded gently to her side and she laid her hand on his rough head. They stared together into the night. To the west, beyond Stoke Point, the squat, bright-lit ferry from Plymouth edged into sight, chugging its way to Roscoff. No other light showed.

'You would have barked, wouldn't you? If anyone were out there, you would have barked. Well, you can stay here now. No more wandering round the house in the dark. On your bed. Go on.'

The great hound obeyed; collapsing quietly on to a blanket of tartan fleece, his eyes watchful, glinting. Cordelia climbed back into bed and pulled the quilt up high, smiling a secret smile; thinking about the morning. Even after thirty years as a journalist she was still excited by the prospect of journeys and new assignments, and this one promised to be fun: a drive into Gloucestershire to find an ancient soke and to interview its almost equally ancient owner – and a meeting on a narrowboat with her lover.

She slept at last but the deerhound raised his narrow head from time to time, listening. Once or twice he growled deep in his throat but Cordelia was sleeping soundly now and didn't hear him.

She woke early and was away, travelling north, by a quarter to eight. It was raining hard. McGregor reclined gracefully on the back seat of her small hatchback. He stared with regal indifference at the drenched countryside and when they turned on to the A38 at Wrangaton, heading north towards Exeter, he sighed and put his head down on his paws. Clearly the brief run on the cliff he'd had earlier was to be his ration for a while. Cordelia chatted to him between bursts of song – she needed music whilst she was driving – and noticed in the mirror that something had been caught under the rear-screen wiper. She switched it on and the fragment – a leaf? – was dragged to and fro across the window but wasn't dislodged.

Cordelia switched it off, hummed a bar or two of 'Every Time We Say Goodbye' with Ella Fitzgerald and thought about the soke and its elderly owner, who was clearly thrilled at the prospect of being written up for *Country Illustrated*. She'd spoken to him on the telephone and he sounded an absolute sweetie. She did a quick mental check-up: had she remembered to pack the spare batteries for her tape recorder? She pulled off at the Sedgemoor service station and got out so as to give McGregor a run. Whilst he paced elegantly along the hedge line, Cordelia removed the small square of sodden paper from behind the windscreen wiper. It almost came apart in her fingers but she could see patches of bright colour and she tried to smooth it flat on the bonnet of the car, squeezing out the moisture, puzzled as to how it could have become wedged. She guessed that it might be an advertisement, tucked there by somebody in the supermarket car park, but she was surprised that she hadn't noticed it before. The rain had done its work and it was impossible, now, to guess at what it had been. She scrumpled the fragment and put it into her pocket. The rain had stopped and gleams of watery light slipped between the rags of cloud that were blown before the south-westerly wind. She opened the door for McGregor to scramble on to the back seat and then went to get a mocha and a *pain au chocolat.*

Angus phoned just after she'd turned off the M5 at Junction 13 and was heading towards Stroud. She pulled in at the side of the road and picked up her mobile.

'Where are you?' she asked. 'Have the boys gone?'

'Yes, they're safely *en route.* Don't worry. The coast is clear. I'm on my way to Tewkesbury, hoping to moor up overnight in the marina. You've got the map?'

'Yes. I'll phone when I've finished at the soke. I've no idea how long it might take. Did they love the narrowboat?'

'It was a huge success. We've all agreed that we want to do it again. Speak later then? Good luck.'

She drove on through Stroud and into the lanes that led to Frampton Parva, stopping once or twice to check the directions. As she turned into the lane signposted to the village she saw the soke at once and pulled on to the verge under the hedge. It stood across the fields at the end of its own drive; golden stone, three storeys high, mullion windows, and, only a few yards further along the lane, a tiny, beautiful church. The combination of church and house was quite perfect and she wondered if the photographer had spotted it.

Cordelia let McGregor out, knowing that he might have to wait in the car for some while, and stood enjoying the scene and the warm sunshine. Now she could see two figures moving outside the soke: one gesticulating, the other slung about with equipment. So the photographer had arrived; she hoped it was Will Goddard. She liked working with Will. She put her hands into her pockets and her fingers came into contact with the ball of paper. She took it out and tried to flatten it into some kind of identifiable shape. It was drier now and she could just make out a picture. It looked like a poorly photocopied photograph; two people in an imposing doorway, at the top of some steps – a hotel, perhaps? – turning towards each other. She half recognized the embroidered denim jacket as her own, but why should it be? Cordelia turned it over to see if there might be some clue on the back of the paper. There had been something written there but the ink was smudged and illegible. She folded the paper more carefully this time and dropped it back into her pocket.

McGregor came loping towards her and she

coaxed him into the car with the promise of a biscuit and settled him again. She checked her bag: tape recorder, notebook, pencil; ran her eye over a list of questions to refresh her memory and drove down to the gateway of Charteris Soke.

Three hours later, on the narrowboat, while Angus made tea, she described the soke: the courtroom with its beautiful judge's seat set within an ancient, barred window, the carved stone fireplace with its coat of arms, and the secret door to the tower, which had once been a fortified treasury; and its charming owner whose family had lived there for centuries.

Presently she stretched and looked about her appreciatively.

'This is fun,' she said. 'And we've got all day tomorrow to ourselves. What bliss.'

'I thought we'd go upriver to Pershore,' he said. 'Let's hope McGregor likes being a water-gypsy. Does Henrietta know where you are? How is she acclimatizing to house-sitting on the Quantocks after her busy life nannying in London?'

Cordelia made a face. 'With difficulty. My poor daughter is in shock but coping.'

'I know you told me about it on the phone but I've lost the plot a bit. What exactly happened?'

'Oh, it's just so sad. Susan and Iain – that's

17

the couple Henrietta works for – have split up. Apparently Iain's been having an affair for ages and poor Susan hadn't the least suspicion until he said he was leaving. It's been a frightful shock for everyone. Well, Susan's parents were planning to go to New Zealand to see their other daughter and they decided that the best thing was simply to take Susan and the children with them to give everyone a breathing space. They all went off last week.'

'And where does the cottage on the Quantocks come in?'

'That's where Susan's parents live. Maggie and Roger. There was no room for Henrietta at the daughter's house in New Zealand, you see, so she's gone down to look after the dogs and the old ponies while they're all away. I've sent her a text and told her I'll be home on Sunday night. And no, I haven't told her I'm here with you – but you knew that. She'll expect me to be in a B & B. That's what I usually do.'

'You'll have to tell her one day, especially now that I've moved down to Dartmouth,' Angus said – and grimaced at her exasperated expression. 'OK, OK. I promise not to mention it again. Not this weekend, anyway. I thought we'd have supper at the White Bear. Then we'll get away early in the morning and I'll cook breakfast somewhere upriver.'

'Sounds wonderful,' Cordelia said. 'Look, d'you mind if I just make a few notes while today's all still so fresh in my mind? Then I can put the soke out of my head and relax, and we'll take McGregor for a walk along the towpath.'

# CHAPTER TWO

Henrietta recognized the voice at once, though this morning the message was a different one.

*'Hi, Roger. It's me again. It's ten o'clock on Tuesday morning. I might pop in later today on my way down from Bristol. Round about four o'clock. Sorry I keep missing you.'*

Instinctively she glanced at her watch: just after eleven.

'It's your fault he keeps missing us, whoever he is,' she told the dogs, who had subsided into furry golden heaps on the cold slates. 'He always phones when we're out for a walk.'

Their feathery tails wagged with polite indifference and Juno, mother and grandmother of the other two retrievers, heaved herself to her feet so as to drink lavishly from the large bowl of water beside the dresser. The kitchen door stood open to the warm September sunshine and a delightful confusion of rich colour: pinky mauve Japanese anemones, crimson and purple Michaelmas daisies, scarlet montbretia all grouped together and dusted by the powdery sunlight. Henrietta made coffee and carried it to the little wooden chair outside the door. She felt that something significant was about to happen: there was a kind of magic in the soft golden glow that overlaid this small court; an expectant, hushed waiting in the deep rural silence. Juno came out to sit beside her, leaning against the chair, and Henrietta slid her arm around the furry neck and laid her cheek on the top of Juno's head.

'You miss them all, don't you?' she murmured sympathetically. 'Well, so do I, but we might as well get used to it.'

They sat quietly together, Henrietta sipping her coffee and wondering about the voice on the answering machine, whilst Juno's heavy head rested against her knee. The first message had been waiting for her just a few hours after Roger and Maggie had left for London on the first leg of their journey nearly a week ago. To distract the dogs from their departure she'd driven them off through the narrow lanes towards Crowcombe, up to the Great Wood, and taken them for a walk on Robin Upright's Hill where she could look out across Bridgwater Bay. When she'd returned to the cottage, the green light on the answerphone had been flashing. She'd hurried to it, fearful that there had been some kind of problem; that the train had been delayed and they'd failed to meet up with Susan and the children.

'*Hi, Roger, it's Joe. Thanks for looking out the books for me. I'll be coming your way soon. Love to Maggie.*'

There had been no instructions about Joe's books, although a carrier bag stood on the chest in the hall. She'd glanced inside and seen that it did indeed contain books: books about boats and harbours. Well, that wasn't surprising given that Roger was a retired naval officer with a very wide knowledge of old sailing boats.

But who was this Joe? Henrietta had the oddest feeling that she knew him; that she recognized his voice – she'd even imagined that she'd met him and that they'd talked. Now, sitting in the sun with Juno stretched out at her feet, she could visualize him: tall, with fair hair, hands sketching shapes in the air as he talked. But where and when? She pulled her long thick plait over one shoulder and twiddled the end, drawing it through her fingers. It occurred to her that he might be a member of one of the naval families with whom she was connected by the network of married quarters, naval hirings and boarding schools. Clearly he was on familiar terms

22

with Roger and Maggie. A new thought, that he also might be of their generation, gave rise to a sudden and quite disproportionate sense of disappointment. Of course she could dial 1471, get his number – unless it was withheld – telephone this Joe and tell him Roger was away but she'd found a bag of books that might be for him. Perhaps she simply wanted to enjoy the mystery for a little longer: to allow her imagination to weave amusing scenarios which distracted from her present problems.

His voice sounded young, she told herself firmly. And that image of him talking, explaining something to her, was the image of a young man. Yet, if they'd met, how could she have forgotten his name? She finished her coffee with mixed emotions: excitement, apprehension, curiosity.

'Get a grip,' she told herself. 'He's probably a boring old fart with a passion for tea clippers.'

Nevertheless, she decided that she'd drive into Bicknoller after lunch and buy something special for tea – a delicious sponge perhaps. Luckily Roger had a very large stock of alcohol, though she'd get a lemon in case Joe liked a gin and tonic. She wondered what she could rustle up for supper . . .

'Honestly!' she cried aloud in vexation. 'What are you *doing*?'

Juno struggled up, alarmed by the sudden cry,

and Henrietta stroked her head remorsefully.

'Sorry,' she said. 'Sorry, Juno. I'm losing it. That's what comes of having nothing to do. I'm missing the children, and Susan dashing in and out, and all the usual dramas.'

Another thought occurred to her. Gently pushing Juno's bulk to one side, Henrietta got up and went into the house. She hesitated for a moment before replaying the message, and then she found her mobile and dialled her mother's number.

Two telephone calls before she'd even got to her desk, which was covered with computer printouts, articles snipped from newspapers and journals, reference books. Wandering between the kitchen and the study, mug of coffee in hand, she was just getting the first sentence of her piece into her head: 'Charteris Soke in Frampton Parva is the only house of its kind known to exist this far south.' Pause there. Was she absolutely certain that this was true? Well, that could be thoroughly checked later. Now. Should it be *'delightful* Charteris Soke'? Or *'charming* Charteris Soke'? Either adjective seemed overused; dull. Anyway, follow that with a bit about what a soke actually is. Cordelia riffled about for a relevant piece of paper, checked the dictionary definition of soke or *soc*: the right to hold a local court; or the territory under the jurisdiction of a particular court. She studied the photographs of the little ancient manor house – the shape of the piece was gradually forming – and then her mobile phone shrieked again in the bowels of the kitchen and she put down the coffee mug and ran out into the passage, finally snatching the phone up from beneath the pile of newspapers on the kitchen table.

'Hi,' she cried breathlessly. 'Hello? Are you still there? Oh, Henrietta. Oh, thank goodness. I thought I was too late and you'd hung up. Did you get my text to say that I was back? How's it going? Are you settling in?'

'I'm fine, Mum. Yes, I got your text. Everything's fine. Look, I just thought I'd check with you. I've had this message on the answerphone from someone called Joe who wants to drop in later and who obviously knows Roger and Maggie very well, so I'm wondering if there might be a naval connection. I feel I recognize the voice. Do we know someone called Joe? My generation, not yours. Does it ring any bells?'

'Jo.' Cordelia cast about amongst her large circle of naval friends and acquaintances. 'Jo. That's short for Joanna, I suppose, or Josephine . . .'

'No, no. Sorry. This is a man not a girl.'

'Ah.' Cordelia revised her ideas. 'Joe. Right. Joseph. No, I can't think of a Joe offhand.'

'Me neither. Only the voice sounds familiar. Never mind. Are you OK?'

'Fine. Wrestling with that piece for *Country Illustrated*. Sure you don't want some company? It must be so odd to be suddenly set down in the middle of rural Somerset with nothing but Maggie's menagerie for company after the house in London with Susan and . . . with Susan and the children. I could come over if you're feeling lonely. Or we could meet in Taunton for a spot of retail therapy.'

'Honestly, I'm fine. Really. And anyway, you're obviously in the middle of your article. I'll let you know who Joe is later on. 'Bye.'

Cordelia went back to her study, her mind all over the place, completely distracted. Had there been a veiled criticism there? *You're obviously in the middle of your article.* Love for her daughter filled her, along with anxiety and compassion and guilt, especially guilt: all the emotions guaranteed to quench any creative flow. She fiddled about, tidying papers, closing books and putting them back on shelves, sipping at the lukewarm coffee whilst a question she'd heard recently on a radio programme nibbled at her thoughts.

*Are we the first generation to need to be friends with our children?*

Well, are we? She thought about her own parents:

26

caring but detached. None of this emotional soul-baring for them; no in-depth discussions of their offsprings' feelings or needs. She could well remember her father's reaction to her own separation and subsequent divorce, his expression of shock fading into distaste when she told him that Simon was leaving her.

'Another woman, I suppose. No, I don't want the sordid details. I can only say that I'm glad your mother is dead.'

No, no. Things relating to the emotions were best kept hidden; not talked of; stiff upper lip.

*Are we the first generation to need to be friends with our children?*

Well, she did need to be friends with Henrietta. She wanted to encourage and support and be there for her. But, oh, the grief and anxiety not to be shown, never to be shown, just gnawing away inside.

Henrietta's little pinched white face: 'Is Daddy leaving us because I got bored of cleaning out Boris properly?'

Boris was the hamster, a handsome, benign, if intellectually limited, creature.

'Bored *with*, darling, or *by*. No, of course he isn't. It's just that sometimes friendships stop working properly.'

27

'But Daddy's still friends with me?'

'Of course he is. And always will be.' Until he'd written to his daughter when she was fifteen; a creamy white envelope containing a message as destructive as a bomb whose fallout was still causing damage nearly twelve years later.

Cordelia sat down and stared at the computer screen, unhelpfully blank just like her mind. How inept she'd been at the time. How ineffectual and helpless. She'd felt exactly the same when she'd arrived in Tregunter Road a month ago to find the place in turmoil.

Suddenly the screen seems to dissolve before her eyes and instead she sees Henrietta's face, her eyes wary, the old familiar shadow slicing down between them like a sword, cutting off any exchange of warmth and love.

She's up in London for a lunch at the Arts Club with her agent. She stays with friends in Fulham but drops in, as arranged, to see Henrietta on the way to Dover Street. As soon as the door opens she knows that something is wrong. The usual atmosphere of busy conviviality is missing. No sound comes from the two big basement rooms from which Susan directs her small but successful mail-order business, and the kitchen is deserted: no Iain snatching a moment from his computer with the morning paper and a cup of coffee; no children running in from the garden to greet her.

Cordelia puts her bag on the table, looks around, puzzled.

'Is it a bad moment?' she asks.

Henrietta's eyes are enormous with shock. 'Iain's gone,' she says. 'He's just packed up and gone.'

They stare at each other. 'Gone?' Her own voice is husky, fearful. 'D'you mean he's left Susan?'

Henrietta nods. Suddenly her expression changes, grows distant. 'Yes, gone. This morning. Apparently he's been having an affair for ages. Susan's gutted.'

They continue to stare at each other; other memories surfacing, resentment stirring. Susan's voice is heard, calling from upstairs, and a child is crying.

'You'd better go,' says Henrietta quickly. 'Sorry, but she won't want to see anyone just yet and I'm trying to keep the children out of her hair,' and Cordelia acquiesces at once, letting herself out of the house, hurrying away to Dover Street.

'Charteris Soke in Frampton Parva is the only house . . .' It was beginning to sound like an estate agent's enthusiastic pitch rather than a feature on a tiny piece of history. When the telephone rang again

Cordelia snatched it up almost fearfully, until she saw his initials.

'Dilly?'

The sound of his voice, the silly, familiar nickname, filled her with joy and relief. As her shoulders relaxed and she took a deep, deep breath she realized how very tense she'd been.

'Darling. Wasn't it fun? When shall I see you?'

'I could be with you about tea-time. Would that be good?'

She could hear the smile in his voice. 'You have no idea how good,' she answered. ''Bye, darling.'

Cordelia stood up and went back to the kitchen, then out on to the wide stone balcony carved from the cliff, which dropped precipitously into the sea below. Hers was the last in the row of coastguard cottages and the most private. The other two were holiday homes, let out for most of the summer and empty for the greater part of the winter. Her windows had an uninterrupted view of the sea, and of the coast that stretched away to Stoke Point to the west and Bolt Tail to the east. Inside the boundary walls she'd planted escallonia, fuchsia, tamarisk, to protect herself from the interested, and even envious, gaze of walkers on the coastal path higher up the cliff that passed a few yards from the front door. She leaned her elbows on the wide wall where feverfew clung in tiny crevices, and clumps of pink and white valerian were precariously rooted. Below her the sea rocked gently as though it were tethered to the cliffs, anchored and going nowhere; a squabble of seagulls screamed insults at one another from sharp-angled ledges. Light streamed down from a wide haze-blue firmament and was reflected back so that there was no distinction between sky and water. Away to the west a single fishing boat ploughed a lonely, shining furrow.

Soon he would be on his way: there would be time for talk, for sharing, and for love.

'It's so silly,' she said to him much later. 'I threw a wobbly. Panicking about Henrietta and how she'll manage while they're all away. Two months! It's such a long time, Angus.'

She passed him a mug of tea, suddenly remembering the remark a mutual friend had once made about Angus Radcliff. 'He's so dishy, he could have been the model for Action Man,' she'd said. 'I rather fancy him, don't you?' Cordelia had pretended indifference but she'd understood what she meant: the disconcerting light-grey stare and strong jaw; the dark, close-cropped hair and compact, well-muscled body.

'So which outfit do you imagine him in?' she'd

asked the friend. 'Resistance Fighter? Helicopter Pilot? Arctic Explorer?'

'Oh, I imagine him in nothing at all,' the friend had answered promptly. 'That's the whole point' – and they'd shrieked with laughter.

Now, sitting down opposite him, she hid her smile. 'And I've been thinking,' she said. 'You know when we were on the narrowboat I was telling you about Susan's marriage breaking up and her parents whisking her and the children off to New Zealand? Well, it occurred to me when I was driving home that surely you must know Roger and Maggie Lestrange? Wasn't Roger at Dartmouth the same year as you and Simon?'

'Roger Lestrange. Yes, of course I know him. You didn't mention his surname. But we weren't the same year. Roger was two years ahead of me and Simon at BRNC, but much later on Roger and I were at the M.o.D. together with Hal Chadwick. Roger and Hal were great oppos. Or should I say Admiral Sir Henry Chadwick?' He pulled a mock-reverential face.

'Dear old Hal,' Cordelia said affectionately. 'He's such a sweetie. And Fliss is so perfect as Lady Chadwick. That clean-cut, patrician face. Couldn't happen to a nicer couple. Remember when they let me do that piece for *Country Life* on that wonderful old house of theirs? The Keep. Hal was thrilled but Fliss insisted that their more personal details were kept right out of it, which was fair enough, I suppose. Apart from the history of the place we decided to concentrate on the organic vegetable-growing business that Jolyon started, Keep Organics. It was great fun.'

'Odd, though, isn't it?' he said thoughtfully. 'They weren't always a couple, Hal and Fliss. We tend to forget it because they seem so right together. They've only been married for about seven or eight years. Fliss and Hal are cousins, you know, and The Keep is just as much Fliss's as Hal's.'

'They explained that when I went to see them,' Cordelia admitted. 'That's why Fliss didn't want too much private stuff put in. It's been such a family house with so much drama that I could have written a whole book about them. It's an amazing place. Actually, the soke reminded me of it but on a much smaller scale. What happened to Hal's first wife? Did you know her?'

Angus frowned. 'I don't think so. Once we'd all specialized we lost touch a bit. Roger and Hal were skimmers; Simon and I went into submarines. I think we were up at the M.o.D. when Hal's wife left him. She took one of their boys but Jolyon stayed with Hal so we saw much more of him. I must say it's so odd when I see Jo on the television these days. He's the image of Hal when he was that age.'

'Jo!' Cordelia clapped her hand to her mouth. 'Jolyon Chadwick. I *am* a fool.'

'Why?'

'That's why Henrietta telephoned. She said someone called Jo had left a message for Roger and she thought she recognized his voice. I never thought of Jolyon. I was thinking Joseph, or Joe with an e. I am a twit. He was going to drop in, not knowing that Maggie and Roger have gone off to New Zealand.'

'Well, that's all right,' Angus said comfortably. 'Henrietta won't come to any harm with Jo.'

'Of course not. But I might just phone. Give her a warning shot across the bows. After all, he's quite a celebrity now, isn't he? She might be cross to be caught in her old jeans and no make-up.'

She found her mobile and pressed the buttons.

'Darling, it's me. Listen. I'm wondering if it's Jo Chadwick who left the message . . . Oh. Oh, he's there now. Right . . . OK. Later on, yes, that'll be fine.'

Cordelia switched off and made a face at him. 'He's already there,' she said.

Angus grinned. 'And?'

Cordelia considered. 'She sounded flustered. But in a nice way. Said she'd speak later on.'

He raised his eyebrows, pursed his lips. 'Not too much later on, I hope,' he said. 'We might be busy.'

# CHAPTER THREE

She'd recognized him at once. He'd paused on
the garden path, a slightly perplexed expression
clouding his face, as if he'd suspected some change
he couldn't quite pin down. Then Juno and Pan
had strolled out of the door to meet him, his
expression had cleared and he'd held out his hands
to them, bending to stroke them. The puppy had
gambolled behind them, prancing and bounding,
and he'd laughed aloud and said, 'Hello, old fellow,'
and crouched to pull the puppy's ears. He'd glanced
up then, and seen her waiting by the door, and his
look of surprise had been almost ludicrous. He'd
waded towards her through the sea of dogs and
said, 'Hello. Is Roger around?' and she'd said, 'No,
I'm afraid not, but come in. I think I've got some
books for you.'

Now, they stood rather shyly together in the cool,
dim hall, looking at the books, and she said, 'So

you didn't know that Maggie and Roger had gone to New Zealand?'

'No.' He put the book back into the bag. 'I'd heard that it was on the cards, but I had no idea they'd gone. And so you're looking after the dogs? And the old ponies.'

She hesitated. It would be easy to allow him to believe that she was an Animal Aunt; no explanations would be needed and he would disappear with his books and that would be that. But she didn't want him to disappear; she had an odd but very definite desire for him to stay.

'Well, I am,' she said, 'but it's not quite that simple. I'm not the Animal Aunt. I'm nanny to Susan's children. They've gone with Maggie and Roger, you see.'

He looked at her more closely. 'I see,' he said. 'Well, I think I do. Look, I'm Jolyon Chadwick. My father is one of Roger's oldest friends. Naval oppos and all that. I know Susan quite well, though I haven't seen her for years.'

She smiled. 'I know who you are,' she said. 'Mainly because of the television, of course, but I expect we've met up somewhere before. My family's Navy, too. Well, it was. I'm Henrietta March. Susan and I were at the Royal Naval School together. That's how I finished up as her nanny. I was between jobs at the same time that her business was really taking off and she had two babies, and it just seemed right somehow. When all this blew up I offered to come down here. Maggie's usual sitter was booked up.'

'"All this"?' he repeated.

She hadn't expected her unconsidered phrase to be picked up quite so quickly. The silence lengthened whilst she wondered how much to tell him; after all, he would very soon hear the truth through the naval grapevine.

'Would you like some tea?' She postponed the moment. 'I've got rather a good cake from the village stores in Bicknoller.'

'Thanks.' He followed her into the kitchen and went down on his knees to play with the puppy that rolled on to his back in ecstasy and nibbled Jolyon's fingers with pin-sharp teeth. 'This fellow's new since I was last here. What's his name?'

'Maggie calls him Tacker. It's the Cornish coming out in her, Roger says. He has a rather grand kennel name but Maggie just began calling him Tacker and it's rather stuck.'

'Well, he is a little tacker,' said Jolyon. 'He's gorgeous. My old fellow, Rufus, died last year but he was just like this once. So.' He stood up and took his tea from her. 'What's it all about then?'

She'd decided not to prevaricate but still she hesitated. 'It's rather embarrassing, isn't it? After all, it's very personal and we don't really know each other.'

'We probably do. Naval families always have some connection. I expect our fathers know each other. I'm just curious as to why Roger and Maggie have dashed off so suddenly without telling their closest friends, that's all. But don't worry if you feel it's indiscreet to tell me. I won't badger you.'

Henrietta sighed as she cut two slices of cake. 'It would be good to talk about it. To be honest, I'm still in shock. Iain has walked out on Susan. He's found someone else and they've split up. Maggie decided that it was a good moment for a sabbatical and has whirled Susan and the children off to New Zealand with her and Roger. Susan's partner is managing the business and looking after the London house and I agreed to come down here so that they could get away quickly.'

'I see. Poor old Susan.' His voice was bleak.

She glanced at him. His expression was grim and somehow this was comforting. 'I'm nearly as gutted as Susan,' she admitted. 'We were all so happy, you see. At least I thought we were. There was no hint of anything. No rows, no shouting, no disagreements. The business going on in the basement and lots of

38

people around. We were like a big family. And this has just blasted us all.'

'Roger and Maggie must be devastated.'

'They are. It affects so many people, doesn't it?' She was silent for a moment. 'My parents are divorced.' She shrugged. 'So what? Big deal, and all that. But it was painful, and now it seems as if it's happened all over again. My second family is all in pieces and it's like I'm in mourning. Oh, I can't explain it.'

'You don't have to. I know all about it, except that I'm luckier than you are. My second family is still in one piece. Rather tough on you, being left alone, isn't it?'

'I don't think they saw it like that. I mean, they weren't really thinking about me in that light. Maggie's one concern was to get Susan and the children away, and I agreed with her. To be honest it was almost a relief. I didn't want to be in Tregunter Road with Iain coming in and out, getting his things.'

'But this is a bit extreme. You need your friends at a time like this.'

'Maggie said I could invite people down. She was great. It's just I don't really want to talk about it yet. At least,' she grimaced, 'not with mutual friends. All that speculation and gossipy stuff; picking over the juicy details. I'm not in the mood.'

39

He nodded. 'I can understand that.'

Her mobile rang. She picked it up from the dresser, glanced at the screen, hesitated, muttered, 'It's my mum,' and pressed the button. She slightly turned away from him, shoulder hunched, and he sat down at the table and began to murmur to the dogs.

'Hi, Mum . . . Yes, actually he's here now . . . Yes. I'll call you later.' She switched it off, looking embarrassed.

'I phoned her earlier,' she told him. 'I'd been trying to decide who you might be after all those messages. I asked her if she knew anyone called Jo and she'd just suddenly wondered if it might be you.'

'Oh.' He looked faintly gratified. 'What's your mum's name?'

'Cordelia Lytton. She reverted to her maiden name after the divorce. She's a journalist; a features writer. She mainly does the big glossies, but she's also written a series of rather off-beat factional books about the black sheep of ancient, well-known families. They've been very successful so her name might sound familiar.'

'Of course, I know her. She did that article about The Keep for *Country Life*. And she's been to some of Dad's parties. She's great fun.'

'Oh, yes. She's great fun,' Henrietta agreed.

40

He glanced at her, alerted by her non-committal tone. 'I'm surprised we haven't met then.'

Henrietta shrugged. 'I'm in London most of the time. In your message you said you were coming down from Bristol. Is that where you live?'

He shook his head. 'I'm still at The Keep. That's our house in the South Hams that Cordelia wrote the article about. It's a funny old place but there's plenty of room and I still like to be involved in the business I started, growing organic vegetables.'

'Before you became a famous television star,' she teased him.

'Hardly a star and certainly not famous. Crazy, isn't it? From gardener to television presenter in three easy stages.'

Henrietta grinned at him. 'You were a nine-day wonder that first summer. My goodness, the grapevine was *very* busy and Mum kept reminding me about the article she'd done about your family. And after that, Roger telephoned Susan every time you were going to be on the box so that we could get our friends in and boast that we knew you, and then we'd all sit round basking in your reflected glory.'

'Oh, stop it. Honestly, it was such a fluke, but I must admit I'm loving every minute of it.'

'It was amazing, though, wasn't it? What were you

doing? Showing a rare rose at the Chelsea Flower Show or something? And next minute you're Monty Don and Ben Fogle rolled into one.'

'It was my great-grandmother's rose. She'd brought a cutting to The Keep when she got married and it thrived but we never knew what it was. It wasn't my idea to take it to the flower show. One of my cousins talked me into it and organized it all, and then the television crew decided to do a little bit about it because of its rarity value and we got on to the history of the family and suddenly it got out of hand.' He shook his head, still baffled by his success. 'The surprising thing was that when we did the live interview I really enjoyed myself. The TV crew were brilliant and we were all just having a good time.'

'And then the offers came pouring in?'

'Not quite like that. Apparently the BBC had loads of emails about the interview we did, and then this producer got in touch and asked if I'd meet him and some of his production team. They asked me to co-present a West Country programme – homes and gardens stuff – and then it went on from there. I've just been up to Bristol to discuss a new project, actually. It's all to do with shipbuilding and old harbours and we're just beginning to research it. That's why Dad asked Roger if I could borrow some of his books. He's a real expert on the sort of thing we're going to be doing.'

He finished his cake and glanced about him, as if preparing to go. Henrietta knew quite certainly that she would be desolate when he left but could think of no way to prevent it. It wasn't only because he was so attractive, with his thatch of fair hair and his easy friendliness; there was more to it than that. There was some quality she recognized and was drawn to, though she couldn't quite define it. She trailed after him as he picked up the books and carried them out to his car, the dogs following hopefully. He stood for a moment, the car door open, neither of them knowing quite what to say.

'Come again when you've got more time,' she said suddenly. 'We could go to the pub or take the dogs for a walk or something.'

'I'd like that. Wait a minute.' He took out his wallet and extracted a card. 'I'll telephone next time I'm going to Bristol but my mobile number is on this, and my home number.'

He gave her the card, hesitated as if uncertain how to say goodbye, then got into the car. She waved him off and then studied the card, which had the words 'Keep Organics' printed on it. Juno and Pan stared despondently after him and the puppy whined miserably.

'I know,' said Henrietta. 'I didn't want him to go, either. Never mind. We'll go out in a minute but I must clear up and put the cake away first.'

It was much later when she rang her mother's mobile.

'You were right. It was Jo Chadwick.' Henrietta paused. Her mother's voice was muffled, as if she were laughing, and there was the sound of a glass clinking. 'Is there someone there?'

'A couple of friends have dropped in for a drink. So it was Jo. Nice, isn't he? Did you like him?'

'Yes.' Henrietta didn't want to talk about how she felt: it was private. 'Yes, he's very nice. Anyway, I won't talk now if you've got friends there.'

'Never mind them. Did Jo stay for supper?'

'No, no, he didn't. Look, I'm going to have a shower and wash my hair. You know how long it takes to dry. Talk tomorrow? 'Bye for now.'

She switched off and fiddled with a strand of clean, shiny hair; she felt guilty at her abruptness but she didn't want to discuss Jo with anyone, especially not with her mother. Familiar emotions of anxiety and resentment threatened to spoil new, happy sensations and she shrugged them away, concentrating on Jo: the way he'd laughed, his face bright with delight, and the way he'd immediately understood about Susan and Iain. She wished he'd stayed but she could understand his caution. She lugged Tacker up on to the sofa beside her and cuddled him.

'I like him,' she murmured to him, and he licked her cheek. 'I really like him.'

'I think she likes him,' Cordelia said. 'Well, she would, wouldn't she? He's a darling.'

'Why did I have to be a couple of friends? Isn't one enough?'

'Certainly not,' she answered. 'Safety in numbers.'

'One day she's going to find us out. Especially now I've moved down. Wouldn't it be wiser to tell her? After all, what harm could it do now?'

'No, no.' Cordelia shook her head. 'Not yet . . . it's too soon.'

He pulled her close against him and she slid her arms around him, head against his heart, holding him tightly.

# CHAPTER FOUR

There had been Chadwicks at The Keep for over a hundred and sixty years. In the early 1840s, Edward Chadwick returned to England having spent a quarter of a century generating a considerable fortune in the Far East. He investigated a number of possible investments and decided to become a major shareholder and director in a company being formed to acquire a large tract of land in south Devon from which to extract the china clay that lay below the surface.

Once this decision was taken, his next step was to find a suitable house. He was unsuccessful. He did, however, find and purchase the ruins of an old hill fort between the moors and the sea and, by using the stones still lying about the site, he had built a castellated tower of three storeys which he named The Keep.

He married a pretty, well-born girl half his age,

but his formidable energies were, in the main, channelled into ensuring the success of the china clay workings so that, before his death, his fortune had doubled and redoubled.

His male descendants, whilst maintaining a presence in the company, made careers within the Royal Navy – but they continued to preserve and modernize The Keep. The wings, two storeys high and set back a little on each side of the original house, were added by a later generation and high stone walls were built to form a courtyard, which was entered from beneath the overarching roof that linked the two small cottages of the gatehouse. Old-fashioned roses and wisteria climbed the courtyard walls and the newer wings, but the austere grey stone of the tower itself remained unadorned. The Keep and the courtyard faced south, whilst to the west stretched the garden, bounded by orchards. To the north and east, however, the ground fell sharply away; rough grassy slopes descending to the river, which came tumbling down from the high moors. From bubbling issues the cold peaty waters raced through narrow rocky beds, down into the quiet, rich farmlands. Moving more slowly then, the river surged onward into the broad reaches of the estuary where it mingled with the salt water of the sea.

\*     \*     \*

Sitting at the breakfast table in the warm quiet kitchen, Hal Chadwick folded the letter and pushed it back into its envelope, saw his wife watching him and gave a little shrug.

'So, then,' he said, rather evasively.

Fliss looked amused. 'You mean "How do we solve a problem like Maria?"' she suggested lightly. When he frowned she grew alert, bracing herself. Ever since Hal's ex-wife had been widowed earlier in the year there had been an unusual flurry of cards and letters from her. 'What does she want?' Fliss asked. She didn't add 'this time' but it was implicit in her tone and he responded to it at once.

'Oh, come on, love,' he said. 'It must be tough for her, all on her own.'

'Of course,' agreed Fliss, spreading honey on her toast. 'I can understand that. It's horrid for her, Adam dying so suddenly, but she's got lots of friends in Salisbury, hasn't she? What I want to know is why, suddenly, are *we* so popular?'

Hal looked uncomfortable. 'Well, we are family, I suppose.'

Fliss suppressed a sharp retort. 'So what *does* she want?' she repeated.

'She's asking if she can come for Jolyon's birthday.' He sounded defensive. 'She wonders if she could stay two nights.'

'I suppose it would be uncharitable to ask why, after how many years – fifteen? – his mother suddenly wants to celebrate his birthday with him? What is he going to think about it?'

'I think she's sounding me out first.' Hal wore a placatory look, willing Fliss to be agreeable. 'She says she so enjoyed that weekend when she came down after Adam's funeral and she'd love to see us all again. She's suggesting that Jo's birthday might be a good time to begin "mending bridges", at least, that's how she puts it.'

Fliss thought: And I shall sound like a real cow if I object.

Aloud, she said calmly, 'Well, I think it's up to Jolyon, don't you? He might have other plans.'

'Well, of course.' Hal's relief was palpable. 'Do you know where he is?'

'He dashed in for some breakfast and then took the dogs out. He's probably still out on the hill or in the office. Do you want some coffee?'

'Yes, please.' He watched her pour it. 'Look, it's not my fault that Maria's lonely. But what can I do, Fliss? She was so dependent on Adam.'

'Yes, she was. Maria is a dependent sort of woman and I don't want her swapping us for Adam, that's all. She left you fifteen years ago and we've hardly ever seen her in all that time. Now, suddenly, we're

49

flavour of the month and I'm worried about it. Apart from anything else, it's not fair to Jo. Ed was always her favourite child – she made no attempt to hide that – and now he's suddenly gone off to the States and Adam's dead and, hey presto, you and Jo are back in fashion.'

'But what can we do?' he asked again. 'We're so lucky, Fliss, aren't we? Can't we spare something for Maria?'

She was silent; he'd made her feel guilty and she felt a very deep sense of resentment.

'I expect so,' she said at last – and turned away from him with relief as Hal's mother came into the kitchen.

Prue Chadwick, eighty-three and looking seventy, assessed the situation (*H'm, a bit of a chill in the air*) and kissed first Fliss and then Hal, as she did each morning and evening. 'Because,' she'd say, 'at my age, I never know when I might pop off when I'm not expecting it. Nothing worse than not saying goodbye.'

They received the light, dry touch of her lips and felt better for it. Fliss smiled at her.

'I'll make you some toast.' She poured coffee into Prue's big Royal Worcester cup with its pretty wreaths of flowers. 'Did you finish your letters last night?'

'Oh, darling, I never seem to *quite* finish. I always think of something else I need to say. Do you do that?'

'No,' said Hal, taking his coffee. 'But then I don't have this feminine urge to communicate in the first place.'

'Well, you'll have to answer this one.' Fliss flipped the corner of the envelope. 'A letter from Maria,' she said to Prue. 'She wants to come for Jolyon's birthday.'

Prue sipped her coffee: so this was the cause of the cool atmosphere. A sense of anxiety and guilt seized her. She had been partly responsible for breaking up the boy-and-girl affair between Hal and Fliss – how foolish it seemed now, that very real fear of first cousins marrying – and she'd been delighted when Hal had married Maria. How could she have known it would finish in separation and divorce, or that Jolyon would be rejected in favour of his younger brother, Ed? Of course, Jolyon had come back to live at The Keep with Hal, and now he seemed really to have found his niche – but would his mother's reappearance unsettle him? Prue's hand shook a little as she replaced her cup in its saucer.

'It's because she's lonely,' she said, not wishing to defend Maria but hoping to engage Fliss's sympathy. 'It's early days, isn't it?'

She fell silent, understanding how Fliss might feel but knowing, too, her son's generosity of spirit and his readiness to offer hospitality. He would not see that there was anything to fear from this poor woman, bereaved and lonely, simply needing the comfort of old friends and family. Prue guessed that Fliss's fear lay in the knowledge of Maria's neediness and dependency on those closest to her, and that this sudden change of heart towards Jolyon might make him resentful. Looking up, she saw that Fliss was watching her and she smiled at her, silently acknowledging her fears.

'After all,' Hal was saying, 'at times like these, old friends are the best, aren't they?'

'Were we her friends?' asked Fliss coolly, putting the toast into the rack and moving the honey towards Prue. 'You were her husband and Jo is her son, and the rest of us were simply just your family, as I remember it. I don't think Maria was particularly close to any of us, was she?' She appealed to Prue rather than to Hal, and Prue shook her head.

'Not particularly but I think I can guess what Hal means. No, no,' she added quickly to Fliss, seeing her expression, 'I'm not taking his side. Really, I'm not. It's just that, at times like this, a shared past is important. I know that Maria and Adam were together for fifteen years, and that her marriage to Hal was a very bumpy ride. Nevertheless, she's known us since she was a girl and she probably finds us some kind of comfort, especially with Ed in America. After all, her own parents are dead and she has no brothers or sisters. I'm afraid that she may well feel that she *is* closer to us than to some of her friends.' She glanced helplessly between the two of them. 'That doesn't mean that we have to feel responsible for her. I'm simply trying to explain how Maria is probably feeling.'

'Exactly,' exclaimed Hal with a kind of triumphant relief. 'That's what I was getting at.'

'However,' said Prue sharply, 'I don't think she should be allowed to intrude on Jolyon's birthday unless he is quite happy about it. That is quite a different case.'

'Well, of course.' Hal finished his coffee. 'I'm going over to the office. I'll see if he's there.'

He went out and there was a short silence.

'The thing is,' said Prue gently, 'that Hal's been so happy with you that he's quite forgiven all the pain she caused him. That's good, isn't it?'

'Oh yes,' Fliss answered rather bleakly. 'It's good. It just makes me feel even guiltier for feeling so . . . ungenerous. I don't want her here every time she's feeling lonely.'

'Of course you don't. That's perfectly natural.

Shall we see what Jolyon thinks? He's a generous, kind boy, but Maria hurt him very badly and he might have something to say about it.'

Fliss stood up and began to load the dishwasher. 'I'm going into Totnes later,' she said. 'Would you like to come?'

'Oh, yes, please.' Prue never refused an outing. 'You mustn't worry, Fliss.' She saw the little frown between her daughter-in-law's brows and smiled reminiscently. 'You're so like your grandmother, you know. She was a worrier.'

Fliss smiled back reluctantly. 'I'll try not to,' she said. 'But I feel . . . helpless.'

'Maria can't hurt you now.'

Fliss stood still, her hands full of plates. 'I have a premonition. Silly, isn't it? I feel that something momentous is about to happen. Sounds a bit fanciful, but I know what I mean.'

Prue watched her soberly; she had no inclination to make light of Fliss's prophecy. 'Perhaps it is. But need it be a bad happening?'

Fliss was silent for a moment. 'Jolyon was in a strange mood last evening,' she said at last. 'It was as if a light had been switched on inside him. Well, you know Jo. He's kind and gentle, and rather reserved. And then, when we saw him on television that first time, we were all amazed, weren't we? There was

54

old Jo, our dear boy, brimming with confidence and authority, and we were all spellbound. And you said – do you remember? – "Well, he's found his niche at last and now the real Jolyon's come to life, and about time too." Something like that. But when he's here, he's still the quiet, self-contained reliable Jo, checking up on Lizzie to make certain the business is still running properly, and taking the dogs out. Well, last night he was just like he is on the television. He came in positively brimming with this . . . magic. He was funny and affectionate and terribly attractive – you can see why he gets all those emails and letters from adoring fans – and I had this premonition that something was going to happen. Maria's letter underlined it some-how.'

'Did you ask him?'

'Ask him what? What could I say? He'd been over to Maggie's on his way back from Bristol to pick up some books that Roger's lending him but he didn't really want to talk about it. He was evasive in a very amusing way. It was almost as if he'd been drinking, but he hadn't. All of a sudden, it reminded me of when he was much younger and out of the blue he'd play mad games with the dogs as if he'd suddenly been overcome with happiness and he couldn't hold it in. He was still like it this morning.'

'Perhaps that's it. Perhaps, for some reason, he's overcome with happiness.'

'But for what reason? And why do I feel anxious?'

Prue shook her head. 'I don't know. Maybe it's the prospect of change. It can be very unsettling.'

Hal came in and both women looked at him expectantly; Hal shrugged.

'Says he'll think about it,' he said in answer to their unspoken question. 'He was rather surprised, to be honest, which is fair enough. Says he's not sure where he'll be. By the way, he told me in confidence that Maggie and Roger have gone to New Zealand with Susan and the children. You won't believe this, Fliss. Iain's left Susan and gone off with another woman. He's been having an affair for ages and nobody guessed.'

'But that's awful.' Fliss was shocked. 'They always seemed so right together, and those two children . . . Oh, poor Maggie and Roger. They'll be gutted.'

'Just between us, remember,' warned Hal.

'Naturally. But how does Jolyon know all this if Maggie and Roger weren't there?'

'The girl was there.'

'The girl?' asked Fliss quickly. Involuntarily, the two women's eyes met.

'Susan's nanny's looking after the dogs while they're all away. She told Jolyon what had happened.

And you'll never guess who she is, Fliss. She's Cordelia's girl. I remember now Cordelia saying something about her working in London and a connection with Susan, don't you, but I never really put two and two together.'

'How nice,' said Prue gently. 'For Jolyon to meet her. And for her too. After all, she must feel rather shaken by all this, mustn't she?'

'I should think so. Jo didn't say. He's dashed off to Watchet. Something to do with this new series he's doing on old harbours.'

'Watchet,' mused Prue. 'That's in Somerset, isn't it?'

'Roger keeps his boat at Watchet,' said Fliss. 'It's only about twenty minutes from their cottage.'

'Jo said not to wait lunch,' said Hal, oblivious to this exchange. 'He said he had other plans.'

'Yes,' said Prue. 'I expect he has.'

# CHAPTER FIVE

Driving towards the Quantocks, Jolyon was hardly aware of the familiar journey: through the lanes to join the A38 at Buckfast, past Exeter, past Tiverton Parkway and then off at Taunton. He'd travelled the road many times with his father, heading for a sailing weekend on Roger's boat, but this morning he was filled with an emotion that was quite new to him. Ever since he'd seen her standing in the doorway with the dogs around her, all he'd been able to think about was Henrietta. He remembered every detail: the quiet, dim hall, as they'd stood together, and her pale profile against the dark red curtains. Her hair flowed over her shoulders in tiny waves, as if she'd just shaken it loose from being very tightly plaited, and he'd been fascinated by the different colours amongst the shining strands: topaz, gold, brown, amber, even black.

'Tortoiseshell,' he'd wanted to say, longing to

touch it. 'Your hair is the colour of tortoiseshell.' And when she'd looked at him, he'd seen that her eyes were the same strange colours; perhaps it was what people meant when they talked about hazel eyes.

He'd liked her reticence, the way she didn't want to gossip about Susan and Iain, and instinct told him that she was wary of relationships; that her parents' divorce had made her cautious. Well, he knew all about that. Nevertheless, he'd felt quite certain that she hadn't wanted him to leave and, although he hadn't had the courage to suggest that he should stay, he'd decided to trust his feelings this morning and telephone her. She'd answered at the second ring, which had cheered him enormously, and sounded delighted at the prospect of another visit. Of course, he'd made sure to explain that he was going to Watchet – he didn't want to frighten her off by sounding too keen – but he'd suggested a pub lunch and a walk with the dogs, and she'd agreed very readily.

He was deeply relieved that nobody at The Keep had questioned the need for this unexpected trip to look at the harbour. Even his father hadn't observed that, after years of sailing out of Watchet, he ought to know the harbour like the back of his hand. He'd muttered things about shipbuilding and other aspects of the new series and hurried away; even the unsettling news that his mother had suggested that she'd like to come down for his birthday hadn't detained him.

'She's lonely, poor old love,' his father had said with his usual tolerant good humour, and Jo knew very well that he was being asked to acquiesce: to forgive the hurts and betrayals of the past and be kind to his newly widowed mother. This was typical, his father was a generous man, but Jo felt resentment stirring. He knew very well why his mother was suddenly eager to repair her connection with the Chadwicks and it wasn't only because she was lonely, although that was a significant part of it. Ever since that momentous interview at the Chelsea Flower Show, two years ago, she'd begun to show a new interest in him; suddenly he'd become worth acknowledging. At last she could be proud of him.

Jo was seized with a paroxysm of anger; his hands tensed on the wheel. Twelve years ago she'd made no attempt to hide her disappointment when he'd told her his vision for the future of The Keep; back then her contempt had been plain to see.

'A gardener?' she'd asked disdainfully. 'Is that the extent of your ambition?'

She'd shown no interest in his idea to convert the

gatehouse into his own quarters, or his plans for growing organic vegetables.

Never once in twelve years had she asked about his work, never invited him to stay in Salisbury. He and Dad were one family and she, Adam and Ed were another quite separate unit. Even now the pain of her rejection threatened to disable him. He pulled into a lay-by and switched off the engine.

'Crazy,' he told himself furiously. 'Crazy to still be affected by this stuff.'

He let down the window on the passenger's side. Beyond the hedge the cattle stood together beneath the sheltering, shadowy waterfall of a willow's branches, their tails twitching against the tormenting flies, and the sunlight casting dappled shade upon their broad creamy backs. Gradually the pain receded and he deliberately schooled his thoughts back into the former channels of happiness. He brought the image of Henrietta's face into his mind: the fine, winged brows, the high, wide cheekbones, and the way her lips curved into a smile. There'd been recognition between them; a kind of exchange. He guessed that she too carried with her a similar form of emotional baggage: the fear of a permanent relationship and the knowledge of what terrible damage failure can do – to yourself and to other people.

Yet, for the first time, he was tempted towards the experiment. No other girl had made him feel like this – and after such a brief acquaintance. He shook his head, bewildered, and turned the key in the ignition.

Maria stood at the window and stared out into the garden that belonged to her dear friend Penelope. The sight of so much beauty depressed her: the perfection of the flower borders, the cunning sweeps and curves of trees and bushes – 'leading the eye on, d'you see?' Penelope would cry – the symmetry of colour and shape. Even now she could see Pen's gardener, dear old Ted, 'loyal and simply wonderful, Maria', chopping savagely away at some poor tree down near the wild garden. And even the wild garden wasn't allowed to be properly wild; oh no, Penelope's idea of wild was a very clear one. None of this 'a weed is a flower in the wrong place' for old Pen. Her wild garden was full of strange and exotic – and very expensive – plants, and woe betide any poor buttercup that dared to put a tendril in it. Dear loyal old Ted gave it very short shrift.

Maria made a face; she'd never liked gardening but she'd kept up the pretence to her friends and let Adam do all the hard work. Adam had enjoyed it. Suddenly, thinking of him, she couldn't prevent a burst of tears. These unexpected attacks of loss were uncontrollable simply because they *were* unexpected: the oddest thing could set them off. She blotted the tears with her handkerchief. To be honest, she was glad to be out of the big house that had been so empty and lonely without Adam – but he could never have guessed the circumstances that had dictated her leaving.

He'd warned her, very tactfully, of course – he knew how defensive she was about Ed and was always careful when he talked about his 'instability' – but he'd warned her against encouraging Ed's wild schemes; worrying about how she'd manage financially if he were to die first and hinting that she'd need to keep a tight hand on the purse strings. Well, he had died – now here, now gone – keeling over whilst he was washing the car and rushed to hospital in a screaming ambulance whilst she'd followed, trembling and terrified, in the car. How she had hated it all: the echoing noise, the hurrying feet, the tubes and dials, and the busy, curt nurses. The terrible A & E waiting room full of uncouth, uncaring, overweight people who stared at a suspended television screen and never stopped eating; a wounded child who had screamed continuously, held by its terrified mother; puddles of some horridly smelling liquid under the chairs.

And then the Sister, long-faced and portentous, calling her name.

She'd known at once, of course, but the whole thing had seemed so unreal, so *impossible*, that she hadn't been able to take it all in. Then Penelope had come – capable, kind Penelope and dear old Philip, putting their arms around her and taking her home; making her a hot drink and being sweet and tactful, arranging things and telling her that in future she must always telephone the minute she needed anything; she *mustn't* be lonely. It was Pen who'd phoned Ed, voice low, throbbing with sympathy, explaining that something had happened and that his mother wanted to speak to him.

She'd taken the phone and waited – rather pointedly – until Pen and Philip had left the room, and then she'd burst out suddenly weeping and poor Ed had been quite alarmed. Of course, Adam hadn't been Ed's father, though he'd lived with him since he was twelve, so she'd been shocked by Ed's very real grief. She hadn't really given much thought to how Ed might feel; she was more concerned with receiving comfort from him. He'd come hurrying down from London, darling Ed . . .

Maria turned away from the window, into the charming, tastefully decorated living room of Penelope's perfect little annexe and stared around her. It was due to darling Ed that she was here. Ed had conceived a brilliant plan that had needed a bit of financial backing – 'Nothing to worry about, Mum, it's purely a formality, I promise' – and she'd signed the document that he'd needed, trusting him and his clever friend who worked the money markets and who'd assured her that it simply couldn't fail. How plausible they'd been; how excited: 'This time next week we could all be millionaires!' And the plan *had* failed. Oh, the terror of that moment when Ed had telephoned to tell her and to warn her that things had gone terribly wrong and that the house would be repossessed: the sick fear that disabled her and haunted the long night hours, the terrified disbelief that this could happen, and the absolute necessity that nobody – especially dear old Pen and clever old Philip – should know the truth.

She'd told them that she was selling, that she couldn't manage another minute all alone in the huge house, and that she'd rent something until she'd decided what to do and where to go. It was Pen who had suggested she should stay in the annexe until she found the little cottage or flat of her dreams. She'd nearly snapped Pen's arm off in her eagerness to accept her offer; oh, the relief of having somewhere decent to go, with old friends close at hand, whilst she tried to regroup. And here she was, fielding their suggestions of this delightful house or some penthouse flat that had just come on to the market. She'd dither, find something wrong with whatever the property in question was; twice she'd been to view houses simply to keep up the pretence. How they laughed about it; suggesting that Maria must be a millionaire now and could afford a luxury pad. Philip was always popping in with the latest offering from the internet, and only her quick wits were keeping the truth hidden. If only they knew that she'd be hard-pressed to afford Pen's annexe, let alone some fancy property in the Cathedral Close!

Maria sat down in one of the armchairs and hugged herself, rocking a little. She'd managed to persuade them that the last thing she wanted was another big house, that she was thinking *really* small and cosy now. Pen had protested when she'd realized that so much furniture was being sold, but she'd been understanding too, and sympathetic that Adam's death had precipitated such changes. Maria closed her eyes against the shrivelling humiliation of Pen's sympathy, and prayed that nobody would ever discover the truth.

Thank God for the Chadwicks. It was a real possibility that they might rescue her. If she played her cards right she might be able to stay with them for a while – there was enough space, after all, in that rambling great place – and then perhaps she'd be able to afford a tiny cottage close to The Keep where she could see something of Jolyon – and Hal. Hal had been so sweet when Ed had decided to go to the States with his partner, Rebecca. Maria braced herself against the pain in her heart. She felt that she'd somehow lost Ed; Rebecca had taken him away from her much more completely and successfully than the move to America could. In her mind's eye she saw Rebecca: short, tiny, perfect. Strong, well-muscled little legs; black hair so smooth it looked as if it were painted to her skull, and a laptop grafted permanently to her tiny, clutching little fingers. Maria's heart lurched again with loss and terror; how could her beloved Ed be happy with such an unemotional, professionally driven girl?

'We're fine, Mum,' he'd said once, impatiently, when she'd tried to question him about his happiness. 'Just fine.'

She'd been warned off – but now, whenever Ed hugged her, she could see over his shoulder Rebecca's cool gaze, so that her pleasure in his affection was diminished. She'd been utterly gutted when, four weeks after the house had been repossessed, Ed had announced that he and Rebecca were moving to New York; that Rebecca had been offered a job she simply couldn't refuse.

'And what about you?' she'd asked – meaning, as well, 'What about *me*? How can you leave me alone now, of all times?' – and he'd said, 'Oh, I'll find something. You know me. This is much too important for Becks to turn down. You know how brilliant she is, and this job's the absolute cream.' He'd looked embarrassed then; put on his small-boy expression. 'The trouble is, Mum, she found out about this last little enterprise and it's a bit of a final chance for me. Take it or leave it. She's got some very good contacts out there and she thinks I'll be able to settle down to some serious work. I'm really gutted that our little scheme didn't work out, Mum. But you'll be OK, won't you? I mean, there's still a lot of investments, aren't there, and there was some money left over when the house sold? God, I'm just so sorry, Mum. Look on it as my inheritance. I promise you I'll never ask you for another penny, ever.' And he'd looked so pathetic and so miserable that she'd forgiven him utterly, and he'd hugged her and that was that.

That was when she'd made her first visit for years to The Keep. Hal had written to her – oh, how thankful she'd been to receive his letter – saying that Ed and Rebecca had been down to The Keep to say goodbye and that she, Maria, must be feeling the draught. They'd all miss them, he'd written, but it seemed a fantastic opportunity and it wasn't that far to New York. She'd enjoy visiting them and seeing the wonders of Manhattan . . .

It had been light-hearted, an encouraging letter, and it had been balm to her aching heart. She'd telephoned – her heart pounding with anxiety lest Fliss should pick up the receiver – but, by extraordinary good luck, Hal had answered. It had been surprisingly easy to talk to him; he'd been sympathetic, kind, and he'd said those magic words: 'If you ever want to come down to The Keep . . .'

Well, to be truthful, she guessed he hadn't really expected her to take him up on it so quickly – of course, she knew that – but she'd been unable to resist the possibility of his offer of warmth, of friendliness. She had her own friends, but Hal was Ed's father and knew how she felt; and there was a connection there, a very special one. You couldn't be married to a man for twenty years and bear his children, and be completely indifferent to him: even Fliss must see that. And she'd even wondered if she should tell him about Ed's disastrous business gamble. After all, it would certainly have increased Hal's sympathy for her situation, yet something had prevented her; some instinct had warned her against it. A big part of it was loyalty to Ed. She knew very well the sort of comments Hal would make about darling Ed's shortcomings. Like Adam, Hal had no illusions when it came to his younger son – and was much more outspoken about his weaknesses. He was extremely fond of Ed but he blamed her and her parents for spoiling him and she simply couldn't bear to hear him spoken badly of – or for Fliss to know that poor old Ed had cocked up so badly. No – she shivered at the thought of such humiliation – she simply couldn't cope with that. But there was more than simple loyalty to Ed. If she told them about the disaster it was possible that they might believe her need to renew the links between them was a financial one. And it wasn't; it really wasn't.

So she'd merely said to Hal that she'd love to see them all and she'd travelled down to the West Country – and, amazingly, it had been wonderful to be back at The Keep. Hal was comfortingly unchanged and Prue was as warm and sympathetic as ever; even Fliss had been sweet, though it had been quite a shock to see how much she had come to resemble her grandmother, that formidable old matriarch Freddy Chadwick. Fliss had that same trick of squaring her shoulders and lifting her chin when she looked at you, which could be a bit disconcerting. And, if she were to be absolutely honest, Jolyon had been slightly awkward, rather uncomfortable when she told him how proud of him she was, but he'd been busy off filming something or other and he hadn't been around for much of the time. Anyway, she'd written again suggesting that she should go down for Jolyon's birthday; that it was time to mend some bridges. And now she was waiting anxiously for Hal's reply. After all, she couldn't stay in Pen's annexe for ever . . .

There was a knock at the door – Pen was very tactful and never just walked in – and Maria glanced at her watch: too early for a drink. It might be an invitation to join them for coffee, or a shopping trip in Salisbury. There were times when she believed that Penelope was very grateful for this instant distraction from dear old Philip's company now that he was retired.

'Come in,' she called, adopting her new expression – cheerfulness with just a hint of brave determination. 'Morning, Pen. I've just been looking at your wonderful garden. Honestly, I still don't know how you do it. I could spend hours at that window.'

# CHAPTER SIX

Alone again, Cordelia returned to her battle with the soke. The structure of the piece eluded her; her words refused to form into an acceptable, cohesive piece of writing and, frustrated, she went out on to the stone balcony. Leaning on the sun-warmed stone she gazed down into the clear green water where thick, dark forests of weed floated, rooted in the rock wall. She knew why she couldn't concentrate: guilt and curiosity strove together in her mind, distracting her utterly from her work. Presently she took her mobile from her pocket and pressed the buttons.

'Hi, Mum.' Was that a hint of impatience in Henrietta's voice?

'Darling,' Cordelia said quickly. 'Listen, I'm sorry about last night. Our timing was awful, wasn't it? First you with Jolyon and then me with . . . the chums. It was so silly of me not to think of Jolyon

in the first place. I was thinking Joe with an "e" and
. . .' She could hear herself rattling on. 'Anyway, I'm
glad it was sorted out at last.'

'Yes.' A hesitation. 'Actually, he's coming back
today. Well, any minute now.'

'Oh.' Cordelia tried not to sound too surprised or
inquisitive. 'Well, that's nice.'

'He's got to go to Watchet.' A defensive note here;
a warning not to read too much into it. 'Something
to do with his new TV series. And we're going out to
the pub for lunch.'

'Great. Well, then.' She wondered whether to say,
'Give him my love,' but decided against it. She didn't
want to muscle in here. 'I'd better get back to work.
'Bye, darling.'

So that was that. Cordelia rested her elbows
on the wall, reassured and hopeful – yet anxiety
persisted. Below her the sea heaved restlessly,
slapping the cliff's face contemptuously with cold
handfuls of water, growling in the deep subterranean
caverns. A cool little breeze polished her cheeks and
tweaked at her hair and she shivered, glad of the
sunshine.

*Are we the first generation to need to be friends
with our children?*

'Wouldn't it be wonderful,' she'd said last night, 'if
Henrietta and Jolyon should fall in love?'

73

'Possibly,' Angus had answered cautiously. 'Possibly not.'

'Why not?' She'd raised herself on one elbow, looking down at him almost indignantly.

'It depends on what follows,' he'd answered reasonably. 'Falling in love isn't an end in itself. You, of all people, must know that.'

She'd subsided back on to the pillow, staring up at the ceiling. 'I do know. But even so . . .'

'What you really hope is that Henrietta would be changed by the experience, enough at least to understand and to forgive you.'

Well, he was quite right about that.

There was the sound of a vehicle on the track; McGregor barked and Cordelia turned her head, listening. It stopped, engine idling, a door opened and there was a burst of noise – the urgent quacking of a radio – and the clang of the letterbox. The regular postie was on holiday and Cordelia waited for the van to turn and disappear down the track before she moved. She liked to have a yarn with old Jimmie but his monosyllabic stand-in was a rather dull youth with no gift for conversation: this morning she simply wasn't in the mood to make the effort.

She turned about, leaning back on her elbows in the sunshine, brooding on her article; she simply must find the discipline to go back into her study and make a start. McGregor barked again, then growled deep in his throat, and a dazzle of light up on the cliff path attracted her attention. A figure moved and there was a glint of sun on glass as the binoculars made a sweep of the coastline before becoming fixed in her direction. For an uneasy moment Cordelia felt that she was being watched. She straightened, staring up at the motionless figure which, after a few moments, turned and disappeared from view. Fighting back her irritation, she wondered whether a walk might start the creative juices flowing, or whether it was simply an excuse to postpone work. The telephone began to ring and with relief she went to answer it.

'Fliss,' she said with pleasure. 'How nice . . . Yes, so I hear. About time, isn't it? It's crazy that they've never met. Isn't it ghastly about Susan and Iain? Poor old Maggie and Roger . . . Well, why not come over and have some lunch? . . . OK, tea, then. I'd love it . . . Great. See you this afternoon.'

Immediately she felt refreshed; this was something to look forward to, and it would be good to talk to Fliss about Jo and Henrietta. Meanwhile she must do some work. Humming, she went into her study: *Charteris Soke in Frampton Parva is the only house of its kind . . .*

Up in her bedroom, Fliss stood for some moments, surprised by her sudden decision to speak to Cordelia. It was unlike her to be so on edge simply because Maria had written to Hal, asking if she might come to stay again. Perhaps it was the very fact that Maria had written *to Hal* – not to them both, only to Hal. There was a possessive, secretive streak in Maria's character that refused to accept Fliss and Hal as an entity. Until Adam's death, this hadn't mattered. After all, letters from Maria had been few and far between. Now things had changed. In the last six months there had been several communications from Salisbury, and Fliss realized that she disliked the fact that Hal was beginning to get letters from his ex-wife that excluded her entirely.

Of course, it was foolish to mind, Fliss told herself. After all, she only had to ask to see the letters and Hal would show them to her, though he had never done so of his own free will. She wondered whether Hal had answered them all – and how he had answered them.

'I might give her a call,' he'd say casually, putting the letter or card to one side, but she'd never quizzed him about it, and later the envelope and its contents would be missing. Once, she remembered, he'd laughed aloud whilst he was reading one of them and she'd experienced a pang of annoyance: jealousy would be going too far, she assured herself now, but definitely a sharp twinge of irritation had shaken her. It would be crazy to suspect Hal of encouraging his ex-wife – and why should she feel anxious at this late date? They'd been married for eight happy years, though she still felt frustrated and resentful if she allowed herself to dwell on all those wasted years they'd spent apart.

At the time she'd never known exactly what Hal's mother and grandmother had said to him that had convinced him that he mustn't marry her, but they'd frightened him.

'They practically accused me of incest,' he'd told her years later, after Maria had left him and Miles had died. 'They said that being brought up like brother and sister, and our fathers being identical twins and all that stuff, made any other relationship between us out of the question. They pointed out how young you were and how I was taking advantage of you. It made me feel like some sort of depraved libertine.'

He was twenty-two, thought Fliss, and I was nineteen, and it never occurred to either of us to rebel. How young and raw we were. And so he married Maria and I married Miles.

The knock at the door startled her. 'Come in,' she called, turning from the window.

Prue smiled at her from the doorway; dressed ready for her outing, and bright with the expectancy of it, she looked young and pretty.

'I didn't want to keep you waiting,' she said happily. 'I wondered if there might be time to stop at Dartington on the way home for a walk in the gardens.' She came a little further into the room. 'What were you thinking about, darling? You look very serious and rather sad.'

'I was thinking about Miles,' Fliss answered, 'and all of us. Me and Maria and Hal. You and Grandmother. And all the wasted time and the mistakes we made.'

'Oh, darling,' said Prue remorsefully. 'How you must have hated us, me and Freddy, when we separated you and Hal. It's impossible now to imagine how strongly we felt about you being first cousins. Later we knew that we'd been wrong, but we couldn't have guessed how deeply you felt about each other. You were both so young. Your uncle Theo was very angry with us, you know.'

'Uncle Theo?' Fliss's expression softened with affection and grief for that diffident priest who had always been on her side. 'Was he?'

'Oh, yes. He and Freddy very nearly fell out over it. He thought the family treated you very badly by deciding that you were too young to be truly affected by it. But, Fliss, many good things have come out of it all. Your lovely children, darling Bess and Jamie. And dear old Miles. We all loved him in the end, didn't we? How brave he was after that ghastly stroke.'

'I know. I'm being silly. I told you earlier, I feel unsettled. I miss the children. Bess and Matt and the children seem such a long way away in America. And now Jamie's been posted to Cairo. I miss having them all around. Come on, let's go to Totnes and get the shopping done and then we'll have coffee at Dartington on the way home.' Fliss paused to pick up her jacket from a chair. 'By the way, I'm going to have tea with Cordelia this afternoon.'

'Oh!' Prue looked at Fliss sharply, approvingly. 'Now that's a very good idea.'

'I hope so,' said Fliss as they went down the stairs together. 'I can't decide if I'm being devious. It's at times like these that I miss Uncle Theo most. He could always cut through the muddle and see straight to the heart of things.'

'Uncle Theo was my dearest friend. He saved me from disaster so many times I've quite lost count.' As they passed through the hall Prue glanced at her watch. 'I wonder where Jolyon is now.'

Fliss chuckled; her anxiety had receded a little and she was looking forward to seeing Cordelia.

'Wherever he is, I bet he's not studying the harbour in Watchet.'

Jolyon was sitting in the sunshine, his elbows on the rough planking of the table outside the pub, watching Henrietta with an expression of amused sympathy.

'As a family we take a bit of getting used to. I think it's why the television crew made so much of it all in the first place. Three generations living in a house that's a cross between a castle and a fort. We're an anachronism, that's the trouble.'

'I can't take it all in.' Henrietta shook her head, drank some beer. She was so happy, sitting in the sun across the table from him, waiting for their ploughman's lunches to arrive. 'It's far too complicated.'

'Not really. I'll go through it again.' He leaned forward, ticking off the names on his fingers. 'There's Granny, Dad, Fliss, me—'

'Hang on, though,' she interrupted. 'You said that Fliss is your step-mum *and* your cousin.'

'Second cousin. That's right. Dad and Fliss are first cousins, childhood sweethearts, though the family wouldn't let them marry, so Dad married my mother and Fliss married Miles. Dad had me and Ed, and Fliss had twins, Jamie and Bess. Then Mum

80

and Dad divorced when I was fifteen and after that I spent all my holidays at The Keep and Dad was there when he was on leave. Dad and Fliss married eight years ago after Miles died.'

She watched him, aware of the turbulent undercurrents beneath the smooth surface of this narrative but seeing that he wasn't ready yet to talk about them.

Keep it light, she told herself. Keep it jokey.

'OK,' she said. 'I've got that. So your granny is your dad's mother *and* Fliss's aunt, and then there's Sam, who's another cousin. His parents died and he's been brought up at The Keep. And that's where Lizzie comes in.'

She could see that Jolyon was steering clear of the tragedy of Sam's parents but she wanted to know about Lizzie: it was clear from his expression when he'd mentioned her that Jolyon had a soft spot for Lizzie.

'Lizzie was Sam's nanny,' he said. 'You'll have that in common with her. Dad and Fliss were rather daunted by taking on a three-year-old, so Lizzie was welcomed with open arms. She'd known Sam all his life, his mother was her best friend, and she was quite happy to become part of the family. It was great for me, too, to have someone of my own age around. When Sam went away to school two years ago there was a question about whether she should move on but she'd already been helping me in the office and knew a lot about Keep Organics so it seemed sensible for her to stay, especially as I was doing more and more work for the television. Anyway, we'd have all missed her terribly if she'd gone. She's part of the family now.'

Henrietta studied him. His face was open, his expression guileless: he might have been talking about a sister, or a cousin.

'Is that it? No more cousins or aunts?'

'Well, not living at The Keep . . .' He hesitated, sitting back to allow the girl to put their plates on the table. Everyone in the bar had recognized Jolyon, and there had been an excited little stir, a sudden murmuring whisper, but Jolyon had remained unruffled, friendly. Now, Henrietta was amused to see that though the girl smiled warmly at Jolyon, he was barely aware of her apart from acknowledging his food with a word of thanks. Henrietta thanked her too, refused the offer of anything else at present, and mimed despair at Jolyon's hesitation.

'No, don't tell me,' she said. 'My brain's signalling information overload.'

'You'll have to come and meet them all,' he said lightly, unwrapping his knife and fork from the paper napkin. 'It's much easier to remember names when you've met the people, don't you think? And, anyway, it's time you met them. They know Cordelia, after all. They'll be delighted to meet you.'

'It sounds terrifying.' She broke open the crusty roll and spread butter, cut a piece of cheese.

'Nonsense. Anyway, I want to show you The Keep. Now there's an anachronism, if you like. It's like a very tiny castle with a castellated roof and high walls round the courtyard, and I live in the gatehouse.'

'Sounds like something out of Hans Andersen. Well, that settles it.' She was simply too happy to be wary or guarded in her response. 'This I must see.'

'Great.' He was delighted. 'That's fantastic.'

'But I have to think about the dogs,' she warned him. 'I can't leave them for too long.'

'The dogs can come too. No problem.'

'Hang on. I can't possibly bring three dogs. Honestly—'

'Rubbish. Dogs are always welcome at The Keep. We've got two bitches at the moment. Sisters. They're descendants from dogs we had years ago and they've inherited their names. Pooter and Perks. They'll love your lot.'

'Pooter and Perks.' She laughed. 'I like that. Any reason?'

He shook his head. 'The original two were before I was born but they passed into the family folklore.

My aunt Kit always named the family dogs. There was Mrs Pooter and, later on, Polly Perkins. We also had Mugwump and Rex and Rufus.'

'Rex seems terribly normal after Mugwump.'

Jo frowned. 'Actually Rex was our dog but my mother wasn't able to cope with him. There used to be terrible rows about him with Dad, and then one day Dad just put Rex into the car and took him down to The Keep to live. I missed him terribly but at least the rows stopped. Well, those particular rows.'

'I suppose,' she said carefully, not looking at him, 'that rows are at least some kind of warning that things are going wrong. My parents didn't row so it was more of a shock when the break came. The same with Iain and Susan. They were even talking of having a puppy. I actually wondered whether Maggie intended Tacker to come to London once he was house-trained. Speaking of which, we must take them for a walk soon. Or I must.'

'We'll go together. We'll take them up to Robin Upright's Hill.'

She raised her eyebrows. 'What time are you due in Watchet, did you say?'

He finished his pint. 'I've forgotten. What a pity. I hope the dogs can wait until we've had some pudding?'

# CHAPTER SEVEN

Cordelia glanced at her watch, reread the last few sentences on her computer screen and pressed the save button. Not a bad day's work on the whole, though it had been a struggle to keep her mind from distraction and to hold at bay that terrible creeping despair that numbs the creative flow. Goodness knows how many times she'd checked the word count – always a bad sign – and on several occasions she'd had to restrain herself from getting up to make yet another cup of coffee or to search for chocolate or biscuits. It was odd how the compelling need to communicate through the written word was dogged by this mental paralysis and lack of confidence. She'd said as much once to a revered and well-known journalist.

'Why is it,' she'd asked plaintively, 'that one is so driven to do something that is such mental agony? You're seized by an idea that seems fantastic, and you get really excited about it but when it comes down to it you find you're doing almost anything else – phoning friends, ironing, walking the dog – *anything*, rather than actually sitting down and getting on with it.'

'I know,' he'd said sympathetically. 'The blank screen, those brilliant phrases that look rubbish in hard print, your confidence leaking away. Still, the vital thing is to keep hitting the keys. Get something down, even if it *is* rubbish, because it will almost always result in moving you on and getting the ideas flowing. You can always wipe out the rubbish later, but there's nothing more destructive than giving in and walking away. It'll be that much harder next time.'

She'd followed his advice, and found that it worked, but there were still days when every phrase she wrote was an act of will born out of desperation and very little inspiration. Today had been one of those days, yet something had been achieved . . .

McGregor growled, there was a movement at the window, a flash of colour, and Cordelia glanced round: had Fliss arrived already? She stood up but there was no knock at the door, no car on the parking space by the garage, only a party of hikers on the cliff path. One of them was lagging behind, pausing to look around. Cordelia shrugged. It must have been a bird at the window, or perhaps one of the hikers had come to have a closer look. Quite often a bold rambler would approach the cottages to stare in; she'd even known one or two to knock and ask questions about the coastguard service.

She sometimes wished that her study had been at the front, overlooking the sea, but when her parents had bought the house in the seventies they'd kept the two small inland-facing rooms, divided by the narrow hall, as study and parlour and converted the seaward-facing rooms into one huge space: kitchen at one end and sitting room at the other. Occasionally she worked on her laptop at the kitchen table, but the view and the sunshine, and the lack of the necessary reference books usually proved too much of a distraction. Anyway, she liked her little study, which still had her parents' books on the shelves and some of her mother's pretty watercolours on the walls.

Ah, there was the car now, and here was Fliss climbing out and looking around her, standing quite still for a moment in the sunshine to gaze out to sea. Cordelia went to meet her, still rather surprised at Fliss's telephone call. She'd summed Fliss up as someone who kept her own counsel and was not given to speculation over the teacups.

'It seems,' she'd said earlier, when she'd phoned,

'that our young have met at last,' but Cordelia had caught something more in her voice than amused pleasure and had instinctively made the offer of lunch or tea and, to her surprise, been readily taken up on it.

'This is great,' she said now, opening the door and smiling warmly at Fliss. She led the way down the hall and into the kitchen.

'I'd forgotten how fantastic it is,' said Fliss, turning from one window to another. 'We came here once before, Hal and I, when you were doing the article. Do you remember?'

'Of course I remember. We had a barbecue down on the beach.'

'You said it could only be done at low tide, and you dared Hal to swim.'

'But he wouldn't take me up on it. I love swimming just when the tide's on the turn and creeping up. It's magic. At high tide the beach is completely covered.'

'I certainly remember all those steps back up the cliff when we'd eaten too much!'

The two women laughed together, the first slightly awkward moment of meeting over. Cordelia moved to the Rayburn and pushed the kettle on to the hot-plate.

'And I remember this fellow. He's nearly as tall

as I am.' Fliss put out her hands to greet McGregor, fondling his ears.

'He's the perfect companion. Big, protective, but quiet with it,' said Cordelia. 'Isn't it nice that Henrietta and Jo have met up at last? It seems crazy that it's taken so long.'

'The Navy's rather like that, though, isn't it?' Fliss had turned back to look at the view. 'You run into the same families over and over again and miss others completely.'

'And, to be honest, I moved out of the network rather early on. When Simon left us I went to London, although Henrietta was still at the Royal Naval School at Haslemere. That's where she met Susan and they became very close friends. I can't believe that she and Iain have split up. Poor Henrietta is devastated and I'm hoping that Jo will cheer her up. When I phoned this morning she was expecting him to arrive at any moment.' She made the tea and glanced at Fliss, noting the lifted chin and the tiny frown between her brows. 'Am I being indiscreet?'

Fliss shook her head. 'Not at all. We guessed as much when he said he had to go to Watchet. Well, Prue and I did. Dear old Hal wouldn't have thought about it.'

'Very astute of you.' Cordelia laughed a little. 'It's the tiny things, isn't it? Henrietta's voice last night

89

was just a shade breathless. Nicely flustered, if you know what I mean.'

'Jolyon was glowing, as if he'd drunk just a bit too much.' Fliss looked directly at Cordelia. 'Would you be pleased?'

Cordelia made a face. 'Would I! I'd be thrilled to bits. Jo is such a sweetie and Henrietta needs to fall madly in love. What about you?'

Fliss followed her out on to the stone balcony and watched as she sorted out mugs and plates and cut a large caramel slice into smaller pieces.

'I'd be delighted. Of course, I'm not his mother . . . My own two are a long way away. Jamie was posted to Cairo last month – he's with the Foreign Office – and Bess and Matt and their children are in Boston. Matt plays the French horn for the Boston Phil and Bess teaches the piano. I miss them terribly but Jo helps to fill the gap. He's always been like one of my own children.'

Cordelia glanced up at her. 'I tend to forget that he isn't. He seems so much part of you and Hal.' A small pause. 'What is his mother like? I don't think I've ever met her.'

'Maria.' This time the pause was much longer. Fliss leaned her elbows on the wall. 'Very pretty. Very insecure. Very needy.'

Behind Fliss's back, Cordelia pulled a different

kind of face. 'Right,' she said. 'That's fairly comprehensive. Sugar?'

Fliss shook her head, turned about and took the mug. 'Thanks. Maria's one of those people that you have ambivalent feelings about. I feel very sorry for her and she irritates me like mad. And I think she's behaved disgracefully to Jolyon. He utterly adored her when he was a boy but she's practically ignored him since he was about twelve, although she became more interested when his television career started. He resents that, and I don't blame him; it makes me cross, too. At the same time I have my own guilt to contend with, which makes me try not to be too hard on her.'

Cordelia was silent; it was one of those moments when she wished that she hadn't given up smoking. She guessed that this outburst was very unlike Fliss and she gave her whole attention to the fair, slender woman who leaned against the wall and sipped her tea. She drank her own tea, and waited.

'Maria's husband died earlier this year,' Fliss said at last, 'and suddenly she wants to be a member of the family again. Hal is ready to accept that – he feels sorry for her – but I suspect that Jolyon will gradually be coerced into responding to his mother's neediness.' She stared at Cordelia, frowning. 'I can't quite decide why that makes me so . . . angry.'

Cordelia was trying to hear a subtext to Fliss's words, something that might give her a clue.

'Maybe Jo won't let himself be coerced,' she said. 'Maybe he understands Maria better than you know. Were they ever very close?'

Fliss shook her head. 'Not really. Jolyon would have liked to have been, but Ed was always the favourite. He's two years younger than Jolyon and very much the baby of the family. He got a scholarship to the Cathedral Choir School in Salisbury and everything, including Jolyon, was sacrificed to it. Jo was sent away to boarding school and encouraged to spend his holidays at The Keep rather than in Salisbury. When the marriage began to fall apart Maria couldn't cope with Jo's loyalty to Hal and it was very uncomfortable for poor Jolyon. He loved her terribly, though. In fact . . .' Another pause. 'Actually, years later, Jolyon accused me – well, me and Hal – of breaking up the marriage.'

Cordelia was frowning, trying to understand. 'Why?' she asked at last. 'How? I mean . . . were you and Hal lovers?'

'No. Maria told Ed that we were, though, and he believed her and told Jo. She said that we'd remained lovers after Hal married her and it had destroyed her confidence. It wasn't true, although we did still love each other. That was the trouble, I suppose, and that's what I mean about feeling ambivalent about Maria. Hal and I were completely loyal to Maria and Miles but, underneath, our love was still there. She sensed it, I suppose. When they separated, and Maria went off with Adam, I was living at The Keep with Miles. He'd had a stroke and I took him home so that he'd be well looked after by the whole family. One day Hal arrived unexpectedly and I was taken off-guard. It was such a stressful, anxious time and, when I saw Hal, I simply flung myself at him. It was such a relief just to react normally with him. Jo saw us but it was later, after Ed told him what Maria had said, that he confronted me; accused me and Hal of deceiving Maria and making her unhappy. He was about seventeen; very hurt, very angry.'

'Gosh. That must have been . . . scary. What did you do?'

Fliss smiled; she drank some more tea and her eyes were wide with memories. 'I gave him the ginger jar,' she said.

'A symbolic gesture?' hazarded Cordelia. 'Sorry, I'm not quite with you. What was the ginger jar?'

'It was given to me by my children's amah out in Hong Kong when we left to come back to the UK. It represented our friendship and the trust and happiness we'd shared, and although later it got damaged it still endured and remained beautiful despite its cracks. I tried to explain something along those lines to Jolyon about friendship . . .' Fliss shook her head. 'Honestly. It would take too long.'

'But I'd like to hear what you said to him,' insisted Cordelia. 'Come on, you can't just stop there. And I've got all evening, if necessary.'

'Jo took me by surprise,' Fliss said, remembering. 'Ed had been down to The Keep for a visit and we found out that Maria had left Adam and gone off with another man. It didn't last, and Adam took her back, but Ed was in a state. It was then that he told Jolyon that Maria had said that Hal and I had remained lovers after their marriage and it had destroyed her self-confidence and ruined her life. After Ed had left, Jolyon confronted me.'

'Why you? Why not Hal? He was his father, after all.'

'Hal had gone back to sea by then. And, in a way, I was the outsider, wasn't I? It would have been easier for Jo to be able to blame me rather than his parents. Anyway. There he was with all his angst and hurt, just not able to contain it any longer, accusing me of ruining his mother's life. I tried to show him how it really was but the truth was very painful. I said that he had to accept that neither age nor parenthood necessarily confers wisdom or perfection on ordinary fallible human beings. It was

94

a very difficult and emotional moment and we very nearly fell out, but afterwards I gave him the ginger jar as a symbol of the renewal of our own friendship and trust.'

'I like that. And what happened then?'

Fliss laughed at her insistence. 'We all lived happily ever after.'

'Sorry.' Cordelia looked repentant. 'I only ask because I want to know. I'm a journalist, remember. It fascinates me how people work, how they think. And this is important. If Jolyon and Henrietta are going to get together then I want to understand him and his relationship with his mother. And with you. Have some more tea and start at the beginning.'

# CHAPTER EIGHT

Later, after Fliss had gone, Cordelia went back into her study to check her emails and to glance over what she'd written earlier. She pressed a key to get rid of the screensaver and sat down to read her day's work. It was a few seconds before she realized with a heart-jerking shock that it wasn't there. The first few sentences were still on the screen but the rest had disappeared. She scanned it again, recognizing some of it, knowing that most of it was missing and all the while trying to remember what she might have done to lose it. She'd saved it; she knew she had. She could recall it quite clearly: there had been the noise at the window and she'd thought it was Fliss arriving – and she'd saved the document before standing up. Perhaps, as she'd stood up, she'd touched the delete key. If so, why had only some of the work been deleted?

She swore beneath her breath, still staring at the

screen, confused and angry with herself – but she knew she had a chance to retrieve her work if she didn't mess up.

'Close down,' she murmured, pressing the appropriate keys.

Up came the words: 'Do you want to save the changes to "Soke"?' She clicked on 'No' and then opened her Articles file and scrolled down to 'Soke'. Fearfully, she pressed 'Enter' and there it was: all her work, quite safe. Very carefully she set it to print off.

She felt quite ill and weak with relief; eagerly watching the printer as it produced the sheets, taking them out and folding them together. Keeping them with her, she went into the kitchen and poured herself another glass of wine from the bottle she and Fliss had shared earlier. The shock of almost losing her work had driven her conversation with Fliss from her mind but now, gulping a mouthful of Sharpham's, she remembered Fliss's story and how Fliss had looked at her when she'd finished telling how she and Hal had been separated and how she'd married Miles; rather embarrassed, surprised at herself, yet hopeful that she, Cordelia, would understand.

She'd said the first thing that came into her mind: 'I didn't love my husband either. Not really. I was in love with someone, just like you with Hal, but he hesitated and then went away for two years. I was terribly hurt and while he was away I had this mad moment and married Simon. I thought it would be OK and I became pregnant and everything was fine, and then he came back into my life.'

'And what happened?' Fliss had asked into the silence that followed.

'I had another kind of mad moment,' she'd answered wretchedly. 'Just the one – but somehow Simon found out and a year later he left me. Henrietta was devastated – she adored him – but he always kept in contact with her. Then, when she was fifteen, he put in for a transfer to the Australian Navy and he wrote to Henrietta and told her in detail why he'd left us and that he was beginning a new life with his new family and he wanted no more contact.'

'Oh hell!'

Now Cordelia smiled wryly, remembering her reaction to the inadequacy of Fliss's response and how they'd laughed together with compassion for each other and a sense of real friendship.

'I know all about guilt,' she'd said to Fliss. 'At least you and Hal played it straight. Henrietta's never really quite forgiven me.'

Fliss had hesitated for a moment. 'What about the other man?'

'Simon was rather clever about that,' she'd said. 'He waited until he, the other man, was married and then he announced that he was leaving us. By then it was too late for me.'

That's when they'd decided to have a drink, and then Fliss had gone back to The Keep.

Dusk was gathering in corners; beneath a rising moon the tide turned, tugging and towing away from the land, dragging its anchors over stony beaches. Cordelia shivered; she went into the hall and dropped the latch on the front door, and then drew the curtains in the rooms on the landward side of the cottage and upstairs. Now, only the big room facing the sea was filled with moonlight. She lit candles and, when her mobile rang and she saw Angus's initials, she gave a great breath of relief.

'It's a good job you didn't stay,' she told him. 'Fliss Chadwick came over.'

'I'm sure you'd have explained me away adequately,' he answered drily. 'A friend of a friend, perhaps? Or a dear old distant cousin. Then there's always the naval connection to fall back on, of course. You'd have thought of something. We're going to get found out one day, though, now I've moved down. Hal and I are bound to run into one another before too long.'

'I know. Listen, Henrietta and Jo were meeting up again today. That's good news, isn't it?'

'Very. Is that why Fliss came to see you?'

'I think so. She's rather worried about Jo's mother becoming a pain now that she's a widow. Having ignored Jo for years it seems that he's about to become flavour of the month and Fliss is rather cross about it. Apart from that, no woman wants an unattached ex-wife hanging about.'

'I can't imagine Fliss is the jealous type.'

'Oh, darling, we're all jealous types. It's just that some of us are able to disguise it better than others.'

In the slightly awkward little silence that followed, Cordelia guessed that any light rejoinder he might have uttered had seemed suddenly inappropriate when he remembered how she had watched from a distance whilst he and Anne had raised three boys within a loving, stable relationship.

'But then,' she said brightly – too brightly – 'that's life, isn't it? The outward show and all that. As long as we can all go on playing happy families, that's all I care about. I don't want anyone else being hurt. We've all done enough of that.'

'And Henrietta?' he asked. 'Has she phoned to tell you how it went?'

'Good grief, no. Well, it's not likely, is it? I can't decide whether it's simply that she doesn't want to talk about that sort of thing with me or whether she just doesn't think I'm that interested. Do you need to be friends with your boys, Angus, or do you let them just get on with it?'

He hesitated. 'I like to know what they're doing. When Anne was alive there seemed to be more communication but that's because she was much better at keeping up with them than I am. I'm lucky that they like to come to stay occasionally. Of course, living in Dartmouth and having a boat on the river is going to be a real attraction. Well, you know all that. Why do you ask?'

'Oh, nothing particular. Just something I heard on the radio. Are we the first generation who needs to be friends with our children? I wondered whether I could get an article out of it. You know? Comparing our generation with our parents'. Anyway, it's not important.'

'I think it's rather an interesting thought,' he said. 'With mobile phones and email it's very easy to be in touch, isn't it? Very tempting.' He chuckled. 'I can just imagine my old father texting! I don't think he telephoned me ever in his life.'

'Well, there you are. I shall do some research on it. So are you out tonight?'

'Yes, I told you. Supper with Tasha and Neil. In fact, I ought to be on my way.'

'Phone me in the morning and we'll make a plan,' she said cheerfully. 'Enjoy yourself.'

Later, as she ate pizza and watched *Corrie*, Cordelia wondered how much more risky their meetings would be now that Henrietta was in Somerset rather than in London and about to become more closely associated with the Chadwicks. She longed to know how the day had gone but resisted telephoning or even texting. She simply mustn't be pushy.

At nine thirty Fliss phoned. 'I thought you might like to know that Jolyon is back and on cloud nine, though he's trying to disguise it.' Her voice was guarded. 'And Henrietta is coming to Sunday lunch.'

'Gosh!'

'Exactly. I wondered if you'd like to come, or whether . . .' she trailed away.

'No,' said Cordelia quickly. 'Henrietta would hate that. But thanks for asking – and for phoning. I can't tell you how much I've been longing to know.'

'I can imagine. Well, Jo can hardly contain himself.' A pause. 'He's even gone so far as to agree to Maria coming down for his birthday weekend. He's not particularly thrilled about it but he's too happy to be able to refuse. Hal got him at a weak moment.'

'Oh, no!'

'Oh, yes! Well, it'll probably be OK, though I wondered if you might come over some time while she's here to give me moral support.'

'I'd love to. I can't wait to meet her.'

'Thanks. I'd better go. Jo might come in at any minute. I just wanted you to know.'

'Bless you for phoning, Fliss. I'm so pleased.'

'Me too. Henrietta sounds very special. Prue is wheedling it all out of him as only a grandmother can. Anyway, we'll speak soon. 'Bye.'

# CHAPTER NINE

Slipping back into the drawing room, Fliss saw that Prue had given up all pretence of watching the television and had turned sideways on the sofa so as to see Jolyon better. He slumped, legs stretched out with the dogs at his feet, his eyes on the flickering screen. Lizzie was curled up in an armchair, a magazine open on her lap, though she looked up at the television from time to time. Hal was entirely absorbed in his newspaper.

'I think it was very thoughtful of you to drop in to see Henrietta again,' Prue was saying. 'It's horrid for those who are left behind at times like these with nothing to do but think. She must have been so pleased to see you.'

Jolyon said, rather guardedly, that he thought she'd been glad to have some company.

'I expect she misses the children,' said Prue thoughtfully.

'Yes, she does.' Jo was surprised out of his caution by his grandmother's insight. 'She says that's the worst thing of all.'

'Well, small children keep you busy; you don't have time to worry about yourself. They don't really care what kind of day you're having. They're only interested in what's happening to them, you see. It's such a relief not to have to think about yourself, isn't it? Too much time to think can be very depressing unless you have a very good opinion of yourself.'

Jo said he hadn't really thought about it and looked relieved when Hal lowered the *Daily Telegraph* and suggested a nightcap. Lizzie shook her head and said that she was going up to bed but Prue beamed at him and said that a small whisky would go down very well. Hal got up and winked at Fliss. She was still cross because he'd had such an easy success over the business of Maria's invitation but she couldn't help smiling back at him. She felt more confident knowing that she had Cordelia on her side, yet the nagging anxiety still persisted. She realized that she didn't want Maria coming back into their lives just now, when Jolyon was making his name as a television presenter and had met Henrietta. Why should Maria, who had caused him such unhappiness and destroyed his self-confidence, suddenly stroll back just in time to reap the rewards of everyone else's hard work? Suppose she were to cause more destruction?

She kissed Lizzie abstractedly as she went off to bed and smiled at Jolyon as he stood up and said that he was taking the dogs out for a last stroll. Pooter and Perks got up reluctantly, stretching, tails wagging, and followed him out.

'A very satisfactory day,' Prue was saying happily, whilst Hal was swallowing his whisky contentedly, and Fliss was seized with another surge of irritation.

'I'm still not sure that it's wise to agree to Maria coming for Jo's birthday,' she heard herself saying, and saw Prue's eyes grow wary and Hal assume a slightly martyred oh-not-all-that-again expression. 'Anyway, I think I'll go on up. I'm going to have a bath.'

She bent to receive Prue's faintly whisky-flavoured kiss, feeling guilty, knowing that she was spoiling Prue's happiness. Upstairs she drew the bedroom curtains, went into the bathroom and turned on the taps, took off her jersey and jeans. Perhaps she shouldn't have allowed herself the luxury of telling Cordelia about the ginger jar; perhaps it had been self-indulgent. Certainly it had stirred up all the old memories and resentments – and certainly it had been out of character. Even now she couldn't quite decide what had led her to confide in Cordelia; she preferred to keep her own counsel rather than have emotional soul-baring sessions with her friends, and she could usually discuss most things with Hal.

Fliss wrapped herself in her dressing gown. This was the difficulty, of course; for the first time they were in disagreement about Maria. Always they'd been on the same side, she and Hal; even when Miles had taken a job in Hong Kong without consulting her, and Maria had decided to move to Salisbury, making family life almost impossible for Hal and Jolyon, she and Hal had agreed that they must stick it out, feeling they must continue to work at their own marriages. Yet, all the while, their secret love for each other had sustained them.

'What are we doing, Fliss?' he'd asked her once, rather desperately. 'Why are we wasting our lives? For God's sake, are we *mad*?'

'No,' she'd answered quickly, 'not mad. Well, probably . . .'

'We love each other,' he'd said urgently. 'Nothing else matters.'

'It's not just us. Other people matter too,' she'd said. 'We don't live in a vacuum.'

'I don't care about anyone else,' he'd said angrily. 'It's our turn . . .'

'But you do,' she'd said. 'You love Jo and Ed. And

you promised Jo you'd hold on. You'd hate being a weekend father, Hal. Driving to Salisbury and taking them out, wondering where to go when it's pouring with rain, having to put them back in through the front door at the end of the day, or taking them to a hotel with a bleak empty evening ahead. That awful brittleness with Maria at the beginning and end of each outing and the boys miserable and awkward. Oh, Hal, you'd hate it and so would they.'

'But what will it matter in the long run?' he'd asked bitterly. 'We've sacrificed our youth, Fliss. We've given it all up. Wasted it. And for what? Maria despises me and is teaching Ed to do the same. What if *she* leaves *me*? What about Jo then? It will all have been for nothing.'

Oh, yes, thought Fliss, testing the water, turning off the taps, we resented *their* behaviour but Hal and I supported each other in spite of it. Actually, of course, it drew us even closer and helped us to cope – and, anyway, back then I still had Uncle Theo to talk to when things were really bad.

She remembered talking to him once about resentment: 'Every time I think I've conquered it,' she'd said, 'it comes back as bad as ever. I wish I could forgive and forget but it's terrible the way the past clings.'

'I've sometimes wondered,' he'd answered,

108

'if that's what Christ meant about forgiving our brothers and sisters seventy times seven. That it's more to do with having to forgive the same hurt each time it comes back to haunt us than forgiving a succession of sins against us. Brooding over the past makes us less able to grow into the future. We have to learn to let things go. Not to bury them down but to truly let them go and trust ourselves to the future, generously and single-mindedly.'

'But how?' she'd asked almost desperately. 'How is it possible?'

He'd remained silent for a long time. 'I believe that only God can make change really possible,' he'd said at last, almost reluctantly, 'and only then if we want it. God will meet us at the threshold of our fear but we are too busy believing that He cannot manage without our tinkering and interfering to put our trust absolutely in Him. We cannot make that ultimate commitment which makes it possible to die to ourselves so as to receive our security at last, for once, from Him.'

Fliss took towels from the heated rail, piled them beside the bath and climbed into the hot, scented water.

It was odd that Theo, naval chaplain and priest, had been so reluctant to talk about his faith: the point was that he'd lived it, and so it had had a much more profound effect than preaching would have done. What would his advice have been now?

She hummed a bar of 'How Do You Solve a Problem Like Maria?', trying to raise her spirits, concentrating on the prospect of meeting Henrietta. It was silly to imagine that Maria could have any real effect on Jolyon now that he was so established, so much more confident. A tiny voice in her head suggested that it might be she and Hal who were more at risk than Jolyon, but this was too foolish to take seriously and she reached for the soap and began, instead, to think about Cordelia.

Downstairs, Hal sat alone nursing his whisky. His mother had gone to bed, pausing on the way out to kiss him lightly and to say: 'I'm sure all will be well. Nothing can come between you and Fliss now. You've loved each other all your lives.'

It was an odd thing to say, although it was true that he was feeling the least bit defensive about Maria coming to stay – but much more because of old Jo than Fliss. It was true that Fliss was being edgy but it was crazy to think that there was anything to worry about. It was also true, what Ma had just said, that they'd loved each other for ever. He could hardly remember a time when Fliss hadn't been there; even as children there had been a special bond between them. Of course, it had been a bad time during those first few months when his three young cousins, Fliss and Mole and little Susanna, had arrived back at The Keep from Kenya, their parents and elder brother murdered by Mau Mau. He'd been told that he must be very kind, very patient, and he'd tried hard to look after them.

Hal swallowed some more whisky, remembering those holidays at The Keep, travelling down from Bristol on the train with his mother and his sister, Kit. The trips to the beach, to the moors, and, years later, the triumph when he passed his driving test and could take the younger ones out in his grandmother's car. Hal chuckled reminiscently, finishing the last of the whisky, settling more comfortably in his chair. What times they'd had together. Drowsing a little, clasping the empty glass in his hand, he slipped between waking and dreaming, remembering the first outing they'd taken, the five cousins, without any adult company. His grandmother had been anxious – all her precious grandchildren in his care – but he'd been confident, with Fliss beside him in the passenger seat, Mrs Pooter curled at her feet, and the other three with Mugwump squashed in the back, the hamper and the rugs and the rounders bat and tennis balls packed in the boot . . .

## Autumn 1961

The picnic party arrives safely at Haytor rocks with only one moment of real anxiety. A car travelling too fast towards them in one of the narrow lanes causes a frightened Hal to turn the wheel sharply, cursing under his breath.

'Bloody fool!' he mutters – and casts a shamefaced glance at Fliss, who is nearly as shocked to hear Hal swearing as she is at the near miss.

She smiles back at him, hiding the shock, not wishing to look prudish. 'He was going much too fast,' she assures him, lest his confidence should be shaken. 'You were jolly quick.'

The three in the back are sorting themselves out, Mugwump pushing his head out at the open window.

'Easy does it,' sings out Kit. 'You had poor old Sooz on the floor.'

Fliss glances back anxiously but Susanna has already scrambled back on the seat and is asking her usual question. 'Are we nearly there?'

'Very nearly,' says Fliss as they bump over a cattle grid. 'Not long now. Hold tight.'

Kit gazes out with pleasure, across the top of Mole's head, as they reach the open moor at last. The deserted road winds between slopes of bracken-covered moorland, which glows with fiery intensity in the afternoon sun, stretching away to the very feet of the high granite tors. Banks of prickly gorse bushes are bright with enamel-yellow blossoms whose excitingly sweet, nutty scent drifts gently in the warm air. Wind-shaped thorn trees, already scarlet with winter berries, offer dappled shade to the grazing ponies, which kick up their heels and clatter away suddenly as the car approaches. A sheep ambles out unexpectedly, crossing the road without a glance, so that Hal has to stand on the brakes and, as the engine slows and idles, Kit can hear a lark singing somewhere high above them.

'Rabbits!' she whispers in Mugwump's ear – and he strains at the open window, whining faintly.

Hal parks the car near Haytor rocks and they lay out the rugs and the hamper on the springy, sheep-nibbled turf and look about them, laughing and stretching, finding it a little strange to be all together without one of the older members of the family.

'Tea first?' asks Fliss, who feels that someone should be in charge of the catering department. 'Or climb? Which?'

'Climb,' says Kit at once. 'We shall be too full after tea to want to climb things.'

They stare up at the grey-seamed rocks, piled high into strange shapes, reaching stony fists and fingers into the pale blue sky; granite islands in a sea of burning bracken.

'Come on,' shout Susanna and Mole. 'Come on, you lot.'

They jump about amongst the bracken, leaping on and off the smaller rocks that lie tumbled about, calling to the dogs questing to and fro, noses to earth, tails wagging.

'Should I stay with the hamper?' suggests Fliss uncertainly. 'What d'you think?'

'No need,' says Hal impatiently. 'It's all quite safe. No ponies about. Roll the rugs up if you're worried. Let's get going.'

'I'll stay,' says Kit suddenly. 'No, really. I want to. I'm a bit fagged, to tell you the truth, and poor old Mrs Ooter-Pooter will never make it to the top. She'll stay here with me, won't you, old lady? Good girl, then. Honestly, Fliss. Don't look so worried. I shall stretch out here in the sun. Go on. Bet you can't get to the top in ten minutes. I'll time you.'

They're off at once, the two little ones running ahead, Mugwump at their heels. Kit watches them for a few moments then lies back, the sun warm on her closed eyelids, listening to the skylarks, her fingers playing with Mrs Pooter's ear. She forgets to keep an eye on her watch, and presently she dozes.

Hal strides out, filled with a joyful sense of

wellbeing and achievement; breathing in lungfuls of the clear air. It had been quite a near thing, with that ass of a driver pushing them into the hedge, but he'd handled it very well, all things considered. He dwells with private satisfaction on one or two moments of the journey and then glances down at Fliss, who is almost running to keep up with his long strides. His heart is filled with a new tenderness for her. He's always been fond of his little cousins but Fliss's faithful devotion and admiration have given her a rather special place in his affections. Last Saturday evening, when she'd appeared in the drawing room, looking shy but excited in her new dress, he'd felt an almost painful sensation in his heart. She'd looked so sweet, so vulnerable – and so different, with her hair all put somehow on the top of her head, emphasizing the slender neck, the swelling of small breasts just evident . . .

He frowns to himself as the climb becomes steeper, loose scree slipping beneath his feet. It seems impossible that little Fliss should be a woman. She is so small and slight, so dear and familiar. Yet, that evening, she seemed strange to him, alight with some kind of inner mystery known only to herself; a mystery that transformed her. He'd felt oddly shy and rather clumsy, glad that he'd seen Kit change from child to woman and therefore had some sort of experience of this sudden transformation. Kit seems capable of passing back and forward between the two spheres of childhood and womanhood, so that he often becomes quite muddled, but the sight of Fliss made him feel protective – and it made him feel something else too. He isn't sure whether it is wrong to be aroused by the sight of his own cousin and he feels guilty – and confused – at this uncontrollable desire because he has the strange idea that it is what Fliss wants him to feel. Yet how could she? She is so young, so innocent – and his cousin.

'Hi!' Mole is shouting from somewhere above him and Hal leans back, looking up to the rocks where Mole and Susanna dance, waving. Fliss is panting up behind him and he puts out his hand so as to haul her up beside him. She is laughing, her face flushed, the shining strands of corn-fair hair blowing loose about her face. She wears an old Aertex shirt that had been Kit's, the faded blue reflecting the colour of her eyes and flattering the warm colour of her skin. Hal feels the strange tightening feeling in the pit of his stomach again as he stares down at her, imagining the breasts that are pressing inside the shirt. He sees her face change, though she still clings to him, and suddenly he wants to kiss her, knows that she wants him to kiss her, and he pulls her closer, his heart crashing about, hammering in his ears . . .

Susanna arrives beside them in a shower of scree, skidding down on her bottom, shrieking with joy and impatience. 'Come on. Oh, do come *on*,' she cries. 'Kit's timing us, don't forget. Mole's at the top already.'

They stare at each other for one heart-stopping second longer before following Susanna up the last steep climb to where Mole waits, high in the autumn sunshine.

'Look,' he says. 'You can see for miles and miles. Like when the d-devil tempted Jesus in the desert and offered him the kingdoms of the world if he would only worship him. It must have looked like this, don't you think?'

'Yes,' says Hal, after a moment. 'Just like.'

He seems to be having difficulty with his breathing, which isn't surprising after that scramble up, and he doesn't look at Fliss, who remains silent.

'Kit's asleep,' says Susanna sadly. 'I've been waving and waving. Now she won't have timed us.'

'Never mind,' consoled Hal. 'We'll do it again soon.'

'After tea?' asks Mole hopefully.

'Perhaps not after tea,' prevaricates Hal. He wishes Fliss would say something. She stands

117

tense and still, staring out over the moor towards Teignmouth, across the blue hazy distances, where the silver sea glints and glitters. 'Although you and Sooz could, if you like, and I'll time you. I can watch you the whole way.'

They cheer loudly and begin to jog back down the way they've come, slipping and sliding and calling to one another. Mugwump shoots out of dead bracken, where he has been pursuing interesting scents, and races after them. Hal clears his throat.

'They've got a mania about being timed for things,' he says awkwardly. 'Everything has to be timed these days, have you noticed? Fox started it with them going round the spinney but now it's getting to be almost anything.'

Fliss nods, still looking away from him, and he wonders if he's got all the signals wrong and she is shocked. Perhaps he's frightened her.

'Fliss,' he says pleadingly. 'Fliss . . .'

She turns to him with a look of such intense love that he is taken aback. So he hasn't got it wrong . . . She does . . . Does what?

'Fliss,' he begins again – but she shakes her head.

'Come on,' she says – and her voice is light and alive, bubbling like running water. 'Look. Kit's woken up. She's unpacking the hamper. Mole and Susanna are nearly there. Race you back.'

She's gone, crossing the rocks, scrambling down the slope, laughing back at him, her plait falling across her shoulder. He follows her, confused, as though he has somehow lost control of the situation and Fliss has gained it. Something has happened but he's damned if he knows what and he feels muddled and faintly irritated. He sees the scene below him: his sister kneeling on the rug, the two smaller children running up, the dogs getting in the way as usual and, as a backdrop, the car. The sight of the car restores his confidence as nothing else could have done, giving him back his sense of superiority and dominance in this family group. He is the eldest, in charge of them all.

He strolls up, hands in pockets, wishing he had a cigarette to add to his show of sophistication, smiling paternally upon them all, avoiding Fliss's eye.

'Tea ready?' he asks. 'So what's it to be afterwards? A game of rounders? Or are you two going to scale Everest again?'

He stretches out on the rug with his hands behind his head, casual and easy, while the girls fuss round, setting out the tea. Susanna falls across his midriff, resting her head on his chest, singing to herself. He tickles her good-naturedly but pushes her off when

Kit offers him a sandwich, rolling on to his side, propped on his elbow. Fliss is sitting back on her heels, frowning as she pours tea from the flask, and he suddenly feels that it is good to be young and strong and just setting out. How terrible to be really old, like Grandmother and Uncle Theo, everything over for them, all passion spent. He'd heard that phrase somewhere and had been struck by the sadness of it. How awful it must be if you could no longer feel passion, not just the sort aroused by pretty girls but passion about driving cars, sailing boats, running, dancing . . .

Fliss is passing him a cup of tea and he grins at her, winking complicitly, drawing her into a private world of their own. To his delight the colour runs up under her fair skin and she presses her lips together as though she might laugh with that same ebullient joy that he is feeling.

'So,' he says, confidence absolutely restored, 'rounders afterwards, I think, and then you two can climb the tor again if there's time. Right. So that's that settled. Where are those sandwiches?'


Hal's empty glass rolled from his fingers and he jumped awake. He glanced at his watch and climbed to his feet. Fliss would be in bed by now but not asleep yet. His dream still clung, the forty-odd-year-old memories clear and fresh, and he wanted to put his arms around her and remind her of that long-ago picnic. Hal put the guard around the fire and went upstairs.

# CHAPTER TEN

Henrietta leaned from the bedroom window watching the sun rising: thick golden sunbeams slipping and sliding swiftly down the steep-sided coombes, probing and chasing dense green shadows that retreated before them. Across the valley a swoop and flutter of birds' wings flickered – now seen, now unseen – between opaque darkness and shafts of brilliant light; and suddenly, as the sun rose above the black rim of the hill, the topmost canopies of the beeches flamed into brilliant, shining colour. The air was cool and fresh, and all around her the Virginia creeper burned crimson on the sandstone walls.

'I'll pick you up on Sunday,' Jo had said when he'd phoned last evening. 'It's quite a drive and you simply must bring the dogs. You can't leave them for a whole day.'

'I'm sure I can manage the drive,' she'd answered.

'But I'm still worried about bringing the dogs.'

'Everyone's looking forward to seeing them,' he'd protested. 'I told you. We can take them out on the hill with ours. Stop worrying.'

'How many of you will be there?' she'd asked with sudden misgiving.

'Just the usual,' he'd reassured her. 'Dad, Fliss and Granny. And Lizzie. Fliss's sister, Susanna, and her husband, Gus, will probably be over for tea. They live near Totnes and have a design and graphics studio in the town. They're really fun. That's all. Not too daunting, is it?'

His voice held a teasing note and she'd laughed suddenly. 'Of course not. I'm much more worried about my dogs than your family.'

'I'll be with you about half past nine,' he'd said firmly. 'That way we can have extra time travelling to and fro together.'

She'd given in gratefully; she hadn't really been looking forward to the hour and a half each way driving Roger's big estate car, but she was still cautious lest Jolyon should take too much for granted too quickly.

'You're so picky,' Susan had said to her once. 'This one's too pushy, that one's too reserved. It's no good looking for perfection, you know.'

Henrietta remembered that she'd felt hurt that

Susan of all people hadn't understood that it wasn't a need for perfection but the fear of making a mistake that made her cautious; the terror of misjudgement that might lead to problems later.

'Give and take,' Susan had said confidently, 'that's what it's all about for me and Iain. You have to take some things on trust.'

She'd often been envious of their relationship; of Susan's ability to organize her family as well as her vintage clothes mail-order business whilst Iain flew to New York and Paris and Brussels. They'd seemed to be able to handle it all – and yet look at what had happened to them.

Henrietta shivered suddenly, rubbing her bare arms and turning back into the room. She'd been so happy with Susan and Iain and the children – life had been so safe and such fun: now it was smashed and nothing would ever be the same again. Yet she couldn't quite despair: a memory, unprompted but sharp, sent her spirits fluttering joyfully upwards. After their pub lunch, up on the hills with the dogs, Jolyon had slipped an arm about her shoulders. They'd been laughing at Tacker, happy and at ease together, and Jo's action had seemed so natural, so comforting – yet exciting, too. After a few moments, she'd put her own arm around his waist – not clutching or clinging but casually – and they'd wandered along, linked like this, until Pan had panted up with a stick and Jolyon had bent to throw it for him. Perhaps it wasn't much, an arm around the shoulders, yet the memory of it warmed her. Henrietta reached for her dressing gown and tying it tightly around her went downstairs to make some tea.

Cordelia drove into Kingsbridge, found a space in the car park at the top of Fore Street, bought a parking ticket and locked the car. She came into the town most Fridays; she liked the bustle of market day and often met up with a friend for lunch. This was her fix, she told her friends; her way of reconnecting with the human race after days of solitude. It was difficult to persuade some of them that she was perfectly happy with only the sea for a capricious neighbour, that great temperamental presence that raged or sulked or basked at her doorstep.

Anyway, she thought, where else could I be so successfully anonymous or more private? I'd never have been able to keep up my relationship with Angus if I'd been living in any kind of community.

Even as she thought about him she saw him on the opposite pavement talking to an elderly couple who had their backs to her. She caught his eye, then let her gaze drift as she walked on. She stopped outside the delicatessen and watched their reflections in the plate glass; they were laughing now. She wondered what he was doing in Kingsbridge and hoped he'd come on the off chance of meeting her.

'We could arrange to meet,' he'd told her just the other day, shaken out of his imperturbability for once. 'It's crazy. When I *do* come over, if we happen to see each other we have coffee together. What's the difference?'

'I know I'm crazy,' she'd agreed, placatingly. 'It's just, if we meet by chance I feel less guilty. My surprise is genuine, I suppose, and I can carry it off more convincingly.'

He'd shaken his head in despair. 'Look. We're both free now. My boys would love to see more of you. They know how fond of you Anne was, and I'm sure they'd be fine about us spending time together. They'd probably be relieved to know I wasn't on my own so much.'

'It's Henrietta,' she'd said wretchedly. 'You know it is. How do I say to her, "Oh, by the way, I'm having an affair with the man your father told you about. Yes, Angus Radcliff, the one who destroyed our marriage"? Each time I see her I tell myself I'll do it, and each time my courage fails me. I know it's pathetic. I'm so afraid she'll think we've been having an affair all these years. And your boys might just think the same. It's too soon.'

126

'I know,' he'd said, resigned. 'It's OK. I'm sure the right moment will come.'

She knew that he hated the subterfuge; it was so out of character for him. She watched his reflection as he bent to say something to the elderly lady, who laughed and put a hand on his arm affectionately – and then a figure came to stand behind her at the window and she could see him no longer.

Cordelia went into Mangetout, smiled at the girls behind the counter and passed through into the narrow café. She ignored the stools at the bar and sat down at a table at the far end, hoping nobody would want to share it with her. A tall woman came in, glanced around and sat on one of the stools, two young women with children crowded on to another table, and a man, immersed and half hidden by a newspaper, was in the corner; then Angus was there, looking round rather vaguely, raising a surprised hand in greeting – 'Hel*lo*. How are you? May I join you?' – and then they were smiling at each other and Angus was sitting down with his back to the rest of the room and making a small private space for them. Yet she felt oddly uncomfortable, as if they were being watched, though nobody was paying them any attention, and she was almost relieved when Angus got up to go and she was alone again.

After he'd gone, and Cordelia was jostling with the

queue at the counter, paying for some cheese and a few other goodies, someone tapped her sharply on the shoulder. She glanced round quickly but there was nobody there, only a man in a navy-blue jersey hurrying out of the shop and disappearing up Fore Street. She turned back to the counter to take her change, puzzled, but with an apologetic smile for the assistant and for the tall woman waiting patiently beside her to pay for her purchases. Cordelia went out into the street, peering after the man in the blue jersey, but there was no sign of him and she turned down the hill towards the chemist.

It wasn't until she'd driven home and was unpacking her shopping that she discovered the small toy koala bear tucked down in her basket. She took it out and stared at it; its black beady eyes stared back at her. It was clearly brand new – the grey fur clean and soft, its black leather hands and feet curled as if it were clinging to some invisible branch – and she felt oddly disquieted by it.

A child must have pushed it into her basket, a toddler, perhaps, playing a game; but wouldn't he – or she – have cried out when it became clear that the toy was being carried away? Of course, the mother might have whisked the child off, not knowing why it was crying, or the child might have been distracted and forgotten it. Cordelia placed the koala bear on the table. Why hadn't she noticed it when she'd put her shopping on top of it? The toy was right at the bottom of her basket, hidden well under the cheese, and she was quite certain it hadn't been there when she'd shopped at the delicatessen.

Cordelia shrugged and began to put the shopping away, but the feeling of unease persisted.

Presently she phoned Angus.

'Listen,' she said, 'I know this might sound odd, but you didn't by any chance put anything in my basket earlier?'

'No.' He sounded puzzled. 'What kind of thing?'

'Well, I found this toy, a koala bear, right at the bottom under the shopping when I got home. It's brand new.'

'Nothing to do with me. Perhaps you knocked it off a shelf with the corner of the basket and it simply fell in?'

'That's possible.' She tried to believe it. 'I might have done.'

'Don't forget that you're coming to supper next Wednesday, Dilly. No cold feet at the last moment.'

'Oh, darling, I don't know. It'll be so odd.'

'You must come,' he insisted. 'You promised. It's just a house-warming thrash. There'll be lots of old friends and it will be a very natural way of getting together publicly. It'll look as if we're just meeting up again after a long time. You promised, Dilly.'

She sighed. 'I know I did. I will come, honestly I will.'

'You'd better,' he said grimly.

'Why didn't you invite Hal and Fliss?' she asked.

He hesitated. 'Hal was never a very close friend,' he said. 'He was senior to me, don't forget, and rose to great heights. And I don't know Fliss at all well. Anyway, I'm leaving them to you. You can give a return party and we'll all meet at your place. I promise you, Dilly, this is the right way to start again. Much better than Henrietta finding out from someone else. It's simply asking for trouble. It was rather different when I was living in Hampshire but now I'm just a few miles away it's much more dangerous.'

'I know. I'm sure you're right. It's just that I'm scared.'

She heard him laugh. 'You and me both.'

The koala bear seemed to be watching her and she gave a little shiver. 'I wish you were here.'

'Well, so do I.' He sounded rather surprised. 'But you said you had to finish your article and that you were going in for a drink this evening with the people on holiday next door.'

'I am,' she said quickly. 'They're so nice, and they're going home tomorrow. It's just that I miss you. Anyway, you've got one of your boys coming for the weekend. I'm fine, honestly. It's just this wretched koala bear has worried me. I can't think where it came from. Anyway. Have a good weekend. I'll see you soon?'

'Absolutely. And let me know how Henrietta gets on with Jo.'

'I will. If she phones me, that is.'

'If she doesn't, I'm sure Fliss will.'

'I'm sure she will. 'Bye, darling.'

The koala bear's black beady gaze seemed to follow her about, and Cordelia picked it up and put it in a drawer. She forced her mind back into work channels: finish the article – it was very nearly done – and then make a few notes about the idea that was running in her mind. *Are we the first generation to need to be friends with our children?* Wondering how Henrietta was, and if a text or a call might be intrusive, Cordelia poured herself a glass of water and went into the study with McGregor, closing the door behind them.

Jolyon was out on the hill with Pooter and Perks. He was following the well-worn sheep paths that led steeply to the river and the spinney, the dogs already far ahead. They'd put up a pheasant, and he could hear its indignant squawking as it rocketed upwards, seeking refuge in the blackthorn hedge. The afternoon was warm, low-slanting sunshine glinting on the bleached stubble of the fields across the river; a gathering of swallows dipped and swerved above his head, twittering sweetly as they headed south.

He couldn't wait to show Henrietta The Keep and to bring her out here on the hill. This was his place, this ancient hill fortress where his ancestors had built The Keep from the stone of the old fort: this was where he belonged, and he wanted to share it with her. Part of him felt strong about that, sure that he'd found the one person with whom he could feel safe within a relationship, but another part warned him that he was taking a huge risk.

'It's head and heart,' Fliss had said to him once about something else. 'Your heart says, "Yes! Yes! Go for it!" and your head is saying, "Hang on! Wait a minute. Are you sure?" It's so difficult to know which is right.'

And the problem was that this whole thing about his mother coming back on the scene was really unsettling him. He felt resentful that she was coming for his birthday when really he wanted to be with Henrietta, and cross too, because he knew that he'd given in to it too easily. He couldn't really blame Dad – he was simply trying to be kind – but he was angry that she felt she could simply walk back into his life now that she was on her own. Could she really have forgotten how she'd treated him?

Every emotional storm, with his mother at their centre, stood like a series of signposts stuck into the map of his childhood; each pointing the way to the final rupture, though some more crucial than others. Since meeting Henrietta the memories of them had become more than usually vivid. For years he'd managed to crush them down, but for some reason they'd begun to surface: that time when she'd rubbished his plans for The Keep, for instance; and the terrible row over Rex. And the odd thing was that the memories were so fresh. He'd imagined that he'd dealt with it all, that he'd grown up and away from it, and it was unsettling to find the scenes replaying so vividly in his head.

The dogs had reached the spinney, and Pooter's excited barking fractured the drowsy peace of the autumn afternoon and recalled Jolyon from the past. He guessed that she'd probably seen a squirrel and was now trying to follow it up its tree. Nothing would persuade the indomitable Pooter that she couldn't climb or fly. He cast aside his disquieting memories and began to run, jumping the last few yards of track and following the dogs into the spinney.

# CHAPTER ELEVEN

Fliss lit the first fire of the year in the hall just after lunch. She'd suddenly decided that the hall should be a warm and welcoming place for Henrietta tomorrow and now she kneeled on the granite hearthstone, making a pyre of kindling in the vast, empty grate and lighting the firelighter beneath the scaffolding of twigs. There was a huge log basket in its own small alcove within the deep recess that housed the fireplace, and which Jolyon kept filled with dry logs, and, while she waited for the flames to take hold, she sat on the little stool that was kept in the other alcove opposite the log basket.

Fliss looked about the hall, unable to decide whether she liked it best in high summer, cool, shadowy, peaceful, with the door open to the court-yard, or in the depths of winter, with the curtains pulled against a wet afternoon and the flames leaping in the granite fireplace.

It was a room within a room: two high-backed sofas piled with cushions faced each other across the low, long table. At the end of this table, opposite the fireplace, stood a deep, comfortable armchair. It was a cosy area within the vaster, draughty spaces of the hall and she could remember so many happy occasions that had taken place here, as well as much simpler everyday events. In the past, tea had always been eaten in the hall and Fliss could readily conjure up the memory of her grandmother, *The Times* open on the sofa beside her, pouring tea for Uncle Theo, cutting a slice of delicious cake.

It was difficult to believe that she, Fliss, was the grandmother now. How wonderful it would be, just at this moment, if the door were to open and nine-year-old Paula were to come running in, followed by Bess with little Timmy staggering beside her. Or darling Jamie, flinging open the door and shouting, 'Is anyone around?' Oh, how she missed them.

Perhaps she would phone Susanna for a chat, a comforting, sisterly gossip about their children and their grandchildren, now all so far from home. Thank goodness that Susanna and Gus lived only a matter of miles away and were still so much a part of the family. Even as she got to her feet the telephone rang and Fliss waited for a few moments, wondering if someone might hear it and answer. The bell was silenced and she could hear Hal's voice speaking. Was it the tone of his voice or some sixth sense that made her feel certain that it was Maria on the other end of the line? The door that led from the hall to the back of the house was open and Fliss could hear Hal laughing, though not what he was saying.

She moved quietly towards the sound of his voice – he must be in the kitchen – and stood in the doorway watching him. He was still chuckling, his face absorbed, and Fliss was seized by the now familiar sense of misgiving. As he turned he caught sight of her in the doorway and his expression changed so suddenly that, had she been in a different mood, Fliss might have laughed. She raised her eyebrows, as if signalling 'Who is it?', but instead of mouthing an answer – as he usually did – he gave an awkward little shrug. Determined, now, not to leave the kitchen, Fliss crossed to the Aga and put the kettle on.

'OK,' Hal was saying cheerfully. 'I'll have a think. I'll let you know if I come up with anything. Give my love to Ed when you phone him. It's great news about his new job, isn't it? . . . Yes. Yes, I will. 'Bye for now.' He switched the telephone off and put it on the table. 'That was Maria,' he said, 'wondering what Jo might like for his birthday. She sends her love.'

'I can well imagine she wouldn't have a clue what to buy him,' said Fliss acidly, hating herself for her bitterness but quite unable to control it. 'It must be such a long time since she's bothered to think about it.'

She kept her back to him, expecting him to react sharply, but he said nothing for a moment; suddenly she felt his arm across her shoulder.

'Come on, old love,' he said quietly. 'Can't we do this together? We've all agreed that she can come for the weekend . . .'

'Have we? Well, I suppose we have, although I think Jo is really upset about it. You got him at a weak moment, you know you did.'

Hal removed his arm abruptly but before he could speak, Prue surged into the kitchen.

'Someone's lit the fire in the hall. How lovely. Was it you, Hal? Oh, and Fliss is making tea. I saw Jo out on the hill with the dogs so he'll be ready for a cup. I love the first fire of the year, don't you? I just wonder, though, if it needs some more logs on it, Hal? Could you come and see to it?'

They went out together. Fliss began to put the tea things on to a tray, partly irritated at the interruption, partly relieved. Always, since she and Hal had been married, there had been other people around: Prue, young Sam, Jolyon, Lizzie. She and Hal had never been alone, although the house was big enough to give everyone plenty of privacy. Sometimes the family irked her but she believed that its continual presence very often held foolish emotions in check and gave silly little storms plenty of time to blow over before they could lead to more serious rows. It was difficult to maintain prolonged silences, to sulk or to say spiteful things with Prue or Lizzie or Jo around. Some friends said that it was unnatural, even unhealthy, to be so constrained, but Fliss believed that it had a rather civilizing effect – and there were many benefits: Prue's eccentric take on life was very wise, and the youthful energy and optimism of Lizzie and Jo and Sam lifted her spirits.

While she waited for the kettle to boil Fliss wandered to the window seat, hitching one knee on to the old patchwork cushion. Outside the two tall windows, the hill sloped away so steeply that the kitchen seemed to be poised high up in the air. She could see the migrating swallows below her, wheeling across the small, neat, multicoloured fields, and beyond them to the high bleak contours of the moor. How often she'd kneeled here as a child; aware of the house around her, as strong and safe as a fortress. The Keep had always been a place of sanctuary, and she'd always felt secure within it; why then should she suddenly feel at risk?

The kettle began to sing. Pooter and Perks came barging into the kitchen ahead of Jolyon, who was still taking off his gumboots in the scullery, hurrying to see if there might be some biscuits for them.

'Wait,' she said to them. 'In a minute, when I've made the tea. Just wait.'

Jolyon came in looking preoccupied and she smiled at him. 'I've just lit the fire in the hall. It's a trial run, really, so that it's all warmed up ready for Henrietta tomorrow. It's always so welcoming, isn't it, to have the fire going?'

His brooding expression fled and he smiled at her. 'I think she's nervous. Well, I don't really blame her.'

'Nobody can be nervous with Pooter and Perks around,' Fliss said. 'And the rest of us will be restrained and very well-behaved.'

He frowned, as if suddenly afraid that he'd committed himself too far, that he was making too much of it. 'It's only lunch after all,' he said defensively.

'Of course,' said Fliss non-committally. 'Well, tea too, I hope. I've made a cake. Susanna and Gus will probably come over as usual but I'm sure Henrietta will be able to cope with them. For goodness' sake, give those dogs a biscuit each and then come and have some tea.'

She carried the tray down the passage and into the hall. The fire was burning well, piled high with logs, and Prue was tidying up the newspapers and books that were scattered across the table so as to clear a space for the tray. Fliss saw that Hal looked quite cheerful; if he'd been upset by her earlier remarks he made no sign of it.

'We need a couple of really big logs,' he said. 'These are so dry they're burning at a rate of knots. Last thing this evening I'll bring in a couple of damp ones to help keep the fire in overnight.'

Fliss knew that he'd guessed why she'd lit the fire, that it was to welcome Henrietta and make it special for her, and his insight disarmed her. She didn't look at him, again, however; she put the tray down and crouched beside the table, pouring tea.

'Where's Lizzie?' she asked. 'Surely she's not still in the office? Oh, here she is.'

Lizzie and Jolyon came in together with Pooter and Perks, and Fliss was seized by a disproportionate sense of relief – as if Lizzie's presence dispelled this clinging miasma of anxiety. Her straightforward approach and natural cheerfulness cut through the shadows of the past, letting in the brighter, fresher air of common sense, and enabled Fliss to breathe more freely.

She thought: What *is* the matter with me? – and,

pouring more tea, was horrified to see that her hand was trembling.

'I've had a letter from Sam,' Lizzie was saying, sinking down beside Prue. 'He's fine. Sends his love to everyone and asks if Jolyon can pick him up for his exeat weekend. He wants to show off his famous cousin.' She flourished the letter. 'Shall I read it to you?'

Fliss perched on the little stool, her mug beside her on the floor, hands linked round her knees; she watched their faces as they listened – amused, interested – and was comforted.

Lizzie stayed on in the hall after the others had disappeared away, curled on the sofa, watching the flames with Pooter and Perks at her feet. After eight years with the Chadwicks she was adept at keeping her finger on the family pulse and just now she'd have said that it was beating a tad too fast. She'd noticed the tension in Fliss's shoulders and hands as she'd sat on the little stool, sipping her tea; she'd been aware of Hal's determined cheerfulness and Prue's watchfulness, and she could almost feel the waves of anxious excitement emanating from Jo.

Well, that was perfectly reasonable; Lizzie smiled to herself. Ever since he'd met Henrietta he'd been beside himself – which could be an uncomfortable place to be. It meant that you were outside of your usual skin, you could see yourself more clearly, and your words and actions took on a new and intense quality. But there was more to it than that: there was the question of his mother suddenly coming back into his life – into all their lives – and it was beginning to cause problems. She could remember that when she'd first arrived at The Keep Jo had been reluctant to speak about Maria and only very gradually, as he and she became friends, had she begun to piece together the history of Jo and his mother, and of the whole Chadwick family.

And what a tragic history it was. Lizzie shifted, no longer smiling. The presence of that matriarch, Freddy Chadwick, could still be felt – possibly because the family still talked about her with such affection and respect. She'd been twenty-two when she'd lost her husband at the Battle of Jutland; left with her twin sons, Peter and John, just a few months old. When the next war had come along John had been killed on convoy duty in 1945, leaving Prue with three-year-old twins. And then, twelve years later, Peter and his wife, Alison, and eldest son, Jamie, had been murdered by Mau Mau terrorists. Lizzie wondered how anyone could survive such appalling loss. She'd often tried to imagine their three remaining children, Fliss, Mole and Susanna, returning from Kenya to their grandmother at The Keep, and how Freddy Chadwick had coped with her own terrible anguish whilst caring for them. That's when Prue had introduced Freddy to her friend, Caroline, who came to The Keep to be the children's nanny.

Perhaps, Lizzie thought, it was because of the strange way the pattern had recurred that she felt she had her own place at The Keep. She'd had an important part to play when, thirty years later, history had almost repeated itself: Mole killed by IRA terrorists before his child was born, and young Sam's mother, Lizzie's closest friend, refusing to tell the Chadwicks about either the relationship or the baby.

'They don't know anything about me,' she'd said to Lizzie. 'They'll think I'm just trying it on. He'd have taken me down to meet them if he'd wanted to, but he thought he was too old for me. He simply couldn't believe I really loved him. But he loved me, I know he did, and the baby was to help him commit; to make up his mind . . .'

Of course, Mole hadn't known she was expecting his baby; their relationship had been such a secret, private thing. And then she'd died too, in a skiing accident, her first holiday for three years, the first since Sam had been born, leaving him with Lizzie. That's when she'd first met the Chadwicks, and Fliss had persuaded her to move to The Keep, to look after Sam.

'You're the bridge,' Fliss had said, 'between Sam's past and his future, and I have this feeling that without you we might all come tumbling down.'

Lizzie leaned to put another log on the fire, remembering. She hadn't needed much persuading to give up her agency work and the tiny flat she could no longer afford. The offer had seemed like a miracle. Of course, the Chadwicks hadn't really hoped or expected her to stay once eight-year-old Sam went off to school at Herongate, but she'd wanted to stay; she loved the Chadwicks. And she'd already begun to work with Jolyon on his new project. It was she who'd really kept it going, once he'd begun to work as a television presenter, by gradually swinging the operation over from being growers to suppliers: to sourcing organic vegetables and meat for West Country hotels and restaurants. She was proud of that. She enjoyed talking to new clients, and finding local farms who were trying to find outlets for their organic produce. Her friends were rather envious of her little suite of rooms up in the nursery wing and the fact that she could walk across the stable yard to work. No, she wouldn't want to leave the Chadwicks just yet – and anyway, she would miss young Sam terribly.

'You and Jo are our generational link with Sam,' Fliss told her, 'just as Prue and Caroline were between us and Grandmother. We all need you.'

It was fun, she and Jolyon driving to Hampshire to watch Sam play in a rugby match or to take him out to tea. And fun, too, to have someone of her own age to go with to the pub, or a film at Dartington or the theatre at Plymouth; though it was possible now, with Henrietta around, that things might change. Lizzie tried to imagine what form the change might take, and how it would affect her, but, before she could pursue the thought, Prue reappeared, looking for her spectacles, and Lizzie got up to help her in the search.

# CHAPTER TWELVE

Maria put the telephone down with a great gasp of relief: goodness, how she needed a drink. Just to hear Hal's voice had been such a relief; to share a joke with him and listen to his infectious laugh. Perhaps it wasn't such a crazy idea to think of moving down to Devon. She'd never imagined that she could be so lonely; she still found herself making tea for two, preparing far too many vegetables, waking at three every morning – always three o'clock – and being struck afresh by aching desolation. Oh, those long, terrible, demon-ridden hours before dawn and the cold emptiness of the big bed. She'd get up and make tea but there was no comfort to be had: the silence was just as much a reminder of her loneliness. And even during the day, even with Penelope and Philip at hand, there were deserts of misery to be negotiated, featureless and pointless; hours that stretched emptily.

At last she could see the point of communal living, of having family and friends near at hand. That's why the Chadwicks were such cheerful people. That strange grouping of all ages under one big roof meant that you need never be lonely or depressed. It was rather odd, though, that she of all people should suddenly be able to appreciate a way of life that she'd once despised. She remembered the cruel, cutting things she'd said to Hal about his family, and how she'd had her own private plans to take over The Keep and throw the old Chadwicks out. She wondered if Hal remembered too, and was unexpectedly suffused with hot embarrassment.

'Don't you think it's selfish for your grandmother to go on living in that big place?' she'd asked Hal, years ago, just after Ed had been born. 'Isn't it time she abdicated in favour of you? We've got a growing family and we need the space—'

'Hold it,' he'd interrupted. 'The Keep is my grand-mother's home. Hers and Uncle Theo's. I'd never try to turn them out. Even if I had the power I'd never do it. And even when we do move in one day, it won't be solely ours. It belongs to us all. That's the agreement . . .'

'It's quite ludicrous,' she'd cried angrily. 'Why should we be obliged to run a kind of hotel for the rest of your family? It's stupid.'

'It's unusual,' he'd agreed, 'and it might not work once the old people have gone. It's an ideal that we could all pull together, share the place and stay close as a family.'

'It sounds like something out of Walt Disney,' she'd answered scornfully. And then Ed had woken and begun to cry and she'd stormed out. She'd been so upset that she'd persuaded her mother to talk to Hal about it but he'd remained intransigent.

'Do you really want to live there?' her mother had asked her, later. 'If The Keep is to be left under those conditions perhaps we should have a rethink. Hal tells me that even if he managed to overturn the trust it wouldn't help you. Fliss's father was the eldest and she would inherit.'

'Well, I can tell you one thing,' she'd said angrily, 'I'm not being a hotel-keeper. If Hal thinks I'm going to move in and be an unpaid housekeeper to his family he can think again.'

'We don't want your inheritance disappearing into some melting pot for the benefit of the Chadwicks, do we?' her mother had said thoughtfully. 'Why should you run a family hotel?'

And she'd gone on to talk rather regretfully about how Hal had changed, and then she'd mentioned Adam and how well he was doing and that his marriage wasn't a happy one . . .

The thin end of the wedge thrust into her own marriage.

Maria pushed the memories aside: it was all too uncomfortable to think about just how ready she'd been to pick up the threads of her old relationship with Adam and seduce him away from his tiresome wife. No, it was much more sensible to concentrate on her visit to The Keep; much more positive to think about the future rather than the past. She glanced at her watch; it was getting on for five o'clock. A little bit early for a drink but she needed one; just a very small one to celebrate her next trip to Devon.

On Sunday morning, with three changes of clothes flung on her bed and her hair in a mess, Henrietta grabbed her mobile, pressed the keys and waited. There was a little delay before her mother answered, her voice a little preoccupied.

'Hello, darling. You're bright and early.'

Henrietta immediately felt guilty. 'Did I get you out of bed? Are you OK?'

'Yes, of course I am. And no, I'm up and having breakfast.'

Henrietta pushed aside a suspicion that there was something wrong, that her mother's voice lacked the usual cheerfulness, the *eagerness*, with which she usually responded to her calls.

'I'm just wondering. Should I be dressing up for this lunch or is it OK to be casual, d'you think?'

'Perfectly fine to be casual, I should think. Not scruffy, but not over the top. The Keep isn't a stately home, you know. It's shabby and comfortable, and Hal and Fliss are very laid-back.'

'It's just, you know, Sunday lunch. People don't really do that much any more, do they?'

'I think a lot of people still have lunch on Sundays, but that doesn't mean that they dress up for it. It's just the family and you, isn't it? Nobody else? Well, see what Jo's wearing when he arrives. You can change if you feel you're not in sync. He'll understand that.'

'OK. Thanks . . . Are you sure you're OK?'

'Of course I am. Just brooding on a new article. And my agent's suggested another short story for the *Mail on Sunday*. They rather liked the last one, which is very good news.'

'That's great. OK. Well, I'll let you know how it goes.'

'You do that. 'Bye, darling.'

Henrietta stared at the selection of clothes on the bed. Perhaps the moleskin trousers with the pretty linen shirt and her treasured cashmere jersey slung casually round her shoulders? She glanced at her watch, swore under her breath, and began to get dressed.

Jolyon arrived ten minutes later. He was wearing cord jeans and a rugby shirt and looked very relaxed. She hurried to open the door and noted his look of appreciation with relief. He refused her offer of coffee and asked if she were ready to go.

'Won't we be a bit early?' Nervousness made her voice sharp. 'For lunch, I mean?'

'I could show you around a bit before everyone gets back from church,' he said. 'Just the two of us. Would that be a plan? I thought it might be fun.'

'Yes,' she said gratefully, trying to be calm. 'Yes, it would.'

Jo began to round up the dogs, encouraging old Juno to her feet. 'Up you get, old girl. Come on, Pan. Good fellow. We'll get Tacker in last. I know a good place to stop on the way to let them have a run.'

'Good.' Henrietta began to gather up rugs and toys. 'I'm terrified Tacker will misbehave. I'm bringing lots of things for him to chew.'

'He'll be with us in the kitchen. Stop worrying.'

She paused, staring at him. 'In the kitchen?'

Jo shrugged. 'I'm afraid so. The banqueting hall is closed for repairs and the ballroom has dry rot. We've even had to pay off the minstrels.'

She laughed reluctantly. 'It's just that The Keep does sound rather grand; and your father being Sir Henry Chadwick and all that . . .'

'Stop panicking and wait until you see it. I'm afraid we eat in the kitchen unless it's a formal dinner party.'

'What a relief. I feel better already.'

He put his arm round her shoulder and gave her a brief hug. 'You're a twit.'

She watched him getting the dogs into the back of the estate car, lifting Tacker in: he was right, she was a twit. After all, she told herself, this was just a perfectly ordinary visit to friends for lunch. But when Jo straightened up and smiled at her she knew that it was much, much more than that.

They drove into the courtyard, skirting the central square of grass, parking by the garage built into the old walls of the gatehouse. Henrietta stared up at the grey stone house. The austere, castellated tower was impressive; odd but striking.

'Wow!' she said. 'I mean, *really* wow!'

Jo looked pleased. 'I want to show you inside first, and we'll have some coffee. Then we'll take all the dogs out on the hill so that they can get to know each other.'

Leaving the dogs in the car, watching anxiously

from the window, Henrietta followed Jolyon up the steps and into the hall.

'Fliss lit the fire yesterday,' Jolyon said. 'She wanted it to feel welcoming. We spend a lot of the time in here in the winter.'

'I can see why.' Henrietta looked around her. 'It's beautiful. I love it. Goodness, if this is the hall, what's the rest of it like?'

'Come and see,' he said. 'Just a quick guided tour to get the feel of it.'

She went with him, glancing through doors, trying to take it all in: an elegantly shabby drawing room, a rather formal dining room, a comfortably untidy garden room. There was a study, rather dark and piled with books, with a computer on a table in the corner, and a large, warm kitchen with flagged floors and tall windows. Two large, rusty-coloured dogs climbed out of their baskets by the Aga and came to meet her, and she went down on one knee to stroke their heads and soft coats.

'Aren't they pretty?' she said. 'Whatever are they?'

Jo shrugged as he made coffee. 'We've never quite known. Border collie crossed with some sort of spaniel is the general idea. Pooter is the bigger one, and don't be deceived, she's a wily, greedy old bitch. Perks is much more civilized, aren't you, Perks? Come on. We'll take the coffee through to the hall.'

153

They sat together on one of the long sofas, with the dogs lying contentedly in front of the fire. Henrietta leaned against Jolyon's shoulder, clasping her mug of coffee.

'It's an amazing house,' she said softly. 'But I want to see your gatehouse too.'

'We'll do that later,' he said comfortably. 'Once you've met the family. They'll be back from church soon. And don't be deceived by Granny, either. She's just as wily as Pooter; she's just more subtle with it.'

Henrietta sipped her coffee. She felt relaxed, at ease with herself and with Jo. It was odd how confident she felt with him, how sure; it was once she was alone again that all her fears and doubts would resurface. At the sound of a car driving into the courtyard, followed by the slamming of doors, however, she was gripped afresh with nervousness. Pooter and Perks were already up and hurrying to the door, tails wagging, and Henrietta set her coffee down on the table, waiting.

Prue was in first, talking as she came, stopping briefly to greet the dogs before she advanced upon Henrietta, who rose quickly to her feet.

'I've been looking at your fellows through the car window,' Prue told her. 'Just a quick peep. I simply couldn't resist the puppy. He's so sweet.'

Henrietta smiled, murmured something about

154

giving them all a walk, liking this sweet-faced woman with her pretty, feathery ash-coloured hair and her warmth and friendliness.

'This is Henrietta, Granny,' Jolyon was saying.

Prue held out her hand. 'I'm Prue,' she said simply. 'And here's Hal and this is Fliss.'

Henrietta took Prue's hand gratefully, her difficulties about how she should address Admiral Sir Henry and Lady Chadwick solved in one neat stroke.

'It's so nice to meet you at last,' said Hal. 'Isn't it silly that we've known Cordelia for such a long time and never met *you*?'

Fliss said, 'Well, we've met you now, which is the important thing. I must change and then look at the lunch. Why don't you bring those dogs in, Jo? I'm sure they'll be fine.'

'We thought we'd take them all out together on the hill. Let them meet on neutral territory first. Here's Lizzie, Henrietta.'

A fair, pretty girl had come into the hall. She looked strong and capable and good-humoured, and, Henrietta guessed, was probably in her early thirties.

'I was putting the car away,' she said. 'Hello, Henrietta. Are you always called Henrietta? Never Hetty or Hattie or Henry?'

Henrietta laughed at this unexpected opening.

'Sometimes, but not generally. There was another Henrietta in my year at school, you see, and she'd always been called Hetty so I was stuck with Henrietta. Because I was at school with Susan, she got used to it too, so there's never been much inclination to shorten it at work either.'

There was a short, slightly uncomfortable silence whilst everyone wondered whether to talk about Susan. It was broken by Hal announcing that he was going to have a drink and was anyone going to join him, and Prue saying that a sherry might be very pleasant.

'Yes, please,' said Fliss, 'but I'll stick with wine. I simply must get changed,' and Jo said that he and Henrietta ought to get the dogs out first. Henrietta wondered if it looked rather abrupt, she and Jo going out when everyone had just arrived, but Fliss was already hurrying up the stairs and Lizzie had disappeared towards the kitchen, crying, 'See you later, then.'

Prue sat down near the fire and beamed upon them. 'Have a lovely time,' she said. 'Go along, Pooter. You're going to meet some very nice new friends. Go on, Perks.'

The four of them went out together and Henrietta clasped Jo's arm and then let it go quickly lest anyone might be watching.

'They're nice,' she said.

'Of course they are,' he answered, lifting the tail-gate. 'I did tell you. Now, let battle commence.'

Pan jumped out quickly, whilst Juno clambered down more carefully and, ignoring Pooter and Perks, began to explore the courtyard. The puppy sat quite still, staring with amazement at the two rusty-coloured animals that came to sniff at him.

'He's rather overwhelmed, poor fellow,' said Henrietta sympathetically, leaning in to comfort him. 'It's OK, Tacker. They won't hurt you. Out you come.'

Jolyon began to herd the dogs towards a green wooden door set in the high wall while Henrietta followed more slowly with Tacker. Passing through the door, out on to the hill, she caught her breath in delight; warm gusts of wind sent cloud shadows racing over the green-and-gold-chequered land that lay beyond the river. A tractor moved slowly, the plough turning the rich crimson earth, a glittering cloud of silvery-white seagulls in pursuit. The hills to the west sloped gently, patched lilac and amber, climbing towards the high moor that sketched its black uneven outline sharply against the pale sky.

On the path below, Jo was watching her; sharing her delight. Suddenly she began to run; jumping

157

and sliding down the narrow sheep tracks, with Tacker scrabbling wildly at her heels, until she reached Jo, who caught her in his arms and held her tightly.

# CHAPTER THIRTEEN

This evening the sea was capricious; whipped to peaks and crests by the increasing wind, stained a fiery gold by the drowning sun, the rising tide dashed itself against the cliffs below the cottage. Cordelia stared down at yellow-eyed gulls contemptuously riding the waves, bobbing fearlessly, drenched by spume and spray.

'Just phoning to tell you,' Fliss had said earlier, 'that the day went well. Just in case you were wondering. Henrietta is an absolute sweetie and we're all holding our respective breaths and praying that Jolyon doesn't mess it up.'

'Poor Jo. Why should he? Henrietta's just as likely to have an attack of cold feet. That's what generally happens.'

'All I can say is that she seemed to like us and nobody said anything embarrassing – though I could see Prue biting her tongue on a couple of occasions. Luckily Henrietta didn't seem to notice. She behaved very well. Prue, I mean. Hal threatened her beforehand that she mustn't put Jo on the spot by unconsidered or tactless remarks. We had a lovely time and I think it was a pity that you couldn't have been here too.'

'I'm just so glad that you liked her. And they looked happy together?'

'They looked utterly right together. What a pretty girl she is! And I think she and Lizzie are going to be good friends. Let's just pray that Maria doesn't put her oar in.'

'Could she? Could she spoil things?'

'I don't know. Jo's been a bit quiet the last few days, and I'm praying that the prospect of Maria's visit isn't stirring up the past too much, that's all. Memory's a funny thing, isn't it?'

'Yes. Yes, it is. But surely Maria has no real power, does she? You said that she's hardly seen Jo or any of you for the last fifteen years.'

'That's true. I know it sounds idiotic but I just don't want her around. Not now when things are going well for Jo.'

'Of course, it might be exactly the right time. The fact that he's in a strong position and feeling confident means that she'll have no power over him.'

'I hope you're right. Come and see us soon.'

'I'd like that.'

She'd gone back outside to watch the sea; the highest tides of the year and gales forecast. Fliss's call had comforted her; Fliss was worrying too, anxious that Jolyon should be happy. How wonderful it would be if Henrietta were to phone now and tell her all about the day and really talk to her, as she might talk to Susan or one of her other friends . . .

Cordelia caught herself up quickly. There it was again: that need to be friends with our children. She wondered if her own mother – that quiet, reserved woman – deep down had seethed with a desire to share in her, Cordelia's, life. Perhaps she too had longed to know what her daughter was thinking and feeling, had been hurt by being shut out from confidences, not allowed to share in the most personal, private joys.

Cordelia thought: But how could I have told her how I really felt about Angus? Or Simon?

And, anyhow, her mother had kept her distance, ready to advise Cordelia on matters like cooking or babies but implying that she was an adult now and should be able to manage. There had been a gentle but firm withdrawal, a kind of dignity that was quite missing in her own relationship with Henrietta. On the other hand, her mother hadn't been riddled with guilt; tormented by the knowledge that with a single act she'd destroyed her marriage and her daughter's confidence. It was difficult to be dignified when you felt guilty all the time.

Perhaps Angus was right: she longed for Henrietta to fall madly in love so that she, Cordelia, might at last be let off the hook. Henrietta would be happy, her confidence in love restored and – but this would be a bonus – she might be able to understand why her mother had behaved as she had.

'Surely,' Angus had said, 'the fact that we're back together after all this time must say something about constancy, if nothing else.'

'It's not that simple,' she'd said. 'She'd want to know how you'd felt about Anne all those years. She couldn't understand why I married Simon when I was in love with you and she used to ask me why you married Anne if you were in love with me. Oh, I *know* you were never unfaithful to her, but it complicates *our* relationship in Henrietta's eyes, you must see that.'

'If it were a Shakespeare play or a Jane Austen novel she'd think it was wonderfully romantic,' he'd said.

'It's different when it's your parents,' she'd answered.

And that was the point, she decided; perhaps it

was impossible to be real friends with your children. There were too many taboos.

It was getting dark, the sunset glow was fading, and her earlier despondency returned. She'd wakened with a sense of isolation. The prospect of the gathering at The Keep had made her feel very much an outsider and, when Henrietta had telephoned to ask about which clothes she should wear, she'd longed to be one of the party. She'd reminded herself that it was neither Fliss nor Hal but Jo who had invited Henrietta to lunch and that there was no reason why he should include her mother in the invitation. Nevertheless, she'd been unable to fight the childish sense of exclusion – and the knowledge that Angus was happily engaged with his son and his family had only pointed up her own loneliness.

She'd wondered if there was someone she could invite to lunch but all of her chums would have been with their husbands or families. It reminded her of those early days as a naval wife, with Simon at sea and Henrietta a small child. How she'd hated weekends. They'd been the most deadly times, normal family life taking place all around and Henrietta enviously watching the other children whose fathers were with them in the park or on the beach.

'Why can't Daddy be here?' she'd ask, and Cordelia

would explain, again, the peculiarities of service life.

She still hated weekends and usually made certain she had things, apart from work, to which she could look forward. Today she'd failed in that respect and, in the end, she'd walked for hours on the cliffs with McGregor, enjoying the glory of the early autumn day and arriving back exhausted. Yet while they'd walked she'd had an odd impression that someone was watching her, that same 'eyes on the back of the neck' sensation she'd had in Mangetout. There were other walkers out on the cliffs, and it was foolish to imagine that she was being followed, yet she'd been unable to free herself of the feeling.

It was very cold now. The wind was strong, scouring along the cliff-top, whirling around her stone balcony. She went inside and lit the candles, pulling the curtains against the darkness.

Later, Fliss lay awake, staring into the darkness, listening to the wind. Hal was deeply asleep, turned away from her, and she was comforted by his bulk, conscious of his warmth. She simply couldn't sleep. The day unreeled before her mind's eye: that first sight of Henrietta, the expression on Jolyon's face each time he looked at her, the way they'd driven off together after tea.

Hal had slipped an arm around her as they'd waved them off. 'Lucky old Jo,' he'd said happily. 'What a gorgeous girl.'

She'd agreed with him, happy for Jo too – and even more anxious now she'd met Henrietta and liked her so much. But why should she feel so anxious? Cordelia was right to point out that now was exactly the right time for Jolyon to show how strong he'd become. All day he'd been calm and confident, despite the presence of his family and Henrietta's nervousness. She'd been careful not to show her feelings for Jo but once or twice Fliss had seen a little glance flash between them, and her heart had gone out to both of them.

'Don't waste time,' she'd wanted to say to them. 'Be happy.'

Perhaps this anxiety sprang out of her own experience. She and Hal had not seized their chance of happiness together but had allowed the family to separate them. Of course, they had been so much younger; too young and inexperienced to stand out against the united disapproval of Prue and Grandmother. Fliss smiled sadly in the darkness. How innocent and foolish they'd been, yet she could barely remember a time when she hadn't loved Hal. All those years ago, she'd waited for some sign from him; for something more than the quick private demonstrations of love that were much more than brotherly or even cousinly; some proof that he was just as serious as she was. She'd allowed her imagination to wander into the future, inventing an endless variety of scenes in which Hal declared himself at last. Oh, the agony of young love . . . Fliss closed her eyes, tucked herself more closely against Hal's back, and slept at last.

On Monday, just after lunch, Cordelia telephoned Henrietta. She'd dithered all morning, arguing with herself and postponing the call, half wondering if Jolyon might still be with Henrietta and dreading that she might interrupt something.

'But what?' she asked herself crossly, nerves on edge. 'If they're in bed they won't be answering the telephone and if not . . .'

The answer was clear: she simply didn't want to give the impression of being an inquisitive mother, asking carefully worded questions. Instead, she prowled: sorting papers, closing reference books and putting them away, finishing the crossword, whilst McGregor rolled a sympathetic eye from time to time in her direction. And all the while her resolution grew stronger: today she would phone Henrietta and tell her about Angus's party.

She decided that she would be quite light-hearted:

'You'll never guess who's just moved back to Dartmouth?'

No, no, said the voice in her head, that's a bit too disingenuous; almost as if you expect Henrietta to be pleased about it.

Something more casual, perhaps: 'By the way, I've been invited to a party on Wednesday. Angus Radcliff. Remember him?'

No, no, that wouldn't do at all: much too tactless. How could Henrietta possibly have forgotten him? No, she needed to be firm, direct and almost indifferent.

'By the way, I'm going to a party on Wednesday evening. Angus Radcliff's moved down to Dartmouth and he's giving a house-warming party. Lots of old friends are going. It should be fun.'

The inner voice was silent and Cordelia rehearsed this once or twice. It seemed to strike the right note. After all, she wasn't asking Henrietta's permission or approval; she was simply telling her *en passant*, as it were. It needed to be dropped into the conversation – which posed its own problem. She could think of nothing to say just at the moment that didn't relate to Jo. And that brought her back to the question of when it would be tactful to telephone. For her reaction to the invitation to be convincing then it needed to be today: not too soon after the invitation had been received, in case it gave it too much importance, but neither too much at the last minute lest she should give the impression that she'd been afraid to mention it.

The voice in her head said that it couldn't matter less, since Henrietta wouldn't know when she'd received the invitation.

She might ask, Cordelia answered silently, and then I shall be able to be truthful.

The voice laughed hollowly.

I *do* tell the truth, Cordelia told it indignantly, even if I don't always tell all of it.

Irritated by the knowledge that she was talking to herself she went back to her desk. She would phone at two o'clock; now she must work. Her mobile began to play its silly tune and she seized it.

Angus said, 'Hello, Dilly.'

'Hi,' she said. 'How wonderful to hear a human voice.'

'Is there any other kind?' he enquired.

'There's the one in my head,' she answered grimly. 'And I promise you that there's nothing human about it. I think I'm going mad.'

He chuckled. 'Poor darling. What's it saying this morning?'

'It's mocking and deriding me. It tells me that I'm a lying, specious woman.'

'Oh dear. That sounds bad.'

'Uncomfortable, anyway. It's too near the truth for my liking. I've decided to telephone Henrietta and tell her that I'm going to your party.'

There was a short surprised silence. 'But that's fantastic, Dilly.'

'Yes, it is. I feel very brave and virtuous, except that I'm trying to decide how soon I can phone her.'

'How soon?'

'Well, in case Jo's still there, you see. I can't bear looking as if I'm a nosy, prurient mother trying to find out if they spent the night together.'

He roared with laughter. 'Even if you are?'

'Well, obviously I want to know, simply because I long for them to be getting along together and I want them to be happy. And I'd like to feel sure that Henrietta isn't going to throw one of her wobblies. She said to me once, "Well, you and Dad must have thought you were in love and look how that finished up." She's afraid to trust her emotions.'

'I think you're being a bit oversensitive about phoning.'

'I *know* I am,' she cried irritably, 'but this is the morning after a big day. She's been to The Keep to meet the rellies and it's a bit difficult to ignore it.' She took a deep, calming breath. 'Fliss phoned last night. She said it went really well.'

169

'That's good then.'

'You don't have to use your soothing voice. I'm OK now.'

'Great.'

She knew he was grinning; she could hear it in his voice. She grinned too. 'I shall phone her at two o'clock and then I'll phone you. Be there.'

'Oh, I will. Are you working?'

Cordelia snorted. 'Are you kidding? I've put in two commas, and taken them out again. That's about the sum total of my output this morning.'

'When shall I see you?'

'On Wednesday, at your wretched party.'

'Fine.'

She felt an irrational hurt that he'd accepted her tart reply so readily; hadn't offered to come over later. She frowned. 'And now I really must do some work.'

'Phone me when you've spoken to Henrietta. 'Bye, Dilly.'

She stared crossly at her computer screen, looked at the small clock in the bottom right-hand corner: twelve forty-three. She could give up and have some lunch or she could force herself to write just one sentence. Experience told her that she'd feel very much better if she could compose even a very short sentence. She set herself to concentrate.

*Are we the first generation to need to be friends with our children?*

An hour later she glanced at the clock and on impulse seized her mobile. A voice informed her that Henrietta's phone was switched off. Cordelia cursed quietly but comprehensively, and went to make herself some lunch.

# CHAPTER FOURTEEN

The village street lay empty and hot in the afternoon sunshine. Henrietta strolled slowly, hands in pockets, relishing the warmth of the sun. On each side the terraced cottages seemed to slump together, drowsing beneath their thatched roofs, rosy sandstone walls crisscrossed about with trellises of clematis and trailing honeysuckle. It was so quiet that she could hear a nectar-laden bee droning as it worked amongst the delicately tinted Japanese anemones. Nasturtiums, gold and yellow and orange, spilled over doorsteps and cobbled paths, climbing sandy banks and cascading down walls. In one small vegetable patch chrysanthemums and dahlias grew among tall runner beans whose late-flowering scarlet flowers drooped upon pale bamboo sticks.

At the end of the street the road forked away to the left, past the church and out of the village, but

172

she continued on the narrower lane that led down to the farm. Here, all along the ditches grew great stands of rosebay willowherb, its flowers turned to fluffy white seed, its leaves glowing glorious, vivid scarlet. A rabbit jinked out of the ditch and dodged beneath the bars of the gate into the field, the flash of its white scut bobbing as it fled down the grassy slope. Henrietta leaned on the gate, arms folded, chin on wrists, and all the while she was thinking about Jolyon. Fragments of conversation, images of what she'd seen, little scenes, all jostled for a place in her mind. Beneath these sensations a secret, un-ruffled continuum of happiness lent extra colour to everything around her; even the ever-present voice of cynicism had been muffled by this extraordinary sense of wellbeing.

Leaning on the gate, she tested her feelings, trying to see Jolyon as her friends might see him. This was a difficult one because he was already well known to them through his role as a television presenter and all her girlfriends fancied him; perhaps it was just as well that she wasn't in London. Seeing him with his family – easy-going, amusing, kind – it might be possible to wonder if he weren't a bit too good to be true, except that she'd seen another side to his character that showed that he was quite capable of anger and resentment.

'My mother's coming down for my birthday,' he'd said, driving home, when they were discussing future meetings.

Glancing sideways, she'd seen a bitter twist to his mouth, and experienced a quick stab of sympathy.

'Not your idea?' she'd asked, and he'd told her a bit more about his childhood and that he was finding it difficult to accept that his mother expected to be able to walk back into his life now she was alone.

Somehow, travelling in the car in the twilight, they both seemed to find it easier to talk about the personal aspects of their lives; exposing certain fears, voicing anxieties that would have been more embarrassing to speak of face to face. The very act of travelling seemed symbolic of the journey they were making in learning about each other; as the car passed through the countryside and small villages, so they were passing through new stages of discovery.

As soon as they arrived back, he lit the wood-burning stove.

'I haven't really needed it yet,' she said, watching him lay the kindling.

'You will, though,' he said, sitting back on his heels. 'Anyway, a fire makes things more cheerful.'

He stayed for supper and, afterwards, he piled more logs on the fire and they sat together on the sofa watching the flames. There was so much to talk about: films, books, friends. The time passed so quickly, though all the while she was hoping he wasn't noticing just how quickly. She didn't want him to go; not yet.

'D'you spend much time on your own in the gate-house?' she asked. She swung her legs across his knees and leaned against him, and his arm auto-matically passed round her to hold her close. 'Do you eat on your own?'

There was a short silence and she knew he was thinking this through, wondering whether he might unwittingly give the wrong impression of himself: a bit of a loner? An immature man who couldn't get away from his family?

'Not often,' he answered. 'It seems crazy when everyone's just across the courtyard to sit all on my own. Sometimes I do, if I want to watch a film or something, but I'm used to having people around, you see; different people. At lunchtime it might be Fliss and Dad, and Sam when he's home from school. Or Lizzie and Granny. Or a variation on the theme. It's the way life at The Keep works and I rather like it.'

She knew that he'd answered truthfully and was now wondering whether she'd be put off; she hastened to reassure him.

'I know exactly what you mean. It's like that in London. Or used to be. There were always people around in the kitchen but not always the same ones. It might have been me and the children and Iain, or Susan and a couple of people from downstairs making some tea, but I liked it too.'

His arm tightened about her and she sensed his relief. 'There are times when it's nice to be alone, like now, for instance, but we're lucky that The Keep is big enough for everyone to have privacy too.'

'Perhaps that's why Iain went,' Henrietta said sadly. 'Perhaps he didn't like it, though he never gave that impression.'

'What will Susan do? Will she have to move?'

She shook her head, her cheek against his jersey. 'I've no idea. She could hardly afford to buy him out of the house and I don't think she could manage to run it without his income.'

'What will you do?'

'I don't know. They went off in such a hurry. Nothing can be decided until they come home.'

There'd been a silence then, as if they'd both known that they were moving on to a very serious level of discussion; she'd given an anxious, quick upward glance and he'd bent his head and kissed her.

Leaning on the gate, remembering, Henrietta

smiled a secret smile, and stretched luxuriously in the warm sunshine.

At the third attempt Cordelia was lucky.

'Sorry, Mum.' Henrietta's voice was apologetic. 'I went out for a walk and forgot my mobile. I was going to phone you to say that yesterday was great. They're so nice, aren't they?'

Cordelia gasped silently with relief and hurried into speech. 'I'm so pleased, darling. Yes, they are, and it's wonderful that you've met them at last. Fliss phoned just now to say how much they'd enjoyed meeting you and to invite me over to The Keep sometime next weekend.'

'Oh.' Cordelia heard surprise mingled with just the least bit of caution in her daughter's voice. 'It's Jolyon's birthday, actually. His mother's coming down for it.'

'Yes, I know.' She was determined not to be warned off here; the Chadwicks were her friends and she mustn't allow this new relationship between Jo and Henrietta to undermine this. 'It's one of the reasons Fliss has asked me over,' she said, almost confidentially. 'She finds Maria a tad difficult.'

Cordelia recognized the quality of the silence that followed. Henrietta was never to be drawn into any kind of gossip; her cool glance would imply that

Cordelia dwelled permanently in a glass house and that the throwing of even the tiniest of stones was to be deplored. Somehow the priggish little silence gave her courage: it made her angry.

'Anyway,' she said lightly, 'I shall be going over to The Keep sometime that weekend, so I'll let you know when a bit later on, after Fliss has worked out exactly what's happening. Meanwhile, I was going to suggest driving over to see you this week. I could take you out to lunch. We could meet at Pulhams Mill. Only not Wednesday. I've been invited to Angus Radcliff's house-warming party that evening. His wife died, oh, just over a year ago, and he's moved down to Dartmouth. There are a lot of old chums going so it should be fun.' A pause, which Henrietta made no attempt to fill. 'I don't think I'd want to do the trip over to you on the same day but I could come tomorrow or Thursday, if it would suit you?'

'Yes, OK.' It sounded as if Henrietta had regained her composure. 'That would be good. What about Thursday, then you can tell me all about the party?'

Cordelia's heart bumped anxiously; did she detect a hint of sarcasm?

'Great,' she said quickly. 'I'll try and get to the Mill in time for an early lunch but I'll be in touch as I come along. Take care, darling. I'd better get on with some work. 'Bye.'

She put the phone down and shut her eyes for a moment: oh, the relief of it. She'd told Henrietta, actually mentioned Angus's name, and the sky had not fallen in; not yet. She'd made no comment, no protest, and she'd agreed to have lunch. Cordelia felt quite weak with the sense of liberation. Soon she would speak to Angus but not quite yet; she needed to savour this moment alone, to revel in it. She poured a glass of wine and took it out on to the balcony to celebrate a private victory in the warm, autumn sunshine.

Maria slipped through the intercommunicating door of the annexe, closed it behind her and paused, listening, in the passageway that led to Penelope's kitchen and the utility room. The noise of Pen's drinks party drifted through from the drawing room: the caw of voices, little shrieks of laughter, the encouraging clink of crystal. She'd already had a very tiny drink, just a nip of vodka, to give her the necessary courage to enter the crowded room. It had become the least bit intimidating, appearing in the doorway, seeing first one guest and then another spotting her and immediately adopting a sympathetic expression, nudging a neighbour warningly. Nobody knew quite what to say since Adam had died. Some, pretending nothing had changed, would utter a few bluff remarks and sidle away; others would seize the opportunity to be understanding. They'd put on special voices, hold her arm comfortingly, smile with a kind of gruesome sympathy.

Phil would materialize at her shoulder, cheerful and comfortingly familiar, like a dear old dog: faithful and loyal. Pen would nod – firm but encouraging at a distance – and raise her glass as if it were a flag and she were urging her old chum to the starting point of a race. Some of Maria's friends had been surprised and rather disapproving of her sudden decision to sell up and move into the annexe. They'd muttered all the old clichés about not doing anything in a hurry, not knowing that she'd had no choice but to sell and that the annexe was an absolute haven. Oh, how she dreaded the news leaking out somehow and then the whispers and the pitying looks; oh, the horror of it. Pen and Philip would remain loyal, of course. They might not even be particularly surprised. They knew Ed very well; knew his inability to stick to a job or be prepared to do anything mundane or boring. Ed had always had spectacular – and very expensive – ideas. Even so, she cringed with gut-churning shame at the thought of these friends of hers knowing the truth, discussing it behind her back. Not that she was destitute – Adam had left some very good investments and she had enough money from the sale of the house to buy a small flat, even here in Salisbury – but she could no longer compete with the social commitments of Philip and Penelope and the gang. Of course, just at the moment, nobody expected her to . . .

She glanced down at her pretty frock with satisfaction. She knew she looked good and that she could still command the reluctant envy of her women friends and the sly admiration of their husbands. She straightened her shoulders, arranged her expression, feeling like a child arriving at a party of older children; hopeful, slightly winsome. And here was darling Phil, just as she'd known he'd be, eye cocked for her appearance, the hand under the elbow.

'That's right,' he said approvingly. 'Gosh, you look good. Now vodka, is it, or a gin?'

# CHAPTER FIFTEEN

Cordelia drove into Dartmouth, found a space for the car at the bottom of Jawbones Hill and sat for a moment summoning up her courage. She'd been determined not to be amongst the first of Angus's guests to arrive and now, glancing at her watch, she was seized with panic lest she should be late enough to draw just the attention she wanted to avoid. She locked the car, walked down Crowthers Hill and turned up towards the house in Above Town. Tingling with nervousness she approached the dark blue door, which was propped open with a weighty doorstop: a beautifully painted cast-iron mallard.

She hesitated, staring at it, recognizing it. She'd seen it many times at the house in Hampshire when she'd been visiting Anne, nearly always when Angus was at sea.

'It would have to be Anne,' she'd cried despairingly all those years ago. 'I can't stop being friends with her after seven years, Angus. How am I to do this?'

'I never thought Simon would leave you,' he'd answered wretchedly. 'God, what bloody awful timing. But I'm committed now. Anne's expecting a baby . . .'

Cordelia could hear the sounds of jollity drifting down the stairs; voices, music: Jacques Loussier playing Bach's *Chromatic Fantasia*. She and Angus loved Jacques Loussier, though she mustn't mention that. She stood quite still, jittery with fear.

She thought: Did I really think that I could get away with this?

She stepped past the mallard into the big room, which was both kitchen and dining room, where a buffet supper had been laid out. Some guests were holding plates and napkins, choosing delicacies, and a pretty girl in a smart uniform was opening bottles at the kitchen end of the room.

'I shall get some caterers in,' Angus had told her, 'if you really won't help me.'

'No way,' she'd answered firmly. 'Absolutely no way. You can't be serious. For God's sake, we might as well put it up in coloured lights that we're having an affair . . .'

'OK,' he'd said equably. 'Just be there.'

183

And here she was, smiling at the girl and miming that no, she didn't have a coat and yes, she'd go on up, nodding cheerfully at the people by the table, and climbing the steep narrow stairs to the first-floor sitting room. And here was Angus, seeing her come into the room, raising an arm high in welcome so that several people swivelled round to see who the newcomer was.

'Cordelia,' he was calling – 'Don't *ever* call me Dilly in public,' she'd threatened him – and she was waving back, crying, 'Wow! What a view! It's nearly as good as mine.' Then he was beside her, giving her a host-like hug and immediately offering her a drink.

'Wine,' she murmured, continuing to beam around, 'whatever,' and waving brightly into the sea of faces: nearly all naval couples. 'Hi, Neil. Tasha. How are you both? Mike, how lovely.' And then, to her utter relief, someone she trusted and loved was moving out of the crowd and coming towards her and, for the first time, she felt as if she might be able to survive this terrible ordeal.

'Julia,' she said with relief. 'Oh, my darling, how are you? You look fantastic. Is Pete here? Oh, yes, there he is. How wonderful to see you.'

'We were so thrilled when Angus said you might be coming,' Julia Bodrugan was saying, embracing her. 'I nearly phoned and then some drama blew up. It's been far too long.'

Cordelia hugged her tightly. 'Much too long,' she agreed. 'We're all so busy these days. But how noble of you to come all the way up from St Breward.'

'It's noble of *me*,' agreed Julia, 'because I've promised not to drink. But it's not noble of Pete. Pete doesn't do noble. He has a simple social rule: if he can't drink, he doesn't go.'

Cordelia laughed and then was engulfed in Pete's bear hug. 'What's she saying about me?' he demanded. 'Whatever it is I deny it. Have you seen this view, Cordelia? He can see right down the river. Look. He can practically see his mooring off Noss. He says that's why he bought the house, because the privately owned moorings went with it. He's even got a running mooring in Bayard's Cove for his dinghy. Lucky devil. Of course, you're not likely to be impressed by a view of the River Dart, are you, not with the English Channel on your doorstep?'

Cordelia squeezed his arm. 'Your own views from Trescairn are pretty good,' she reminded him. 'But this is lovely. Different from my view but just as beautiful. I love seeing all the little boats.'

Standing between Julia and Pete she felt safe; as long as she didn't say anything compromising. Angus brought her a drink and she smiled her thanks, not looking at him, gesticulating at the river and making polite noises.

'I might get a bit of sailing in before I have to take the boat out of the water for the winter,' he said. 'What about it, Cordelia? Fancy a run up to Salcombe one fine afternoon?'

She saw how his jokey invitation was giving her an opportunity to establish their supposedly casual relationship publicly. 'It shows how little you remember about me,' she retorted. 'I get seasick on the Lower Ferry. No thanks.'

Someone called to him, claiming his attention, and he turned away.

'Isn't it nice that Angus has got so many friends to help him settle in?' Julia was saying. 'I hope the boys will make the effort to get down to visit him.'

Cordelia stopped herself just in time from saying that one of them had been down this last weekend, and was seized anew with terror. How easy it would be to make a mistake. And now Lynne Talbot was approaching with her thin, vinegar smile and cool, penetrating stare.

'Cordelia,' she said, offering her cheek, 'Jeff and I were just saying the other day that we hardly ever see you. Scribbling away as usual, I suppose.'

'That's my job,' agreed Cordelia amiably. She held her drink to one side and touched her cheek very lightly to Lynne's. 'I don't have a grateful government paying me a whacking great pension like you and Jeff. And I've never been one for the sailing club; not really my scene. Like I just told Angus, I get seasick on the Lower Ferry. And I can't seem to master the intricacies of bridge. I'm a social disaster. Are you well?'

'Pretty well. Julia and I were just talking about grandchildren. How's Henrietta?'

'Childless so far,' said Cordelia promptly. 'But that's fine. You had two the last time I saw you. Is there any advance on that?'

'No, still just the two. Someone – who was it? – was saying that they saw you upcountry a few weeks ago. Oxford, was it? Coming out of The Randolph with some man? No? Oh, well, she must have been mistaken. It's good to have Angus around, isn't it? He's coming over for lunch next week. Perhaps you'd like to come too.'

Angus was back; she could feel him just behind her, smell the scent of his aftershave. Lynne was watching her with that familiar, narrowed stare, the faintly knowing smile on her lips, and it occurred to Cordelia that she might give much more away by behaving stiffly with Angus than by being her normal self.

She turned, took his arm, made big eyes at him.

'Darling,' she said, 'Lynne's matchmaking already. We're having lunch with her next week. Are you ready for this?'

He grimaced comically, miming pleasurable anxiety. 'I can see that I shall have to be careful. Anne always said that you were a dangerous woman.'

It worked perfectly. As she glanced around she saw tiny mental connections being made: 'Of course, Anne and Cordelia were friends, weren't they?' and approving smiles: 'Isn't it nice to see Angus happy again?' and meanwhile Julia was laughing, and Angus was asking everyone to go downstairs and get some food. Cordelia released his arm quite naturally and turned away with Pete and Julia to fetch some supper. She felt confident now; the worst was over.

She left quite early: that was planned too.

'You could pretend to go,' he'd suggested when they'd talked about the party, 'and come back after everyone's gone.'

'And how would I know?' she'd demanded. 'Do I hide under a rug in the car and count everyone out? You must be joking.'

So she waited until three or four people had already gone and then glanced at her watch and said she'd be on her way. There were the usual polite protests and she hugged Angus quite naturally. It was Pete and Julia who came downstairs to see her off and remind her of the new plan for her to drive down to Trescairn for the day.

'I'll phone tomorrow,' she promised, 'when I've looked at my diary. It'd be wonderful.'

She got into the car, light-headed with relief, and drove home: out through Stoke Fleming and Strete, along Torcross Line, through Kingsbridge, and then plunged into the narrow winding lanes that led to the cliffs.

She let herself into the cottage, greeted McGregor and, still high on adrenalin, flung her jacket and bag on to the table. Her phone rang just as she'd made herself some camomile tea.

'Are you OK?' Angus asked. 'You did so well, Dilly. Bless you for coming. I really thought you might chicken out at the last minute.'

She sat down in her rocking chair, hugging a little patchwork cushion, longing for him.

'I nearly did. I had a really terrible attack of cold feet but I'm glad I made it. It was . . . OK. And fantastic to see Pete and Julia. Why don't I like Lynne?'

'Troublemaker,' he said succinctly. 'Always was. Tiny innuendoes and carefully worded comments that spread gossip. She can't hurt us. Not now.'

'No,' Cordelia agreed cautiously. 'But you were right about telling Henrietta as soon as possible now. When I saw Lynne I thought how it might be if

189

Henrietta were to be told by someone else and I felt quite ill. It was a great party, Angus. But it was scary at times. Pretending that I'd never been to the house before, for instance.'

'You looked very calm,' he assured her. 'Very poised. The professional journalist.'

She chuckled. 'Lynne took pains to mention my scribbling. Are we really going to lunch with them next week?'

'I think it's a brilliant move if you can face it. Just what we want, isn't it? To look as if we're re-establishing an old connection. It would be a perfectly natural thing to do, wouldn't it?'

Quite unexpectedly she was shaken by an irrational bitterness.

'Do you mean my connection with Anne or with you? Would Anne consider it perfectly natural, I wonder?'

There was a silence. 'I think it's too late in the evening to pursue this line of conversation,' he said evenly. 'And especially on the end of a telephone.'

'Yes,' she said tiredly. 'Yes, it is. We'll speak tomorrow. Sorry, darling. Suddenly, I'm very tired. Reaction, I expect. It was a great party. Goodnight, Angus.'

She sat in silence with McGregor stretched beside

her, racked by the old, familiar sensations of resentment and hurt.

'You went away,' she'd suddenly wanted to shout at him. 'After that amazing year of love and happiness we had you just went away for two years. Said you were too young to commit, that you needed time to see the world. And then you come back and break up my marriage and then proceed to devote yourself to one of my friends for the next twenty-five years. And now she's died and so it's my turn again. I can be taken out of the cupboard and dusted down and put back in your heart.'

Cordelia rocked to and fro, clutching the cushion, aghast at the strength of this emotion, which she believed she'd conquered. She wondered if by keeping Angus at arm's length she was subconsciously punishing him for leaving her all those years ago. Perhaps fear of Henrietta's discovery had simply been a convenient excuse for keeping control over the relationship. So what now: now there was no longer any excuse?

Tomorrow she would see Henrietta, and describe the party, and so begin to lay the foundation for the future. She remembered Lynne's remarks about being seen in Oxford – and quite suddenly she thought about the piece of paper stuck under the windscreen wiper. Could it have been a photograph of her and Angus outside The Randolph? But who could have taken it – and why? Fear reasserted its grip: whatever happened, the growing relationship between Henrietta and Jolyon must not be put at risk. Thoughtfully Cordelia finished her tea, put the cushion to one side and went upstairs to bed.

# CHAPTER SIXTEEN

Jolyon was pottering in his tiny sitting room in the gatehouse. He was only half listening to the voice of Lea Delaria singing 'Losing My Mind' whilst he held his mobile and tapped a text to Henrietta with one hand and swung the guard in front of the dying fire in the grate with the other. As the weekend approached he grew less confident about how he should handle the meeting between his mother and Henrietta. Resentment lurked, reminding him that he was under no obligation to present Henrietta for inspection to the woman who had made him so unhappy.

Jolyon sent the text message, put the phone down and picked up Roger's books, which were piled on the sofa and the floor. He put them on to the shelf and paused, his attention caught by the softly gleaming pink and blue glaze of the ginger jar. Jolyon stretched out his hand and touched it, tracing the cracks, remembering when Fliss had given it to him.

She'd talked about how each person had to face crossroads in their lives: had choices, decisions to make . . .

Well, this was one of them – and he would decide now. There was no way that he was prepared to expose Henrietta to the kind of humiliation he'd suffered; he wouldn't be coerced into it. The music drifted into silence and he turned away. Switching off the radio and the light, he picked up his mobile and went up to bed.

Across the courtyard Fliss was sitting on the window seat in the little sitting room that adjoined her and Hal's bedroom. Once it had been her grandmother's room, a private place of sanctuary, and very little had been changed: here was the bow-fronted bureau with its shallow drawers, a tall glass-fronted bookcase full of well-loved books, the small inlaid table with its bowl of flowers, and the Widgerys hanging on the pale walls.

Fliss watched the light go out downstairs in the gatehouse and another flash on upstairs.

'I can't decide,' Jolyon had said to her earlier, 'whether I want my mother to meet Henrietta yet.'

He'd glanced sideways at her; defensive, embarrassed that he even needed to be mentioning it to her, yet somehow requiring her support. She'd been surprised at a sharp sense of triumph; that he was appealing to her as if he and she were on the same side – against Maria.

'You must do what is right for you and Henrietta,' she'd told him. 'It's tricky with new relationships, isn't it? They need nurturing.'

He'd flashed a look of relief at her. 'That's it. It's very early days . . . Only Dad thought it might be nice to get Henrietta over for lunch or something . . .'

His voice had tailed off, and she'd touched his shoulder encouragingly. 'If I were you I'd play it by ear,' she'd advised. 'Don't make any plans till you see how you feel once Maria's arrived.'

He'd nodded, given her an awkward, grateful smile and gone out.

Now, sitting at the window, Fliss suspected that she was somehow conniving with Jo against Maria and Hal; that she was taking sides. She knew very well that Hal's suggestions sprang from his natural generosity and self-confidence, but she was less sure about her own reactions. Old antagonisms and fears had resurfaced since Maria's visit a few months ago and, as she stared out at Jolyon's light, she tried to pin them down. She felt cross with Hal for putting Jolyon into an awkward position, yet it was something much deeper than partisanship for Jo that was gnawing at her peace of mind. Maybe it was simply that it was impossible to be indifferent to Maria. After all, she was Hal's ex-wife; they'd been married for twenty years and she'd given him two sons.

This is the crux of it, thought Fliss. She and Hal had twenty years together. We've had eight.

Looking back, it was hardly possible to believe that she and Hal had given in so readily to being separated; had acquiesced without a fight. But then – a bitter little thought – *she*'d never had the chance to fight. It had been a *fait accompli* between Hal, his mother and his grandmother, and suddenly she could visualize the scene, could remember exactly how he'd told her why they could never marry.

## Spring 1965

It is a cold day in early spring and the house is very quiet. There is nobody around and Fliss wanders into the drawing room and seats herself at the piano. She likes to play, and she selects a Beethoven sonata from her grandmother's music. It is here that Hal finds her.

She swings round to greet him, her eyes alight with pleasure at the sight of him. He looks cold and almost stern as he stands beside her, rubbing his hands to warm them. As usual she finds it difficult to speak when they are quite alone and so she simply sits smiling at him, waiting for him to say something. When he does begin to talk to her she is unable to take it in. She frowns, watching him, feeling suddenly frightened. His words sound stilted, as if he has been practising them, and he continues to look aloof. At one point she puts out her hand to him, hoping to stop him, to make him look at her properly. He holds her hand tightly but drops it almost immediately.

'It's you I'm thinking of, Fliss,' he is saying. 'You're very young and then there's all your training to get through . . .'

He sounds quite desperate – and very unhappy. She shakes her head, puzzled, wanting to comfort him. Surely he must know that she'd wait for ever for him? Now he is talking about being cousins, the problems, children . . .

'We couldn't take the chance, you see. Think how you love children. Supposing you . . . we were to have a child that wasn't normal. It would break your heart. We mustn't take the risk. It's bad enough for ordinary cousins, but our fathers were identical twins. It was silly of us to get carried away but we'll go on being close, won't we?'

There is silence. His voice has stopped and she can hear the grandfather clock ticking weightily, the logs sighing into ashes in the grate. He stands quite still beside her and she notices that he is wearing his old blue Shetland jersey, which is very slightly too small for him. Presently she looks up at him. His face is pinched with anxiety, clenched with misery.

'But I love you.' She says the words quite simply, as if they will cure everything.

She watches him close his eyes and pass his hands over his face, sees his breast lift with a deep sigh. He lays the back of his hand to her cheek, touches her hair.

'It's no good, Fliss,' he says gently and very sadly, looking at her properly at last. 'We have to accept that it wouldn't work. Everything's against us. I love you too. But it's got to be a different kind of love from now on.'

'But how? How are we just to stop?' she asks dully. His misery is passing into her, filling her up so that she can barely breathe.

'We just must.' He is crouching beside her, watching her anxiously. 'Don't look like that, Fliss. Please don't. I can't stand it. Look. You've never had a boyfriend. You simply don't know what you want yet. *Please*, Fliss.'

His last desperate plea pulls her together as

nothing else can. She sees that he is suffering too, and instinctively wishes to protect him from it, realizing that she must be the strong one now. She swallows, nodding, accepting. He grips her shoulder, relieved, grateful.

'Try,' he pleads. 'Try not to let it change us, Fliss. We can still be close. Don't let this spoil everything.'

She shakes her head, agreeing, her smile woefully awry. 'No . . . No, I won't.' Tears blind her and she turns away. 'Go on, Hal. Just leave me. I'll be OK. Only please go away now.'

He stands up awkwardly, pausing only to kiss her neat fair head before plunging out of the room . . .

How odd that the memory should be so clear and fresh. It was her cousin Kit, Fliss remembered now, who had comforted her once Hal had gone, made her tea, and attempted to help her make sense of his words. The frustration and pain she'd suffered then unexpectedly struck anew at her heart, and anger shook her. Surely she and Hal could have made a fight of it? He should have stood up to them instead of backing down; he'd given in at the first blast of matriarchal manipulation.

Fliss frowned; was she angry with Hal, then?

Could it be possible that her fear of Maria was simply masking a deep resentment that Hal had not loved her enough to fight for her all those years ago; and – yes, now another grievance slipped up out of her subconscious – that, even when they were both free at last, it had taken nearly a year for him to make that final declaration?

Hugging her knees, Fliss felt fearful and lonely. Staring out into the dusk, and seeing the lights streaming out across the courtyard, she experienced a sense of *déjà vu*. Back then the lights had been switched on by Hal, who'd been looking around the empty gatehouse, sizing up its potential to make it habitable for Jolyon. She'd been sitting up here on the window seat thinking about her uncle Theo and wishing he were still alive so that she might talk to him about the anguish of trying to contain her love for Hal alongside her loyalty to Miles. Now, she wished that she could present Theo with this new dilemma: was her self-righteous championship and loyalty for Jolyon the result of a subconscious desire to take revenge for a long-buried resentment, and a disguise for her fear of Hal's ex-wife?

She knew that Theo would have understood. Nothing had ever shocked him, he'd never preached or remonstrated, yet she'd always had an odd kind of horror at the thought of disappointing him. Miles had once said something so true about Uncle Theo that she'd never forgotten it.

'If you were to let him down,' Miles had said, 'you'd be endangering something far more precious than your skin or your pride. In fact, you'd be letting down this vital thing inside yourself, not him at all, and he'd be alongside you in the gutter, holding your hand while you wept with the grief and the pain of it.'

Theo had known that she'd married Miles as a shield against the pain of Hal's engagement to Maria, known that her love for Hal remained unchanged through the years of her marriage to Miles, yet he'd always been on her side.

Now, dropping her head on her knees, she longed to see Theo's smile, to feel his hand on her shoulder, and his strength communicated, flowing into her . . . As she sat there, remembering, the words of a prayer slid into her mind. She'd found it written on a paper in his Daily Office book; he'd recited it to her once, and she'd read it many times since his death.

Who can free himself from his meanness
    and limitations,
If *you* do not lift him to yourself, my God,
    in purity of love?

How will a person
brought to birth and nurtured in a world of
   small horizons,
rise up to you, Lord,
If *you* do not raise him by your hand which
   made him?

How indeed? Fliss raised her head and looked out into the darkness. The lights in the gatehouse had been switched off but she no longer felt alone. She could remember the last words of the prayer and saw again, in her mind's eye, Theo's small clear writing.

so I shall rejoice:
You will not delay, if I do not fail to hope.

It was a promise, and back then, in that time of crisis, she'd clung to it; perhaps she might need it again in the days to come.

# PART TWO

# CHAPTER SEVENTEEN

The train was packed. Maria wrestled with the door handle of a first-class carriage and glanced around hopefully for some strong male to help lift her case on to the train. Philip and Penelope had driven away early to a lunch with friends in Hampshire and she'd been obliged to take a taxi to the station. A young woman pushed past impatiently, climbed on to the train and disappeared, and Maria began to bump her case up on to the step, manipulating the small wheels with difficulty, watched indifferently from the platform by two men in suits, clasping laptops and deep in conversation.

'OK, love?' one of them asked cheerfully, once she and her case were safely aboard.

She entered the carriage, pulling her case behind her, mourning the days of porters and young men with good manners, consulting her ticket and checking out the numbers on the seats. Her heart sank:

a large young man was sitting in her reserved seat. She peered again, making the action quite pointed now, and smiled placatingly.

'I'm so sorry – ' though why should *she* be sorry? – 'but I think you've taken my seat.'

He stared at her combatively, clearly expecting her to back down – after all, there were quite a few empty seats including the one next to him – but she stared back at him, remembering Peggy Ashcroft's performance in *Caught on a Train* and determined to stand her ground.

She held her ticket under his nose. 'D'you see?' She smiled at him now, almost enjoying the contest – she could always call the guard if he remained intransigent – and repeated the number loudly and clearly, but very sweetly. Other passengers had begun to be interested; his face grew sullen and he glanced pointedly but silently at the empty seat beside him, but she took him up on it at once.

'I always book a window seat if I can. I feel sick if I can't look out. Do you get that too? Perhaps that's why you sat there.'

He gave in, getting up with very bad grace, taking his case down, while she waited, still smiling.

'Thank you so much.' She put her ticket away, wheeled her case to the space by the door and when she got back to her seat he'd disappeared.

She was relieved; it might have been rather stressful to have to sit beside him all the way to Totnes. She pulled down the little shelf from the back of the seat in front and put her bag on it. It never ceased to surprise her that, unconfident though she was, she absolutely refused to be bullied. Adam had always teased her about being a tough cookie, though he was the only person who'd ever truly known her, and had loved her despite her weaknesses.

Maria's eyes filled suddenly with tears. She bit her lips, feeling for her handkerchief. The train was pulling out of the station and she stared at the blurred buildings and sheds, blinking away her tears. She simply couldn't forgive herself for wasting so many years. They should never have been parted, she and Adam: she'd been too malleable, too anxious to please her parents. All those years married to Hal when she could have been with the one man who'd truly loved her, yet the odd thing was that it was to the Chadwicks she was turning in her grief, and she was so relieved to be going to The Keep now; to see Hal and Jolyon and darling old Prue. Hal's mother had always been kind to her.

The only fly in the ointment – although that was a terrible way of putting it – was Fliss. Fliss had always been the stumbling block; from the very beginning it was Fliss who'd shaken her confidence and made her feel inadequate. Staring from the window, Maria recalled other journeys to The Keep in the early days of her marriage to Hal.

## Summer 1972

During the journey from Portsmouth to Devon, Maria sits wrapped in preoccupation while Hal talks about his posting to the frigate HMS *Falmouth*, the fun of returning to Devon, the possibilities of the married quarter available in Compton Road near Manadon in Plymouth. She murmurs appropriately, trying to inject enthusiasm into her voice, but her thoughts are busy elsewhere. The prospect of their few days of leave is ruined by the knowledge that Fliss is at The Keep. Maria had been delighted when Hal suggested that they should go down to see the married quarter, staying for a few nights with his grandmother. She loves to be fussed over by Prue, to be approved by old Mrs Chadwick and Uncle Theo, spoiled by Caroline. She feels like a beloved child returning home from school – and Hal is such a favourite with his family. Although she stares straight ahead she can visualize his face; determined, confident, handsome, open. People take to him, warming to his friendly smile and good-natured laugh. He has a handclasp and a redeeming word for all; everyone loves him.

This, of course, is where the root of the matter lies. Maria does not want everyone to love Hal or, rather, she wishes he were not so indiscriminate in his returning of this love. In her more rational moments she knows that Hal's easy affection is given to male and female alike – but when was jealousy ever rational? It comes at her from nowhere, swooping in to undermine her fragile confidence, to shake her belief in his love for her. It drives her to be bitchy and cruel, it keeps her awake at nights when he is away; it makes her dread the other wives' gossip, hating to hear that he is enjoying himself in any way that might involve other women. She knows that, wherever the ship docks, the officers are invited to parties and dinners, entertained royally during their 'showing the flag visits', fêted when they are in foreign ports. She waits eagerly for his letters, for the occasional telephone call, for any constant reaffirmation of his love.

This sunny June morning, as the road flees away behind them, she wonders if it would have been the same if Hal had never told her about Fliss. Was it Hal's 'confession' – that he and his cousin had been romantically involved – that is to blame for her insecurity? It is so unfair. Manlike, he has been determined to get it off his chest, unaware of the effect on her. He's explained that it was adolescent and quite innocent, but there is something so horribly Romeo-and-Juliet-ish about the whole business and, or so it seems to Maria, if his family hadn't forbidden it then presumably he and Fliss would have continued to love one another. She has never been quite able to pin him down. Hal's stance is 'well, it didn't happen so what's all the fuss about? I'm married to you now and that's that'.

Maria thinks: There's something still there, though, I just know it. I can feel it when they're together. I'm second best, that's the problem. How can I compete with her? God, I hate her!

The truly irritating thing is that Fliss is so nice to her. In fact, during one of Hal's longer patrols at sea, she accepts an invitation to stay with Fliss in her little house in Dartmouth. For a brief, sane moment, Maria sees that she might neutralize the whole thing by making friends with Fliss; they will form an alliance so that she has nothing to fear from her.

To begin with it actually seems as if it might work. Without Hal around, the two girls settle into a delightfully friendly relationship and have a wonderful week together. Fliss introduces her to the beaches and moors, takes her into the small market towns, they even go to choral evensong at Exeter Cathedral after a glorious morning of shopping in the city. They barely mention Hal, except as he relates to Maria's being utterly miserable when he's away. His absence allows her to talk about him as if he were a different Hal, one whom Fliss knows only slightly but whom *she* knows intimately. She is worldly-wise, tolerant about his shortcomings, joking and light-hearted about his lack of domesticity. Fliss makes no attempt to be proprietorial, makes no mention of her own particular knowledge of Hal. She is so understanding, so sympathetic, and they laugh together over the problems facing the naval wife. By the end of the week Maria is convinced that she's laid the ghost and her certainty lasts until the next visit to The Keep.

They are in the hall with Uncle Theo, having arrived much earlier than they'd expected to, when Fliss comes in with Caroline, helping her to carry the tea things. They are laughing together and pause just inside the door to finish their conversation, heads bent together and looking suddenly serious, before they turn to look at the group around the fire. Maria's heard the phrase about faces 'lighting up' and, at that moment, she knows exactly what it means. Fliss's small face smooths out, her eyes widen and her lips curve upward. Glancing involuntarily at Hal, Maria sees that his face too is bright with love. It is as though something invisible but almost tangible stretches between them. Her heart beats fast with terror and she knows a longing to smash something, to scream, anything to snap the thread that seems to draw her husband and his cousin together.

She overreacted then by chattering wildly to Uncle Theo; her voice too high, her gestures too exaggerated but knowing that she must do something to break the tension between Hal and Fliss. Then Prue appears and the charge of electricity falters, dwindling into the affection of two members of the same family greeting each other with perfectly natural friendliness. Maria melts into her mother-in-law's hug with relief and gratitude. Prue is so motherly, so sweet, so delighted to see them . . .


The train was pulling into Honiton, sliding past the waiting passengers grouped on the platform. Maria stared unseeingly at them. She'd hated the married quarter in Compton Road; been jealous when she'd discovered that Fliss was pregnant, relieved when she'd heard that she and Miles were going to Hong Kong for two years. And now, thirty years later, Fliss still had the power to make her nervous; make her heart beat anxiously. How foolish: Fliss couldn't harm her now. They were all friends together – old friends. Now was the time to build bridges and mend broken fences, especially with Jolyon. She wanted so much to make things up with Jolyon. And it wasn't just because darling Ed was in America and she missed him terribly. No, Adam's death had shown her how precious people were, how fragile love was, and she was beginning to realize what harm she'd done in her own crazy pursuit of love.

And this was a beginning, the thin end of the wedge – no, that made it sound a rather contrived and calculating effort to worm her way back into favour; but it was a new start. She must make a special effort with Jolyon, because she *was* proud of him now that he had a really great career – and he looked so much like Hal. It was uncanny, actually, and rather heart-wrenching, to see him quite so like the young Hal she'd once been married to, and loved. She *had* loved Hal, though she still tried to persuade herself that without her parents' pressure she'd have remained with Adam. But they'd been so knocked backwards by the handsome, confident young naval officer. And, let's face it, so had she. If she were to be brutally honest, she couldn't remember a single occasion on which she'd defended her affection for Adam. Oh, yes, her parents had encouraged and persuaded, and been so pleased with her for being malleable, but she hadn't put up much of a fight.

'He'll go far,' her father had prophesied. 'You'll see,' and he'd been right. Actually, it had come as a bit of an unpleasant shock to discover that Fliss was to be Lady Chadwick; rather as if Fliss were reaping the reward without putting in the work. After all, it was she, Maria, who had been at Hal's side through those early years, not Fliss.

'No regrets?' Adam had asked, watching her across the table as she read the announcement in the *Daily Telegraph* – and she'd ignored that ever-ready thrust of jealousy of Fliss and answered, 'Of course not. All those social events? No thanks.'

Had he believed her? Too late, now, to ask the question. Pain clutched her heart and she bit her lip. The guard was approaching, checking tickets, and Maria summoned up her friendliest smile and reached for her bag.

# CHAPTER EIGHTEEN

It was Hal and Prue who drove into Totnes to meet the train.

'Does she want us to wait lunch for her?' Fliss had asked when Hal told them at breakfast that Maria would be arriving at one twenty-five.

There was a brittle sharpness about the question, as if it weren't really anything to do with her, that this was Hal's guest and a rather tiresome one at that, and Lizzie glanced up quickly and then looked back at her porridge. The tension she'd noticed earlier in the week was still there, vibrating in the quiet morning warmth of the kitchen.

'I didn't ask,' Hal answered. 'And she didn't mention it. I doubt she'll get much on the train, though, and she'll probably be starving. We'll wait for her. It won't be a problem, will it? Nobody will mind a late lunch for once, will they?'

Fliss stood up to make some more toast; her body

language said very loudly that it would matter *very much indeed* but her voice was quite calm if chill.

'I don't imagine so. Just as long as I know.'

Lizzie saw Hal's swift upward look, noted his expression of controlled irritation, and wondered if it would be tactful to finish her porridge quickly, forgo her toast and leave them to it. As if Fliss guessed her thought, she put the toast rack directly in front of Lizzie's plate and refilled her cup from the cafetiere.

'So who's going to collect her?' asked Hal innocently, stepping even further into the lion's den. 'I'm probably the best person – ' Fliss raised her eyebrows – 'or Jo, of course,' he added quickly, 'but I've got a meeting later on this morning with one of our suppliers and I don't know what Jo's up to. Could you meet her if I get held up, darling?'

Fliss said, rather tightly, that it might be difficult to cook the lunch *and* drive to Totnes, and that to travel at a later time might have been more sensible. She didn't add the word 'considerate' but it seemed to echo in the silence after she'd spoken.

'I think there was a later train,' Hal said cheerfully, 'but it meant that the poor old love had to change at Westbury. Or Exeter. You know how she hates that. Not a great traveller, Maria.'

Lizzie saw Fliss's thin hand clench on the butter knife and hurried into speech.

'I could fetch her,' she offered. 'Not a problem.' She looked from one to the other, hoping this was a tactful suggestion. Fliss stared at her toast, Hal stared at Fliss. 'Or I could cook the lunch,' Lizzie added more cautiously.

'That might be nicer,' Hal said, still watching Fliss, as if for guidance. 'After all, she doesn't really know you very well, does she, Lizzie?'

'How well do you have to know somebody before they qualify for picking you up from the station?' enquired Fliss brightly. 'Taxi drivers seem to manage,' and Hal smothered an impatient exclamation whilst Fliss bit her lip, as if regretting her sharp remark.

Prue came in, took the temperature (*Unsettled conditions; storm brewing*), kissed them all and sat down. Lizzie smiled at her; sometimes Prue's entrances were so appropriate that Lizzie wondered if she listened at doors.

'I'm rather late this morning,' she was saying. 'I woke up thinking about darling Theo and that Collect he loved. Well, he loved so many of them, didn't he? But it was that one about evil thoughts that may assault and hurt the soul. He thought that was so important, didn't he? I was trying to find it. Do you remember which one it is, Fliss?'

Lizzie saw that Fliss looked taken aback, as if Prue had struck a blow below the belt, but she answered rather mechanically: 'I think it's one of the Collects for Lent,' and began to spread butter on her toast.

'Of course,' said Prue contentedly. 'How clever of you, Fliss. Dear old Theo, how we miss him. Thank you, Lizzie. I'd love some porridge if there's some left. So what's the plan for today?'

'Maria's coming later on. Rather inconvenient because her train gets in at half past one,' Hal said, sounding more certain of himself with his mother present. 'We're trying to decide which of us should pick her up.'

'Oh, I think you should, darling,' said Prue at once, receiving her bowl of porridge and sprinkling it lavishly with brown sugar, apparently oblivious of Hal's gratified nod. 'And I shall come with you. We can just pop into Totnes on the way. I've got one or two things I need to get. Market day, too. That's splendid.'

Even Fliss couldn't control a tiny smile at the change in Hal's expression, and Lizzie grinned openly at Prue, who beamed back at her.

'Hal's so good at finding a parking space,' she said, 'and he never minds waiting on a yellow line for a few minutes when I've got held up, do you, darling?'

'Perhaps you'd better cancel that meeting,' said Fliss to Hal. 'Looks like you'll need to allow plenty of time.'

He looked resigned but also relieved, and Lizzie noticed that somehow the tension had evaporated; Fliss was deciding what they'd have for lunch and Prue was eating her porridge and making a shopping list. Lizzie finished her breakfast and slipped out to find Jolyon.

He was in the office checking emails, the dogs lying beside his desk.

'Hi,' she said. 'Are you around today? Not off to Bristol – or anywhere?'

He glanced at her rather suspiciously. 'Unfortunately, no,' he answered. 'No, I shall be here. I've got a bit of catching-up to do.'

'We've just been deciding who shall fetch Maria,' she said casually, sitting at her own desk. 'Hal's been chosen from a host of applicants and Prue has decided to go with him. Via a shopping trip to Totnes. Just what he needs on market day with a train to meet.'

Even in his glum mood, Jolyon couldn't help smiling. 'Good old Granny,' he said reflectively. 'She always manages to keep things just a tad off balance. You never quite know where you are from one minute to the next.'

'I don't think he was utterly thrilled,' agreed Lizzie, 'but it successfully distracted everyone's attention from the argument as to who was to be the taxi driver.' She switched on her computer. 'Is Henrietta coming over this weekend?'

Jolyon scowled at his screen. 'We haven't decided yet. I don't want her to feel she's being . . . weighed up.'

Lizzie shrugged. 'You didn't think of that when she came last Sunday.'

'I *thought* about it but I knew that . . . nobody would upset her.'

She looked at him curiously. 'Do you think Maria would upset her?'

'I don't know. That's the whole point. You can't trust her not to. I could trust all of you, that's the difference.'

Lizzie was silent for a moment. 'You might find that bereavement has changed her a little,' she suggested.

Jolyon shrugged. 'Maybe. But I'm not exposing Henrietta to any bitchy remarks. I'll wait and see.'

'Fair enough.' The telephone began to ring and she made a little face at him. 'Here we go.' She lifted the receiver. 'Keep Organics. Oh, hi, Dave. Did you get your worksheet? Your fax seemed to be playing up a bit . . .'

Jo stared at his computer screen, partly listening to Lizzie joking with one of the drivers, partly worrying about the day ahead. He glanced at his watch; breakfast would be over and the kitchen would be empty. This was his favourite time to make himself coffee and think about life. He stood up, smiled at Lizzie and, followed by the dogs, went out into the yard. However hard he tried to dismiss them, the old, painful memories came thick and fast and he wondered where he could possibly find the strength to combat them. Coming in through the scullery, a shadow seemed to accompany him; a much younger Jolyon seeking the comfort and silence of the kitchen, trying to come to terms with the fact that his mother didn't love him . . .

## Autumn 1990

Jolyon comes in from the scullery and looks round the empty kitchen. He's been busy since early morning chopping logs from the remains of an oak tree, which was uprooted in the gales during last spring. It formed part of the boundary hedge beyond the orchard and two ancient apple trees were brought down with it, its great weight smashing them into matchwood. During the summer holidays he's gradually filled bags with twigs and the smaller branches for kindling and the huge trunk has been sawed up into manageable pieces, which he is now chopping into logs. This work gives him a great sense of satisfaction as well as a good appetite and, although he had a big breakfast, he's beginning to feel hungry again. He lifts the lid and pushes the kettle over on to the hotplate. Rex sighs deeply and Jolyon bends to stroke him, murmuring to him, glad that he is there. Rex opens one eye whilst his tail thumps once or twice in recognition. Crouching beside him Jolyon remembers Rex as a fluffy puppy, always getting into mischief, and his eyes fill with the ready tears that humiliate him so often lately. He is dreading going back to school, knowing that everyone knows about his parents' separation and that he is often unable to hide these treacherous emotions. Keeping his head low lest anyone should come in, Jolyon strokes Rex's soft ears, trying to come to terms with the bitter knowledge that his mother doesn't love him. Rex settles contentedly, enjoying the attention.

Calmed alike by the mechanical process of stroking and the undemanding company of his old friend, Jolyon reminds himself that Mum hadn't liked Rex much either. She'd shouted at him and locked him in the garage and he, Jo, had been powerless to defend him. He hadn't been able to defend Dad either, or himself, come to that. He and Dad tried hard to make it work, he knows that, but it wasn't enough. The painful truth is that Mum simply doesn't love either of them. Not as much as she loves Ed and Adam Wishart.

He sits right down beside Rex as the pain in his heart doubles him up. It's silly and girly to behave like this but he just can't help himself. He loves her so much and she just doesn't care about him. Try as he might he can't see why she is able to love Ed but not him and Dad. Dad's simply great, much, much nicer than that boring Adam Wishart, who looks as if his hair is sliding off backwards, like a quilt off a bed.

'I don't like him as much as Daddy,' Ed admitted when he came down to The Keep for a few days at Easter. 'Of course I don't. But what can I do about it?'

The thing is, he doesn't really know what Ed could do, either, but there is something, well, almost disloyal in the way Ed is so nice to Mummy and Adam. He was really uncomfortable here at The Keep during the Easter holidays.

'I don't belong here like you do,' he said at last. 'My home's in Salisbury now, with my friends and school. I don't feel right here, really.'

Jo knows that Dad was really upset by the way Ed

behaved and, when he drove him back to Salisbury, Jo insisted on going too. That's when he saw how nice Ed was to Adam. There was a really awful bit with Mum and Adam and Ed all standing together like a proper family, staring at Dad as if he were an unwelcome stranger and he stood beside Dad and held his hand. Dad held it terribly tightly and he was determined that he wouldn't show that it was hurting. He didn't like Adam's house and he knew that Mum was cross because Dad was selling their old house. He overheard them talking when he was packing up some of his things at Easter and she called Dad a dog in the manger.

'You've got that big place down in Devon,' she said, 'but you grudge me having this.'

'I've never grudged you having this house,' Dad answered. 'But do you seriously suggest that not only should I stand by while Adam Wishart takes my wife and my son but that I should offer him my house as well? He's got a house of his own. You've moved into it, remember?'

'It's much smaller than this,' she said in a whining sort of voice – and Dad said, 'Bloody tough!' in a really frightening voice and he, Jo, had hurried into the room just in case they had a row.

She hugged him then, and he wanted her to, although he felt he was being really disloyal to Dad, and she pretended that he had a home with her and Adam and Ed even if there wasn't a bedroom for him. She said that if Dad hadn't wanted to sell the house they could have stayed in it and he could have kept his old bedroom, making it sound as if it was all Dad's fault, but he was really upset at the thought of Adam moving in and taking Dad's place and he said he didn't mind all his stuff going down to The Keep.

'You can always sleep on a Put-u-up in Ed's bedroom,' she said and he could see that Dad was only just holding on to his temper so he said that he'd like that, just to keep the peace.

'I've let you down, Jo,' Dad said later, driving down to Devon. 'I'm sorry, old son. It's not that Mum doesn't love you just as much as Ed but he has to be there because of school . . .'

'It doesn't matter,' he said quickly. 'I'd rather be at The Keep anyway. There's more room and you'll be there too now.'

'Of course I will,' he said. 'Every spare minute.'

He was, too. Of course, he had to be at *Dryad* most of the time because he was the Principal Warfare Officer and, when he went to stay with him at *Dryad* for half-term, Dad showed him the room where D-Day was planned and the map of the landings in Normandy, and it was really great.

Dad had booked some riding lessons for him at the stables in Southwick and afterwards he took him to The Chairmakers for a pub lunch although he wasn't old enough to have a pint of beer. Dad dropped him off in Salisbury for two days and it was really good to see Ed, even if he did have to sleep on the Put-u-up, but Mum was all over Adam, as if she wanted to make certain that he, Jo, knew just how happy she was. It was as if she were showing off all the time and Adam made a fuss of Ed too, as if to prove that Mum and Ed were happier with him than they'd been with Dad. They certainly didn't need *him*. He hugged Mum tightly the morning he was leaving.

'You mustn't be so silly,' she said, laughing but impatient too. 'And you mustn't be jealous of Ed. He's still only a little boy, remember. Try not to be a baby . . .'

The kettle is boiling. Scrubbing at his cheeks with his wrists, Jolyon climbs to his feet and fetches a mug. The door opens suddenly and Caroline dashes in.

'Lost my purse,' she says. 'No, here it is on the dresser. Just off to Totnes, Jolyon. Are you OK here or do you want to come?'

'No, I'll get on in the orchard,' he says, fiddling about with his mug and the jar of instant coffee, careful to keep his back to her. 'See you later.'

The door closes behind her and he sighs with relief. He's quite good at that now, making his voice quite bright and cheerful, even though his heart is a tight little ball of pain in his chest. He had this silly hope that Mum might have discovered that she didn't like Adam so much after all, and that, this summer, things might have been put right between her and Dad, but he can see now that it is just wishful thinking. He stirs his coffee and sits down at the kitchen table, looking about him at the familiar scene: the gleam of china on the dresser shelves; the patchwork curtains, which match the cushions on the window seat; bright rugs on the worn flags; the geraniums on the deep windowsill. He likes to be alone here, listening to Rex snoring and pretending that at any moment Ellen or Fox might come in. Fox would have been chopping wood in the orchard, just like he'd been doing earlier, and Ellen would say, 'Sitting here drinking coffee at this time of the day. Whatever next, I wonder?' Ellen died before he was born but he could just remember Fox. He feels he really knows them, though, because of all the things Fliss has told him about them. Fox looked after The Keep, making sure that it was in good repair and that everything worked properly. It must have made him feel good, looking about and knowing that things were running smoothly because of his hard work. Ellen would have felt like that too, taking care of all the people who lived in The Keep, cooking delicious meals for them and making them happy.

For a moment he feels that they are with him, there in the quiet kitchen – Ellen pottering at her tasks, Fox taking his ease in the rocking chair by the Aga – and he is part of them, part of a long human chain: another Chadwick looking after his home and the people who live in it . . .


The door opened and Fliss came in. 'Having a quiet moment?' she asked, smiling at him.

'I was seeing ghosts,' he answered. 'Myself when young. Caroline. Ellen. Fox.'

'I see them too.' Fliss took a large casserole dish from the dresser and began to assemble the component parts of their prospective lunch on to a chopping board. 'The Keep is full of ghosts, but they're benign, wouldn't you say?'

'Oh, yes. Poignant, though, sometimes.'

Fliss began to chop vegetables and herbs, she sliced meat, took a jug of stock from the fridge.

'Do we ever get over things?' Jo asked suddenly, angrily. 'You think you have, and then it comes back at you from nowhere and it's . . . frustrating. And

228

disappointing. You feel so limited, as if you haven't grown.'

'"Who can free himself from his meanness and limitations . . ."' muttered Fliss, still with her back to him, chopping and slicing.

'Sorry?' he frowned, puzzled.

'Nothing,' she said. 'Just a quote from something. The trouble is, the past catches up with us unexpectedly and poses problems we thought we'd dealt with. It takes us unawares.'

'I don't even know what to call her,' he said wretchedly.

Fliss didn't pretend not to understand. 'There's nothing worse,' she agreed. 'In the end you try to avoid using anything at all, but it's such a strain. I knew someone years ago whose mother-in-law insisted she called her "Mother". And my friend simply couldn't manage it. "She's not my mother," she'd say. "I've got a mother of my own. It's just not right." It was easier for me. I dropped the Aunt and kept up the Prue.'

'It's just so difficult to pretend that nothing's happened,' Jolyon said. 'When she came down a few months ago it wasn't too bad, because it was like she was in shock over Adam dying. Very muted, very quiet; nobody saying much at all. But now it sounds as if she wants to make a new start and I don't see how that's possible. Not after all the damage.'

Fliss swept all the ingredients into the dish, put it in the oven and turned to look at him.

'I feel exactly the same,' she said. 'I feel just as negative and cross about it as you do.'

He stared at her, surprised but comforted. 'Do you? Dad seems so . . . well, so cool with it. He makes me feel small. After all, he suffered as much as any of us.'

Fliss leaned back against the towel rail on the Aga and folded her arms. 'Hal has a straightforward approach to life in general,' she said thoughtfully. 'In this instance it seems that he's dealt with it emotionally and put it aside, and perhaps that's why he can afford to be generous.'

'He had you,' Jo said rather bitterly. 'I suppose that was the difference. Do *you* think it can work?'

'Perhaps. It depends how much Maria wants it to. Even when there's been a lot of damage it's possible that something good can still be retrievable.' She smiled at him. 'Remember the ginger jar?'

He smiled too, though reluctantly, and she sat down opposite him.

'I had an idea,' she said cautiously. 'When I knew that Maria was coming down I invited Cordelia over. We haven't yet decided exactly which day but

230

I thought that to dilute the family with an outsider might be a good idea. How about Cordelia and Henrietta coming over together? It would look quite natural – they're old friends of ours – and it would take the heat out of it a bit for you just to begin with. We can say that Henrietta and Lizzie are old friends too. I know that Henrietta's a few years younger than Lizzie but that needn't matter. Do you think it would be an idea?'

Jolyon was silent, staring at his coffee mug as he turned it round and round. He shook his head. 'I simply don't know,' he said at last. 'Someone might say something embarrassing. Granny, for instance. I don't think Henrietta wants to be rushed into anything. And neither do I.'

'It's a risk,' Fliss admitted, 'but Granny knows the score and she's not stupid. We're on your side, Jo. You can trust us to be tactful. It was OK last Sunday, wasn't it?'

He nodded. 'I could ask Henrietta, I suppose. See what she thinks.'

'You do that. After all, if Maria is going to come back into our lives then we might as well start as we mean to go on.'

# CHAPTER NINETEEN

Cordelia climbed the steps from the beach slowly, pausing to look back over her shoulder, McGregor at her heels. The horizon had vanished into soft vaporous cloud that drifted over the shining grey surface of the sea and dimmed the sun to a pale silver disc. The snaking breeze was clammy and chill, and she shivered, carefully holding in one hand her small treasure trove – a perfect blue-black mussel shell, a piece of smooth green glass – the other hand thrust deep into her pocket for warmth. At the top of the granite staircase she stood for a moment, catching her breath. A pair of walkers were striding on the higher path, with a third some way behind turning to look back over the way they'd come. She opened the little gate into the wide stone balcony and put her treasures on the weathered teak table whilst McGregor went to his bowl and drank thirstily. A stone trough stretched across one corner of the balcony and here she kept her sea-gleanings: strangely marked stones, undamaged shells, small glass bottles.

She was exhilarated by her climb and by a new and wonderful sense of relief. Yesterday she'd had such a good day with Henrietta – a delicious lunch at Pulhams Mill and a bit of retail therapy in the Barn Shop afterwards – and she'd talked lightly and easily about Angus and the party, and Henrietta hadn't once been sarcastic or cold or judgemental. She'd listened, asked a few questions in a very casual way, and said that she'd love to see Julia and Pete again. It was clear that a tiny miracle had happened and that Henrietta's blossoming love for Jolyon was making her more human. In fact, she'd seemed much more concerned about Maria staying at The Keep and how Jo would manage than about Cordelia's relationship with Angus. There were still dangerous areas concerning infidelity, betrayal and divorce, where Cordelia had feared to go: Susan – and by extension, Maggie and Roger – was one of the minefields around which she'd found it wise to tread carefully.

Nevertheless, it was a beginning. That evening she'd spoken to Angus. She was so happy that she felt really guilty for snapping at him on the night of the party, but he'd made no mention of it, merely sounding delighted that Henrietta had accepted the fact that he was around and that Cordelia had taken the first vital step in re-establishing the relationship.

'It's early days,' she'd warned, 'and I want to be very careful not to rush her. Anyway, it's a good start. I was right. Falling in love with Jo is softening her heart.'

They were so relieved, so happy – and they'd arranged that he should come for supper on Monday – yet she was still thinking over those unexpected sensations of hurt and resentment that had resurfaced after the party, and part of her was secretly pleased that there was still a very good reason to continue to go warily for a while.

Cordelia opened the French door and went into the kitchen; she was very hungry, it was later than she'd realized, and she wondered what she might have for lunch. On the deep, stone windowsill the red eye of the answerphone was winking at her and, as she began to take off her jacket, she bent to see if a message had been left. The little screen was flashing; she pressed the buttons and Fliss's clear voice filled the room.

'Hi, Cordelia, it's Fliss. Could you give me a buzz when you get a moment? Thanks.'

Turning away from the window, Cordelia

hesitated, puzzled: something was wrong. She couldn't immediately place the cause of her unease but as she looked around she became aware of odd discrepancies. For instance, a photograph of Henrietta and a pot of geraniums had changed places on the small shelf, and the heavy Windsor chair stood sideways to the table and in its wide lap was a faded gingham-covered cushion from one of the other chairs. The small wooden lectern that was kept on the table so as to enable reading whilst eating now held two books, neither of which she'd read for years. The books were closed and standing side by side; both were Georgette Heyer paperbacks: one was *Simon the Coldheart*, the other was *The Reluctant Widow*.

One arm still in her jacket, Cordelia stared at them. Panic shivered up her spine and she shuddered, taking a deep breath and willing herself to be calm. It was possible that someone had come in – foolishly she'd left the back door unlocked again – but why move her belongings around? The sudden realization that the intruder might still be in the house filled her with terror. She called to McGregor and then stood quite still, listening intently, but there was no noise other than the usual sea-sounds. McGregor padded in and went to sniff at the Windsor chair but he gave no sign of wariness. Moving quietly,

Cordelia opened the door into the hall, listened again, but all was silent, and some strong instinct told her that the house was empty of any presence but her own. Her fear quite suddenly evaporated. She went into her study and looked quickly around. Everything seemed to be in its place, the computer screen blank, her laptop just as she'd left it on the desk.

She ran across the hall and into the little parlour. Nothing here was out of place either; no paintings missing from the walls, no objects taken from the small glass-topped table. Upstairs all was just as she'd left it: no jewellery or trinkets taken, and her bag was lying on the dressing table with her purse and its contents intact. Back in the kitchen she checked the small Wedgwood bowl into which she put her small change ready for parking machines. It was more than half full with one- and two-pound coins and fifty- and twenty-pence pieces, and the ten-pound note put out in readiness for the window cleaner was still stuck under the corner of the cheese dish.

Cordelia sat down at the table, baffled and uneasy. Surely an opportunistic thief would hardly waste time moving the furniture and books around whilst ignoring an expensive laptop and ready cash? It was crazy. She'd been gazing almost unseeingly for some seconds at the intricately worked wrought-iron candlestick before she saw the koala bear. It had been carefully placed on one of its branches so as to look as if he were climbing amongst the pretty, painted metal flowers. His black leather paws clung to the delicate black stem and his black beady eyes stared out at her from amongst the foliage. She stared back at it fearfully, disbelievingly.

But, she told herself, you put the bear in the dresser drawer.

She stood up and went quickly to the dresser, dragging open the middle drawer, staring down. The soft, grey toy lay on its side, its empty black leather paws reaching forward, curling and grasping. Cordelia slammed the drawer shut: now she was really scared. This was something worse than some light-fingered stealing, more frightening than being the victim of a sneak thief.

She felt in her jacket pocket for her mobile phone, unlocked the keypad – and then hesitated. She knew that Angus would insist that the police were called, and what could she tell them? That nothing of value was missing; that some furniture and objects had been moved and that someone had put a toy koala bear amongst the foliage of her candlestick. Cordelia shook her head. They'd think she was potty. Angus would be cross too. He'd often bawled her out for being so casual about locking the kitchen door.

'I was only out for ten minutes,' she'd say. 'I'd just pottered down to the beach with McGregor. Good grief, we only get ramblers up here and no cars are allowed up the track except for residents' use. Anyway, the back gate isn't visible from the path. Stop fussing.'

All the same, she wished that he was with her, angry or not; she'd feel safe with Angus there. She moved to the table and stared at the two paperbacks. She'd recognized the covers at once but why should these two books be selected from her extensive library? An idea occurred to her and she went into her study. Her books were kept in alphabetical order and it took only a few moments to find her own copies of the books were missing.

Her mobile phone began to ring and she ran into the kitchen and seized it: it was Henrietta.

'Hello, darling.' Cordelia forced her voice to a bright tone; Henrietta mustn't suspect that anything was wrong. 'How are you?'

'I'm fine. Listen, Jo just phoned. You know his mother is due at The Keep any minute and you said you might be going over this weekend?'

'Yes.' Cordelia struggled to concentrate. 'Yes, I did, didn't I? And there was a message from Fliss when I got in a few minutes ago so that's probably to arrange something.'

'Well, Jo's wondering whether you and I might go together. We don't want his mum to think there's any big deal and this might be a kind of casual way of doing it. Old friends of the family sort of thing. What d'you think?'

What did she think? An hour earlier she'd have been delighted; pleased that Henrietta felt that she could trust her with something that was so crucial to her. At the moment she felt confused, frightened, and quite incapable of rational thought.

'Are you there, Mum? Are you OK?'

'Yes, yes, of course I am. I was just thinking. It sounds a very good idea and I'm sure we can carry it off. Shall I speak to Fliss and find out when she thinks would be a good time? Or did Jo discuss that with you?'

'No, he didn't. We were just talking about whether we'd be able to manage it without giving anything away.'

'Fine. Well, I'll phone Fliss and then I'll come back to you. Is that OK?'

'Great. Thanks, Mum.'

Cordelia gave a great gasp; tried to slow the beating of her heart. She could barely breathe. She was afraid to move either of the books, or to hide the koala bear, or put the photograph and the geranium and the Windsor chair back in their original places. Partly this was because she simply didn't want to touch any of the things that had been moved; partly she was afraid that she ought not to, in case it destroyed some kind of evidence: fingerprints, for instance.

She stood for some moments in silence and then she heard the sound of a car coming up the track. Quickly slipping into her study, standing well back from the window, she saw the car stop outside the furthest of the three garages and the young couple who were staying at Number One climb out. Cordelia relaxed; she watched them take the bags and the baby from the car and walk together to their gate. Her confidence returned and, without stopping to think about it, she went into the hall, took some gloves from her coat pocket and went back into the kitchen. Quickly she returned all the things that had been moved to their original places: the chair and its cushion, the photograph and the geraniums. Carefully she edged the koala bear out of its hiding place amongst the leaves and flowers and put it in the dresser drawer with the other one.

Whilst she was staring at the two novels on the lectern her mobile rang: it was Henrietta again.

'Mum, Jo and I have had another idea. How would

it be if I came to stay with you for the weekend? It would make it all a bit easier and a bit more . . . well, genuine.'

Cordelia was silent for a moment, torn between fear and joy. 'It's a great idea,' she said. 'But what will you do about the dogs? Or will you bring them, too? That wouldn't be a problem. But what about the ponies? I couldn't manage them, I'm afraid.'

'There's a girl in the village, Jackie, who is happy to do weekends. She often helps out and Maggie cleared it with her just in case I needed a break. She's quite happy to come in later on today until Sunday evening. If you're sure?'

'Of course I'm sure,' answered Cordelia, heart pounding. 'I haven't spoken to Fliss yet. I thought they'd probably be finishing lunch. So, shall I come and get you?'

'No, no. I'll drive over. I'm insured to drive both the cars so I'll take Maggie's Polo. That'll be OK. I'm not quite sure what time I'll get to you but I'll text you as I come along. Great, Mum. Thanks. See you later. 'Bye.'

Cordelia said goodbye and put her mobile on the table. 'And what do I do,' she asked herself silently, 'if this nutter comes around while Henrietta is here? What then?'

She looked again at the titles of the two paperbacks

and a fragment of an idea edged into her brain. She remembered the tall figure with the binoculars up on the cliff the day Fliss had come over for tea and how, later, she'd lost part of her work from the computer. She remembered the sharp tap on her shoulder in the deli and the man hurrying out of the shop as she'd turned round; the photo tucked beneath the windscreen wiper.

The telephone rang and Cordelia jumped: it was Fliss.

'They're on their way from the station as we speak,' she said. 'Has Henrietta told you our cunning plan?'

'I think it's a very good plan,' Cordelia said, 'and Henrietta is driving over this afternoon. When shall we come to you?'

'We were thinking late morning tomorrow, ready for lunch? How would that be?'

'That's fine. I agree that it will look much more natural this way.' Cordelia briefly wondered whether to tell Fliss about her strange experience but decided that it wouldn't be fair; not now, with Maria due to arrive at any minute. 'See you tomorrow then,' she said cheerfully. 'Good luck.'

She checked that both doors were locked, and the windows firmly fastened, and went upstairs to make up a bed for Henrietta.

# CHAPTER TWENTY

Maria dropped her bag on the bed and looked about her with a sigh of satisfaction; all was well. First, dear Hal striding along the platform to meet her and the relief of being able to give herself unreservedly to his great bear hug without the awareness of Fliss's quizzical gaze to spoil it. And then Prue, waiting out in the car; actually Prue had come as a bit of a shock, because it had been rather nice imagining the drive back to The Keep, just her and Hal, without anybody else around. And, of course, old Prue was firmly ensconced in the passenger seat, which made conversation much more difficult. But still, it was kind of her to come along; after all, as a mother-in-law – especially an ex-mother-in-law – Prue could be forgiven for harbouring a pretty strong grievance if you came to think about it.

And then, when they'd arrived at The Keep, Fliss had come out to meet her and she'd managed to quell that little instinctive flicker of anxiety and antagonism, hurried forward and given Fliss a hug. Well, it wasn't quite a hug – Fliss wasn't the sort you could really hug. She was rather too formal, and thin, much too thin. It was always more difficult to embrace angular people. Anyway, Fliss had been welcoming, that was the great thing. She'd made a delicious lunch which she said was all ready for them and that she hoped Maria was hungry. And then Jolyon had come through into the hall, just as they'd all got inside, and he'd looked so handsome and so fit and strong that she'd been quite overwhelmed. He really was ridiculously like Hal at that age; and he'd been very sweet, if a trifle cool and reserved.

Maria touched the pretty white cotton embroidered quilt cover, glanced approvingly at the pile of fluffy white towels and snapped open the locks on her case. It was too much to hope for an en-suite bedroom at the dear old Keep but at least the water would be hot. She began to put her clothes into the drawers of an ancient bow-fronted chest and hung two skirts and her coat in the cavernous cedar-smelling mahogany wardrobe: no built-in cupboards either. The Keep simply didn't do modern, but somehow it didn't matter; and oh! how pleased she was to be here and to see how little had changed.

With an uncomfortable little pang of self-honesty she admitted to herself that if it had been left to her there would have been many changes to this old house, and this very atmosphere, which was so soothing to her now, might have been utterly destroyed. It was odd how your values changed as you grew older. Things became less important whilst people, friends . . . She sat down suddenly on the bed, her hands full of underclothes, and wept. It was terrible how these fits of grief came from nowhere and she was unable to control them. Suddenly it seemed quite impossible that she should be here alone at The Keep, whilst Adam . . . She doubled over, her face amongst the sweet-scented underclothes, her cries of anguish muffled. She wished, now, that she'd been kinder to her mother when Dad had died but her mother had seemed so contained; her stiff upper lip had never so much as quivered. Maria straightened up, feeling inadequate, and shrugged. Well, that wasn't new – her mother had always had the power to make her feel deficient in one way or another. It was her mother, after all, who had promoted her marriage to Hal and, just as skilfully, assisted in the detaching from him when it appeared that her daughter was not destined to be the chatelaine of The Keep. They'd been so afraid, her mother and Dad, that their money would all vanish into the Chadwicks' coffers. They'd hated the prospect of losing control of their property and their daughter and their grandsons, especially Ed. They'd been so proud of Ed, winning the scholarship to the choir school, though Jolyon had been too much like Hal – and too loyal to him when the chips were down – to inspire the same devotion. How ironical it was that it should be Ed who had lost the house her parents had left to her!

Maria wiped her cheeks on a pair of soft cotton knickers and stood up. As she finished her unpacking there was a knock at the door and Lizzie put her head in: 'Everything OK?'

'It's wonderful. Just like old times. It's so good to be here.' She wanted Lizzie to approve of her and to be on her side. She needed approval; it warmed her. 'And it's so cosy. I feel the cold terribly just lately. I think I'm still in a kind of shock. It was all so sudden.'

She smiled rather pathetically at the younger woman, waiting for the little look of sympathy that would comfort and lift her. Lizzie nodded understandingly.

'In that case you might like a cup of tea. Fliss is just getting it organized. See you in the hall when you're ready.'

She disappeared and Maria brooded. Part of her

liked the idea of being treated like a special guest, but part of her needed to be accepted as one of the family; to come and go as she pleased. She frowned, slightly irritated. They might have guessed that she'd know that they'd be having tea in the hall. Even if the apocalypse were destined for half past four in the afternoon, and the whole world had been informed, there would still be a Chadwick having tea in the hall at The Keep . . . Maria caught herself up sharply; made herself smile. Picking up her cashmere cardigan, she went out and down to the hall.

Jolyon followed his mother into the hall, watched her sit down near the fire beside Prue and saw how the older woman smiled sweetly at her.

He wondered how they were all managing to look so naturally happy; even Fliss was behaving as if Maria were a dear old friend, despite what she'd said to him earlier. He could barely contain the anger that surged in him when Maria slipped her arm through his, or gave him a little hug, or patted his hand in a motherly attempt to demonstrate their special relationship. He had to subdue a violent urge to shake her off; to shout, 'It's too late.' It was impossible to return her affectionate looks or to call her 'Mum': he simply couldn't do it.

He heard Fliss coming through from the kitchen

and turned, glad to take the tray from her, to have something to do. Their eyes met and he saw that her face was very serious, almost grim, and he realized that she was not as happy as she was making out. He raised his eyebrows, signalling understanding, and she smiled gratefully. They went in together and as he put down the tray he was able to position himself on the opposite side of the low table so that when he sat down he would be at a little distance away from Maria.

'We were just saying,' she said to him, 'how much you look like your father when he was your age. It's quite uncanny.'

She put her hand to her heart in a foolishly theatrical way, as if the memory were in some way deeply moving, and although he managed to smile vaguely he was unable to respond because the anger had seized him again.

He wanted to shout: 'You mean you can remember when Dad was my age and there were all those rows and shouting and sulking? And you were carrying on with that bloody man Keith Graves, and beating Rex up for coming from the garden with muddy paws and then screaming at Dad about it whenever he got in from the base.'

He poured tea, biting his lips, aware of Fliss beside him setting out the cups and shielding him from Maria's view. He saw her concerned sideways glance at him.

'Forgot the milk,' she muttered and hurried out. He saw that there was a jug of milk on the tray but it was too late to call her back, and then Lizzie came in.

'Jo,' she said, 'sorry to break up the party but there's a rather important telephone call. Could you come over to the office?'

He straightened up, barely able to contain his relief, smiled vaguely at the two women.

'Sorry,' he said, ignoring Maria's look of disappointment. 'It probably won't take long.'

'Here we are.' Fliss was there again with a jug of milk. 'You and Lizzie can have yours later, Jo.'

He followed Lizzie out; when they reached the kitchen she put out a hand to him.

'There isn't a telephone call, Jo. Fliss just thought you might need a break.'

He closed his eyes for a moment, shaking his head. 'Was it that obvious? I honestly don't know what's wrong with me. I think I'll go over to the office anyway. I'm hoping Henrietta's on her way by now – she might even be with Cordelia. I'll phone her. It might calm me down.'

'You do that. Send Hal over to help Fliss out. I'm going out on the hill with the dogs. We're trying to keep them out of the way as much as possible while Maria's here.'

He nodded. 'She's not a dog person. Thanks, Lizzie.'

He went out across the yard and into the converted barn. His father glanced up from his desk.

'Everything OK?'

Jo shrugged. 'I don't know,' he answered coolly. 'I feel as if I've been cast in the role of the prodigal son when I haven't asked for the part and I don't like it much.'

Hal leaned his elbows on the desk, chin in hands. 'I'm sorry, old son. When Adam died and Maria asked to come down to see us I really thought it might be an opportunity to get all this out of our systems. Perhaps I was wrong. I just hate ill feeling and bad-mouthing people and no-go areas, and I hoped that now might be the right time to sort it all out.'

Jo sat down at his desk and stared at his computer. 'I don't intend to feel guilty,' he said angrily.

His father looked surprised. 'Why should you feel guilty?' he asked. 'Nobody can blame you for any of it. *You* were the scapegoat. *You* took the flak. My God, Jo! Why the hell should *you* feel guilty?'

'Because I can't forgive her,' he shouted. 'I don't want her here suddenly playing the devoted mother.

250

I thought I'd got over it, dealt with it. And now she's brought it all back again. I can remember all the bloody pain and I don't need that just now.'

'I'm sorry.' Hal was beside him, his hand on his shoulder. 'I'm so sorry, Jo. Fliss was right. I've completely misjudged this. You're right too, though, about bringing it all back. When I first saw Maria at the station it was almost like looking at her mother however many years ago. Really odd.'

Jo didn't look at him; he didn't want any confidences, any heart-to-hearts about the past. 'Well, we'll just have to deal with it,' he muttered. 'Fliss might need some help, though. They're having tea, and I want to make a phone call. I might be a while.'

His father went out and Jo waited for a moment, then took out his mobile. Henrietta answered after a few rings.

'Hello,' she said. Her voice was warm with love, and he felt his heart move in his breast. 'How are you managing? Has she arrived?'

'Yes. We've done the lunch bit and she's unpacked and now they're having tea. You're an important business call. Where are you?'

'I've just pulled into a lay-by not far from the M5.'

'I wish I could see you,' he said. An idea occurred to him and he sat up straight. 'Listen, I've had a

251

brilliant idea. If I give you directions we could rendezvous on the A38 in about half an hour. What d'you think?'

'Great,' she answered calmly. 'But you'll have to make the instructions very clear. I've only driven to Mum's once before from here. I'd love to see you, though.'

His spirits swooped upwards. 'Listen,' he said, 'I'll be on the end of the phone all the time, and I'm setting off now, but this is what you do . . .'

Hal crossed the yard. Jo's outburst had upset him and he was worried. He wondered if he'd so completely misjudged the situation that, instead of it being the start of a healing process, Maria's visit would be a catastrophe. There was no question that he'd underestimated the depth of Jo's hurt; well, he could understand that Jo hadn't forgotten how Maria had rejected him, nevertheless he was shocked by the bitterness in Jo's voice and he was kicking himself for going along with Maria's wishes. Fliss had been against it from the beginning and he should have listened to her. The trouble was, he felt guilty; guilty that he hadn't stood up to his mother and grandmother in the first place and insisted that he and Fliss should be together; guilty that he'd ever told Maria about Fliss and undermined her fragile self-esteem; guilty that Jo had borne the brunt of his and Maria's failing relationship.

It was damned odd, though, how that look on Maria's face had reminded him of her mother and an unpleasant scene when she'd accused him of misleading them about his inheritance. When she'd seen Prue sitting in the car in the station car park Maria's expression of irritated indignation, though it was gone in a flash, had brought back the past with a sharp shock. He shrugged: well, they'd have to go through with it now. He passed through the scullery and into the kitchen, took a deep breath, bracing himself.

Fliss glanced up as he came into the hall and he saw the tension on her face and smiled at her, sending her a tiny wink.

'Jo's going to be a while,' he said. 'That's what comes of doing two jobs at once, but he's happy. That's the great thing.'

'It is indeed,' agreed Prue comfortably, tackling her slice of cake. 'I was just telling Maria that you've got some new photographs of Ed and their flat. Or apartment, do they call it? So clever, this method of sending photographs on the computer. Maria hasn't got a computer, darling, so I said you'd show them to her.'

Fliss nodded encouragingly, slipping him a quick

look, which, interpreted, meant: 'Please do. It will fill the next half-hour!'

'I'd love to see them,' said Maria. 'I'm afraid Ed and Rebecca aren't very good letter-writers. And as to phone calls . . .'

She looked rueful, deprecating the non-communication of the young, inviting a sympathetic response and Hal chuckled.

'Ed takes after me, I'm afraid,' he said cheerfully. 'Luckily email and the internet make things a bit easier for busy people. I'll go and get them.'

# CHAPTER TWENTY-ONE

Jo managed to postpone Maria's guided tour of the gatehouse until after breakfast. By the time he'd got back from his rendezvous with Henrietta the previous evening it had been nearly dark and despite his mother's gentle protestations that she couldn't wait to see his quarters he'd managed to stand firm. He was surprised that he'd been able to withstand her request and knew that it was his meeting with Henrietta that instilled the courage to refuse.

'I don't know what's got into me,' he'd said, sitting in her car, holding her hands. 'I feel so angry. I'm not usually an angry person and I can't understand it.'

They'd turned sideways to face each other and he'd stared into those strange-coloured topaz eyes and known that here was someone who completely understood him.

'I do,' she'd said quietly. 'Unintentionally our parents undermined our belief in love. Our homes and families were torn apart and we can never quite forgive them for it. And we can never really trust that the same thing isn't going to happen to us. That there might be something in us, some similar gene, which makes it possible that we might do the same thing. We can't really trust love, them – or ourselves. Or forgive them for that betrayal.'

They'd stared at each other. Jo nodded. 'That's absolutely it,' he'd said. 'But what can we do about it? Until I met you I never wanted to take the risk of a serious relationship.'

Her clasp on his hands tightened. 'Me, too. It's why I became a nanny. I'd decided never to marry and have children of my own so this was the next best thing.'

'And now?'

'Now I think – I *think* I think – I might want to take a chance.'

He'd let go of her hands then, and put his arms round her. They'd sat for ages, holding on to each other, and she'd said, 'I still don't know how you manage Maria, though. It's easier for me. Mum was always there, though I've been pretty awful to her at times. It was Dad who went; though I've always been on his side. Crazy, isn't it?'

He'd nodded. 'Fliss said to me once that children expect their parents to be perfect simply because they're adults, but that it's an unrealistic expectation because nobody is without faults and weaknesses. All I know is that I love you. I shall always love you. That's how it seems to me now.'

'I love you too. But I still don't want to rush things.'

He'd held her tightly, his heart bursting with joy, his face buried in her soft shining tortoiseshell hair. 'We won't. When we meet tomorrow I'll just be friendly and casual. Like I am with Lizzie. I shall hate it, though.'

She'd held him away from her, studying him: 'Promise you won't cheat. Not for a minute.'

'Not for a minute,' he'd promised. 'You can trust me.'

'Yes,' she'd said on a deep breath. 'I think I can.'

Now, as he watched Maria looking round his small sitting room, he experienced a twinge of pity for her.

'It's not very big, is it?' he said, taking her criticism for granted, bracing himself for it. 'But I like it here. It's given me independence, though it's nice to know that I can have company when I want it just across the courtyard. Best of both worlds.'

'It's a perfect set-up,' she agreed, her face

thoughtful. 'I'm beginning to realize how bad I am at being alone. I hate it.'

Jo stiffened, warding off pernicious temptation to his former reactions to her attempts at emotional blackmail.

'It's bound to take a while to grow accustomed to it,' he said calmly. 'It's very early days. But you've got lots of friends in Salisbury, haven't you?'

Maria looked at him almost reproachfully but he met her eyes squarely: he would not feel guilty or responsible. She turned away, examining his rack of CDs and his bookshelves, studying the two paintings, both by David Stead, and then paused to examine the ginger jar.

'How pretty,' she said. 'It looks valuable. Is it?'

He hesitated. 'It is to me,' he said at last. 'Fliss gave it to me years ago.'

'Really?' Her interest sharpened. 'Where did she get it, I wonder?'

'She brought it back from Hong Kong. It was given to her by the twins' amah as a token of the love and friendship they'd shared. Fliss left it behind at the house in Dartmouth during one of her moves with Miles, and her tenants broke it. They got it mended but Fliss could never forgive herself for being so careless with something which meant so much. She gave it to me as a symbol.'

'A symbol of what?'

He hesitated again; reluctant to admit too much. 'Of loyalty and friendship. She said that though a relationship might be damaged it didn't necessarily mean that it was irretrievably destroyed. Sometimes it could even become more special.' He shook his head, cross with saying too much, for betraying something Fliss had said in a private moment. 'Something like that, anyway.'

He was fearful that Maria might cross-question him but she wasn't looking at him. She touched the ginger jar gently, tracing the cracks, her head bent.

'It's very beautiful,' she said at last.

She turned, and he saw that her face was serious; for once she was making no attempt to create an impression and suddenly, despite the make-up and the carefully tinted hair, she looked her full age. A familiar treacherous shaft of pity pierced him again, though he resisted it.

'Do you want to see upstairs?' he asked, trying not to sound reluctant.

But she shook her head. 'Just this room,' she said. 'This says all I needed to know. Thank you, Jolyon.'

She went before him out into the courtyard and he followed her, surprised but relieved.

\*　　\*　　\*

When Cordelia and Henrietta drove into the court-yard an hour later it was Fliss who went to meet them.

'Are you surviving?' muttered Cordelia in her ear as they hugged, and Fliss snorted with frustration and said, 'Only just,' before letting her go.

She waved across the roof of the car at Henrietta, who was looking very beautiful and faintly formidable. Fliss smiled to herself; she knew only too well how she, herself, looked when she was frightened. Miles had summed it up once: 'A clear, cool look that can make you feel awkward. You feel school-boyish, and you wonder if you need a haircut or if your shoes are clean. It keeps you up to scratch but at the same time it keeps you at arm's length and lets you know you're found wanting.'

Fliss knew it – and regretted it – but only she knew that behind that look was a requirement to protect herself; few people guessed how shy and uncertain she could be. Her cool look was a wonderful defence and it was just such a look that Henrietta was using now.

'It's lovely to see you,' she said warmly. 'Isn't this weather vile? I hate these sea mists. Susanna and Gus will be over later for tea. Come and have a drink.'

Jo was nowhere to be seen but Hal was busy at

the drinks tray, Prue beside him, whilst Maria sat on one of the long sofas looking pensive. Fliss made the introductions and Maria and Cordelia shook hands whilst Henrietta remained behind the other sofa and said 'Hello,' to Maria and 'Is Lizzie around?' to Hal.

Lizzie and Jo came in together just then, and Fliss saw that Jo smiled and said 'Hi' to Henrietta and waved a greeting to Cordelia, who mouthed 'Happy birthday', and then went across to his father and grandmother. By now Cordelia and Maria were deep in conversation and silently Fliss blessed Prue, whose idea it had been to show Maria the article Cordelia had written about The Keep. A copy of that particular *Country Life* was kept in the guest room and Prue had drawn Maria's attention to it and to two of Cordelia's books.

Maria had been suitably impressed and rather excited by the prospect of meeting an author. Watching her, Fliss suspected that it had certainly distracted her from any speculation on the relationship between Jo and Henrietta.

'She's bringing her daughter with her,' Fliss had told Maria when they'd talked about Cordelia. 'Henrietta's staying with her for a few days. She and Lizzie are great friends, though Henrietta lives in London and we don't see her too often. We've known them for ever, of course, but I'm not sure you ever met Cordelia, did you? Anyway, I know you'll like them both.'

It was clear that Maria was much more inclined to approve of a well-known journalist and her daughter coming to lunch on Jo's birthday than any old naval chum, and now Fliss glanced at Prue to see if she'd noticed how well her plan was working. Prue smiled sweetly at her, raised her glass, and Fliss couldn't stop the laughter that bubbled up.

Lizzie and Henrietta were chatting away together – as if they were indeed old friends – and Jo lounged beside them, joining in occasionally but talking to his father about the rugby; all was well. Fliss took her glass of wine from Hal and he smiled at her, such an odd smile that she was overwhelmed with affection for him. She stepped forward and raised her glass.

'Shall we drink to Jo and get it over with,' she said, 'and then he can relax until tea-time when he gets his presents.'

He grinned at her, and they all turned, raising their glasses and saying, 'Happy birthday,' and the awkward moment was passed.

The mist was thick and chill when Henrietta and Cordelia drove home after tea. Cordelia could feel

Henrietta beside her, rigid with pent-up emotion, and she sought for the right words to help her to relax.

'We got through it very well,' she said at last. 'Don't you think so? I really like Susanna and Gus, and Jolyon was great.'

Henrietta took a great breath and visibly relaxed, shoulders dropping, hands unlocking.

'He was very convincing,' she admitted. It was odd that, though she'd made him promise that he'd give nothing away, she was rather surprised at how very well he'd hidden his feelings for her. At no time would anyone have suspected that they were anything but old friends, just as she'd instructed; odd then – and very silly – that she should feel almost hurt. It had been horrid to leave him without some reassuring word or smile.

'And what did you think of Maria?' Cordelia was asking.

Henrietta thought about it. 'She wasn't too bad,' she said at last. 'Quite sweet, really. She puts on a bit of an act, though, doesn't she?'

'Just a bit.' Cordelia slowed down, peering ahead. 'I hate driving in these mists. It's weird how it makes everything look quite different.'

'You did well, too,' Henrietta said. 'You rather deflected her attention away from us.'

'She was very impressed with my article about The Keep,' Cordelia admitted, pleased by her daughter's approval. 'And my books. They helped to distract her a bit. She's thinking how I might do an article on her.'

'You're joking! Or does she live in some amazing place?'

'I don't think so. She's just one of those people who love to be noticed. I led her on a bit, talking about the different effects of bereavement, so as to keep her attention.'

Henrietta chuckled and then made a face. 'Jo was doing so well I'm not sure you needed to bother,' she said rather bitterly.

Cordelia hid a smile. 'I thought that's what you wanted.'

'I did,' Henrietta admitted. 'But I'm rather shocked that he was so good at it. Silly, isn't it?'

They both laughed and travelled on together in a companionable silence.

Henrietta was thinking: I'll send him a text when we get in. He could have come out to say goodbye instead of just waving from the steps, but Mum's right. It was the way I wanted it.

Cordelia was thinking: I'm glad Henrietta's with me tonight. These sea mists can be a bit creepy. I hope there's nothing there when we get in. Thank

God for McGregor. He'll frighten off anybody if they try to get into the house.

She slowed right down and turned off the high road, and the car plunged down into the narrow lanes that led to the coast.

'Thank goodness, it's over,' Fliss said later to Hal as they were getting ready for bed. 'Jo did brilliantly, didn't he?'

Hal pulled off his jersey and began to unbutton his shirt. 'I must admit that if I didn't know better, I'd say that he and Henrietta had known each other from childhood, and he had no more interest in her than he has in Lizzie. They were amazing. Quite frightening, really. I'd no idea Jo was such a good actor. It's very difficult pretending you're not in love with someone for five or six hours on end.'

There was a little silence.

'Oh, I don't know,' said Fliss rather bitterly as she took out her earrings. 'We managed it pretty well for twenty-five years.'

Hal stood for a moment, his face shocked, and then he went to her and put his arms round her where she sat at her dressing table, pulling her to her feet.

'Oh, Fliss,' he said remorsefully. 'We didn't always manage it, though, did we?'

She shook her head against his chest. 'Not always.'

They stood locked together, recalling the past.

'Do you remember,' he murmured against her hair, 'that night I brought Rex down here?'

'Oh, Hal,' she said sadly. 'I remember everything. How could I forget? I didn't think you did, though.'

'Just lately,' he said, still holding her tightly, 'certain moments come back to me. I'll never forget that one.'

'I was here with the twins, and Grandmother was dying,' Fliss said.

'It began to snow,' he said. 'I remember the snow.'

Still holding Fliss in his arms, his cheek against her hair, Hal was filled with sadness.

'I shouldn't have agreed to Maria coming,' he muttered. 'I didn't think it through properly. I was a tad high-handed, wasn't I?'

She freed herself and looked up at him gravely. 'It's like opening Pandora's box. None of us knows what might come out. It's a big risk.'

'Is it?' He stared down at her. 'Do you really believe that, Fliss?'

She turned away and sat down again at the dressing table. 'It could be. Certainly for Jolyon, who's in an emotional state at the moment . . .'

'And for us?'

'Like you said, it brings back memories. I'm not sure that's always a good idea.'

'There was something left at the bottom of Pandora's box,' Hal said, pulling off his shirt. 'What was it?'

Fliss watched him through the mirror for a moment. 'It was hope,' she answered.

# CHAPTER TWENTY-TWO

It was Fliss who took Maria to the train on Monday morning.

'I don't want to go,' Maria said, twisting to look back through the arch of the gatehouse to where Prue stood on the steps, waving. 'Silly, isn't it? Well, I am a fool. You know that.'

She turned back again and settled herself while Fliss, confused, wondered how to answer her.

'It's wretched for you,' she began cautiously, 'having to cope with being alone. But, to be truthful, I've never seen community living as your scene somehow.'

'Absolutely not,' agreed Maria readily. 'That's what's so crazy, really. When I was young, the set-up here horrified me, I admit it. Now, it seems very attractive.'

Fliss was surprised by such honesty – and slightly

anxious. 'I expect it seems safe. It's frightening being alone, isn't it?'

'It is for me. I've been thinking about it a lot just lately and I can see that I've always had someone controlling my life. First my parents, then Hal, and then Adam. I was used to having someone telling me what to do and how to do it. As an only child I was cosseted and organized, and even now I look for someone to be in charge. It's pathetic but I can't seem to help myself. It was different for you, being orphaned so young.' She looked at Fliss compassionately. 'How on earth did you manage?'

'With difficulty.' Fliss drove through the winding lanes towards Staverton, remembering how frightened she'd been. 'I wasn't allowed to show it because of Mole and Susanna. I remember a ghastly woman telling me that I must be a little mother to them and I can remember how resentful and angry I felt deep down because I didn't want to be a little mother. I felt that I'd been deprived of my right to mourn simply because I was older than they were. It was such a relief to come back to The Keep and to Grandmother, and to pass some of the burden over.'

'You always made me feel so immature,' said Maria reflectively. 'Well, I was. But it didn't help, knowing that Hal loved you.' She saw Fliss's instinctive gesture of embarrassed denial and smiled. 'Sorry. I know you hate this kind of emoting and stuff, but it's true. Don't you feel resentful for the way our lives were messed up by the adults in our families? I should have stuck with Adam but my parents were bowled over by Hal – and so was I, of course. He was so confident and mature. But without pressure from them I think I'd have been quite happy to stay with Adam. And as for you and Hal, well, that was crazy, really, wasn't it? All that first cousin stuff. Even if your fathers were identical twins I can't see why there was such a fuss about it.'

'I do think that we gave in too easily,' said Fliss. 'But we forget how it was all those years ago. It was hard to go against the wishes of our elders and we were all so young.'

The car passed over Shinner's Bridge, past the waterwheel, and Maria looked down into the glittering shining river.

'It's been a mess,' she said sadly, 'and I've been such a fool. I can't tell you how much there is that I regret. Thanks for letting me come down; it's been important.'

'You're always welcome,' Fliss answered with an effort, still taken aback by such plain, unaffected speaking. She couldn't decide whether this was another piece of play-acting on Maria's part: the role of the penitent prodigal, perhaps?

'Am I?' Maria was looking at her rather quizzically. 'I'm not sure Jolyon feels that way. Or you. Hal doesn't really care either way, of course. Why should he?'

'I think Jo has a lot of trust to rebuild.' Fliss decided that they could both play the honesty game. 'You can't do that in one weekend.'

Maria bit her lip. 'No, I realize that. I know how it looks to him. To all of you. Adam's gone, Ed's gone. Who shall I turn to now? I can't deny it. But Adam's death was a terrible shock and it's woken me up to certain things. Maybe it's too late to make amends, but I've got to try, and especially with Jolyon. Is that wrong?'

They drove into the station yard and Fliss pulled up near the fence and sat for a moment with the engine idling.

'No,' she said at last, 'of course not. But you've got to remember that people can't simply forgive and forget to order. *You* might have had an epiphany but *he* hasn't.'

Maria looked at Fliss. 'You see things so clearly,' she said rather wistfully. 'I've always envied you your clear-sightedness. I seem to spend my life in such a stupid muddle. Thanks for the lift. Don't come on to the platform. I can manage.'

'Of course I shall come,' Fliss said. 'I'd worry in

271

case the train didn't turn up or you were waiting for ages. Look, you climb out so that I can pull in against the fence and then we'll get your case out.'

'And after all that,' Fliss said to Prue later, 'I invited her down for Hal's birthday and then I drove home regretting it and feeling quite cross. As if I'd been manipulated.'

'No, no.' Prue put her book aside and shook her head. 'You did quite right. Poor Maria. It's clear that the shock of Adam's death has opened her eyes to many things and it can be so painful. That was kind of you, Fliss.'

'I didn't feel kind. Part of me thinks she's getting off lightly. It's a bit like the Prodigal Son, isn't it? He behaves disgracefully and then wanders in saying, "Sorry," and everyone is expected to be thrilled to bits.'

Prue laughed. 'Do you remember saying that to darling Theo when you were small? You were terribly upset that the elder son was so undervalued, and Theo had to try to explain that there were faults on both sides.'

'Did he?' Fliss frowned. 'I don't remember that.'

'You were a bit young for it, I expect. The gist, as I remember it, was that, although the younger son had been wild and thoughtless, the older son was resentful and angry. There was a lack of generosity in his self-righteousness that was just as damaging in its way as the profligacy of his younger brother. At least, that's how Theo saw it.'

Fliss was silent, still frowning, and presently Prue picked up her book again and left her to her thoughts.

On the train, Maria sat in a trance of surprise and delight.

'Why don't you come down for Hal's birthday?' Fliss had said, just as the train appeared around the bend in the track. 'Think about it and let me know,' and then there had been the bustle of finding the right carriage and saying goodbye, and now she sat quite still, hardly believing her luck.

There was no need to think about it – the answer was 'Yes, please,' – but she felt rather relieved that she hadn't been too pathetically eager. Now she had something to look forward to; to plan for in the empty days ahead. Suddenly, at the prospect of the tiny annexe, the endless silence, the pointless meals for one, Maria fell prey to a sinking, gut-churning misery. No Adam talking about his plans for the garden, or a fishing trip, or coming home with tickets for the theatre; no Adam in the big, cold bed or sitting at the kitchen table with the newspaper.

She stared resolutely through her tears, thinking about the warmth and companionship at The Keep and how once she'd despised it.

'I've never seen community living as your scene,' Fliss had said – and how right she'd been.

It was the prospect of that community living, thought Maria, as the train pulled in at Exeter St David's, that was the thin end of the wedge. It was my first real step away from Hal and back to Adam. I don't regret going back to Adam but I wish I could have done it with less damage. What a selfish prat I was.

There was a little twist of pain in her heart when she thought about Jolyon; he'd been the scapegoat. Hal had Fliss and she'd had Adam and Ed – but poor Jolyon had borne the real brunt of the rupture: he'd endured the rows and scenes, and then being sent away to boarding school while Ed stayed at home, cherished and beloved, and went daily to the choir school. When she'd finally moved in with Adam there hadn't even been a bedroom for Jo in that first little house in Salisbury. He'd had a Put-u-up in Ed's bedroom and she'd actively encouraged him to spend his holidays at The Keep whether Hal was at home there on leave or not. Jo's unswerving love for her – and the way he looked so much like Hal – had made her feel guilty and resentful. Remembering,

Maria burned with a scalding shame. She wondered if it would ever be possible that Jo might forgive her. She'd noticed that he couldn't bring himself to call her 'Mum' or to be really at ease with her but maybe, if she persevered, she might break down the barrier between them.

'You might have had an epiphany,' Fliss had said, 'but he hasn't.'

She thought about Fliss; how strong she was, how upright: that cool, clear look that shone like a merciless beam of light upon her own shortcomings. Maria shuddered away from the shame of her memories, from the muddle and mess of the past. Suddenly she remembered what Jolyon had said about the ginger jar, that it was a symbol of loyalty and friendship: '. . . though a relationship might be damaged it didn't necessarily mean that it was irretrievably destroyed. Sometimes it could even become more special.'

They'd been Fliss's words, he'd told her, and Maria wondered why Fliss had given the ginger jar to Jolyon in the first place. How miraculous if the words could, sometime in the future, apply to the relationship between her and her son.

# CHAPTER TWENTY-THREE

They'd parked on Robin Upright's Hill and were now walking away from the car, arm in arm, whilst Juno and Pan ran amongst the rusty bracken and Tacker splashed joyfully through the earth-red puddles on the deeply rutted track.

'I can't see it,' Jolyon said gloomily, 'I really can't. It's been such a shock realizing how resentful I still feel about her.'

Henrietta squeezed his arm sympathetically. 'I can understand that. Well. You know how I feel about Mum.'

'It's different, though, isn't it? You're angry with Cordelia because she made a mistake and broke up your family. But, actually, it was your father who walked away from it, wasn't it? How would you feel if he suddenly wanted to come back into your life now?'

Henrietta tried to imagine it. Just at this minute,

all she could really think about was Jo; holding his arm and feeling him close.

'It would depend how he was,' she said at last. 'I can't imagine how he could talk away all that rejection. I can imagine him being angry with Mum and wanting to hurt her, but to stop all communication with me ten years later . . .' She shook her head. 'How do you get over that?'

They walked for a while in silence. The dogs were far ahead but Tacker still skittered at the track's edge. Bulky black clouds, gold-edged, crowded the sun and, through the gaps in the hills, they could see far across the sunlit spaces of Somerset towards the coast; the island of Steep Holm rose from the silver shimmer of the sea like a hump-backed whale dozing in the misty sunshine.

'Perhaps the first thing we have to do is to convince ourselves that it's their problem, not ours,' suggested Jolyon thoughtfully. 'We blame ourselves, don't we? We tell ourselves that because they couldn't love us there must be something wrong with us? Even when we try to persuade ourselves that there might be something wrong with *them* we can't quite believe it, can we? I tell myself that because my mother loved Adam and Ed it must be my fault that she didn't love *me*. It makes me feel inadequate. Fliss tried to explain it years ago when she gave me the ginger jar. She said that there were lots of people who loved and valued me and that it was destructive to dwell on the one person who didn't. She tried to show me how it might be my mother's problem, and I believed I'd come to terms with it. That's what's really upset me: the fact that I feel that I've made no progress at all.'

'I think it's one thing coming to terms with it when the person concerned isn't part of your life, and quite another when you're asked to welcome them back with open arms and pretend it never happened. That's a different adjustment, isn't it? You'll need time. I'm beginning to think I've been a bit hard on Mum. I resented her for causing the break-up in the first place, but I think I've blamed her for Dad walking away simply because she was there. I've projected my anger and hurt on to her instead of him.'

'Why did he wait so long?' asked Jolyon. 'I mean, ten years later seems a bit odd.'

'It was odd,' she agreed. 'My mum and Angus Radcliff were in love when they were young but he didn't want to commit and went to Australia for a two-year exchange with the Australian Navy. Mum married my father and then five years later she and Angus met up again when he and Dad were based in *Dolphin*. Mum and Angus had a weak moment and Dad found out and he left. He wrote to me when I was about fifteen and told me all the details. Apparently, Mum had a telephone in her study and Angus phoned her the day after their indiscretion. Dad had been suspicious that they might be getting friendly again and he picked up the extension and listened in. Mum was telling Angus that they must never ever do it again and that she wouldn't leave me and Dad. Stuff like that.'

'I suppose he just couldn't hack the fact that she'd been unfaithful. Is that why he left?'

Henrietta shrugged. 'Possibly. The odd thing was that he waited nearly a year before he confronted her. By then Angus was married.'

'A *year*?' Jolyon was shocked.

'I know. He wanted to make certain that Angus and Mum couldn't marry, I suppose.'

'That's . . . that's really chilling, isn't it? And she didn't know he knew, all that time?'

'No. Mum said he felt things very deeply. He was very intense.'

'And calculating, by the sound of it. You mean he waited a year before he confronted her and then another ten years before he told you why and that he was going out of your life for good?'

'He said he'd met someone in Australia and was starting a completely new life.'

Jolyon grimaced. 'He sounds a bit of a cold fish, to be honest, doesn't he?'

Henrietta nodded; her face serious. She clutched his arm more tightly. 'I don't think I'd want him back in my life. Not now. To tell you the truth, I'm beginning to feel guilty that I've been a bit of a cow with Mum.'

He returned the pressure of her arm. 'I can understand, though. Philip Larkin had the right of it, didn't he? I'm probably overreacting too. Perhaps I need to lay the ghosts properly. I just don't know how.'

They stood together listening to the whistle of the steam engine echoing over the hills from Stogumber.

'Angus Radcliff's moved down to Dartmouth. His wife's died and he's on his own again,' Henrietta said. The sun disappeared behind the great banks of cloud and she shivered a little. 'Mum went to his house-warming party last week.'

Jo looked down at her. 'Is that a problem?'

She made a little face. 'I don't know. I'm trying to decide how I feel about it.'

'Does it matter after all this time?'

'I don't *want* it to matter,' she explained, almost crossly, 'but it's just a bit difficult imagining how I might react if they get together again and I have to meet him. It's a bit like you and Maria, in a way. He's coming back into my life and I have to work out how not to feel resentful about him.'

'It's odd, isn't it?' said Jolyon thoughtfully. 'Your mum and mine and Fliss. Falling in love with one man and then marrying another.'

'It's scary,' answered Henrietta. 'I mean, how do you know? Really *know*?'

They stared at one another, her hand slid into his and his grip tightened. Heavy drops of rain began to fall, splashing into the puddles, plopping in the soft red earth, and they started to run back along the track with Tacker at their heels, shouting to Pan and Juno, who came racing out of the bracken. They opened the hatchback so that the dogs could jump in, lifted Tacker in, and then fell, panting and out of breath, into the car, laughing at each other, wiping the rain from their cheeks. Henrietta pulled off her hat and shook her head, and her wild tortoiseshell hair flew about her cold face. Jo reached out and seized her by the shoulders, smiling at her.

'Will you marry me?' he asked – and, to his surprise, he felt quite free of fear and doubt and was able to wait with joyful certainty for her reply.

She beamed at him. 'Yes, please,' she said, and kissed him.

\*　　\*　　\*

Lizzie kicked off her boots, gave Pooter and Perks a biscuit each and went into the kitchen. Prue was stirring soup.

'Is Fliss back from the station?' asked Lizzie. 'I'm starving.'

'Yes, she's back. Maria's train was on time, which is a miracle, and Fliss has invited Maria down for Hal's birthday, which is an even bigger miracle.'

'*Has* she?' Lizzie took an olive from the dish on the table and crunched it with relish. 'I think I'm surprised.'

'So is Fliss,' said Prue cheerfully. 'Nothing is more surprising to us than making a truly charitable gesture. Have you noticed? It's followed by such confusion. At first we feel rather elevated by our great-heartedness and then we're furious that we've allowed ourselves to be taken in. Don't you agree?'

Lizzie chuckled. 'I don't think I've ever thought about it,' she said, 'but I'm sure you're right. Which is Fliss feeling at the moment?'

'I rather think that she'd worked through her sense of self-satisfaction by the time she'd driven home and now she's in a fit of exasperation at what she sees as her weakness. She's in the drawing room playing the piano. Rather gloomy Brahms.'

'Do you think it was weakness?' asked Lizzie, amused.

'No, no. I think that a true act of generosity should never be regretted, but poor Fliss fears that she might have been manipulated.'

'Well, that's possible. Maria's rather good at that, isn't she?'

'Yes,' sighed Prue. 'Poor Maria finds it hard to relax. She is fearful because she's insecure and so she needs to feel in control all the time. It's very sad.'

'I was expecting her to be more of a cow. You know, making bitchy remarks and putting the cat among the pigeons. She was very subdued when she was here in the spring, but I put that down to her bereavement, and I was expecting more ructions this time.'

Prue put bread and cheese on the table, and a bowl of salad. 'Adam's death has shocked her,' she said. 'Maria was always immature, putting her own needs before those of her children, looking to Hal and then Adam to make difficult decisions and look after her. She could never see that we are each responsible for ourselves and now, suddenly, she's completely alone. I think, in the end, that she truly loved Adam and his death has opened her eyes at last. She's left it late to grow up but perhaps not too late. We must hope not.'

'And what about Jo?'

'Ah, yes. Well, Jo was expected to grow up too quickly. Maria forced him into that and he might find it very hard to be sympathetic now that it's her turn.'

'You think he ought to forgive her?' asked Lizzie diffidently.

'Oh, yes,' said Prue at once. 'For his own sake, if not for hers. Anger and resentment are so bad for the soul, aren't they? So destructive. Perhaps, especially now, he can afford to be generous.'

'Why especially now?'

'Henrietta,' answered Prue succinctly, 'the wonderful thing about love is that it's all-encompassing. He might find he has a little left over for Maria.'

Cordelia came out of the Harbour Bookshop and stood for a moment, tucking her parcel into her basket. A tall woman with a familiar face emerged from the doorway behind her and Cordelia stood to one side to let her pass.

'I think you dropped this in the bookshop.' The woman smiled at her, holding out a pretty silk scarf. 'They asked me to give it to you. It is yours, isn't it?'

'Yes, it is. Thank you so much.' Cordelia hesitated, wondering whether to make a friendly observation, but before she could say anything else her mobile

284

phone began to ring. She rolled her eyes, shrugged, and the woman laughed and moved away.

It was Henrietta. Cordelia hurried across the road towards the car park on the quay, her phone to her ear.

'Hello, darling,' she said. 'How are you?'

'Fine. Really good. Actually I've got some news for you. Jolyon and I are engaged.'

Cordelia stood quite still; she closed her eyes. 'Oh, darling,' she breathed. 'What fantastic news. It's wonderful. I'm so pleased.'

'I knew you would be.' Henrietta's voice was jubilant and Cordelia felt that she might weep with joy. 'Listen, Jo's here and he wants to speak to you.'

Jolyon was talking before she could pull herself together and she clasped the phone even tighter, listening eagerly to his voice.

'Hello, Cordelia. Henrietta says you're pleased. Isn't it fantastic? I know I should have asked your permission first and all that but it was a bit spur-of-the-moment stuff so I hope you'll overlook it . . .'

'Oh, darling Jo, it's the most wonderful news. I couldn't be happier. Oh, I want to shout with joy but I'm in the car park in Kingsbridge. Where are you?'

'I'm with Henrietta. We're at the cottage. Look, I haven't talked to anyone at The Keep yet so if you should speak to Fliss or Dad before we do I'd be grateful if you didn't mention it.'

'Of course, I understand. Let me know when you've spoken to them.'

'I'm hoping to do that now but Henrietta wanted you to be the first to know. Here she is again.'

'Hi, Mum. Listen, we're only telling just the immediate family at the moment. Nobody else. I don't want Susan to find out from anyone but me. I'll catch you later but Jo wants to speak to his family now. OK?'

'Absolutely. And I won't tell a soul. Of course not. Oh, darling, I'm just so happy for you.'

She stood for a moment beside her car, quite incapable of getting in and driving away; too happy to do anything but revel in her joy. *Henrietta wanted you to be the first to know . . .*' How sweet those words were; Cordelia clasped her hands to her heart and swallowed down her tears.

'Are you OK?'

It was the tall woman again, unlocking her own car door in the row opposite and looking at her with friendly concern.

'Yes.' Cordelia made an effort to behave normally. 'Yes, I'm fine, thanks. Just some rather wonderful news from my daughter, that's all.'

'That's good then.'

286

'Oh, it is. It is. I'm so happy.'

'I can see that.' The woman nodded, smiling. 'Drive carefully.'

'Thanks. I will.' For a moment Cordelia longed to share her news with this kind woman, but she remembered Henrietta's injunction and held her tongue, simply raising her hand in farewell to the woman as she drove away. She unlocked the car and got in, wanting to be at home. With any luck Fliss would telephone and she'd be able to share her happiness. Still, she paused long enough to dial Angus's number.

'It's nearly four o'clock,' she said, 'and I'm on my way home now so you could come any time you like.'

'Great,' he answered. 'I can't wait to hear how the weekend went and what Maria was like. I'll be with you in an hour at the most.'

287

# CHAPTER TWENTY-FOUR

It was Hal who took the phone call. He talked first to Jolyon, then to Henrietta and then to Jolyon again. Taking the phone into the little study he found Cordelia's number and dialled it.

'I gather you've heard the tidings of great joy?' he enquired. 'Isn't it wonderful? . . . Of *course* I'm pleased . . . Well, she doesn't know yet. No, listen, Jo and I have made a plan. He's staying with Henrietta tonight, doing some research around Appledore and Bideford tomorrow, and he'll be back here late afternoon. We're going to have a little party when he's back but we're keeping it a secret until then. I think it will be nice for Fliss and my old ma and Lizzie if he tells them himself. What d'you think? . . . Fantastic! So will you be here? Come early and have some tea . . . Of *course* we want you here. You're part of the family now . . . Don't be daft. We need you here. It's just a pity Henrietta can't be here too, but the logistics are a bit tricky. I talked to her about it and we've agreed to do it all over again on Sunday when Jo can go and fetch her over for the day, so book out Sunday lunch as well . . . Oh, yes. Good thinking. Look, I'll tell Fliss that you rang up for a chat and that I've suggested that you drop in for tea tomorrow. OK? . . . That's great. And remember, not a word to anyone. See you tomorrow.'

He came out of the study and came face to face with Fliss.

'I thought I heard the phone,' she said. 'I just won-dered . . .'

Her voice tailed away and despite his excitement, he saw the signs of strain in her face, the little lines between her brows, and he was seized with anxiety.

'What's the matter, love?' he asked. He took her thin, cold hands and drew her into the warmth of the kitchen. 'That was Cordelia. She's over this way tomorrow and I told her to drop in for tea. That's OK, isn't it? Gosh, you're cold. I'll light the fire in the hall and we'll have some tea. What is it, Fliss? Not still worrying about Maria?'

'Not really.' She looked away from him. 'Though I still wish I hadn't invited her for your birthday. I'm worried about what Jo will say when he finds out.'

Hal turned away to push the kettle on to the

hotplate, longing to tell her that Jo was in such high spirits that he probably wouldn't care.

'So what is it, then?' He had a tiny flickering memory, a sense of *déjà vu*, as if he and she had been here before, and turned back to her. 'You still think we're taking a risk? That I've opened Pandora's box and we're going to be hurt by the fallout?'

She sat down at the table. 'I just don't know. It's brought back memories, like we said before.'

He sat down too, turning his chair towards her.

'That's true. I've suddenly realized that I feel guilty about quite a lot of things I thought I'd forgotten. That I didn't fight harder for us when we were young, for one thing. And I shouldn't have told Maria how I felt about you, for another. Looking back I can see that she was much too insecure to deal with something like that. And I feel guilty about poor old Jo. He was the scapegoat and now I've forced him into an untenable position. I should have listened to you, Fliss.'

She tried to smile. 'I think it's me, really,' she admitted. 'At least now, doing it your way, some kind of healing might be possible. It's just that I feel so muddled. Yes, it's raised all kinds of feelings I didn't realize were there. Resentment because we gave in so easily all those years ago, and anger at Maria because she thinks she only has to say sorry

290

and we'll forgive her, and guilt that I can't be more generous about it all.'

Hal couldn't help laughing, just a little. 'Poor old love,' he said sympathetically. 'That's pretty comprehensive.'

He saw the instinctive flash of annoyance give way to a reluctant amusement.

'Uncle Theo stands at my shoulder,' she said. 'Do you remember that thing he used to say? "We are as big or small as the objects of our love." I'm feeling very small. It's complicated though, isn't it? Can I forgive Maria for the damage she's caused to Jo? Anyway,' she shrugged, 'if I'm honest, it's not just about Jo. It's not even about Maria. It's about me. Maria's reappearance has made me see myself more clearly. Yes, I suddenly realize that I *do* feel resentful that you didn't fight for me when we were young. And that you took so long to getting round to proposing to me after Miles died. Crazy, isn't it? It's eight years ago, for goodness' sake, but suddenly all these feelings have come from nowhere.'

'Pandora's box,' he repeated bitterly. 'I don't know what to say. I can repeat the old well-worn phrases, of course, explaining why: I was too young to know what I wanted and what I was doing in the first place; and that we'd got into a kind of rut in the second. But they just sound like excuses, don't they?'

'I'm being stupid,' she said. 'I know how it was back then. Of course I do. It's lots of things, really. We're all getting older and we feel vulnerable . . .'

'But it's more than that, isn't it?' He stared anxiously into her down-turned face. 'What is it really, Fliss?'

She stared at her clasped hands and he felt a real fear. Suddenly she looked up at him.

'I miss the children,' she said woefully. 'I miss Bess and Matt and Paula and little Timmy. It was bad enough when they were in London but now they're in Boston they seem so far away and I get this pain in my heart and I long to see them. It's so hard. I know that you're going to say that it's not so bad and we can get a flight out whenever we like and all that, but it's not the same. And now that Jamie's been posted to Cairo . . .'

She stopped, biting her lip, staring down at her hands, and Hal's heart twisted with pain for her. He covered her cold hands with his warm ones.

'I miss them all coming down for weekends and holidays,' she said. 'All the noise and the fun and watching the babies grow up. And I tell myself to get a grip. I think of how Grandmother must have felt when my father and mother moved out to Kenya when I was little and it was so much more difficult to travel. And I worry about Jamie . . .'

Hal remained silent: no point trying to assure her

that, though her son was a member of MI5, he was not in any kind of danger. They all knew the risks involved.

The door opened and Prue came into the kitchen; her eyes met Hal's above Fliss's bent head.

'The kettle's boiling. I'll make some tea, shall I?' Prue said. 'Hal, why don't you light the fire in the hall?'

Hall nodded, gave Fliss's hands one last squeeze and went through to the hall. He wished that he could break the news about Jolyon's engagement – it would cheer Fliss up, make her happy again – yet he knew he must keep it secret until tomorrow: he'd promised Jo. Whilst he laid and lit the fire and then went out to fetch logs his mind was busy with that little tag of memory, the sense of *déjà vu*, and suddenly he remembered another secret celebration, eight years ago; his mother's seventy-fifth birthday party and the day he'd decided to propose to Fliss. His sister, Kit, had come down from London and it was she who'd shown him how stupid he was being to let things drift.

## Spring 1998

Leaving Fliss and Caroline in the kitchen, Hal and Kit stroll in the garden together. The air is sweet and cold, and a thrush is singing in the orchard. The rain has drawn off at last, leaving a tender blue-green sky, and the western hills are washed in luminous golden light. Sparkling raindrops shower over her hands as Kit breaks off a spray of *Ribes oderatum* and inhales the fragrance of its yellow flowers.

'Ma hasn't got a clue what's going on,' she says. 'I've brought her masses of freesias and smuggled them into Fliss's bathroom. She's looking a bit stressed out, I thought. Fliss, that is. Not Ma. It occurs to me, little brother, that you two still haven't got your act together.'

He frowns, not looking at her, and she glances at him sharply.

'Don't tell me you're both still doing the "just good friends" bit? Oh, I don't believe it! Honestly, Hal. I don't want to sound callous but Miles has been dead for nearly a year. What the hell are you both waiting for now? Some divine intervention? Authorization from the Pope?'

'Oh, shut up!' he says angrily. 'It's not funny. And it's not that bloody simple, either.'

She watches him, eyebrows raised, lightly brushing the spray of *Ribes* to and fro across her lips.

'Sorry,' he says presently. 'It's just . . . not a joking matter.'

'No,' she says. 'No, I can see it wouldn't be. Not

294

for you two, anyway. But it's getting silly, Hal. Fliss has got that end-of-tether look about her. That little frown is back and her jaw is all clenched. She's too thin, too. What's going on?'

'We can't seem to take the plunge,' he says slowly. 'I know it seems as if it should be easy. We've loved each other all our lives, and we've been under the same roof for years, but now we're both free at last we can't seem to break out. I honestly think that none of the family would give a damn. After all, we're not going to have children so the old fears don't apply, but even so . . .'

'It's sex,' says Kit cheerfully. 'Amazing how it always comes back to it, isn't it? That's what's blocking it. Well, there's nothing to stop you both now, is there? For heaven's sake, just get on and do it.'

'You make it sound so easy,' he says irritably. 'Just think about it. The whole family has got used to our situation. They take us for granted now. How passionate would you feel if you knew that Ma was likely to come wandering into your bedroom at midnight with an attack of insomnia? Or that Jolyon might burst in with some brilliant new idea for his damned market garden? And how do we behave the next morning? Do we subtly imply with loving gestures and caresses that the Rubicon has been crossed and that we are now the equivalent of a married couple? I'm sure you'd manage splendidly but Fliss and I are very conventional people and we don't get too much time together to iron out the problem. The other thing is that she's never really recovered properly from Mole's death. I thought she was coming to terms with it but just lately she's been rather odd.'

'I know that's been a nightmare for her.' Kit looks grave. 'Like her parents and Jamie all over again. It was a terrible thing, appalling, but I thought she was more or less over it. Maybe this new peace agreement has brought it all back again. It's rather bitter to think that such people might be walking about free in a few months' time, isn't it?'

'I don't think it's that.' Hal shakes his head. 'I can't describe it but she's . . . oh, I don't know. Abstracted. Not quite with me.'

Kit stops quite still so that Hal is obliged to pause too. He looks at her, surprised at the serious look on her face.

'You've got to do something,' she says urgently. 'It's gone on too long, Hal, and soon it will be too late. You can't expect Fliss to make the running. Like you said, she's too conventional and she might be anxious about the family's reaction. Especially Ma and Jo's. Just do it, Hal. No, I don't mean the great seduction scene. I agree you're both a bit too old for creeping along landings or going away for the weekend. It's too ridiculous and undignified. You've just got to tell them. Don't even ask Fliss. Just do it. There are times when a man needs to take the initiative, never mind about how emancipated we women are or how high our consciousnesses have been raised.'

He is staring at her. 'But how can I not tell Fliss? She'll be a bit miffed, won't she?'

'Of course she won't,' Kit says impatiently. 'She might be embarrassed, anxious, surprised, but she won't be angry. Take my word for it. She'll feel an overwhelming relief. Poor old Flissy has had a rotten deal. She's loved you all her life, Hal, but if you're not careful her love will pass its sell-by date and go bad on her and she could finish up bitter and miserable. Just trust me and do it. Tell the family that you're getting married, set a date for it and afterwards go away for a few days together. Then come home and settle down. It will be so simple, I promise you, if you'll just do it. You were the one who told her first time round. You took the responsibility and made the final decision. Now you've got to do it again.'

'You're right.' He is looking past her and she knows that he is thinking back to a spring over thirty years before. 'You're absolutely right.'

'There's another thing,' Kit tells him. 'You took

my advice then, little brother, so take it now. It's the same advice but for different reasons. When you've told them, don't stay around. It'll be embarrassing and mawkish and you'll both find it hard to handle. Say your piece and say it loud and clear. Name the day, tell Flissy you love her and then clear out. Ma and Caroline will be delighted and she'll have quite enough on her plate without you hanging about like a star-struck lover.'

'I've been a bloody fool,' he says. 'Bless you, Kit. You're so right and I just couldn't see it.'

'You're too close to it,' she tells him, 'and it's gone on so long. She looked after Miles for all those years and now he's dead and for the first time she's free. She doesn't know how to handle it. She's lost her bearings and I suspect that deep down she's scared stiff. The poor girl's all at sea . . .'

'Very nautical.' He's grinning at her, relief and excitement in his eyes. 'I'll go and polish up my anchor.'

'Oh, shut up.' She aims a blow at him and drops her spray.

'What are you two up to?' Fliss is coming across the lawn. 'Dinner's nearly ready and I wondered if you'd like a drink?'

'An unnecessary question, little coz.' Kit finds the *Ribes* and picks it up. 'Just lead us to it. I was telling

298

Hal about Ma's freesias and he was trying to persuade me to let him in on it. He's forgotten to get anything, as usual.'

'I gave her a present on her birthday,' he says, unperturbed by his sister's aspersions. He slips an arm about Fliss's shoulders and gives her a hug and she smiles up at him. Remembering Kit's words he feels a thrill of fear. How terrible if he should lose her now through procrastination. 'Play to us?' he suggests. 'Play to us until dinner's ready,' and they cross the grass together and go through the French doors into the drawing room.

All through the last few days of his leave he waits for an opportunity to follow Kit's advice. Looking at Fliss with new eyes, he sees the lines of strain about her mouth, the tiny frown between her feathery brows. There is a tense, coiled look about her, as if she is waiting, wound as tight as a spring. Anxiety washes through him leaving fear in its wake. Supposing she has ceased to love him? He knows that she is deeply fond of him, no question of that, but supposing her love for him has already begun to go bad on her and she is dreading the question she is expecting him to ask? It might explain her prevarication, her reluctance to discuss the future.

As soon as he's identified his fear he acts upon it and takes her up on to the moor. As he drives through Buckfast, towards Holne, he sees how her thin hands clasp and unclasp on her knees, notes her introspection. He sets himself the task of relaxing her, talking idly, pointing out small indications of spring's arrival: a chiffchaff swinging on a branch of budding crab apple; a clump of early purple orchis on a grassy bank; two painted ladies fluttering above a patch of violets that cling in the crevice of a dry-stone wall. The moor shows a placid, smiling face: fold on fold of blue distant hills, smooth grey stone, wooded valleys misting into a new tender green. Venford Reservoir is a dazzling shield of water, blue as the sky that overarches it; a secret shining jewel set deep within the surrounding ink-black pines.

They walk out to Bench Tor and stand together looking down into White Wood; seeing the gleam of water far below between the branches of the trees that cling to the coombe's steep sides; listening to the river thundering through the narrow rocky chasm. Sheep scramble, sure-footed on the piled granite, watching them with narrow yellow eyes, whilst ponies graze undisturbed on the lower slopes.

Across the valley a cuckoo calls and suddenly they see him, unmistakable with his pointed wings and long tail. They watch his dipping flight as he drops down towards Meltor Wood and disappears from sight. They laugh, delighted, hugging each other.

'Odd, isn't it?' says Fliss. 'He's such a rogue and yet we love him.'

Looking down at her, Hal sees that the signs of strain are gone and her face is as carefree as a child's. He pushes back the fair strands of hair that blow about her face and bends to kiss her. Her arms tighten about him and her response tells him all that he needs to know. In his relief he clasps her closely to him but before he can speak there is the sound of yelping and thudding feet. A dog appears over the rocks, sheep scattering before him, and behind him comes a young man, shouting threats, brandishing a lead, gasping for breath.

'Sorry,' he cries when he sees them. 'He's only a puppy, really, but I should have kept him on the lead. A sheep broke right in front of him . . .'

They acknowledge his dilemma, sympathize, agree that the puppy must be controlled, but by the time the fuss is over, the moment has passed. Once or twice, on the journey home, Hal attempts to find appropriate words, to warn her of his intention to tell the family, but each time he opens his mouth, Fliss begins to speak and he is forestalled. Nevertheless, he no longer doubts that Kit's advice is sound; it is simply a matter of timing, of finding the right moment.

It comes on Sunday afternoon, hours before he is

due to leave for the station. He's been down in the stable yard with Jolyon, and when he comes back into the hall, Jolyon at his heels, they are sitting by the fire: Caroline and his mother; Fliss and Susanna. Tea is in progress and they are laughing. Fliss glances round at him and he sees that the old expression is back; a kind of patient resignation that is worlds away from the happy face that had laughed into his, up on Bench Tor in the warm spring sunshine. He clenches his fists, pushing them into his pockets and walks into the circle of firelight and warmth. They all look at him now and he smiles at them, swallowing down a ridiculous spasm of terror.

'There's something I want to say,' he announces. 'It might come as a shock but it shouldn't, not after all this time.' They are all silent now, watching him. 'Fliss and I are going to get married. You all know that we've loved each other since we were children and now there's nothing to prevent us being properly together. I think it's best if we have a registry office ceremony as soon as possible and then Fliss and I will have a few days away somewhere. We don't want a huge fuss . . .'

The echoing surprised silence crashes into a noisy hubbub of words and laughter. Prue is in tears, Caroline is hugging Fliss, and Susanna sits in open-mouthed amazement. Hal stands quite still, feeling

302

almost foolish, undecided as to what he should do next, trying to gauge Fliss's reaction. It is Jolyon who carries him through. Hal feels his arm seized in a fierce grip and then his son is hugging him, thumping him on the back with his free fist, congratulating him. Hal barely has time to register his gratitude before Jo releases him and turns to Fliss, opening both arms to her. Her eyes meet Hal's at last and, in that brief moment before she is engulfed by Jolyon's embrace, he sees that they are bright with pure joy, shining with unutterable relief.

# CHAPTER TWENTY-FIVE

Driving to Bristol on Monday morning, Jolyon covered whole stretches of the familiar road without seeing them; his vision was still filled with other joyful images and though he reminded himself from time to time that he must concentrate on the journey, nevertheless another happy memory would distract him and he would give himself up to this unfamiliar sensation of exhilaration; even his translation from the grower of organic food to popular TV presenter hadn't given him such happiness.

He was loved, desired, wanted, for himself: not as a son or a brother or a cousin but simply for himself. And by such a gorgeous, wonderful girl. Jolyon shook his head and pulled obligingly into the inside lane as a BMW tailgated him, lights flashing. The driver leaned to glare at him as he swept by, fingers raised insultingly. Jolyon beamed blindingly at him and raised his own hand in a kind of benediction. The BMW powered past, baffled, deprived of its victory, and Jolyon was filled with a benign compassion for all poor fellows who were so sad that such actions gave them pleasure. Clearly they had no Henrietta in their lives; clearly they did not know – or had forgotten – what it was like to be exalted by love. And it wasn't just him – the whole family was exalted.

He'd got back to The Keep quite early in the evening to find them all – Fliss, Granny, Lizzie and Cordelia – sitting by the fire in the hall surrounded by the remnants of tea, just as he and Dad had planned. They'd greeted him as usual, Cordelia hardly daring to meet his eyes lest she should give the secret away, and then Dad had appeared and said, 'Hail, the conquering hero comes,' or some nonsense like that, and they'd smiled and Granny had offered him tea. But Dad had said, 'Hang on a minute, I think Jo wants to tell us something,' and they'd all – except Cordelia – looked puzzled, turning to him.

He'd felt nervous and a bit silly, but he was still so elated that he'd been able to walk into the little group and stand with his back to the fire so that he could see them all.

'Yes, I have,' he'd said. 'It probably won't be too much of a surprise, actually. I've asked Henrietta to marry me and she's said "yes" . . .' The rest of his little speech was lost in the reaction of his family. Cordelia was beaming at him, tears in her eyes; Lizzie was crying, 'Wow! Great. Gosh, you clever old thing,' and Granny was sitting quite still, with her hands clasped, and saying, 'Darling Jo. Oh, how wonderful.' Miraculously, Dad had produced a tray with glasses on it and was opening a bottle of champagne, but it was Fliss who leaped to her feet and came to him, her arms opened wide and her eyes bright and shining with joy. They'd held each other really tightly, her cheek pressed against his as she whispered her happiness into his ear, and then Dad was there, glass in one hand and seizing his, Jo's, free hand with the other, pumping it up and down and congratulating him.

He'd never been so happy, and he'd longed for Henrietta to be there with him – but, at the same time, it had been very special, that little moment with those dearest to him, who had supported and encouraged him for so many years. And then, on Sunday, they'd done it all over again, with Henrietta. He'd driven over and fetched her and the dogs, and they'd had another celebration – 'This is what The Keep does best,' Dad had said to her. 'We love celebrations' – and she'd looked so happy and so relaxed, and he'd been so proud . . .

And now he'd nearly missed his turning; Jo laughed aloud. He glanced at his mobile, lying on the seat beside him. As soon as he could he'd pull in and send a text to Henrietta, who'd asked him to let her know when he was safe at Bristol – and how strange that was; to have someone special waiting to hear from him, caring where he was and what he was feeling. He wondered what she was doing right now.

Henrietta was on her knees, clearing up a large pool of sick from the flagstones in the kitchen.

'And that is what happens,' she was saying severely to the chastened Tacker, 'when you eat nasty things when I've told you not to.'

Tacker's tail beat feebly, his ears flattened as he watched her. She wrapped the newspaper together into a ball, gave the floor another wipe with a clean sheet of paper and then stood up to fetch the bucket and mop. Juno and Pan watched from their beds, keeping themselves aloof from such behaviour.

'And it's no good,' Henrietta warned them, 'looking holier-than-thou. You're just as bad as he is.'

They pricked their ears and looked reproachfully at her, wounded by such an accusation.

Henrietta mopped the floor vigorously whilst Tacker made cautious advances on the sweeping mop, his spirits already rising. She pretended to chase him with it and he turned tail, barking excitedly, but then rushed back to pounce on it again. Henrietta laughed and took the bucket outside to empty it into one of the flowerbeds. Glancing at her watch, she wondered how soon she might hear from Jo; it was too early. Her heart bumped with this exciting new happiness and she wished that she wasn't alone; that she had someone with whom she could share her news. One of her London friends was coming for a few days – and that was great – but she daren't tell Jilly, not until she'd told Susan.

'I must tell Susan myself,' she'd told Jo. 'It'll be another shock for her and I shan't want to leave her in the lurch. I'll need to go back to London with her when she gets home until she can sort out a new nanny.'

He'd understood that but they'd decided to go away, just the two of them, for Christmas; she'd always wanted to spend Christmas and the New Year in Scotland, and Jo knew a hotel – an old castle – where they could be together.

'And perhaps an Easter wedding,' she'd said, 'if we can get organized that quickly. Where shall we get married?'

He'd been rather diffident when he'd suggested The Keep and the local church, hoping he wasn't being pushy, but she'd been thrilled at the idea: The Keep would be utterly perfect – and, after all, it would be a bit much to expect Mum to do it all from the cottage.

They'd sat together, curled up in front of the fire, talking, making plans, making love . . .

'We could live in Bristol,' he'd offered tentatively. 'You know, to begin with. Until we know how everything would pan out.'

'But wouldn't it be easier for you to be at The Keep?' she'd asked. 'Your television work seems rather peripatetic but you need to be at the office quite a lot, don't you?'

'Well, it would be easier,' he'd agreed, 'and we'd be in the gatehouse, of course. But I don't know quite how you feel about being there with all the family around. Bristol's got more going for it; your friends could easily come down from London. I could commute down to The Keep.'

'But I told you I like having people around,' she'd protested. 'And I want us to be together as much as possible. We could give it a try, at least. Perhaps I could help out with Keep Organics until I reinvent myself. I can't go on being a nanny once we're married. At least, I don't think I'd want to. We want our own children, don't we, Jo?'

She'd looked up at him, pulling his arm more tightly round her shoulders, holding his hand, and she'd seen an odd expression on his face then:

shock, wonder, almost disbelief at such a prospect.

'Yes,' he'd muttered at last. 'Yes, of course we do,' and he'd looked down at her and kissed her . . .

The dogs were staring at her expectantly and she gave a great sigh.

'OK,' she said. 'Walks time. Where shall we go? Somewhere we can let Tacker play around and you two can have a good run. Come on, then.'

Her mobile rang and she seized it up. 'Hi. Where are you?'

'Nearly there,' Jo said. 'Though I almost missed my exit, thinking about you. What about you?'

'The usual,' she said. 'Taking the dogs out for a walk. Then some shopping to get ready for Jilly. It'll be hell not being able to tell her. Wondering what sort of ring I want.'

He laughed. 'It ought to be a topaz, with your hair. Must dash, I'm going to be late. Love you.'

'I love you too,' she said rather shyly.

The dogs stood at the door, watching her, and she put the phone in her pocket and grabbed her coat.

'I love him,' she told them happily. 'Good, isn't it?'

Maria was watching television: Simon King's *Big Cat Diary*. Never in her life had she watched so much television, but then she'd never realized that each day could last so long when there was nobody else to share it. Penelope and Philip were wonderful, simply wonderful, but she had her pride and she couldn't rely on them too heavily for company – and, anyway, they were out this evening.

She took another sip at her gin and tonic: the lioness was watching her four cubs playing in the long grass. How sweet they were; they looked just like golden retriever puppies, just like Rex had looked at a few months old. Maria frowned; the memory irked her: the wretched animal had caused so many problems. Let's face it – and this needn't be a criticism – she wasn't a dog person; mud all over the floor and hairs everywhere, always needing a walk or a feed. No, she could manage nicely without all those demands, thank you very much. She'd blamed Hal for Rex's misdemeanours and finally, after a monumental row, he'd been carted off down to The Keep. Poor Jolyon had been heartbroken . . .

Now the mother lion was looking about her, scenting danger, and here it came in the form of a large male, and Simon – what a sweetie Simon was – was explaining that the male would kill the cubs if he could get close enough. Maria shivered, holding her glass. He'd kill the babies simply because they weren't his, just for the hell of it: so bloody typical. Sometimes she wondered why she watched these nature programmes: always full of death and destruction; one species eating another; tiny, vulnerable creatures swallowed whole by larger, brutal ones; distraught mothers flapping about helplessly. It was all rather depressing . . . She took another glop of gin.

Simon was really upset; he really cared. Jo had this same kind of appeal that Simon had; he drew you in, made you want to watch. There was an intimacy about Jo's presentation – and it helped that he was so good-looking, so like Hal. And, oh God, now the lion was coming closer and the cubs were all scattering about, terrified, and he was roaring and pouncing, and suddenly the lioness was attacking him savagely, so savagely, that he was actually turning tail and fleeing, and she was racing after him and seeing him off, and it was so exhilarating that Maria was shouting, 'Go, girl, go!' and waving her glass and half laughing and half crying.

She got up to pour another drink – was this her second or third? – feeling slightly unsteady on her feet. Once, ages ago, she'd had a bit of a drink problem; well, fair enough, Hal had been at sea for weeks at a time and she'd been lonely. Dear old Jo had worried about her, making her cups of tea, running her bath. He couldn't have been more than seven. Once he'd broken the sugar bowl while he was making the tea and she'd screamed at him . . .

Maria steadied herself at the kitchen counter. She must simply stop this pointless brooding on the past. It did nobody any good. She sloshed some gin into the glass, poured in some tonic, and went back to her chair. Simon was explaining that only one cub had been saved, two must have been killed, and the fourth was so badly injured that he now simply lay down and refused to move. The mother stood over him, licking him, trying to restore him to life whilst the other cub watched and tears poured down Maria's cheeks.

She reminded herself that her problem was that she was just so soft-hearted, too sensitive; she'd always been the same. Dear old Pen, so stalwart and community-minded, was always trying to persuade her to take up good works, down at the hospice or amongst the elderly. It was OK for Pen; she was tough as old boots, always had been. She and Pen had been at school together, best friends from the first day, and she'd been like it way back: a Brownie and then a Girl Guide, dibbing away, doing good by stealth. Mind, she'd been a rock, had Pen, always looking out for her shyer, gentler best friend.

Maria staunched another flood of tears and stared at the screen. The mother lion wasn't giving up,

Simon was telling the viewers. She'd gone back with her remaining cub to the den and now stood amongst the flattened grass, calling for her young. Well, of course she would: she was a mother, wasn't she? But how could they have survived that deadly attack? Honestly, it was simply too heart-rending, and any minute that huge chauvinist lion would come back and do for them both.

'Run away!' Maria wanted to cry. 'Run away!'

But wait, now the grasses were stirring and here was a cub, unharmed, running to its mother, and dear old Simon's voice was wavering, and now another cub – oh, good grief, this was so fantastic – another cub was coming out of its hiding place, and the three cubs and their mother were having a reunion. Maria gulped some more gin, and wept, and so did Simon – well, there were tears in his eyes, bless – and by the time she'd mopped her own eyes and looked again they'd all moved on to meerkats, but she'd had enough traumas for one evening and she was perfectly certain that there would be more ahead. A predator who just adored raw meerkat would be hovering somewhere at hand and it would begin all over again.

Maria channel-hopped for a few minutes and then switched the television off. The lioness had made her think about family, about Jo. Family was important, more important than anything else. OK, so she'd got a few things wrong in the past but there was absolutely no reason why things couldn't be put right. She could buy a little cottage, or a flat, in Staverton or Totnes, not too far away from The Keep but not absolutely on the doorstep, and make a new start. Maybe, while she was looking for this little place, Hal might suggest that she should stay at The Keep. That would be so good; give everyone plenty of opportunity to mend fences.

Of course, Pen would put up a fight. She'd already said that it was best for Maria to be amongst her friends in Salisbury, where she'd lived nearly all her life. Well, Pen would say that, wouldn't she? There was no question that she enjoyed having her old friend next door – and they had some good times together, no doubt about that. Once or twice, to be honest, she'd wondered whether she'd ever do better than to be in this very comfortable little annexe with the use of the garden, demanding no effort on her part, and a couple of very good mates just a shout away. After all, they had lots of mutual friends and darling old Phil was just the kind of bossy boots who was only too happy to organize things and sort out problems. She simply had to put on a particular expression – a tiny frown, a nibble at the lower lip – and old Phil's arm would be round the shoulder, comforting, wanting to help. Of course, in these days of equality it was an absolute godsend for an old-fashioned chap like Philip to be able to defend a helpless woman. Pen wasn't having any of that kind of patronizing nonsense, thank you very much, so she knew that Phil really appreciated her own rather delicate helplessness. Adam had been just such another, and it was child's play to have them eating out of her hand. Of course, she had to be careful. She didn't want to upset darling Pen; no killing of the goose that laid the golden eggs.

Maria finished her drink. Nevertheless, Pen and Philip weren't her family. She'd explain that to them, very tactfully, and put forward this new plan. Hadn't Pen talked of going down to their cottage in Salcombe quite soon? That might be an excellent place to start: she could go down with them, have a look at the market, go and see Hal and Jo . . .

Her spirits flew upwards and she felt excited, quite giggly and happy. Humming to herself, Maria got up, holding on to the chair's arm for a moment, just to get her balance, and went to make some supper.

# CHAPTER TWENTY-SIX

Cordelia put the car in the garage, collected the shopping and found the front door key. Great gusts of salty air poured over the headland, whisking her hair around her face and tugging at the paper bags in her basket. The sea, glassy and transparent, mirrored the majestic, swift-moving cloudscape: cream and gold and white. She stood for a moment, relishing this new sense of happiness, recalling tiny, special moments that had occurred over and over again during the last week. Henrietta had been so sweet, so warm, that it was as if a whole new side of her daughter had been revealed.

She let herself into the cottage, picked up the letters that were lying on the mat and carried them into the kitchen. McGregor came to greet her and a quick glance assured her that all was well, but she remained anxious. She was fearful lest there should be another visitation, a further development in the mystery that surrounded the events of the last few weeks. Several times she'd been tempted to confide in Angus, although she knew exactly what he'd say: call the police. It was a sensible idea yet something stopped her, though she couldn't say quite what it was: some instinct that told her that she was not actually in real danger but rather being forced to be an unwilling partner in some drama that had to be played out. Angus would say that she was a fool; that she was taking a huge risk. Perhaps she was; but after all, what could she actually tell the police that would be of any help? She'd pieced together a fragmented sequence of events: a photo tucked into her windscreen wipers; a tall figure up on the cliff watching her through binoculars; some of her work destroyed whilst she was out on the balcony with Fliss; the sharp tap on her shoulder and the man hurrying out of the deli, followed by the discovery of the koala bear in her basket; the visitor who'd left another koala bear and moved her books whilst she was down on the beach. It was all so pointless. Surely the police would think that it was simply someone playing practical jokes on her, and she was inclined to agree, but who might it be? She had thought about it endlessly and only one person fitted the bill, as far as she could see, but her suspicion seemed so preposterous that at first she could hardly admit it to herself and she'd certainly been unable to talk about it even to Angus.

Cordelia riffled idly through her letters: two bills, three catalogues and two envelopes – one handwritten, one typed. Dropping the bills and the catalogues on to the kitchen table she opened the handwritten envelope first: a card from an old friend asking if Cordelia might manage the trip to Oxfordshire to celebrate a wedding anniversary.

Janey had written: '. . . thirty years!! Can you believe it? And it seems only minutes ago we were all at Smuggler's Way in Faslane. Do you remember the drying area and how we used to puff up and down all those steps with the nappies?!!'

Cordelia smiled reminiscently – *only minutes ago*' – and was still smiling when she opened the second envelope. A photograph fell out into her hand and she stared down at it, her smile fading into bewilderment. The young Cordelia beamed back at her, Simon beside her in his navy jersey with his lieutenant-commander's stripes on its shoulders; he held a small, laughing Henrietta between his hands: a happy little family, kneeling together on a patch of grass.

She turned the photograph quickly and saw three fuzzy black patches, where it had been torn from the black page of an album. Instantly, in her mind's eye, she pictured the album: a rather expensive leather book with gold tooling that she'd filled with the best of the photographs that had been taken from the time of Henrietta's first birthday until Simon had left them. There had been other photographs, stuffed into big manila envelopes or made into montages and framed, but the album had been the place for those special recorded moments.

Cordelia picked up the envelope and shook it but there was nothing else inside. She examined the typed address but there was no clue there. The second-class stamp had missed the franking machine, although it had been crossed through in biro by the postman, so there was no date or postmark either. An idea occurred to her and with it a sense of relief: the photo was from Janey. Perhaps she'd meant to put it in with her letter, forgotten it, and sent it on in a different envelope. The photograph of the little scene, with the rather ugly concrete wall as the backdrop, might easily have been taken at Smuggler's Way, probably by Janey herself, and removed from her own album, and this would tie in with her letter. Cordelia pictured the scene: Janey arriving back from the postbox to find the photograph lying on the table.

'Oh, Richard,' she might have said crossly. 'I've forgotten to put the photo in,' and Richard would have said, 'Don't worry, love. I'll print an envelope off on the computer.'

Cordelia tried to take comfort from this scenario but her relief was short-lived. It was most unlikely that Janey would be so tactless as to send a photograph with Simon in it: she knew what a painful time it had been for her friend, and all that had happened since; surely she would never just send such a reminder out of the blue. Of course they talked about the past and on these occasions Simon's name might crop up quite naturally, but to post the photo . . . No, no. It was simply an extraordinary coincidence that it should arrive with her letter.

She put the photograph on the table and went into her study. The big rosewood chest of drawers had travelled with her for years; it had belonged to her grandmother. She knew exactly where the album would be. It would be lying at the back of the bottom drawer underneath all the folders and envelopes of photographs that had amassed over the years. She'd offered it to Henrietta years ago, after Simon's letter had arrived, but she'd refused it.

'I've got my own album, thank you,' she'd said stonily, accusingly. And so she had: a large unwieldy book with the photos pasted in all haphazard, and uneven writing beneath each one in coloured ink: 'Me and Daddy at Salcombe'; 'Me and Daddy at the

Boat Float'. She'd ostentatiously let Cordelia see that there were very few of 'Me and Mummy'. Later, the entries were more sophisticated – simply a place and a date – but still very few pictures of Henrietta with her mother.

And why should there be, thought Cordelia defensively. After all, I was with her all through that time. She didn't need photos of me.

Getting down on to her knees, she pulled out the heavy drawer. Carefully she took out folders that threatened to spill their slippery contents all over the floor, and there at the back was the album. She lifted it almost gingerly, smoothing the cover with her fingers before opening it, and felt a shock to her heart. Several photographs were missing. Quickly she turned the thick, black pages, unevenly weighty with glue and photos, and packed with memories.

They'd been removed with care: on this page two were gone, on this only one, on some none at all had been taken. Cordelia sat back on her heels, fighting down a growing sense of unease. The likeliest person to take the photos was Henrietta – but why should she? And why secretly, without mentioning it? Perhaps it hadn't been done in secret; perhaps she'd simply decided one day to remove some of them. She wouldn't have needed to ask permission.

There was another person who might have taken

them – and this confirmed her suspicions: Simon. Simon the Coldheart. That's what she'd called him after he'd so cruelly written to Henrietta explaining exactly why he'd left them and telling her that there would be no room for his daughter in his new life in Australia. Cordelia had written to him, addressing him as Simon the Coldheart and accusing him of inhuman behaviour. It was the title of the novel that had been left on her lectern, although the other title – *The Reluctant Widow* – was less apt. She guessed that it was the closest he could get to his new state: his wife must have died and he'd come back to England to pursue some kind of revenge. But why? Perhaps he was unhinged by grief. Simon had always been a very intense character. She remembered how resolutely he'd pursued her once Angus had gone to Australia, sending funny notes, flowers that had folklore meanings, and even, occasionally, small, strange gifts. In her state of misery at Angus's defection, she'd been touched by Simon's unfaltering love, flattered by his persistence.

It was Angus who had introduced them, and they'd both been amused by the younger man's complete infatuation for Cordelia. They took him along with them sometimes, humouring and teasing him as if he were a child or a pet; confident in their own power and happiness, graciously allowing him the crumbs of friendship from their cornucopia of love.

'I think he'd kill me if he could,' Angus had once told her laughingly. 'He's utterly besotted by you. He's a funny chap, old Si. Very single-minded.'

Now, Cordelia shivered. She wondered if Simon had been out there on the cliff, watching through his binoculars, on the occasions when Angus had been with her. Quite suddenly she remembered the photograph tucked beneath the windscreen washer: had it been of her and Angus? *I think he'd kill me if he could*. Closing the drawer, she stood up and went back into the kitchen. She seized her mobile, scrolled to Angus's number and waited.

'Dilly.' His voice was warm. 'How are you?'

'Worried,' she said briefly. 'Something I need to talk to you about. Could you come over?'

'Yes, of course.' He sounded anxious now, and puzzled. 'I'll be with you in half an hour.'

Typically, he asked no questions and she was grateful, but while she waited she wondered if she should have gone to him instead. If it were Simon out there, watching, then Angus's presence might inflame him further. These strange happenings had begun just after Angus had moved to Dartmouth and she imagined Simon watching them both, following her when she went shopping and even farther afield, and making a note of her movements and routines. Perhaps he'd been in Mangetout when she and Angus had had coffee together, and had slipped the Australian koala bear into her basket whilst she waited to be served.

She began to put away her shopping, glancing at her watch from time to time, listening for the sound of the car. When she heard the engine she slipped into her study and looked out of the window but there was nobody on the cliff path and she opened the front door with relief and hurried Angus inside.

'What's up?' he asked, following her into the kitchen. 'Is it Henrietta? Nothing's wrong, is it?'

'No,' Cordelia answered, turning to look at him, folding her arms across her breast. 'It's me. It sounds crazy, Angus, but I think I'm being stalked.'

# CHAPTER TWENTY-SEVEN

'I can't believe you didn't tell me before,' Angus said for the third time. 'And to think you've been here all alone. Anything might have happened. For God's sake, Dilly!'

'It seemed so silly,' she said wearily. 'Just foolish little things. And I've got McGregor, don't forget. I thought you'd want me to go to the police and I simply can't face it. I can't, Angus.'

'So what do you plan to do?' he asked angrily. 'Wait till you get a brick through the window? Or he jumps you one dark night when you're getting out of the car when you haven't got McGregor with you? And what if he goes after Henrietta?'

She stared at him fearfully. 'But why should he? He always adored her.'

'Dilly, these are not the actions of a sane person. If you really think it might be Simon then you must take precautions.'

'Do *you* think it's him?'

He stared at her white face and his expression softened. 'My poor darling, it's very likely, isn't it? Who else fits the bill? The koala bear signifies Australia, and the book titles seem to be a serious clue to his name and state. And then there are the photographs . . .'

He paused and she nodded. 'You see? It's not much to go on, is it?'

'But who else would do such things? And why?'

'How should I know? It's so utterly weird.'

'One thing is certain. You mustn't be alone here. Honestly, Dilly, when I think of these last few weeks . . .'

'I know, but where can I go?'

'You can come to me. Or if you won't do that then tell Fliss what's going on and ask if you can stay at The Keep.'

'But for how long? I have work to do. And I don't want to leave my home empty and unprotected. The point is, how will something like this be resolved?'

Angus took a deep breath, shrugged his shoulders. 'How the hell do I know? Well, I'm not leaving you alone, Dilly, so don't think I will. And I'm anxious about Henrietta, all on her own, too.'

Cordelia pressed her fingers to her lips. 'What

shall we do? I never thought of Henrietta being at risk. It almost seemed like a silly game.'

'Silly games can turn nasty,' said Angus grimly, 'and Simon was always a very intense kind of man. We need to speak to the Chadwicks. If necessary, Jo will have to move in with Henrietta for a few days while we decide what to do. I think we shall have to go to the police, Dilly.'

'On the strength of two koala bears and a couple of paperbacks?' She held up a placating hand at the expression on his face. 'OK, OK, sorry. But it's just so silly. They'll simply say that it's a practical joke. And it's going to mean another black mark against us from Henrietta, isn't it?'

'Better a black mark than something much worse. I'm sorry, I know you think I'm overreacting, but I just don't like this, Dilly.'

'Neither do I,' she said miserably. 'OK. Let's talk to Fliss and Hal, see what they think and go from there. Henrietta's got a friend from London staying for a couple of days but it might be wise to alert Jo.'

He looked at her curiously. 'I think I'm surprised that you're not more frightened.'

'I have moments of real terror,' she admitted, 'but deep down some instinct tells me that this is more a war of nerves than something more serious.' She shrugged. 'I know it sounds crazy but that's how it feels.'

'But what's the point?' Angus asked, baffled. 'What is it that Simon hopes to achieve?'

'I don't know.' She shook her head. 'Could it be that he hopes it might come between us somehow?'

'Well, if he thinks that then he's certainly crazy.'

She hesitated. 'We weren't very kind to him, I suppose, were we? When we were young, I mean. We were a bit high-handed, allowing him a few crumbs from the rich man's table. Perhaps he wants to punish us for the way we patronized him.'

Angus shrugged. 'He got you in the end, didn't he?'

'Well, you didn't want me,' she flashed. 'It was you who went away.'

He was silent for a moment. 'I was a callow youth,' he said reluctantly, 'who didn't know what he wanted until it was too late. But it was Simon's decision to leave, wasn't it? You didn't throw him out. He knew you were prepared to stay with your marriage.'

'But he knew that it was you I loved,' she answered sadly.

'Darling, I'm sorry. Perhaps you're right and this is some silly payback for his hurt and humiliation all those years ago. Look, telephone The Keep and see if we can go over sometime today. If you won't let me call the police at least we can have another point of view, though I think I know what Hal will say.'

'So do I,' said Cordelia glumly. 'I think I'm going to be outnumbered.'

'I've got another idea,' Angus said. 'We could simply tell the police that someone's been in the house. No mention of koala bears and books but just enough to get them round here, and that might frighten Simon off. If it is Simon.'

'It's a possibility.' Cordelia struck her hands together with frustration. 'It's just the timing, Angus. I don't want to upset Henrietta just now. It's all going so well and she was so sweet this last weekend at The Keep . . . We were all so happy together.'

Angus was shaking his head. 'Sorry, love,' he said. 'But we can't take risks. Nothing's worth it. There's a pottiness about all this that I don't like. I don't understand it.'

Cordelia sighed. 'I'll phone Fliss,' she said, resigned. 'But it's going to sound very odd.'

There were two telephone calls whilst Hal and Fliss were having lunch with friends at The Sea Trout in Staverton. Prue took both messages and waited anxiously for their return. Cordelia had sounded quite calm although it clearly wasn't just a friendly call.

'No, no,' she'd said. 'It's nothing to do with Henrietta and Jo. No, just that I rather wanted Fliss and Hal's advice about something.' There'd been a little pause and Prue had heard another voice, a man's voice, in the background. 'Could you ask Fliss to phone me, Prue?' Cordelia had asked. 'When she gets in? . . . Great. Are you well? . . . Yes, I'm fine. 'Bye for now.'

The second call had been even more unsettling: Maria this time – also asking for Hal or Fliss.

'Just to say,' she'd said, once she and Prue had exchanged pleasantries, 'I've been thinking that I might look at some properties in Devon. A friend of mine is coming down to her holiday cottage in Salcombe for a few days at the weekend and she's offered to bring me with her. I'd love to see you all but I can't quite say when. I'll phone again once I'm down, to make a date to come over. Perhaps you could tell Hal and Fliss? . . . Thanks. See you soon, then.'

Prue replaced the receiver, feeling anxious: this would put the cat among the pigeons. She clasped her hands together, staring from the hall window, waiting for Hal's return. Perhaps it would be wise to tell Hal first and plan how they might break the news to Fliss. Prue shook her head distressfully; Fliss had been so happy since the news of Jolyon's engagement. All those little anxious worry lines had been smoothed away; her fears laid to rest.

'It's wonderful, Prue,' she'd said. 'Oh, I feel so happy I don't know what to do with myself. I've been so anxious, deep down, that Jo would never take the final step. I believed that between us, Hal and Maria and me, we'd made him emotionally incapable of committing to anyone. He's always been fearful that he'd never be able to sustain a relationship and then there would be all that mess and muddle over again. And when I knew Maria was coming down, I thought she'd undo all his confidence once more. Isn't it a miracle? I feel that he's won through all his insecurities and now he's safe.' She'd laughed at herself. 'I know it's silly but that morning, d'you remember, Prue, when Maria's letter came, I was so fearful that something awful was going to happen.'

Prue went to sit by the fire that Hal had lit before he and Fliss had gone out. She sat staring at the flames, remembering Fliss's relief and joy, and trying to think what it reminded her of, and Lizzie found her there when she came into the hall, followed by the dogs, who settled in front of the fire.

'I'm going to make a cup of tea,' Lizzie said. 'Jo's holding the fort in the office and I need a break.

Would you like one?' She paused, struck by Prue's immobility. 'Are you OK?'

'Maria has phoned,' Prue answered without preamble. 'She's coming down again this weekend to stay with friends at Salcombe. She's decided that she wants to come and live down here.'

'You're kidding?' Lizzie came closer, staring down at her. 'Down here? Where down here?'

Prue shrugged helplessly. 'I don't know where. She didn't say. But I gathered that she'd suddenly decided that it might be nice to be closer to us.'

'Nicer for whom?' asked Lizzie bluntly. 'Sorry, but you know what I mean. Is she thinking this through properly?'

'I doubt it,' answered Prue. 'I believe it's true that she's had an epiphany with Adam's death, and I believe that she sincerely wants to try to repair the damage she's done. But Maria is still Maria. She'll act first and think about it afterwards, and her view will be particularly biased towards her own needs. I think she'll believe that simply because she wants something to happen, and that it is ostensibly a good thing for everyone, then it's simply a matter of will. Rather like Mr Blair,' she added obscurely.

'But it's one thing mending bridges gradually over a period of time and from a distance, and quite another coming to live on the doorstep,' said Lizzie, ignoring the political aside. 'Fliss'll have a fit.'

'Oh, I know,' cried Prue. 'And things were going so well. She's been so much more relaxed since Jo's engagement. I've just remembered when I last saw her so happy and that was when Hal told us they were getting married. We were all here together in the hall. Oh, it was such a wonderful moment.'

'And that's another thing,' said Lizzie thoughtfully. 'Maria's going to think it's a bit odd that Jo and Henrietta are engaged when they were so casual together when she was here last, isn't she? Jo said he planned to break it to her very gradually, assuming that she wasn't going to be around much. Oh hell. Will she be over this weekend, d'you think?'

'That seemed to be the purpose of the call.' Prue sighed miserably. 'And we were all so happy.'

'I think someone should be honest with her,' said Lizzie robustly. 'She needs to know that miracles don't happen overnight and that she should give Jo some space.'

Prue looked up at her. 'And who do you think should tell her?' she asked. 'It would have to be done very tactfully. Would Hal do it, or would Fliss be more . . . kind, d'you think?'

Lizzie shook her head. 'I don't think either of them

should do it,' she said. 'I think Jo should do it. He's a big boy now and he should deal with it himself. I'm going to make that tea.'

She turned to find Jo standing behind her at the end of the sofa. She gave a squawk of surprise and Prue turned quickly, peering to see who had come in.

'Deal with what myself?' asked Jo. He had his hands in his pockets and he looked wary and rather grim. 'You're quite right, Lizzie. I'm a big boy now. What do I need to be dealing with?'

Both women stared at him. Prue's heart pounded alarmingly; Jo looked extraordinarily like Hal and with that cool, measuring expression she suddenly saw quite clearly why her son had risen so high in his career. She felt quite frightened. Lizzie was made of sterner stuff.

'Maria's just phoned,' she said. 'She's suddenly taken it into her head to move to Devon. She'll be down at the weekend and Prue and I were just wondering how surprised she'll be at your engagement to Henrietta, given the way you were both behaving when she was here. We were saying that it's great that she wants to mend bridges and all that stuff but she should be a bit more intelligent about it and give you some space. And that perhaps someone should say so. You know? Point it out in words of one syllable. And I was saying that, if anyone were to do it, it ought to be you.'

Prue felt quite weak with anxiety; never a confrontational person, she was always full of admiration for anyone who approached a problem directly. She stared at Jolyon, praying that he would understand Lizzie's forthrightness.

'I think you're right,' he said calmly. The wariness had vanished and he now looked simply very serious. 'Now that Henrietta and I are engaged I don't have a problem with that. She can't harm us now.'

Prue heaved a silent gasp of relief. 'Of course she can't,' she said warmly. 'She no longer has any power of that kind. But she needs to realize that mending fences takes time, and living on the doorstep might make things worse, not better. But how could anyone tell her that? I genuinely believe that she wants to make up for her behaviour in the past, don't you?'

She looked pleadingly at her grandson, who smiled at her. 'Don't worry, Granny,' he said. 'I shan't deprive her of her good intentions but I think it's time we talked properly. I feel ready for it now. So she's down again this weekend, did you say?'

'Staying with friends at Salcombe,' said Prue quickly. 'Not here. But she's hoping to come over.'

Jolyon nodded. 'Fair enough. It works in very

well, actually. Henrietta's got a girlfriend staying until next Monday so I shan't be seeing much of her. It's a bit tricky keeping it a secret but she wants to tell Susan herself and she's trying to decide whether to write to her or ring her up. It's going to come as a bit of a shock and Henrietta's a bit sensitive about it. Anyway, I'll have plenty of time to sort things out here. I came over to say that you're wanted in the office, Lizzie.'

'Blast,' said Lizzie.

She went out and Jo moved to put some more logs on the fire, stepping over Pooter and Perks, whose tails moved gently.

'D'you remember when Hal and Fliss announced they were getting married?' Prue asked him. 'Your engagement reminded me of it. We were all so happy.'

He straightened up and looked down at her. 'Yes,' he said, after a moment. 'I remember it very well.'

'Fliss is so pleased,' she said, 'that you're happy. It means a great deal to her.'

'I know.' He stared down into the flames. 'I owe Fliss a lot. She was very honest with me once, years ago. And very brave. I've never forgotten it.'

'She misses Bess and Jamie much more than we realize,' Prue said. 'You've always been like another son to her.'

He nodded. 'I've come to the conclusion that it's not so much to do with blood relationships; it's not necessarily whether someone's a son or a father or an uncle that matters. It's having someone who's on your side that is important. Fliss has always been on my side. She's special.'

Prue nodded her agreement; she couldn't quite bring herself to speak. Jolyon touched her lightly on the shoulder and went out, and Prue was left alone.

# CHAPTER TWENTY-EIGHT

Hal laid down the newspaper as Fliss came into the drawing room to sit beside him on the sofa. It was growing dark and pools of lamplight glowed on polished mahogany, reflecting off dark wood panelling and the brass fender. Portraits of long-dead Chadwicks stared down at them from the walls.

'So what was all that about?' he asked. 'Has Cordelia got a problem?'

'It's all very odd,' she said, tucking her legs underneath her and turning towards him. 'In fact, I had some difficulty in understanding all of it. Do you remember Cordelia's ex-husband? Simon March? He was a submariner.'

Hal shook his head. 'Name doesn't ring a bell.'

'What about Angus Radcliff?'

'Oh, yes. I know Angus. We were at the M.o.D. together. Why?'

Fliss sighed. 'It's a bit of a long story. Cordelia told me some of it but it's got rather complicated so you'll have to concentrate.'

Hal listened with interest as she told him about Angus and Cordelia's first love affair, and how he'd gone to Australia, and then explained how Cordelia had married Simon and why he'd left her and how he'd written to Henrietta. When she embarked on the story of the koala bears and the books, however, Hal's interest rapidly changed to disbelief and he grew impatient.

'This is crazy,' he said. 'Honestly, Fliss. Surely it's just a practical joke?'

'Even so, you can see how horrid it is for her,' Fliss protested. 'And if it *is* a practical joke, who's playing it? Remember that the person actually got into the house. Cordelia admits that she's casual about locking up, but even so, think about it. Who would wander into someone's house and put a koala bear all amongst the candlesticks and take two books from her study and put them in the kitchen? And what about the photograph?'

Hal was still disinclined to take it seriously. 'Is she absolutely certain that she didn't move the books herself? I mean, it's so easy to do something and then forget you've done it?'

'And what about the koala bears. Two of them?

She knows they aren't hers.'

Hal shrugged. 'Honestly, Fliss. It sounds ludicrous.' A thought struck him. 'I suppose it couldn't be Henrietta playing tricks?'

'Of course not,' cried Fliss impatiently. 'It's not a bit like Henrietta. And she's hardly likely to play tricks about something she still feels very sensitive about.'

'So they think it's Simon come back to haunt them?'

'I know it sounds weird,' admitted Fliss, 'but the Australian touch with the bears, and the book titles seem to hint at it. And then there's the photograph that came in the post. Who else would know where to find it, let alone send it?'

'He sounds like a nutter,' said Hal.

'Exactly. That's why Angus is worried about Cordelia out there all on her own. He wants her to call the police but having listened to your reaction I'm not confident that the police would be particularly helpful.'

'Come on, love. They'll just think she's potty. So what *are* they going to do?'

'Well, that's why Cordelia phoned. I think Angus is hoping you'll weigh in on his side and make her take it more seriously. He's worried about leaving her alone.'

Hal looked at her, eyebrows raised. 'Are they having an affair?'

Fliss shrugged. 'Probably. After all, he's a widower and Cordelia's alone. Why not?'

'No reason. Perhaps Simon has come back and doesn't like the idea of them getting together.'

'Exactly. That's the whole point. But what can they do?'

Hal sat in silence, staring at nothing, whilst Fliss bit her lips anxiously and twirled a strand of hair.

'I don't know,' he said at last. 'I simply don't know. I honestly think that the police are much too busy to take this kind of thing seriously. They might just think it's a hoax call. Although, if Cordelia reports a break-in they might manage to get someone round eventually. Of course, if this fellow is a bit unbalanced . . .'

Fliss folded her arms across her breast and shivered. 'It's beastly. I can't imagine how Cordelia has stayed there all on her own with this going on, though of course she's got McGregor.'

'Isn't she frightened?' asked Hal curiously. 'You make it sound as if it's Angus who's doing the panicking.'

'She says she has moments of terror but deep down she feels certain that it is simply a kind of war of nerves, nothing more than that.'

Hal raised his eyebrows. 'Women's intuition?'

Fliss made a face. 'Angus certainly doesn't go along with it. But what can he do?'

'Well, if it were me, I'd move in with her and wait and see what happens. I really can't see that they've got any alternative. They should report the break-in, even if nothing comes of it.'

'So that's your advice?'

'If they're asking for it, yes. Can you think of anything better?'

Fliss shook her head. 'She could come here but, like she says, she doesn't really want to leave her cottage empty and she's got work to do. It's so frustrating.'

'Well, tell her she's welcome here at any time. What a tiresome thing to happen, and especially just now when everyone's so happy.'

'Well, that's the other fear. If it *is* Simon, he might start on Henrietta. And she's all on her own too.'

'Oh my God!' Hal looked anxious. 'I hadn't thought about that. Does Jo know?'

'Not yet. But I shall tell him and see what he thinks about it. We don't want to frighten Henrietta, and at least she's got a friend staying at the moment. And all the dogs, of course, but even so . . .'

'Even so,' repeated Hal thoughtfully, 'we'll have to pray that Cordelia's intuition is correct. Jo will have to go and stay with Henrietta until it's sorted, that's all there is to it.'

'But that's the point,' said Fliss. 'How does this kind of thing get sorted? It could go on for months. If it *is* Simon he could keep it up indefinitely. If only we could be certain.'

'Hang on a minute,' said Hal. 'I'm sure I can find out what's happened to him. Well, up to a point, anyway. If he transferred to the Australian Navy there must be a way to check him out. Let me think about it.'

'That would be something,' said Fliss. 'I'll phone Cordelia and tell her. And, by the way, what about Maria's news?'

Hal groaned. 'Don't. Talk about a disaster. I'm sorry, darling, I really am.'

He looked so remorseful that Fliss leaned forward and kissed him. 'Prue says that Jo's going to have a serious talk with her. I've got a feeling that somehow this is the right thing to happen. Something good will come out of it.'

He pulled a face of mock alarm. 'Not more women's intuition?'

She grinned. 'Possibly,' she said. 'Don't knock it,' and went away to talk to Cordelia.

\*     \*     \*

'So what did he say?' asked Angus. He paced restlessly, hands in pockets, and Cordelia went to sit in her rocking chair, willing him to be calm.

'Hal's had rather a good idea,' she told him. 'He thinks the police would simply think it a hoax but he's going to see if he can track Simon down through naval channels; find out what's happened to him. It might help, mightn't it? Could he do that?'

'Probably. He's got lots of clout – and it's a very good idea – but I'm sorry he's not more positive about the police.'

'He did say that we should report a break-in but he's not particularly sanguine once it comes to giving details. It's like I said, it all sounds so ludicrous.' She smiled at him, seeing his disappointment. 'He thinks you should stay with me, though. He agrees with that.'

'It's not a subject for negotiation,' Angus said more cheerfully. 'Was he . . . were they surprised when they heard I was here?'

Cordelia shook her head. 'No. Should they be?'

'I just wondered. You're happy that I stay for a bit, then? At least until Hal finds out what he can about Simon?'

'I'm a bit worried about Henrietta but we'll have to go with it, I think. At least she's got Jilly with her. Let's hope Hal finds out something helpful. The point is, can you just put everything on hold and move in with me?'

'I'll have to go over to Dartmouth on Saturday morning. The boat's being taken out of the water for the winter. And I'll have to go back now to pick up some gear, but otherwise I'm rather looking forward to it. I wouldn't mind coming face to face with Simon again.'

'Thanks,' said Cordelia.

He laughed. 'Sorry, Dilly. Naturally, spending time with you in an official capacity is a bonus.'

'"An official capacity"?'

'Well, you know what I mean. Since you're so pathologically determined to keep us low-key I welcome any opportunity to be with you with the blessing of our friends and family. Does that sound better?'

'No,' she said crossly.

'OK. How about we drive over to Dartmouth to-gether and I collect some clothes?'

He watched her pick up the photograph and stare down at it reflectively.

'I suppose it could be tested for fingerprints?' she asked – and stood it up on the shelf. 'Yes, let's go and fetch your stuff. To be truthful, I'm glad you're staying, Angus. It's getting silly, isn't it? To begin with, after that thing with the bear and the books, I

346

imagined Simon would just suddenly appear – jump out from somewhere and give me a fright and then that would be that. I really believed that he was hoping for some kind of reconciliation and didn't quite know how to start it off. Being Simon, he'd need to be in control of it and so he'd want me to be on the wrong foot, so to speak. But I don't feel quite so sanguine about it now. It's dragging on a bit, and the photograph is odd. He must have had it all these years. There's something rather horrid about the idea of him brooding on it all this time . . . And I'm worried about Henrietta. He can't hold anything against her, quite the reverse, but I'm beginning to think he might be a bit unbalanced – and that puts a different light on it.'

'If anything happened we'd never forgive ourselves,' Angus said. 'I agree that, so far, it's the kind of rather childish trick Simon might play but he's carrying it too far.'

'D'you think that if he sees us together all the time it might force him into the open?'

Angus nodded. 'Something like that.'

She looked at him quizzically. 'It sounds as if you're looking forward to it.'

He looked at her. 'I must admit that I'm rather enjoying the prospect of having a pop at Simon,' he said.

# CHAPTER TWENTY-NINE

On Saturday morning Fliss wandered in the garden looking for some late-flowering blooms and thinking about Jo's imminent meeting with Maria. He'd been rather quiet these last two days and Fliss's heart had ached for him. The exhilaration was muted now – although part of that might be due to the fact that Henrietta had her friend Jilly staying with her. Jo and Henrietta had agreed that it would be wise to keep a low profile, especially with Jo being something of a personality. Jilly was Susan's friend too, and Henrietta was still dithering over whether she should telephone Susan or wait until she came home at the end of the month. Meanwhile, Jolyon was keeping his distance and preparing for a heart-to-heart with his mother.

Fliss cut a few Michaelmas daisies, remembering Cordelia's question: Are we the first generation to need to be friends with our children?

Fliss found the question an interesting one. Since her parents had died when she was only eleven years old, she had no benchmark with which to measure her relationship with her own children, but she suspected that she *did* want to be friends with them: to share their joys and sorrows, to have girly chats on the phone with Bess, and to hear about Jamie's ideas and what he was thinking and reading. She leaned to cut a spray of berries from the honeysuckle bush that climbed the old stone wall behind the herbaceous border.

'We might like to think that we're all friends,' Cordelia had said. 'But do we continue to have the same authority that our parents had? My mother could still quell me with a glance up until the day she died, but then we weren't friends in that sense. And in insisting on being friends with our children do we deprive them of a safe place to go when they have real problems?'

Here again, Fliss had no yardstick with which to compare her own experience. As she crossed the lawn and went into the garden room to put her gleanings into a vase she found that she was thinking of that formidable matriarch, her grandmother. There had never been any question of authority there.

Fliss thought: Yet we felt so safe with her. So secure.

349

Was Cordelia right? If one were to become too friendly with one's children, might it deprive them of some crucial area of security? How essential her grandmother's authority had been when she and Mole and Susanna had returned from Kenya; how vital to feel safe and to know that someone was in charge.

'You remind me of old Mrs Chadwick,' Maria had said to her. 'You're not so tall but there's something about you . . .'

She'd tailed off then and talked about something else but Fliss had an inkling of what she'd meant. Other people had remarked on it too. Yet, she didn't feel anywhere near as confident and strong as her grandmother had been. She certainly didn't have her authority. Finding a vase, turning on the cold water tap, Fliss looked about her. She remembered her grandmother working here, and herself as a small child, just back from Kenya, curled up in the old wicker chair, watching her. Quite suddenly she was seized by the remembrance of the fear and anguish of those far-off days – and, along with the fear, that all-important sense of security she'd found at The Keep and in the presence of her grandmother.

'Are you OK?' Jolyon was standing at the door, the dogs at his heels, and Fliss gave a little jump.

'You startled me,' she said. 'I was miles away,

thinking about when we first came back to The Keep all those years ago. It seemed like a fortress to us. A sanctuary. I was so relieved to be able to pass over the responsibility of Mole and Susanna, and Grandmother was so wonderfully reassuring.' She looked at him thoughtfully, noting the strain about his mouth. 'You don't remember her, do you? She died when you were a very small boy, but she'd have been so proud of you, Jo. Yes, she would. Her greatest wish was that The Keep should be a kind of refuge for the whole family, not just for one or two, or the person who could afford it, but for all of us. She'd have been utterly thrilled to have seen the way you've developed Keep Organics, and the fact that it goes a huge way to supporting The Keep. I know you're going to say that we've got our china clay shares, and that Hal's pension goes into the pot but, without you, Jo, The Keep would probably now be a dozen flats or a hotel. You've done utterly brilliantly, and we're all proud of you.'

He looked awkward and rather embarrassed, but pleased too. 'Thanks,' he muttered. 'It just seemed the natural thing to do. To make the place pay for itself. For it to be self-supporting.'

'Yes, but *you* were the one to think of it. Nobody else did.'

He nodded. 'I suppose that's true. It always seemed

sad to see so much of the land going to waste. I remember talking to Uncle Theo about it and it was he who said that maybe we could develop the land beyond the stables and that he'd talk to Dad about it. That's what got me started.'

She grinned at him. 'And Miles giving you the poly-tunnel for your eighteenth birthday – don't forget that.'

He grinned back at her. 'As if I could. That was a great turning point. Miles was brilliant. He did my business plan for me.' His face grew sad. 'I used to sit with him in the evenings, after he'd had that stroke, and tell him all my ideas. He was so enthusiastic, and he used to write on that pad of his, d'you remember, because he couldn't speak properly?'

He broke off, seeing the tears in her eyes and came to her and put his arms round her.

'Sorry,' he muttered. 'Sorry, that was tactless.'

'No,' she said, looking up at him, trying to smile. 'Not tactless. Just remembering, which is good. Miles would have been proud of you too, wouldn't he? What did you tell me? A turnover of one and a half million this year, and a fourteen per cent net profit, and seven vans out on the road. And now you're a famous TV presenter into the bargain. You're a true Chadwick and a worthy guardian of The Keep, Jo.'

He flushed brightly and she turned back to her flowers so as to cover his embarrassment.

'I'm just off to meet . . .' He hesitated, and Fliss came to his rescue.

'You're meeting Maria at the White Hart, aren't you? That's a good choice. You can walk in the gardens afterwards and talk things through. You're quite right to want to be honest, Jo. About Henrietta and this proposed move to Devon. I think Maria genuinely wants to heal the breach but she needs to give you space too. You'll know what to say.'

'I hope so,' he said, his expression bleak again. 'I'm going to get changed. I'll see you later.'

Fliss watched him go, the dogs following him, and picked up the vase. Hal was in the hall, standing with his hands in his pockets, looking preoccupied. She put the vase on the table and raised her eyebrows.

'Problem?'

'Probably,' he said. 'Alan phoned. He's given me some feedback about Simon March.'

'Oh my God,' she said, frightened by his sombre expression. 'What is it? Is he back in England?'

'No,' he said. 'Simon died of cancer earlier this year.'

Fliss stared at him, horrified. 'That's awful,' she said. 'I mean it's awful that he's died but it's awful in another way too. Because if it isn't Simon then who can it be? Did Alan talk to his wife? I mean widow.'

'That's even odder,' Hal said. 'Simon never married. There's no wife, no children, no second family.'

'But that was why he cut all connections with Henrietta, so that he could commit totally to his new family.'

Hal shrugged. 'Nevertheless, those are the facts.'

She stared at him anxiously. 'What shall we do?'

'We'll have to tell Cordelia and Angus. But in some way this makes it more worrying, doesn't it? I felt that between us we might have been able to contain Simon. This puts a different light on it all. Shall you phone or shall I?'

Fliss bit her lip, thinking about it. 'You phone,' she said at last, 'and let's hope that Angus answers the phone. I've got a feeling that Cordelia is going to find this very difficult to handle.'

All the way to Dartington, Jolyon rehearsed the various things he might say to his mother. Fliss had given him more courage than she could possibly have guessed. It was so incredible that she'd talked about those very things that his mother had once spoken of so contemptuously; his desire to see The Keep supporting itself from its own land had been only the first step. His heart swelled with gratitude and pride when he recalled Fliss's words: *You're a true Chadwick and a worthy guardian of The Keep.*

And it *was* true, he told himself: nobody else in the family could have managed to save it as a private house into the twenty-first century. The knowledge of this gave him confidence as he parked the car at Dartington and walked into the courtyard of the great medieval house – and saw Maria, standing outside the White Hart with another woman. She was looking out for him and she waved when she saw him, and he raised his hand in return. The other woman looked at him curiously, rather excitedly, and he knew exactly what she was going to say.

'I've seen you on television.' She was right on cue. 'Maria's promised to get your autograph for me. We all think she's so lucky to have such a famous son.'

Her greeting and the following introductions made it easy for him to gloss over his meeting with his mother. He smiled as he shook Penelope's hand, said all the right things, agreed that they'd see each other again later on, and she went rather reluctantly away, smiling back at him.

'She was hoping we were going to invite her to join us for coffee,' said Maria complacently, clearly enjoying her privilege, 'but we don't want that, do we?'

He shook his head, opening the door for her to go into the bar, sitting down at the table by the window. The fire had been lit and it was a cheerful, cosy scene. He went to the bar to order the coffee and some *pain au chocolat* and went back to the table, his heart beating unevenly.

'This is fun,' she said. 'Thanks for coming, Jolyon. It's nice to be on our own for a change, isn't it?'

The question was an uncertain one and, looking at her, Jolyon saw the nervousness in her eyes and the anxious determination of her smile. It was odd that the carefully coloured hair and well-applied make-up, the brightly varnished nails and smart clothes, rather than achieving the desired effect actually made her seem slightly pathetic. He remembered how pretty she'd been, how stylish, and he felt a stab of compassion.

'Yes,' he said. 'Yes, it's nice. And rather necessary. I need to talk to you.'

Once again he saw that tiny flicker of anxiety behind her bright smile. 'What about?' she asked. 'No problems, I hope?'

Their coffee and pastries arrived, and Jo waited until they were quite alone again before he answered. He gathered his courage, remembered

Fliss's comments and took the plunge.

'I haven't been quite honest with you, I'm afraid,' he said quietly. 'When you came to stay I wasn't quite certain of how the future lay and I misled you on a rather important matter.'

It wasn't coming out quite how he'd planned – it sounded very stilted and a bit pompous – but he couldn't quite find a more natural approach.

She was making big eyes at him, guying it up a bit, but he knew now that she was just as nervous as he was, and it gave him courage.

'That sounds serious,' she was saying. 'Whatever can it be?'

'I'm engaged to be married,' he said – and saw the smile fade from her face and her eyes widen with shock.

'Married,' she repeated faintly. 'Good heavens. But who . . . ? Is it Lizzie?'

'No, not Lizzie.' He drank some coffee. 'Do you remember Henrietta March? She came to lunch on my birthday.'

'Yes, of course I remember her.' Maria seemed to speak with difficulty, as if her lips were stiff. 'But why didn't you tell me? You both seemed so . . . indifferent, I suppose. I never guessed for a moment.'

'We didn't want you to.' It was brutal but he could

see no way out of it. 'We weren't engaged then, and neither of us wanted you to know that we were . . . romantically involved.'

She was staring at him, coffee and pastries forgotten. 'You mean, everyone else knew? Fliss and Hal . . . ? And Cordelia?'

'Yes,' he said reluctantly; he was hating this. 'Yes, they knew but they'd promised us, you see. Only the family knew.'

'But I'm family too,' she said; she sounded furious. 'I'm your mother.'

He simply looked at her, a measured look, and presently her gaze dropped.

'You mean I didn't deserve to know?' she said at last.

She drank some coffee and he tried to think how he should answer her: only the truth would serve.

'I couldn't trust you,' he said. 'In the past, you've never hesitated to make your feelings very clear about how you thought about me and what I did, and I couldn't risk that with Henrietta. I wasn't certain how you might react. Of course, things have changed a bit lately, I realize that. Adam has died and Ed's gone to the States . . .' He hesitated, unable to add, 'and I've become a well-known TV personality.'

She said it for him rather bitterly. 'And you're

358

famous now. Yes, well, I knew that you'd think that had something to do with my visit.'

'Didn't it?'

She looked at him; her anger had fallen away and she looked defeated. 'I don't think so. I really don't. It's true that being all alone has made a huge difference, I can't deny that. When Adam died I suddenly realized how easy it is to take people for granted and how precious love is. It was a shock. Then Ed decided to move so far away – not that I'd seen much of him since he and Rebecca got together – and that was another blow. It doesn't reflect very well on me, I can see that, but I wanted to try to make a new start with you. I can't pretend that I'm not thrilled that you're famous but I don't think that's why I came to see you. Hal wrote such a nice letter after Ed had gone. It was as if he understood how empty my life must be, and I suddenly needed to be in contact with all of you again. Not just you, but with Hal and Prue and The Keep. I've been a fool, I know that, and I've said some pretty awful things to you in the past and behaved very badly, but I hoped that we might, well, try again. Are you saying that it's too late?'

She looked desolate and he felt guilty, remembering how happily she'd waved at him and her expression of expectation. He thought of her plans

359

to move to Devon and of everything she must have been hoping for. He'd crushed all her future dreams.

'No,' he answered cautiously. 'I'm not saying it's too late but I think you're expecting too much too soon.' She was watching him eagerly now, hopefully, and he tried to remember what he'd planned to say.

'I like Henrietta,' she was telling him, almost pleadingly. 'She's a lovely girl. I can't imagine why you should think I wouldn't have been pleased.'

'Look.' He still couldn't bring himself to call her 'Mum'; she was almost a stranger to him. 'Whether or not you like her isn't the point as far as I'm concerned. The point is that you decided more or less to cut me out of *your* life when I was very young and you can't simply expect to walk back into *my* life now as if nothing has changed. I'm sorry if that sounds brutal but if we're going to start again then we need to know where we both stand. I'm glad you've had a road-to-Damascus experience if it means that we can make a new start but there's a lot of mending to do along that road. We can't just pretend that we've been a close, happy family for the last twenty years – at least, I can't – but it doesn't mean, either, that there's nowhere to go.'

She nodded, drank some coffee, but remained

silent. He sat back in his chair and glanced around. It seemed light years since they'd come in and the noise of chatter and laughter struck his ears suddenly as if, until that moment, he'd been deaf.

'I know what you're saying.' She spoke at last and he turned back to her. 'And you're quite right, of course. I got carried away. I so enjoyed my last visit to The Keep and seeing you all that I felt we'd made some real progress.'

He watched her warily, refusing to feel guilty, and after a moment she looked away from him.

'Don't worry,' she said lightly. 'I shan't do anything rash, like buying a cottage in Staverton. It was a crazy idea, I can see that now.'

He felt as if he'd hit her but he knew that he mustn't back down. 'It's too soon,' he said, as gently as he could. 'Much too soon. Can't we take it a step at a time? You're coming down for Dad's birthday, aren't you? Well, that's something to look forward to, and you'll be able to celebrate our engagement with the rest of the family. Until then I'd be grateful if you didn't speak of it to anyone else.' He added as some kind of comfort, 'Even Kit doesn't know yet.'

'It'll be odd to see Kit after all these years,' she said quietly.

He felt uncomfortable, but relieved; he'd made

his point but he hadn't closed the door on the future. She was smiling at him now, as if she could sympathize with how he was feeling.

'Penelope's meeting me here for some lunch,' she told him, 'and if I know her she's probably planning to wheedle you into joining us. She's a terrific fan, you know. I wonder if it might be a good idea for you to make a getaway while you can.'

For the first time he felt a tremor of real affection for her and he nodded gratefully.

'Thanks for the warning,' he said, 'and we're all looking forward to seeing you in a couple of weeks. Everyone sends their love.'

She nodded smilingly, quite in control of herself again, and he got up, hesitated and then bent to kiss her quickly on the cheek.

'Thanks for the coffee,' she said, and he smiled awkwardly and then hurried out.

He almost ran to the car park, dreading that he might see Penelope, relieved that the meeting was over, anxious that he'd messed it up. Once in the car he dragged out his mobile: he needed to talk to Henrietta.

# CHAPTER THIRTY

Maria sat on, a little half-smile pinned to her lips lest anyone should think anything might be wrong. Several people had recognized Jolyon and she was so glad that he'd kissed her when he left because nobody would guess at the terrible things he'd said. *I couldn't trust you*, he'd said. And, *Whether or not you like her isn't the point as far as I'm concerned.* It was difficult to keep her little smile in place when she was in such pain but she couldn't bear that any of these people, some of whom still glanced at her from time to time, should suspect for a moment that she and Jolyon didn't have a special relationship.

She'd been so thrilled to meet him in such a public place – Penelope had been green with envy and had dropped heavy hints about how she'd love to meet him – and it had been rather sweet to see that Jolyon wasn't really aware of people staring and nudging one another. And it was fun to see people looking at her and wondering who she might be, but she hadn't expected him to be so hurtful. He'd looked so like Hal. How odd that little Jolyon, always so eager to please her, to win her love, had grown into this rather tough, focused man. As a little boy he'd dreaded arguments and angry voices, gone out of his way to be the peacemaker; he'd loved her so much – and she'd hurt him so badly.

It was impossible to keep smiling now and she opened her bag and pretended to look inside it. The remains of her coffee were cold but she hadn't the will to go up to the bar and order some more. Anyway, she needed a drink: a serious drink. She felt rather weak, as if she'd been struck a blow, and in a way she had been, yet a part of her knew that nothing Jolyon had said had been untrue or unfair. As usual she'd been looking at things from her own point of view and not thinking properly about anybody else. This plan for moving to Devon, for instance, had been an impulsive idea. With the weekend so fresh in her mind the possibility of moving west had seemed a wonderful opportunity, something exciting to plan. She hadn't thought it through or imagined how the Chadwicks might see it, Jolyon in particular; but then, looking back, she was obliged to admit that she'd never much worried about what Jolyon had felt about things. She'd ignored him, and used him, and cast him aside in favour of Ed and Adam. And now he was getting married and he didn't care whether she liked his bride-to-be or not. After all the years of rejection he was now utterly indifferent to her feelings.

Instinctively, as if to hurry away from the wrenching pain in her heart, she closed her handbag, got up and went to collect a glass of wine from the bar. Waiting in the small queue she reflected on the humiliation of spending that whole weekend at The Keep with everyone else knowing about Jolyon and Henrietta. She felt hot with the shame of it. How they must have laughed behind her back – and how difficult, now, to go for Hal's birthday. How would she manage it? Yet she saw, dimly, that if there were ever to be some kind of reconciliation then she must accept the humiliation and hurt patiently, and work through it. Somehow, Jolyon had conquered his own hurts and her rejection of him, and had become a strong and successful man, loved by his family and by a charming and pretty girl. Now, she must try to win back just a little of the affection he'd once felt for her.

She saw with dismay that Penelope had come in and was looking about with bright, expectant eyes. She was early, damn her, in the hope of catching Jolyon. Maria waved, mimed a drink and pointed to her table. She took a deep breath, summoning her courage and some shred of gaiety; Penelope must never guess that anything was wrong.

Neither Angus nor Cordelia answered Hal's telephone call. They'd left the cottage at the same time, in separate cars, and were planning to rendezvous at Angus's house in Dartmouth for a late lunch.

As they reached Kingsbridge, and Cordelia and McGregor turned off towards the car park, Angus flashed his headlights and headed on to Dartmouth. Cordelia drove into the car park with a lightening of heart. Fond of Angus though she was, this moment of freedom was delightful. She hadn't realized how unaccustomed she'd grown to having somebody around all the time and she was finding it the least bit claustrophobic. Of course, she could disappear into her study to work – but each time she was seized with feelings of guilt that Angus was bored and wondering what to do, and she couldn't concentrate. He insisted on going with her even to buy the newspaper in the village and she was beginning to believe that she'd rather take her chance with Simon than continue to endure this feeling of being a prisoner. She was rather shocked at her feelings but, after all, she'd been alone for the last twenty years and her solitary routine was a difficult habit to break overnight. Yet she loved Angus; she'd always loved him.

Enough to live with him? asked the small familiar voice brightly in her head.

'Shut up,' she muttered and got out of the car and went to the ticket machine. She felt depressed and anxious as she fed money in and scooped out her ticket.

'Hello again,' said a voice from behind her. It was the tall woman who'd returned her scarf outside the bookshop and Cordelia greeted her in return and stood aside so that she could buy a ticket.

The woman smiled and then looked at her more closely. 'Are you OK? You're looking rather glum this morning and you were so happy the last time we met.'

Cordelia summoned a smile, touched by her enquiry. 'I'm fine. A bit of a problem, nothing much.'

'I'm sorry to hear that.' The woman hesitated. 'Would a cup of coffee help? I'm just going into Mangetout to have one myself.'

'Thanks,' said Cordelia, surprised. 'That would be nice.' She waved her ticket. 'I'll just put this in the car and I'll be right back. I'll meet you on the corner.'

They went together into the delicatessen and sat

at a table at the far end of the café. They ordered coffee and Cordelia glanced around. It was here that she'd sat the last time she'd met Angus and suddenly she remembered something else.

'I think I saw you in here a few weeks ago,' she exclaimed. 'You were sitting on one of the stools. I knew I'd seen you before.' She smiled. 'Shall we introduce ourselves?'

'Oh, I know who you are,' the woman said, looking at her intently. 'You're Cordelia Lytton, the famous journalist.'

Cordelia raised her eyebrows. 'Hardly famous, unfortunately. How did you know that? Oh, I know. It was Pat Abrehart, wasn't it? When you picked up my scarf in the bookshop. Pat and I are old friends.'

'Oh, I knew all about you before that,' she answered.

'Don't tell me that you've read one of my books,' Cordelia said lightly, embarrassed – and was relieved when the coffee arrived so that she could change the subject. 'You haven't told me your name.'

The woman put sugar in her coffee, smiling to herself as if she were considering her answer.

'How about Elinor Rochdale?' she suggested.

Cordelia was puzzled by the way she phrased her answer. 'It sounds familiar,' she answered slowly, unsettled by the woman's amused expression. She began to feel uncomfortable. '*Have* we met before? I'm not talking about seeing each other in the town but somewhere else. I feel that I'm being stupid and that you're waiting patiently for the penny to drop.'

'We haven't met before. Not officially. But I know a great deal about you.'

Quite suddenly the penny *did* drop and Cordelia experienced a tiny tremor of fear. Elinor Rochdale. She glanced round; all the tables were full and the shop was busy. She was quite safe and it would be foolish to panic.

'Elinor Rochdale,' she repeated. She looked directly at the woman, determined to appear quite calm. 'Very clever. I like it. So you are Simon's wife. Or . . .' she hesitated, less sure of her ground, 'in light of the name, should I say his widow?'

The woman stared back at her. 'Neither,' she said. She drank some coffee and set the cup back in its saucer. 'I was his mistress.'

Cordelia was silent. She refused to be jockeyed into either sympathy or curiosity. 'In that case, why "Elinor Rochdale"?' she asked calmly. She wondered if her hand would tremble if she lifted the cup and chanced it anyway. 'Surely that was the heroine's name in *The Reluctant Widow*? That's the book you put on my lectern, isn't it? Along with *Simon the Coldheart*? What was all that about?'

The woman rested her elbows on the table, staring at Cordelia with light grey eyes. 'He wouldn't marry me,' she said. 'I was crazy about him and he was crazy about you.'

Cordelia's composure deserted her a little. 'Do you mean he wasn't married at all? But he told us that was why he was cutting all communication with Henrietta. Because he was going to Australia to have a new life with a new family.'

Her *vis-à-vis* shook her head. 'No wife, no children. Just me. He told me all about you until I felt that I knew you almost better than I knew him. You were an obsession.'

'But he left me.' Cordelia leaned forward, keeping her voice low. '*I* didn't want to break up our marriage. It was he who decided to go. If he loved me so much why did he leave me and Henrietta?'

The woman raised her eyebrows a little. 'Who said we were talking about love?' she asked softly. 'Obsession isn't love. Obsession is all about insecurity and neediness and wanting to possess. It drives you crazy. It drove Simon crazy. He cursed himself sometimes for walking away from it, though he made sure he'd ruined your chances of happiness first. When the satisfaction of that began to pall he

370

decided to ruin Henrietta's – and put the boot in for you at the same time. He guessed that it would be just as devastating for you if she knew exactly why he'd left, and by that time he'd gone beyond having any real feelings for her.' She shook her head. 'Poor bastard. Yet there were times when we were so happy, and I'd really believe that he was getting over it, but there was always something that would set him off again. What a waste.'

Cordelia stared down into her coffee cup. 'I gather that he's dead?'

'Yes. He died from cancer in April. My family's still in England, in the Border country, so I decided to come home. I needed to see you. To find out exactly who it was that destroyed his life. And mine.'

'So you stalked me?'

The woman snorted with amusement. 'It was so easy,' she said reflectively. 'Of course, having a coastal path a few feet from your front door was a godsend. I could always be coming or going or looking as if I were at the tag end of a group of ramblers. I used to watch you through binoculars; see you out in your little garden. I followed your car a few times, took a few photos. And then there was your habit of leaving the door unlocked. After a while I decided to get a bit closer.'

Cordelia clasped her hands in her lap; she was

determined to show no sign of the clammy fear that trickled down her spine and crept in the roots of her hair.

'What did you hope to achieve?' she asked coolly. 'Did you want to frighten me?'

The woman considered the question. 'Possibly,' she said at last. 'I just had a need to be near you. You've got to remember that I felt I knew you already. Simon talked about you so much that I felt we were a threesome. It was very odd, after all those things he'd told me about you, to be so close to you physically. After a while, tracking you lost its charm and I decided to chance my arm and come into your cottage – of course, I had excuses ready if you caught me in the hall. "Sorry, I knocked at the door but you didn't hear me" kind of thing, but I wasn't certain I'd get away with it. That was part of the thrill of it, of course. I tried it first when I knew you had someone with you, out in the garden. I just opened the door and slipped in. I knew which room your study was and I went in and fiddled with your computer. A few days later I followed you in here and put the koala bear in your basket.'

'But I saw a man going out?' Cordelia was confused. 'He tapped me on the shoulder.'

The woman shook her head almost reprovingly at her naiveté. 'That's such an old trick. Look. I'm standing on your right, beside you at the counter. I reach behind you and tap your left shoulder. You turn round and see a man leaving the shop while I'm putting the bear into your basket. Easy.'

'And the other bear and the books. Was that easy too?'

'I'd begun to gain confidence by then. I saw you go down the steps to the beach so I knew I had plenty of time. I'd brought copies of the books with me, just in case. But Simon had told me that you were an absolute devotee of Georgette Heyer and had all her books so I thought it would be more interesting to use yours. He told me how you called him Simon the Coldheart and I thought that *The Reluctant Widow* was the closest I could come to really giving you a clue.'

'So you were hoping that I would discover you?'

The woman shrugged. 'It was getting a bit boring,' she admitted. 'I wanted to get close to you. Can you understand that? We'd been three in a bed and I wanted more than just following you and frightening you a bit. I needed you to see me and for there to be some communication. I thought you'd begin to guess but I didn't want to make it too easy. You did, didn't you?'

'I thought it was Simon,' said Cordelia. 'I thought that it was you – or, rather, his wife – who had died

373

and that he'd come back hoping for a reconciliation. It would have been an odd approach, I agree, but it was Simon's style somehow.'

She looked genuinely pleased at this. 'I thought so too. He always had an oddball take on life.'

'So the scarf,' Cordelia prompted her. 'Was that genuine?'

'I was looking for an opportunity to speak to you so I just edged it out of your basket while you were talking to the woman in the bookshop and when you'd gone out I picked it up off the floor and hurried out after you.' She paused, frowning.

'And what then?' asked Cordelia curiously.

'It was strange,' she said slowly. 'When you looked at me and spoke to me, everything changed. At that moment it was real, and suddenly you were just an ordinary woman. The spell was broken. And then we spoke again in the car park and you looked so happy, and somehow the focus shifted completely. You'd been a kind of presence in our lives and you'd had such an extraordinary and powerful effect that suddenly being so close to you, face to face, was a shock . . .'

'And?' prompted Cordelia.

She shrugged. 'Something changed. The fun went out of it. You see, I'd been feeling for the first time since I'd known Simon that it was *I* who had the upper hand. *I* was in control. But when we spoke it wasn't like that any more. It was as if quite suddenly everything regained its proportion and I realized that I didn't have to go along with it any more.'

'But you sent the photograph anyway?'

The woman shook her head. 'I wished I hadn't but I'd already posted it. I couldn't do anything about it but I regretted it. The whole thing had begun to seem rather silly, as if I were still allowing Simon to control me by continuing to punish you, to try and keep the hatred and the obsession alive, and I didn't want to be part of it any longer. I decided I'd try to meet you and explain. And say that I'm sorry.'

'But how do I know that's true? It could just be another clever move in the game. My friends are trying to persuade me to report all this to the police. How do I know that you won't keep following me about – or push me off a cliff?'

The woman sat back with a sigh and drank some coffee. 'You don't,' she said. 'You'll have to take my word for it. It was a moment of madness and the spell's broken. I suddenly realize that I don't like to feel that I'm being manipulated from beyond the grave. I was in thrall to Simon for years and I want to break that power he had. Now that he's dead and we've met properly and talked like this, I believe I can do that. I've wasted quite enough time and now I plan to get on with my life.' She gave another deep sigh, as if she were breathing clean, fresh air for the first time for a long while. Her expression was calm, even peaceful. 'I don't expect you to believe me but I promise you that you're quite safe.'

'Oddly,' Cordelia said, 'I always believed that. It was other people who were anxious on my behalf. I had one or two brief moments of terror but deep down I was never truly frightened.'

The woman smiled. 'I'm glad,' she said. 'We're both free then, after all these years. And what will you do now? Will you be able to pick up the pieces with Angus Radcliff or have you found that Simon has managed to put it out of court? He hated Angus but he felt that he'd managed to . . .' she paused, seeking for the appropriate word, 'neutralize him.'

'Why was Simon so certain about that? We might have gone on being lovers.'

She shook her head. 'He said he knew Angus too well for that. He said that once he was married he'd be much too honourable – and too scared.'

For the first time Cordelia smiled, genuinely amused. 'He didn't say that *I* was too honourable to play around with another woman's husband?'

The woman smiled too. 'I gather that the woman was one of your best friends. Simon felt that was deterrent enough.'

Cordelia's smile faded. 'He waited for nearly a year. All that time, until Angus was married, and he must have hated me for every minute of it.'

'For someone like Simon it wasn't always easy to tell the difference between hate and love. And what about Angus? It *is* Angus I've seen you with, isn't it? And I know he's a widower now. Oh, yes, Simon kept tabs on him too. He was furious when Angus put up his fourth stripe.'

'And did it never occur to Simon that I might marry again?'

She shook her head. 'Oddly enough, no. He said you were a one-man woman and that you only married him because he wouldn't let you alone and because you thought you'd lost Angus.'

'Well, he was right. And then Angus came back and we had that brief, crazy moment and it all started up again. After Simon left I knew that second best simply didn't work and I never wanted to chance it again. And it was too late for me and Angus. My God, what fools sex makes of us all.'

'Who was it who said that it was like being chained to a madman? Well, my chains are broken. I'm free at last.' She picked up her bag and nodded to the coffee cups. 'I'll get these,' she said. 'Good luck, Cordelia.'

Cordelia watched her go to the counter and pay for the coffee; then she turned, raised her hand and was gone.

# CHAPTER THIRTY-ONE

'The woman's crazy,' Hal said for the third time. 'Creeping about on the cliff, breaking into your house and leaving books and bears about, and sending photographs. Sorry, love, but it's crazy. And you sat there drinking coffee with her.'

'What would you have done?' asked Cordelia, trying to smile.

She was beginning to wish that she hadn't suddenly decided to drop in at The Keep on the way to Dartmouth, yet she'd needed some kind of reassurance; some ordinary human companionship. She hadn't wanted to be alone until she met Angus much later in Dartmouth.

'Hal would have made a citizen's arrest and tied her to her chair until the police came,' said Fliss cheerfully. She could see the strain in Cordelia's face and she shook her head at Hal, willing him to calm down.

Hal saw her gesture and was irritated by it. Surely they could see how potentially dangerous this was?

'I've always said that I never believed that I was in any danger.' Cordelia was trying to reassure him. 'And I believe it even more now that I've met her. I think it was just some kind of terrible fascination on her part. Well, I can understand that, can't you?'

'I can,' said Fliss quickly, before Hal could answer. 'You'd want to see who your rival was, wouldn't you? It got out of hand, that's all. Like a silly game played by children. It crossed the barrier between reality and fantasy, but then she got a grip again when she actually spoke to Cordelia. Poor woman, I feel rather sorry for her.'

Hal was staring at her as if she were crazy too, and Fliss stifled an urge to burst out laughing.

'Perhaps it's a woman thing,' she said soothingly – but Hal was not to be comforted.

'And you didn't even get her name. Calling herself something out of a book, it's ludicrous. I think it's a ruse to lull you into a false sense of security.'

'It was a silly game,' said Cordelia wearily. 'Nothing more, I'm sure of it.'

'Well, we'll see what Angus says.' Hal got up. 'I'm going to chop some wood before the rain comes in.'

He kissed Cordelia and went out into the scullery where they could hear him putting on his gumboots and talking to the dogs, who'd followed him out. Fliss raised her eyebrows interrogatively at Cordelia, who made a little face. They heard the scullery door close and Cordelia sighed.

'Perhaps I am being a fool,' she said. 'I don't think so. My gut instinct says that I'm not in danger. You're right. It was like a game that went a bit too far but it's over now. I want to forget it and get back to normal.'

'And will Angus let you do that?'

'Do you know, I felt just a tad irritated when Hal said that. "We'll see what Angus says." As if it's up to Angus to decide how I should go forward. I've managed to live without him for most of my life, after all.'

They sat together at the kitchen table in silence for a moment.

'I quite see that,' Fliss said at last. 'But you did call him in on it, didn't you? He's bound to feel involved.'

'Yes,' admitted Cordelia crossly. 'I know I did. That was when it occurred to me that if it *were* Simon playing these jokes, then he might have it in for Angus too, and so it was only right that he should be warned. Well, I feel quite confident now that it's

381

all over and I don't want . . .' She paused, frowning, and Fliss watched her thoughtfully.

'You don't want Angus playing gaoler?' she suggested.

Cordelia looked at her with an odd expression: guilt mixed with shock and disappointment. 'I never imagined that it would be so . . . so *claustrophobic*,' she said defensively. 'I've been on my own for so long, you see, and then again, Angus and I are . . . Well, we're not used to being particularly domestic when we're together.'

Fliss grinned. 'You mean you still behave like lovers. You are courteous to one another and intimate moments are still rather exciting. You don't bicker about mundane things like who's lost the car keys or taking out the rubbish. Or argue about forgetting to pass on telephone messages and whose turn it is to walk the dog. You still wear sexy underwear, and Angus has a shower and puts on a clean shirt before he comes to supper.'

Cordelia was laughing, relaxed now. 'Honestly,' she said, 'I hadn't realized how dull cohabiting could be. Or how inconvenient. I'm not used to sharing the bathroom. I like to work at odd hours, when the mood takes me, and meals are pretty erratic. Angus is an utter darling but he's very . . . punctual. He gets a bit irritated from time to time when I work past lunchtime, or I suddenly need a gin and tonic at half past three in the afternoon, and once or twice I've had to stifle the urge to hit him with a blunt instrument. It's all very well to laugh, Fliss, but what am I going to *do*?'

'Why do anything?' asked Fliss calmly. 'Let this silly business die down. Meet him halfway on any protection suggestions, and see what happens. By the sound of it, Angus will, even as we speak, be thinking how very pleasant it is to be on his own in Dartmouth with his boat just down the river. Do nothing and behave as if nothing has changed.'

'I hope that's possible. Though it's odd, isn't it? It seems as if Simon has had the last laugh after all. I hate thinking that he's won.'

'Look at it the other way round. This might have prevented you from making a terrible mistake. Be thankful for it.'

Cordelia sighed. 'It worked for you and Hal.'

'Yes, but Hal and I had very close contact all our lives. We were family, we were always meeting up. When Miles was in Hong Kong for two years and I moved back to The Keep with my children, Hal was based at Devonport and lived here too with Jolyon. Oh, it was all very proper – not much choice with all the others around – but we were always very close friends. It's odd, though, isn't it, that you and I and Maria have one thing in common? We all fell in love with one man but married another. Poor Maria. She's down with friends in Salcombe for the weekend. Jo met her earlier on and told her in words of one syllable that she couldn't just stroll back into his life as if nothing had happened. She's suddenly decided that she'd like to move to Devon.'

'Oh, no.'

Fliss shrugged. 'Well, she's got every right to live where she likes but the point is that she's lived in Salisbury for the last twenty years and it's too soon after Adam's death to make such a big move. I think she'd rely very heavily on us for friendship and entertainment and I don't think Jo's ready for that. He hated being so outspoken, though, and he said she was clearly hurt but being brave. I can't decide whether to invite her over or whether it would slightly undermine Jo's good work.'

'Does she know about him and Henrietta yet?'

'She does now. He decided that it was unfair to keep her in the dark any longer, and he feels very much more secure about telling her now they're engaged, but she was clearly humiliated by the fact that, when she was here, we were all keeping it a secret from her. Poor Maria. I feel so sorry for her but I'm afraid to interfere. Anyway, she's probably not in the mood to come and see us.'

'Supposing *I* were to phone her,' suggested Cordelia. 'Ask her over for coffee or something. How long is she down for?'

'Until Tuesday, I think she said. Could you cope with it? It's rather a nice idea. A kind of sop to her pride. I'm sure she'd love it. The only trouble is, she hasn't got a car and the woman she's staying with is a bit pushy, according to Jo.'

'I'll go and fetch her,' Cordelia said. 'Have you got a phone number?'

'Somewhere around. She left it so that Jo could call her.' Fliss got up and began to look amongst the papers on the dresser. 'Are you certain?'

'Absolutely. I agree that it would be difficult for you but I think it's the right gesture just at the moment. The lump of sugar after the medicine.' She took the piece of paper. 'I'll do it straight away, shall I?' Fliss passed her the handset and she dialled the number, waited. 'Oh, hello. Is Maria there? Could I speak to her? My name's Cordelia Lytton.' She grinned at Fliss and nodded. 'Oh, hi, Maria. How are you? . . . I was just talking to Fliss and she said you were down and I gather you've heard the glad tidings. What a wonderful surprise, isn't it? I could hardly believe it. Listen, how about I come over and pick you up and bring you back to my cottage for coffee one morning? . . . What about Monday? . . .

385

Great! . . . No, that's no problem, I shall be coming into Kingsbridge on Monday morning so it'll take no time at all to drop into Salcombe. Quarter to eleven-ish? Right. Give me the address . . . Fine. See you then. 'Bye.'

'I can't tell you how relieved I feel,' said Fliss. 'Thanks, Cordelia. Jo had to be tough but I can't help feeling sorry for her. She behaved very badly to him but, when you really think about these things, it's so difficult to be black and white about them, isn't it?'

Cordelia nodded. 'I go round in circles thinking about Henrietta and feeling guilty about how it's all affected her. Was it Angus's fault because he left me in the first place? Was it my fault for being unfaithful with him when he got back? Was it Simon's fault for leaving me and abandoning Henrietta? We all had a hand in it.'

'That's where I've got to,' said Fliss. 'I used to think it was Maria's fault because she left Hal and more or less abandoned Jo, and so I was always able to occupy the moral high ground about it all. But I've begun to see that the problem started much earlier. Hal and I should have stood up to my grandmother and Prue when they decided that we shouldn't marry, and Hal should never have told Maria about the way we felt about each other. Hal and I always loved each other but because we stayed physically faithful to Miles and Maria we felt that *we* were rather noble and that *their* behaviour was indefensible. In truth, we all contributed, one way and another, and it was Jo who suffered. And is still suffering. I'm so glad that he and Henrietta have got together, Cordelia.'

'So am I. Henrietta is so happy it's heartbreaking. I live in terror of something going wrong. And now I've got to tell her that Simon is dead. I'm still in shock about it, actually. I know I haven't seen or heard from him for twelve years but he was part of my life once. And hers.'

'Were they ever really close?'

Cordelia shook her head. 'There was too much separation in the early days – well, you know what it's like being a naval wife – and he walked out when she was five. After that he used to take her out when his leaves and her school holidays allowed but there was no real bonding. He was living in the Mess so he had nowhere for them to go. And when she was fifteen he went to Australia and that was that. But she's still bitter about it, understandably, and I'm fearful that all the resentment will resurface, just when we were beginning to be so happy.'

'Make sure that Jo knows that Simon is dead,' Fliss said. 'Hal and I decided not to say anything to him until we'd talked it over with you. But now he needs to be ready to comfort Henrietta and talk it all through with her. She'll need to do that.'

'Yes,' said Cordelia after a moment. 'Yes, you're right. She'll probably be able to do that more easily with him than with me. Is he around?'

Fliss shook her head. 'He went to Exeter to see a friend and they were going to the cinema. He'll be back later.'

Cordelia thought about it. 'Look, do you think that perhaps you could tell him when you next see him? After all, it doesn't matter who tells Jo. He's not going to be affected one way or another, is he? And then I don't have to worry about when I tell Henrietta. I need to choose my moment. Make sure he knows that he mustn't tell her that we told him. Oh dear, is it fair to embroil him in it, do you think?'

'Jo will understand exactly why we're doing it. I'll tell him this evening and then you'll know he'll be ready to stand by.'

'Thanks, Fliss. I must go. I've got poor McGregor out in the car and Angus will start panicking and think I've been pushed off a cliff. I'll let you know how we go on.'

'Please do. And thanks for doing this for Maria. I'm really very grateful. I hate to think of her going back to Salisbury feeling miserable. Take care, Cordelia.'

Cordelia grinned. 'You sound like Hal,' she said. 'Give him a kiss from me and tell him that I'll attend to Angus's every utterance. I'll phone you on Monday once I've taken Maria back to Salcombe.'

Fliss waved her goodbye and went back into the hall. Hal was piling logs into the log basket set in the recess of the huge granite fireplace.

'And don't start talking to me about women's bloody intuition,' he said crossly, breathing heavily from his exertions. 'It was *you* who was in a state about Cordelia, remember. And *I* was the one who said it was just a practical joke.'

'I know I was,' said Fliss placatingly. 'I panicked a bit, I admit, and I *did* want you to check on Simon and so on, but I think we have to trust Cordelia's . . . reactions. Now she's met this woman, I mean. It does sound crazy but I believe her when she says she thinks it's all over.'

'Until we find her body at the bottom of the cliff,' he muttered.

'And she's invited Maria for coffee on Monday,' Fliss said, determined to maintain a positive note. 'That's good, isn't it?'

'Now that *is* kind of her.' Hal straightened up and dusted his hands together. 'Lets us off the hook but makes Maria still feel part of the family.'

'Exactly.' She glanced at her watch. 'Prue and

Lizzie should be back from Totnes quite soon. If you light the fire, I'll make some tea. We may even have five minutes on our own.'

He smiled at her then. 'Do you mind living in a commune, Fliss?' he asked. 'Do you ever wonder what it might have been like to be normal? To be on our own together?'

Fliss thought about what Cordelia had said earlier, and her own views about the civilizing effect of having other people about.

'I've lived like this since I was eleven years old,' she said. 'And then, when I was married to Miles, he was away for such a lot of the time. First with the Navy and then in Hong Kong. You were the same. We've never done normal, have we? I think this suits me.'

'Just as well,' he said. 'Let's hope Henrietta feels the same way.'

# CHAPTER THIRTY-TWO

The moon balanced on the rim of the hill, its light pouring down on bleached fields and casting sharp shadows beneath thorn hedges. It seemed to roll along the summit, bouncing gently over peaks and across valleys, until it rose at last, lifting itself clear of the earth.

'One night,' Jo had said, 'when there's a full moon, we'll go up to Crowcombe Park Gate and along the top of Harenaps. It's amazing how much you can see by moonlight. You'll love it.'

Standing at the window, Henrietta pulled her warm, crimson pashmina more closely around her. Her feet were bare and she wriggled her toes into the soft thick rug. Tomorrow Jilly would be gone and she would see Jo again: it was five days since she'd seen him, though they'd texted each other several times a day.

'We simply can't risk it,' she'd told him. 'Jilly and

Susan are very old friends and Jilly will go straight back to London and tell everyone. It wouldn't be so bad if you weren't so well known but she'll be so excited. I know it's frustrating to keep it a secret but I still can't decide how to tell Susan that I shall be leaving. She's going to find it really hard. First Iain and then me. Part of me is tempted to wait until she gets back, so I can do it face to face, and part of me feels it's only fair to telephone her so as to give her plenty of time to think about it.'

She shivered in the bright moonlight: odd how the moon seemed to grow smaller as it rose higher. Henrietta leaned her forehead against the cold glass, one knee on the window seat. The trouble was that she didn't quite know how to open such a conversation. Would she chat as if nothing had happened and then introduce it into the conversation? Or start straight off with the news?

Maggie had telephoned to check that all was well, and had sent Susan's love and said that the children were missing her; and Henrietta had said, very casually, that everything was fine and that Jolyon Chadwick had been to collect the books. She'd had cards from Susan and the children, but the messages had been strictly of the tourist variety and she still had no clue about how Susan was feeling. It would have been good to talk it over with Jilly – after all, she knew Susan really well – but it simply wouldn't be fair to swear her to secrecy.

'I want to tell my friends myself,' she'd said to Jo. 'I don't want other people doing it for me. Anyway, it's not official yet, is it? I can't wait to go and choose my ring.'

He'd called her after his meeting with Maria, still sitting in his car at Dartington. He'd sounded odd and flat, as if all emotion had been drained out of his voice, and she'd wished they'd been together then. She was glad Maria knew now; that Jo had felt strong enough to tell her. It seemed almost impossible to believe that she'd once dreaded anyone suspecting anything was going on between her and Jo, when now she felt so happy about it all that she wanted everyone to know about it. That afternoon at The Keep when he'd behaved so indifferently, as if they were indeed just casual friends, she'd utterly hated it. Just for a while his indifference had seemed real and, as she'd watched him with Lizzie, she'd felt frightened that she'd lost him; that her almost paranoid fear had somehow put him off. That's why she hadn't wanted him to come over while Jilly was with her: she simply couldn't go through that again – and, anyway, Jilly would have smelled a life-size rat.

She suddenly made up her mind. Tomorrow, once

393

Jilly had gone, she would telephone Susan and tell her the truth. It was foolish to drift on, making everyone keep the engagement a secret, afraid to see Jo if friends were around. They would go to Bath together and buy the ring and then anyone could know and they could be free and happy.

Having made the decision she was filled with exhilaration; she took a deep breath, longing for tomorrow when she would see Jo. She tried to imagine them together, living in the gatehouse.

'You'll want to change a lot of stuff,' he'd said. 'It's a typical bachelor's pad. I've always had The Keep across the courtyard if I needed home comforts. We'll want to be more independent.'

She wondered how she would manage; whether communal life would suit her once she was married. She could see no real reason why not. After all, she'd loved the life in London – and she'd spoken to Lizzie about it too, just to get a feel of life at The Keep.

'I think you have to have the right kind of temperament,' Lizzie had said. 'I lived in a flat with three other girls before I came here and I'd never known it any other way. It works fine for me. I've got my own quarters but the Chadwicks are brilliant about making you feel part of the family while respecting your privacy. I suppose it must be rather like living in a convent, or on board a ship. The point is that they've always been used to it too. Luckily there's masses of space, and a nice generational cross-section. It might not work if it were, say, two families with young children trying to do it together but we've got Sam, who's nearly twelve, at one end, and Prue at eighty-three at the other and everyone else in between. Sam brings his friends home at half-term or in the holidays, and his uncle, Charlie, and my two brothers come down to stay, as well as the other Chadwicks, so it's great. If you like that kind of thing. I come from an army family so I'm used to a lot of coming and going.'

'It sounds like fun,' Henrietta had said.

She'd meant it; she'd been lonelier than she cared to admit during these last weeks and she wondered how she'd have managed these two months without Jo in her life. She was really looking forward to having people around again, and to having some work to do. It had been rather a treat, at first, to have no commitments but to walk the dogs, check out the two aged ponies in the paddock, and sit and read in the warm autumn sunshine. Now, she'd begun to feel restless; the wet days seemed endless and she was ready to move on. Of course, she'd stay with Susan until she found a new nanny – and it would be fun to be in London again for a while – but now everything was different and she couldn't wait to be with Jo, and to start their new life together.

'So Simon is dead.' Angus stood at the window watching the moon's reflection in the black, choppy, river water. 'And this woman . . . To be honest, I can hardly take it in. And you just sat there talking to her as if you were old friends.'

'You sound like Hal,' Cordelia said drowsily. 'Honestly, darling, I'm exhausted. Do you think we could just go to sleep?'

He turned towards her, coming back to the bed and sitting on its edge. 'I can't seem to relax,' he said. 'And I still feel anxious about your being alone, even with McGregor there.'

'That's why I stayed tonight,' she told him. 'It seemed silly to go back again when we could be together here. And it's been so nice to have an evening at the pub and then to walk back without worrying about drinking and driving, hasn't it? It's been fun, after the anxieties of the last week. Or perhaps I'm being heartless? I mean, Simon is dead.'

'No,' Angus said quickly. 'Not heartless. After all, you and Simon have been out of touch for such a long time. Poor old Si.'

'I do feel sad,' she admitted. 'A part of me hoped

that all this nonsense *was* Simon, working himself up to a reconciliation. I feel that an opportunity has been missed and that's what makes me sad. And I really don't know how Henrietta will take it. Oh, I'm sorry, Angus, I really am. You must be sick to death of me going on and on about Henrietta, but I just didn't need this now when she's so happy and I really believed that she and I were beginning to move forward.'

'I feel responsible too,' he reminded her. 'We're all involved.'

'I know.' She watched him affectionately – and rather guiltily. Her love for him had become stronger again now he was back in his own place. He belonged here, and she was happy to be his guest, and the ease between them had returned; just in the same way that it worked so well when he visited her. All her instincts told her that this was how it must be for them both and, as soon as they'd met again earlier, she'd guessed that he'd been feeling exactly the same. Their particular kind of intimacy was very special. It might not have the depth and understanding that forty years of ups and downs of marriage and parenthood brought to a relationship, but their friendship worked very well. Why risk it by demanding more? This last week together had given them both a great deal to think about and neither of them had been foolish enough to put those thoughts into words.

'I just wish I could really believe it's over,' he was saying. 'What you've told me is so utterly bizarre that I'm afraid that it's just another trick. You know?'

'Trying to lull me into a false sense of security?' Cordelia suggested. 'You really *are* beginning to sound like Hal. We've been through all this once and it's too late to go through it all again. Come back to bed, Angus. Let's sleep on it.'

He stood up and pulled the curtains together; she opened her mouth to protest – she loved to see the moonlight pouring in – and shut it again. His house, his rules: she put out her arms and pulled his chilled body close, holding him in her arms, warming him.

As they drove through the lanes and out to the coast, Maria could feel her spirits rising. Cordelia's telephone call, coming so soon after the meeting with Jolyon, had done much to restore her confidence. It had been so good to be able to say very casually: 'Oh, yes, that was Cordelia Lytton, the journalist. I'm sure you've heard of her,' and Penelope and Philip *had* heard of her – Pen had read some of her books: 'Terrific fun, Maria, but informative too. I'll lend you one' – and she'd been able to bask in their envy. If only she could have said that Jolyon was engaged to Cordelia's daughter, but she hadn't dared break her promise to Jolyon and, anyway, that disclosure would be something to look forward to later on. It had been just a bit embarrassing to have to say that the Chadwicks hadn't invited her over and that it didn't seem as if she'd be seeing Jolyon again this weekend. ('Would you like to invite him here?' Penelope had asked hopefully. 'We could have a little drinks party.') Maria had had to tread rather carefully, implying that Jolyon was very busy with his new TV programme and that, anyway, she'd really just come down to look at a couple of houses. And that was humiliating in itself, because now, after what Jolyon had said, there was clearly no point at all in looking at houses, though she'd had to go through the motions of being keen and excited about the cottages Philip had found on the internet. She'd been quite clever about that, pretending that she was still undecided and telling Penelope about a really rather wonderful flat in the Cathedral Close in Salisbury; but then of course old clever clogs Philip had asked all about the flat and had said he'd have a look at it on the internet so that Penelope could see it too. Not that it really mattered – after all, it wasn't a lie; there *was* a flat in Sarum St Michael – and Philip had printed off the details, but then, of course, Penelope had pointed out that

399

it was only a one-bed flat, not knowing it was all she could afford, and she'd asked where the boys could stay when they came to visit her, and it had all been a bit tricky. And so she'd hastily said that there was another flat in Century House in Endless Street, which was the one she'd *really* love and, of course, Philip had to find that one too, and then old Penelope had really gasped and stretched her eyes at the price and she, Maria, had had to point out that it *was* in a Grade II listed Georgian building and it had two bedrooms, as well as a parking space – 'Gold dust, Pen, I promise you,' – and she'd made a big point about how she might miss her friends and the bridge club if she moved to Devon . . .

'Rather nice,' Cordelia was saying, 'to have chums with a holiday cottage in Salcombe.'

'It makes a change from The Keep,' Maria said quickly, wanting to give the impression that she had choices. She felt suddenly shy, wondering how to introduce the subject of Henrietta and Jolyon whilst still smarting from the knowledge that she'd been excluded from their secret. Cordelia saved her the trouble.

'Isn't the news wonderful?' she asked, so naturally and easily. 'Such a surprise to us all. The engagement, I mean. And isn't it tiresome to be sworn to secrecy about it? Honestly, the young can be so intense, can't they? But I'm afraid you must blame my daughter for it. Did Jo mention the reason to you?'

'No,' said Maria quickly. 'No, not exactly.'

How could she say that Jolyon hadn't trusted her enough even to tell her that they were in love; that he'd feared she might have made some unkind and hurtful remark to his beloved? Of course she couldn't and, anyway, Cordelia surely knew that already; she'd been at The Keep that weekend. Humiliation threatened to weaken her again and she tried to concentrate on what Cordelia was telling her. She was saying something about Henrietta needing to explain to her employer, Susan, that she'd be leaving her when she got married and she didn't want anyone else telling her first because Susan's husband had walked out and she was in a bit of a state . . .

To be honest, she didn't care too much about the details because she was so relieved that Cordelia didn't seem to know about how things were between her and Jolyon, and she was able to relax and look about her and allow herself to feel happy. And when she saw the row of coastguard cottages perched at the end of the cliff she gave a cry of delight, probably overdoing it just a tiny bit because she wanted to reward Cordelia for being so kind to her.

Though when she got inside there was no need

to fake her amazement. She walked into a room that brimmed with brilliant, shaking light; the sea and sky were just one immense bowl of tremulous radiance that made her gasp and stand in silent awe. Even the great hound that rose up so regally from its bed seemed all part of the magnificence. Cordelia opened the French door for her so that she could step out onto the big stone balcony, and she stood in silence, overwhelmed by the glittering expanse of water and by an odd, unsettling sense of infinity. For a moment, she was seized with a sense of absolute peace, as if the light had somehow drenched her soul in its purifying lustre and washed away all her weakness and pettiness: a baptismal process that cleansed her, lifted her above the foolish striving of this world and set her down in a new place. She gulped the sweet, salty air and suddenly realized that her cheeks were wet with tears.

She turned, dazed, but Cordelia was busy making coffee, taking no notice, and she quickly wiped her cheeks and licked her salty lips and frowned into the brilliance, holding on to the stone wall.

'Is it warm enough to have coffee outside?' Cordelia was coming out, followed by the great hound that went to sit against the wall. 'I often sit here swathed in shawls and rugs simply because I love it so much. After all these years I can never get enough of it.

Yes, I think it will be. There's no wind, is there? The chairs will be wet, though. Don't sit on them until I've wiped them with a cloth.'

The business of wiping the chairs and setting out the coffee helped to get her over her first reaction, although her gaze was drawn over and over again to the vision of infinity beyond the stone wall. Cordelia poured the coffee out and sat down. Maria sat down too. Any need to gush or exclaim seemed to have vanished away. The stark, sheer cliffs and the dazzling expanse of water seemed to have reduced all emotions to one simple requirement: truth.

'It's extraordinary,' she said, and she noticed that her voice was almost expressionless; no wheedling lilt or determined jolliness; not even the familiar whine of irritation and disappointment. 'Do you ever get used to it?'

Cordelia shook her head. 'It's hardly ever the same, you see. And it's always amazing. Having the sea as your neighbour teaches you that you're never in control and, after a while, you accept that and relax into it. It's extraordinarily freeing, if you know what I mean?'

'Yes, I think I do. Except that it wouldn't last, would it? Not if you couldn't be here all the time.'

Cordelia was watching her thoughtfully. 'Only so long as any uplifting experience stays with you.

You have to make an effort, don't you, to remember what it was like and, well, practise it, I suppose? Like meditation. Or contemplative prayer. You have one brief moment of glorious clarity before you descend again into the vast plains of doubt and anxiety.'

Maria remembered her earlier conversation with Jolyon. 'Like Paul on the Damascus road?' she asked. She sipped some coffee: the first shock was over and she was able to behave more normally. Even so, she didn't have the usual desire to plunge into speech, to project the image – charming, amusing, winsome – with which she instinctively masked the insecurities and inadequacies that made up her persona. It was surprisingly restful not to have to act, to pretend.

'The trouble is,' she said, sipping some more coffee, 'I feel so guilty all the time lately.' She frowned, she hadn't meant to say that, and she felt slightly alarmed, as if she were indeed out of control.

'Tell me about it,' Cordelia was saying, laughing rather bitterly. 'Guilt seems to drive us all, doesn't it? I wonder why. There doesn't seem to be anything particularly life-enhancing about guilt, does there, that makes it necessary to the survival of the species?'

'It's just that Adam dying seems to have opened my eyes to so many things and I blame myself for a lot of mistakes in the past. I always manage to

404

put the responsibility on to other people but I'm beginning to find it difficult to do that any more. I feel so ashamed. I go over and over the past and just tear myself to pieces.' She sighed rather sadly. 'Well, I suppose humility is good for the soul, at least.'

Cordelia frowned. 'But self-blame is not necessarily humility, is it? Often it's a form of self-rejection. True humility is something quite different. I think it's rather dangerous to assume that because we're beating ourselves up we're actually addressing the real problem. We can even feel complacent about it instead of asking *why* we feel guilty. Perhaps feeling guilty lets us off actually looking honestly at ourselves, asking why it is we are rejecting ourselves, and then doing something about it.'

Maria felt confused; anxiety nibbled at the fringes of her new peacefulness. 'How do you mean?'

Cordelia smiled ruefully. 'Take no notice of me,' she said. 'It's just a theory I'm working through in an attempt to cure myself of this debilitating guilt. We all make mistakes, and other people suffer because of them, but surely there must be a moment when we can ask forgiveness of them and let it go.'

There was a little silence.

'And then?' asked Maria tentatively.

Cordelia shrugged, pursed her lips. 'And then, perhaps, we allow plenty of space all round and start practising true humility. We respect them and ourselves equally, and try to work together for good; not just *our* good, but *their* good, without assuming that we naturally know what that is. How does that sound? Confusing? Pretentious?'

'It sounds . . . good,' said Maria cautiously.

Cordelia grinned. 'Great,' she said. 'I think I'll write an article about it.'

Maria began to laugh. 'You make it sound terribly easy.'

'Writing it might be, though I doubt it; getting it published by a magazine, now that's something else.'

Maria accepted more coffee and gave a sigh of pure pleasure. How good it was to sit here in the autumn sunshine with this odd, likeable woman, feeling no strain or stress.

'Isn't it odd,' she remarked, 'that we're going to be co-mothers-in-law? There's something quite . . .' She hesitated, seeking for an appropriate word.

'Random?' suggested Cordelia. 'Haphazard? I couldn't agree more. Their children will share our genes. Now there's a scary thought.'

'I've got to move soon,' Maria told her, quite calmly, 'and I don't know where to go. I can't stay in

Penelope's annexe for ever. That's another random thing, isn't it? I could go anywhere – and nobody would stop me.'

Cordelia glanced at her quickly – an odd, penetrating look of compassion – and Maria made a little face as if agreeing with something Cordelia had said aloud.

'I know it sounds pathetic but I'm not used to making decisions, you see,' she explained. 'There have always been people, my parents, Hal, Adam, who have done it for me. I'm afraid of getting it wrong, and nobody would care. Nobody would actually stop me from making a terrible mistake. I'm really rather frightened.'

'Do you have to move just yet?' asked Cordelia gently. 'Maybe the decision will become clearer if you give it time.'

'It's getting a bit embarrassing,' she said, 'just sitting there being dependent. I don't want Pen getting fed up with me, though I think she actually likes having the company, but I'd rather jump than be pushed, if you know what I mean. There's something else. My younger son, Ed, made a terrible business loss and my house was standing security for it. I had to sell up. Nobody knows. Not even Pen and Philip. I simply can't bear the humiliation or the pity. Oh, I'm not destitute, I've got some good investments and enough over to buy something small, but it's been a rather scary experience.'

She looked out over the shining sea, surprised at herself at making such an admission, at not bothering to keep up any kind of pretence. She glanced at Cordelia, who was exhibiting no signs of pity or disdain but merely murmured, 'Isn't life hell?' and continued to drink her coffee thoughtfully. The relief of having finally told the truth was so exhilarating that Maria took another brave step.

'I suddenly thought that I might move down here. To be nearer to Jolyon and the Chadwicks.' She grimaced. 'Jolyon wasn't frightfully keen on the idea – and that's putting it mildly.'

'It's too early,' Cordelia said – and, turning again to look at her, Maria realized that she was not bothering to pretend either. 'Don't you think,' Cordelia continued slowly, rather as if she were thinking it through as she talked, 'that what we see as rejection in other people might simply be their need to protect themselves from our neediness? They might not be capable of supplying all the things we want from them so they withdraw to give themselves a little space. And then we feel hurt. But we don't have to blame ourselves – or them – we just need to accept that we all have limitations. Perhaps Jo needs space at the moment. After all, he's entering a momentous period of his life, isn't he? I think that this engagement is a big step for both of them. This is your chance to show Jo just how much you love him, isn't it?'

'By keeping out of his way?'

'By not pressing or pushing,' corrected Cordelia. 'By allowing him to see that you're thinking about him and his needs, now, not you and yours.'

There was a little silence.

'It's a bit depressing, isn't it?' Maria said wistfully. 'Not doing anything, just waiting.'

'Oh, but tremendous things can happen when everything is lying fallow,' exclaimed Cordelia. 'Think of the wintertime with the earth sealed and silent, but all that growth going on underneath. And then the spring comes . . .'

'You think it will come?'

'Of course it will come. You've made the first move, which was brave, no matter what your reasons were, and there has been a response. It's begun, the wheels are in motion. You've been invited down for Hal's birthday and the engagement party for the family.'

'Yes, that's true. Though I'm rather dreading it. I shall feel such an outsider with the whole Chadwick clan there in force, and after all these years. My track record's pretty rubbish, isn't it? I'm rather frightened of Kit. I haven't seen her for years and we were never good friends. Never mind.' She straightened her shoulders as if instinctively bracing herself for battle. 'It will be good practice for me to show Jo that I really mean to be different. The Chadwicks *en masse* can be quite powerful.'

'I can imagine that it would be a bit daunting,' admitted Cordelia. 'Listen, I've had a thought. Would you like to stay here for the weekend? We can go and come to suit ourselves, and we'll invite Jo and Henrietta over for a cup of tea or something. They'll probably be quite glad to get away too.'

Maria stared at her in amazement. 'Do you really mean it? But that would be wonderful. Are you sure?'

'Sure I'm sure. We mums-in-law must stick together. We mustn't allow ourselves to be overwhelmed by Chadwicks, delightful though they are.'

'Thank you very much. I honestly don't know what to say.'

'No need to say anything.' Cordelia got up. 'We'll have a drink while I think about lunch. Don't get up. I can't bear people watching me while I prepare food.'

She went into the cottage and Maria sat in absolute happiness, her mind quite still; none of the usual restlessness, no turning the last half-hour into an amusing little scene to be recounted to Philip and Penelope, no anxiety as to whether she'd acquitted herself well; just this amazing peace.

# PART THREE

# CHAPTER THIRTY-THREE

Thick grey mist, blank as a wall, blotted out the valley and the distant hills. Only the very tops of the tall beeches were visible, rising sharp and clear out of the cloud: each naked twig shining, vivid. Jolyon stood on the hill below The Keep wishing that he had the skill to paint this rather surreal scene, glad that the weekend, so long anticipated, was over. He couldn't quite remember at what point the plan for his father's birthday celebrations had tipped over into becoming a much more significant event; he was just relieved that Henrietta had been happy to go along with it and allow their engagement to be the cause of such jollity.

Kit had come down from London, Sam had brought two school friends home – after all, it was also half-term – and the rest of the family had been busy with the preparations for days beforehand. Jackie, from the village, had been called upon again to house-sit and look after the dogs and the ponies, and he'd picked Henrietta up on Saturday morning to drive her to The Keep. She'd been white-faced and tense and he'd felt anxious and guilty that his family had rather taken over.

'It's really Dad's birthday,' he'd said, so as to alleviate her anxieties, 'and Kit's, of course, since they're twins, and it's Sam's half-term. Lizzie picked him up yesterday. He's got two friends with him so there's pandemonium but it's always like this at this particular time of the year. It always has been. It was my great-grandmother's birthday too, you see, as well as Dad and Kit's, and since it generally coincided with half-term it became an institution. Us being engaged is not all that important, honestly.'

She'd grinned at him. 'Thanks for that,' she'd said.

'You know I didn't mean it like that,' he'd protested. 'I'm just trying to say that we're celebrating lots of things so you needn't feel too embarrassed,' and she'd given him a hug and they'd both relaxed a bit.

'It's just a tad overwhelming,' she'd admitted. 'There are rather a lot of you, you know – Fliss says some of Susanna's family are going to be there – and being an only child I'm just not used to it. I like it, though, and I'll be fine when I've met all these new ones. It's lovely that they're all so pleased about it. I'm being silly, really.'

He knew that part of her difficulty was that Susan had taken the news rather badly and this had upset Henrietta.

'I was half expecting it,' she'd told him after the telephone call to New Zealand, 'which is why I kept putting it off, I suppose, but she was almost bitter. It wasn't personal, she says she's very fond of you, but she asked me if I was really sure, and stuff like that. Well, the timing's not too good, is it? She's been really let down so you can't expect her to feel terribly positive about the married state. It was awful, doing it on the phone, but I'm glad it's over now. I told her I'd stay with her until she found a new nanny but she was rather negative about the whole thing and said she didn't know how she'd tell the children that I'd be leaving too.'

Jo turned his back on the cloud-filled valley and began to climb the hill, calling to the dogs, whose barks could be heard somewhere below him, echoing in the almost eerie silence. Susan's reaction had affected him too, resurrecting his old fear of commitment, and it had been difficult for either of them to regain the exhilaration of the earlier few weeks.

415

Luckily, the prospect of the weekend at The Keep had forced them to raise their spirits and, in the end, it had been easy – and fun. Having three lively twelve-year-old boys around had kept the focus away from the newly engaged couple, and it was clear that Hal and Kit had no intention of letting anyone steal too much of their thunder. It was a family celebration and very soon both he and Henrietta had been able to unwind. It had helped, too, that his mother had been staying with Cordelia; it had taken the pressure off him. It was odd, on reflection, that both mothers had been content to behave as if they were very close friends rather than to be in control. It had somehow made it less stressful for him, and for Henrietta, and he'd been aware of a stirring of admiration for his mother. After all, it couldn't have been easy, given the past, to confront such a gathering of Chadwicks, and she'd done it well, with an unusual quietness and self-effacement. It was clear to him that Cordelia was unobtrusively supporting her and giving her confidence.

'I really like your mum,' he'd said, driving Henrietta back to Somerset on Sunday afternoon after a walk on the cliff and tea with Cordelia and Maria at the coastguard cottage. 'She's just great.'

'I thought yours did pretty well,' she'd said. 'She seemed much more laid-back this time and happy just to be in the background. She seems to have taken on board what you said to her at the White Hart. I got on with her really well.'

After their walk on the cliff, when they'd been having tea, his mother had given Henrietta a pretty bracelet: a delicate chain of silver and coral.

'My grandmother gave it to me when I was eighteen,' she'd said. 'I've always adored it but it needs a more delicate wrist than mine now. I'd love you to have it. I just hope that it isn't politically incorrect to wear coral because it's an endangered species.'

As usual Jo had been seized by the instinctive anxiety that manifested itself whenever Henrietta and his mother were together; all his protective instincts were aroused lest she make one of those light hurtful comments that might wound Henrietta as they had once wounded him. But to his relief, Henrietta had slipped the bracelet on at once, and given his mother a kiss, and Cordelia had raised her teacup in a toast to 'happy families'. And there *had* been an atmosphere of real happiness, a true sense of family amongst the four of them, and the fact that Cordelia had made such a friend of her disposed him towards his mother even more kindly.

The dogs had appeared now out of the curling mist, their coats damp, and barged past him, racing up the hill towards the green door in the wall. He paused in a small homage to other dogs who were buried here, under the wall, then he opened the door and they all passed inside.

Hal was just leaving the office when Jolyon appeared.

'I've got a few phone calls to make,' he said to his father. 'See you later on.'

Hal left him to it and made his way back to the house, hunching his shoulders slightly against the encroaching mist. He was still filled with a pleasurable satisfaction at the memory of the birthday weekend, and he wanted to get an email off to Ed telling him all about it, but there was a tiny edge of discomfort; something that he didn't particularly want to think about, that nevertheless continued to nag at his consciousness. It had been a terrific success, he told himself; everyone had enjoyed it. Even old Maria had behaved incredibly well. Hal grimaced to himself; that sounded a bit patronizing but, might as well admit it, they'd all been a bit anxious about how it might work out with Maria there. And there was that memory again, all tied up with another great occasion, though he couldn't just put his finger on which one; there had been so many celebrations at The Keep.

There was nobody in the kitchen and he went into the hall. His mother was dozing by the fire, the damp dogs stretched before the flames. Their tails thumped gently in welcome but his mother didn't stir and Hal picked up the newspaper and wondered where Fliss was. She and Lizzie had worked so hard to make the weekend such a special one that she was taking a little while to recover. She'd been so happy, though, once the preparations were over and everything was actually under way, but she was always like that, dear old Flissy: anxious and preoccupied until the first person arrived and then all her fears were swept away and she was like a child again, loving every minute of it. And she'd looked really good, too; once or twice he'd seen her amongst all the family, talking to Kit and Susanna, or joking with young Sam and his friends; coming in to the hall with a tray of glasses for the champagne, her face alight with pleasure . . .

Hal frowned a little. He was remembering now and he could see it quite clearly: another weekend party at The Keep, one summer thirty years ago; plans for it spiralling out of control so that invitations had been extended to others apart from family members. He and Maria must have been at the quarter in Compton Road in Plymouth by then; oh, how Maria had hated that quarter after the pretty little cottage that had been their first home in Hampshire. And, even then, he'd been aware of how daunting Maria found these big family get-togethers, and he could remember that she'd been so uptight that he'd telephoned his mother and asked her to come to the party to give Maria some moral support. Hal looked across affectionately at his mother, still asleep, her head sliding sideways against the cushion. She'd always been sweet to Maria in those early years, so encouraging and patient.

'Please come down, Ma,' he'd pleaded. 'I don't think Maria can face it without you. She's wound up about Fliss being pregnant – you know how she's longing to have a baby – and Kit's inclined to tease her. All in good fun, of course, but Maria's a touch sensitive just at present . . .'

She'd come by train from Bristol, he recalled, and he and Maria had met her in Plymouth and she'd stayed with them for the weekend. Kit and a group of her friends had travelled down to The Keep from London, and Fliss and Miles had come over from their house in Dartmouth, of course; Miles full of his imminent posting to Hong Kong. And then during the party he'd bumped unexpectedly into Fliss as she was carrying a tray of glasses into the garden and his love for her had suddenly threatened to overwhelm him; he hadn't wanted her to go to Hong

Kong, to be so far away from him. He'd put out his hands and covered hers with them so that they held the tray between them – and Maria had seen them, and later there had been a terrible row.

He remembered that he'd denied his love for Fliss and accused Maria of jealousy, turning it back on her, making her feel guilty . . .

Prue woke suddenly. Hal was sitting opposite, staring at nothing in particular, his face grim. She watched him fearfully for a moment, knowing that he was thinking about something that was causing him a great deal of pain. She stayed quite still, casting her mind over the various things that might be concerning him. After all, it'd been such a happy time, and everyone was still basking in the afterglow of the weekend. Fliss had been so happy, despite the fact that she'd wished that dear Bess and Jamie could have been there with them all. And darling Jo with that sweet girl beside him; oh, how handsome he'd looked, and so much like Hal at that age . . . And Maria had behaved wonderfully well; not overacting to mask her insecurities as she'd done when she was young . . .

Prue sat upright, disturbing Hal, who still wore that rather forbidding look as though he wasn't really seeing her properly.

'Thinking about the past,' she began, uncertainly,

hardly knowing what she was saying, 'can be so unsettling.'

Hal didn't look at her. 'Opening Pandora's box,' he said. 'That was what Fliss called it and she was right.'

'But sometimes,' Prue said, 'it can be a good thing.'

'I don't see how it can be particularly good to be aware of all the mistakes you've made when it's too late to do anything about them.'

'We've all made mistakes,' she said gently, still feeling her way forward. 'None of us is free from guilt. To be fair, though, we have to try to remember how things were at the time.'

'Fair to whom?' he asked rather bitterly.

'To everyone,' she answered. 'Feeling guilty about someone can do just as much harm as making the mistake did in the first place. It can put pressure on a relationship and throw it out of balance.'

'Oh, well, that's all right then,' he said flippantly. 'We can just forget all about it.'

'I didn't say that nothing should be done,' she said. 'I was trying to point out that guilt, all on its own, is a singularly destructive emotion. Healing, on the other hand, is a special grace.'

He looked at her with such an odd expression on his face – a mixture of disbelief and hope – that she felt terribly anxious and completely inadequate. 'And how do we achieve that?' he asked almost derisively.

Prue shook her head helplessly, and then for some reason thought of Theo. 'By simply wanting it more than anything else,' she answered.

He put the newspaper aside. 'It's odd,' he said, 'and rather unsettling, how these little memories keep coming back after all these years.'

She saw with relief that he was looking more like his usual self. 'It's been an emotional time,' she said. 'Adam dying and Maria coming back into our lives. Jolyon and Henrietta meeting and falling in love. It's bound to stir up the past. I still think that good will come of it all.'

'If you say so.' He got up. 'I think I need a drink.'

'Now that,' said Prue warmly, 'is a very good idea. And since you're on your feet, darling, you could put some more logs on the fire.'

# CHAPTER THIRTY-FOUR

'The trouble is,' Cordelia said, 'that I've kept putting off telling Henrietta that Simon is dead and now I simply don't know how to do it. Or where. I know I'm being tiresome, Angus. No. Don't do that gentlemanly thing and be polite about it. I *know* I am but you can see what I mean, can't you? To begin with: *where* do I tell her? Oh, I know that you think that it doesn't really matter where it is but I don't want her to be left alone afterwards and I can see difficulties either way. And *don't* say that I'm just making trouble for myself. I can hardly drag her all the way over here without telling her why, and I really don't think I ought to do it on the telephone. And even if she *were* to come here, then she's got to drive all the way back on her own, mulling it over in her head, unless she gets that girl in from the village again to look after the animals so she can stay here. But then I'd have to give her some reason as to why

424

she'd need to stay. Of course, I could go over there – and I know you said I could stay there with her if necessary, and that's a possibility, but generally I don't go to the cottage. It's a long drive for me. We usually meet somewhere for lunch, like Pulhams Mill, and I can hardly tell her there, in public. So after lunch I'd have to say, "Let's go back to the cottage", and I think she'd find it a bit odd and wonder why I hadn't simply told her straight out.

'And that's the other thing. *How* do I actually tell her? The more I think about it the more I lose my nerve. Oh, I wish I'd done it straight away, but first of all Jilly was with her and then, as soon as Jilly left, she decided to phone Susan and tell her she was engaged and she was really wound up about that so I thought I'd wait, and then, of course, it was the great weekend at The Keep and I didn't want spoil it for her. So it's got quite out of proportion and OK, so you're saying, "In that case just get on and do it and get it over with," but how? It's really not quite that easy. I simply can't see myself phoning her and saying, "I just want to tell you that your father is dead." I know you think that I'm making a fuss, and at least she hasn't seen or heard from him for ten years so it could be much, much worse. I *know* that. But I still can't quite see how to do it and I simply don't want to spoil things. It's been so much better between us since she got engaged to Jo, I've been so happy, and I just know that this is going to rake up the past again and I shall feel the need to justify myself and all that stuff. And it's no good telling me that I don't have to tear myself apart and all that, I just simply can't *bear* it when it's all being so good and I just *know* I'm going to cock up in a really big way over this one . . . Oh damn, that's my mobile. Where the hell is it? Oh, here it is. Oh, my God, it's Henrietta.

'Hello, darling. How are you? . . . Oh, is he? Oh, that's lovely . . . Oh, just until tomorrow morning but still, that's good. Give him my love . . . No. I mean yes. Yes, quite alone . . . Do I? Well, actually I *am* in a bit of a state, to be honest. I've got some rather sad news, darling. I've just heard that your father died earlier this year from cancer . . . Yes, I know. A terrible shock . . . A mutual friend told me, and I'm so sorry, darling . . . Well, that's true, of course. I can imagine that's how you'd feel. Shocked but rather detached. After all, we'd all been out of touch for so long . . . Yes, of *course* it's terribly sad and I'm so glad you've got Jo with you . . . No, no. I'm fine. Don't worry about me . . . It's sweet of you to think like that but I shall be quite OK, as long as you're all right . . . Yes, we'll talk again tomorrow. 'Bye, darling . . .

'Golly. Wasn't that extraordinary, Angus? Fancy it happening just like that. After all the scenarios I've painted and it just happens out of the blue. And she's OK. She was fine about it. Worried about *me*, actually, being on my own. And *don't* look at me like that, Angus. You've got to admit that it wasn't just *quite* the moment to say that you of all people were here at nearly ten o'clock at night, was it? But she was OK. Oh, I can't get over it. Very calm. She said she felt detached about it. Shocked but detached. Thank God Jo was there. Well, I wouldn't have told her if he hadn't been, of course. Oh, the relief. Don't just sit there, darling, *say* something. No, on second thoughts, just pour me a drink. A very big one.'

'Dad's dead,' Henrietta said. 'I can't quite take it in. Poor old Mum just blurted it out. I think she was in shock, actually. Well, I suppose she would be, wouldn't she? After all, they *were* married, even if it was a long time ago and they haven't been in touch. It's still a shock, isn't it? Oh, yes, please, Jo, I think I will have another cup of tea. I know it's a bit late but I'm kind of, like, numb. It might warm me up a bit. I can't believe it, to tell you the truth. It was cancer. Oh God, how beastly. And he wasn't very old, either. Oh hell, I just wish he could have known about us and I could have asked him why he went away like that. And I *know* what you've said about him obviously being a very black and white, intense kind of guy, and that he simply couldn't cope with Mum being unfaithful, or with having a relationship with me as well as starting a new life for himself. I *know* all that, but I still wish we could have just made our peace, if you know what I mean. I mean it's one thing sending me a letter when I was too young to know how to handle it and another actually having closure – if that's the right word, sounds a bit formal – between two adults. I mean, I really think that you and Maria have got a bit of a chance to make that kind of peace now, and I feel I've been cheated out of it. I'd actually been wondering whether I might send a letter to him, I expect someone could have traced him, just to let him know about you and me. I mean, it's been so great these last few weeks and I've felt differently about a few things, and I just thought I could have sort of let him know that. No, no, it's fine. I'm not crying, really, I'm not, and I'm not really upset, honestly, because actually I didn't particularly want him back in my life. I'd have felt very nervous about it because, like you said, there was something so cold and calculating – and, OK, creepy – about the way he behaved to both me and Mum and I wouldn't have felt very happy about that, especially when we have babies, if you know what I mean. I wouldn't have been able to trust him and it could have been really embarrassing and difficult. Oh God, that sounds awful, doesn't it? You know what I mean, though, don't you? But, well, it *is* a shock. It's bound to be, isn't it? Because he was my father, after all, and he was part of my life, even if I don't remember much about when we were a proper family because even then he was at sea so much. And then, after he left, we had to fit meetings in between me being at boarding school and his leave so it was really difficult, and he didn't write much and when we did meet up we never had much to say to one another and it was difficult to know how to fill the time up. So, one way and another, it didn't really work. Oh, thanks, Jo. Lovely hot tea. Come and sit beside me and give me a cuddle while I drink it.'

Lizzie finished her porridge and sat for a moment, enjoying the unusual silence in the kitchen. Jo had already driven away to Bristol, and Hal was over in the office checking any overnight emails and faxes. It was a bonus for all of them that Hal's long years in the Navy resulted in this habit of being up early in the morning; he'd be back for coffee once he'd made certain that everything was under control but on the days when Jo was away, Hal's self-discipline let Lizzie off the hook a bit and she was grateful for it.

She reached for some toast and, using her butter knife, she slit open the first of her two letters. It was from her mother, and she laid the sheets on the table beside her plate whilst she spread butter and marmalade on her toast. It was a cheerful letter, full of news about the family and the dogs, telling her about their inability to make a decision about getting a puppy; asking if Lizzie would be coming home for Christmas . . .

Lizzie folded the letter and put it back in its envelope. It had been her intention, this year, to spend Christmas with her parents at Pin Mill but that was before she'd known that Jolyon would become engaged and that he and Henrietta would decide to go to Scotland for Christmas and the New Year. It would be strange enough without him but she wondered how young Sam and the others would manage without either of them if she decided to go away too. Fliss had been right when she'd said that she, Lizzie, was the bridge between the older members of the family and Sam – but Jo, too, had proved to be a very strong and necessary part of that bridge. They'd cope without them, of course they would, but she had a good idea of how very different it would be and she felt the stirrings of guilt.

She got up to make some coffee. Part of her guilt was wrapped up in the knowledge that Bess and her little family wouldn't be home this year either, and Jamie had already made it clear that his plans were very uncertain, so it was beginning to look as if it would be a very quiet Christmas at The Keep. Putting the cafetiere on the table, fetching a mug from the dresser, Lizzie looked thoughtfully at the letter addressed to Admiral Sir Henry and Lady Chadwick. She recognized Maria's handwriting and wondered what news it might contain. Fliss came in whilst she was pouring her coffee and she felt a twinge of apprehension, remembering that other morning two months before when a letter from Maria had caused so much disturbance. Fliss said, 'Wasn't it cold last night? There's quite a frost this morning,' glanced at the letter – and glanced quickly again and more closely – but hesitated for a moment and then left it where it was and went to collect a mug instead.

Lizzie poured some coffee for her, wondering whether to mention her plans for Christmas. She decided she'd wait to see what Maria's letter contained; it might not be just the moment to break her own news to Fliss. Instead, she continued to eat her toast and watched out of the corner of her eye whilst Fliss opened a bill, put it to one side, and unwrapped a catalogue. Prue came in and Lizzie smiled a welcome and accepted Prue's kiss with real affection; she was very attached to Prue.

'Ah,' said Prue at once – no hesitation here, Lizzie noted with amusement – 'is that a letter from Maria?'

Fliss affected a slight show of surprise. She picked up the envelope as if to study the writing more closely and said yes, she thought it was.

'And addressed to you both,' observed Prue, as if this were something rather special, and Fliss nodded.

Prue was now waiting, watching Fliss with unfeigned anticipation, as if she expected Fliss to be as pleased as she was to have the letter, addressed to both Fliss and Hal. And it occurred to Lizzie that, previously, letters from Maria had indeed been addressed only to Hal. She discovered that she was just as keen as Prue was to see if this were to be a special communication. Still, Fliss hesitated.

'Perhaps she wants to come for Christmas,' Prue said brightly – and Lizzie felt a little shock, as if Prue might have guessed at her own dilemma – and Fliss snatched up the envelope rather hastily and slit it open. Prue beamed at Lizzie and asked if there might be any porridge left and Lizzie got up, smiling back at her and trying to analyse exactly

432

what it was about Prue that was so very endearing. She was very sweet-tempered, which was part of it, although she could be surprisingly firm with Sam if he overstepped the mark, but also – and perhaps this was the really good thing about Prue's character – she was non-judgemental; she wasn't sentimental or vapid, but she looked at people and situations from her own balanced, compassionate and rather eccentric standpoint.

Lizzie spooned porridge into a bowl and put it down in front of Prue, who thanked her but did not take her unwavering gaze from Fliss's face. When Fliss let out a little 'Oh!' both of them sat expectantly, watching her.

'Maria's decided to stay in Salisbury for Christmas.' Fliss put down the letter and picked up her mug of coffee. 'She says that Christmas will be very odd without Adam but she's been invited next door for Christmas Day and she's planning to do her own drinks party on Boxing Day. She's also decided to stay in the annexe for a while. Her friends want her to and she's decided to rent it officially for six months and see what happens then.'

'Well, that's a relief,' said Prue candidly, and Lizzie wanted to burst out laughing at the slight look of surprise on Fliss's face.

She finished her own coffee and got up. 'I'll

send Hal over for some coffee,' she said. 'See you later.'

'That was very tactful of Lizzie,' Prue said approvingly, after she'd gone. 'She knows that you find it difficult to be really outspoken about Maria in front of her.'

Fliss began to laugh. 'I didn't realize that I wanted to be outspoken,' she protested, though she knew deep down that her relief was very great. 'I did have a slight fear that Maria might hint strongly about Christmas and that Hal would feel sorry for her and then I'd feel guilty if I vetoed it. But to be honest, there really is no point in her coming if Jolyon's away in Scotland. If they are going to put things right between them then it's better if she comes down in the New Year when he's back again. It was good of her not to try it on, though. I shall tell her that he's going off to Scotland with Henrietta and then she'll feel that her nobleness has been worth while.'

Prue was eating her porridge contentedly. 'I think that it will all work out splendidly,' she said. 'Though it will be odd to have Christmas without Jolyon.'

'Yes,' said Fliss, rather shortly. She experienced the now familiar little pain of desolation in her heart when she thought about Bess and Matt and the children, and her darling Jamie, so far away at Christmas. And this year there would be no Jo to joke and mess around with Sam, and to make them all laugh. At least Susanna and Gus would be with them.

'Soon we shall have Henrietta with us too,' Prue was saying gently, 'and then she and Jolyon will be having babies. Won't that be fun? And Bess is talking about them coming over at Easter for the wedding. Perhaps little Paula could be a bridesmaid. Goodness! There's so much to plan and to look forward to, isn't there?'

Fliss bit her lip, willing herself not to cry, furious with herself: these days she was so emotional. She tried to smile at Prue, wondering how the older woman managed to remain so positive, remembering how brave she'd been after Caroline died; her real friend and confidante and the last person of her own generation at The Keep. Suddenly Fliss thought how terrible it would be if anything were to happen to Prue: she'd been there since those very first days after their return from Kenya, her warm motherliness embracing the three small orphans.

Prue had finished her porridge and her warm hand was holding Fliss's cold one, and then Hal was coming in saying, 'Goodness, it's quite chilly out there. Is there any coffee? Morning, Ma,' and Fliss was able to squeeze Prue's hand, and give her a little nod to say that she was fine, and the moment passed.

'I must say,' Hal said later, when he and Fliss were alone, 'that I'm very glad that Maria hasn't suggested coming for Christmas. And I think she's very wise to stay with her friends since they're happy to have her there.'

Ever since he'd come into the kitchen he'd seen that there was a change in Fliss. Her reaction was nothing like it had been when that other letter had come and all hell had broken loose. There was no antagonism about this letter; he didn't feel the usual requirement to play it down, or defend Maria in any way, and this was a great relief. Fliss had referred to it quite casually, almost indifferently, and simply gone on to say how strange it would be with Jo going away for Christmas and that it was a pity that none of Susanna's family would be down until the New Year. But there was more to it than that. Looking at her, he could see the stress and strain had been smoothed away from her small face and he guessed that whatever threat she'd imagined a widowed Maria might be to them all had finally been neutralized.

Hal stood up and began to collect the breakfast

436

things together. Actually, he'd noticed the change in other small ways, starting when Maria had come down and stayed with Cordelia, and again after the birthday weekend. Of course, Fliss had been emotional about missing her twins at such a big family occasion – and he could understand that – yet that terrible bitterness that he'd begun to fear might seriously damage their relationship had gradually disappeared. There was absolutely no question that part of it was to do with the fact that Jo had faced up to his mother, put his cards on the table, so that it seemed very unlikely now that she could hurt him. But part of it, too, was that he and Fliss had been able to talk about their own feelings together and that's what had made the real difference; he'd told her he felt guilty about the things that had happened in the past and he'd accepted his share of the blame, and somehow this had brought a kind of shared healing. It had been odd, the way those little scenes from the past had haunted him the last few weeks. Not like him at all to do that introspective stuff. He couldn't explain it, didn't want to – no point in dwelling on it – he was just glad that the air had been cleared and they could all move forward.

Of course, the wedding would be a vital thing for focusing minds away from the past – the women were all beginning to get excited about it – though

it was a pity that Christmas was likely to be an un-
usually quiet affair.

'I've had an idea about Christmas,' he said now,
to Fliss, as he loaded the dishwasher and she sat at
the table finishing her coffee. 'Why don't we invite
Cordelia over for Christmas Day? She gets on really
well with Susanna and Gus and I imagine she'll be
on her own, won't she?'

Fliss looked at him rather oddly, as though he
were missing some point, and he raised his brows.
'What?'

'Well, you remember I told you about Angus?'

'Yes. But . . . Oh, I see. You mean they're back together again, officially?'

Fliss bit her lip, shook her head. 'Well, probably
not. Not officially. I think Cordelia won't do much
about that until Henrietta is married, and even then
. . . She's been alone a long time.'

'So what are you saying?' He felt impatient with all
this pussy-footing about. 'Ask them *both* to Christmas lunch. After all, he's on his own now, isn't he?
Good grief, we're all adults. Surely there's no need
to play games?'

'No,' she said, 'but it's up to them, isn't it? I'd rather
sound Cordelia out first and see what she's got in
mind. After all, Angus might be going to one of his

boys, or they might be coming down to Dartmouth. It's a nice idea, though.'

'Well, then. I'm just going to check emails and see if there's anything from Ed. He's really enjoying his new job. Let's hope it lasts.' He felt pleased, happy again. He couldn't really be doing with all this emotional stuff and he was relieved that things were getting back to normal. He went into the study and switched on the computer.

# CHAPTER THIRTY-FIVE

She recognized the voice at once.

*'Hi, Henrietta, just to say we've just got back to Tregunter Road. We're all fine but pretty exhausted after the long flight. We're going to stay here for a couple of days to get Susan and the kids sorted but we'll be with you some time on Thursday. Everyone sends their love.'*

Henrietta switched off the answerphone. Roger and Maggie would be back on Thursday, which meant that in three days' time she'd be travelling back to London. It seemed impossible that it was only eight weeks ago that she'd first met Jo; so much had happened since then. And how strange it would be to be back in London with Susan and the children, picking up the old routine – and much further away from Jo.

She went into the kitchen and sat at the table; it was too cold this morning to sit out in the small court, though the sun shone in at the window and lit the berries on the little spray of hawthorn to a bright, rich crimson. Juno came to sit beside her, her head on Henrietta's knee, and Tacker scrabbled at her feet with his rubber bone on a frayed rope. He shook it fiercely and tossed it up and pounced on it again, inviting her to throw it for him. She kicked it across the floor and he bounded after it, scrabbling over Pan's recumbent form. Henrietta was pierced with sadness: she'd miss it all terribly, the little cottage and the dogs and the two old ponies; the walks on the Quantocks hills, Jo coming in on his way back from Bristol and lighting the wood-burning stove, and then sitting with him late into the night, talking and planning, and making love. Just for these two months they'd been able to step out of the world and be private and alone together, with only the dogs for company.

How would it be in London, with Susan not really approving of their engagement and nowhere to go to be with Jo to have a quiet talk? It wouldn't be very easy to find the right moments to have time together away from Tregunter Road – and Susan would need her even more without Iain there, especially at weekends when the children weren't at nursery.

'We'll manage somehow,' Jo had said comfortingly.

'After all, it's not your fault that Susan's marriage has broken up, and you simply can't be expected to become a surrogate father. I know it will be difficult, and we shall miss the wonderful freedom we've had here, but we'll set the date for the wedding and that will make Susan see that she must find another nanny as soon as she can. We can't dither around; that would be fatal for everyone, especially the children. They need to settle down as quickly as possible with the new routine.'

'But I've promised her I'll stay until she finds a new nanny,' Henrietta had said anxiously, feeling trapped between Jo's determination and Susan's needs. 'It just makes it so much more difficult now I know that she disapproves.'

'Susan isn't so stupid as to believe that because it hasn't worked for her it won't work for you. She's just upset at the timing – and, I agree, it isn't ideal. But we can't put our lives on hold indefinitely, and it's the sort of thing that could drift if a date isn't set. Anyway, we want an Easter wedding . . . don't we?'

There had been a sudden anxiety in his voice, as if he were wondering if she'd changed her mind, and her heart had brimmed with love for him.

'Of *course* we do,' she'd answered vehemently. 'Mum and Fliss and I are beginning to work it out together. Oh, it's going to be fantastic. It's just . . . oh, poor old Susan. I feel guilty being so happy when she's so miserable, that's all.'

He'd held her tightly. 'I know how you feel but we'll just have to do what we can for her until Easter. Thank God we got Christmas booked and she's not making a fuss about that.'

It was Maggie who'd helped out there. She'd said that she and Roger would be spending Christmas with Susan and the children in London, and this information had given Henrietta the courage to go ahead and book the hotel in Scotland. Quite suddenly she remembered how she'd wondered whose voice it had been on the answerphone all those weeks ago, and how she'd dashed over to the stores in Bicknoller to buy a cake. And then a few hours later Jo had arrived and her whole life had been changed. Even her father was dead . . .

Henrietta bent down to stroke Tacker and subsided on to the floor beside him, hugging him. It was so difficult to come to terms with this knowledge. Yes, she knew that it had been her father's decision to go, to cut her out of his life – and she'd been too shocked, too hurt, and, at fifteen, too inexperienced to fight it – but, later on, she might have been able to track him down and make him explain why *she* must be made to suffer for her parents' faults and inadequacies. Instead it had been easier, less painful, to blame her mother; she'd punished her in a thousand tiny ways, subconsciously some of the time, but now she felt differently: more compassionate and very sad. She wished she'd had her photograph album with her so that she could look at the photos of them all together as a family, just to prove that she had some happy memories.

'Probably it's just as well you haven't,' Jo had said. 'Not while you're on your own so much. That sort of thing can get out of proportion and you can lose control and never stop crying. It's so difficult to remember the past exactly how it was and sometimes you find you're overwhelmed with guilt and remorse. You have to be very balanced and contented to remember happy times in a positive way. It can so easily segue into sheer sentiment, followed by regret and all sorts of other emotions. It's best to do it with other people around.'

It had sounded odd when he'd said that, but she knew what he was trying to tell her. It was because he'd been through it all himself that he understood the way she was feeling; his own experience had given him a strength and stability that sustained her. She kissed Tacker's soft head, stood up, reached for her mobile and texted a message to Jo: 'C u l8er. Luv u x'.

She looked around her sadly: this was the last

night they'd spend together at the cottage. Suddenly she picked up the phone again and dialled.

Two telephone calls before she even got to her desk, she'd mislaid a crucial telephone number from a magazine editor, and her coffee was cold – but she was too happy to care.

Cordelia sighed contentedly and sat down to stare at her computer screen; even now she couldn't concentrate. The first call, not long after breakfast, had been from Henrietta.

'Jo's just gone,' she'd said rather wistfully, 'and this is my last whole day here alone. Maggie and Roger will be back sometime tomorrow, and I feel so, well, so disorientated. It's just really weird. To be honest, I feel a bit panicky about going back to London and seeing Susan and the children again after all this time, and I'm really going to miss the dogs, especially Tacker, and the cottage. It seems like I've been here for ever. The point is, Mum, I suppose you couldn't manage to get over for some lunch, could you? I expect you're working but we could meet at Pulhams Mill and have a walk at Wimbleball Lake afterwards.'

'Of course I can come,' she'd said at once. 'Not a problem. Let's say one o'clock. What fun! You can choose your Christmas present in the craft shop . . . I promise, it's not a problem. See you later. 'Bye darling.'

Cordelia smiled. *Are we the first generation to need to be friends with our children?* That article, along with the one about the soke, had been accepted and she was now working on the idea she'd talked about with Maria, when they'd stood on the balcony and discussed the difference between self-blame and true humility. It was complicated and probably out of her league but she really wanted to have a try at it.

The second phone call, from her agent, had filled her with a different kind of delight. She'd emailed Dinah with a synopsis of an idea for a novel and then waited in terror for her to tell her that it was rubbish. To her amazement Dinah had been very excited and told her that she couldn't wait to see the first three chapters.

'Terror with a humorous twist!' she'd said. 'Difficult to bring off but I like the idea. It'll be interesting to see how you handle it. Have you had much experience of being stalked?' She'd chuckled at the absurdity of such a possibility.

Cordelia had laughed too. 'You'd be surprised,' she'd said lightly.

The ideas were seething in her head: characters, fragments of conversation, bits of plot, the crucial decision about where to set it. She'd already begun to block it out, knowing exactly how it must end, and now she needed to make some notes before she went off to see Henrietta. When her mobile rang she had to leap up and search about for it; she'd left it in the kitchen.

'Angus,' she said, out of breath. 'Sorry, darling. I couldn't find the damned phone. Are you OK?'

'I'm fine,' he said. 'Still OK for this evening, Dilly?'

'Absolutely OK. Listen, Henrietta just phoned and asked me to meet her for lunch. Isn't it great? *She* invited *me*. Without prompting. I didn't have to hint. I'll be back late afternoon, though, so come over at about six.'

'Sounds good,' he said, 'and so do you. Is it just Henrietta's invitation that's put that note in your voice? What else has happened?'

'Oh, darling,' she said, 'something *is* rather good but I don't want to tell you over the phone. And it's very early days . . . Look, I'll tell you tonight. Promise. But it must be a secret.'

'I can't wait. As long as it's nothing to do with that wretched woman.'

'No, no. That's all over. I told you there was nothing else to worry about there.'

'Mm,' he said non-committally. 'OK. Well, see you later, Dilly.'

Cordelia went back into her study and stood for a moment, thinking about the last few weeks. She picked up a postcard that was propped against the clock. She studied the picture of a dramatic north country scene and then turned it over and reread the message on the back: 'I'd forgotten how beautiful this country is. I've decided to put the past right behind me and settle near my family here. It was good to meet you. Good luck and goodbye.'

It was signed 'Elinor Rochdale'. Cordelia stood the card back on the shelf: she too was learning how to allow the past to settle into its proper place. No doubt the black clouds of guilt and sadness would continue to roll by but that didn't mean that she must put her head in them: she could choose not to. She went back to her desk and with a sigh of pleasurable anticipation she settled down to work.

# CHAPTER THIRTY-SIX

A few weeks later Prue was sitting by the fire in the hall watching Jolyon and Sam setting up the Christmas tree. When he first heard the news, Sam had been dismayed at the prospect of both Jolyon and Lizzie going away for Christmas, but Jolyon had been determined that there were certain things that he and Sam must do together before he went: setting up the Christmas tree, bringing in the enormous Yule log and cutting holly out on the hill. There were other important tasks Jolyon was entrusting to Sam in his absence: the care and welfare of the dogs, and the filling of the log baskets in the hall and the drawing room. This was very clever of Jolyon. The idea that Sam was in charge of certain things, and a necessary link in the smooth running of the daily routine, had given him a sense of importance and responsibility and it was clear to Prue that a part of him was almost longing for Jo and Lizzie to be gone so that he could take complete charge.

From time to time Sam glanced at Prue, just to be certain that she was watching his heroic efforts, and she would nod her approval and admiration and he would redouble his efforts in hauling the great tree upright. Jolyon winked at her and she smiled at him, feeling so proud of him, and very grateful. She knew just how lucky she was to be a part of this family; loved and cared for and valued. As she grew older she blessed her mother-in-law, Freddy Chadwick, for inviting her to make her home here at The Keep with those people she loved best, and just for a poignant moment she recalled the Bidding Prayer for Christmas Eve: 'We remember those who worship with us but on another shore and in a brighter light'. They were all gone now, those friends of her young womanhood: Ellen and Fox, who had worked so hard to make The Keep a home; Uncle Theo, with his great wisdom and staunch support; dear Caroline, her oldest, closest friend – oh, how she missed Caroline – and Freddy herself, of course: that autocratic woman who had held them all together through those difficult years, after the three small children, Fliss and Mole and Susanna, had arrived from Kenya.

As she watched, Prue found that her thoughts were

450

wandering to other times and other Christmases. Sometimes Jo looked like his grandfather, her darling Johnny, just before he'd gone away to war, and sometimes he looked like Hal; and Sam was so like his father that, every now and again as he beamed proudly across at her, she could believe that it was Mole struggling to hold the tree upright whilst Jolyon stacked large stones round its base in the huge earthenware pot.

Fliss came in with the cardboard box of decorations she'd fetched down from the attic, and smiled at the workers.

'Here we are,' she said. 'Well done, Sam. What a fantastic tree.'

Both of them stood back to admire their efforts and then Sam began to unpack the decorations while Jo strolled over to the fire and continued to gaze upon his handiwork.

'It's a good tree,' he said. 'It'll be nice to have it up and dressed before I go, though it's a few days earlier than usual.'

'Are you ready for the great trek to the North?' asked Fliss. 'I'm glad that you're going to see Maria on the way. She must be so thrilled about that.'

'She is,' he said. 'It seemed the right thing to do. My problem is that I haven't got a present for her yet.' He frowned. 'It seems to be proving more difficult than it ought to be but I'm probably being oversensitive about it.'

'I think I know what you mean,' Prue said. 'It's important, isn't it? When there's been a breakdown and then a coming together again, the first present you give is significant, isn't it?'

He looked at her gratefully. 'That's exactly it. After all, she might so easily have made Christmas a bit of an issue but she didn't. She took on board what I said to her about giving us all space and I respect her for that. It was my idea that I should drop in and see her on my way to London to pick up Henrietta. She's put no pressure on at all. I'd like to show her that we've got a future. Just buying a box of chocolates or some soap seems a bit mere. Anyway, I shall have to make a decision very quickly. I thought I'd go into Totnes this afternoon and have a look round. Hang on, Sam. Don't try to reach too high or you'll have the whole tree over. Anyway, we ought to get the lights on before we decorate it. Wait a sec and I'll go and get the little stepladder.'

He went out.

'Isn't it wonderful?' said Prue contentedly. 'The dear fellow seems so much happier, doesn't he? And being able to forgive his mother is so much a part of it. Nice for Maria, but even more crucial for Jo. If he can be generous to her it will bring *him* such healing as well as new strength and confidence. All will be well, I feel sure of it.'

'Yes. Yes, I think so too,' Fliss agreed rather abstractedly. 'Actually, you've just given me an idea. Shan't be long.'

She followed Jolyon out of the hall, and Prue settled again in her corner. She watched Sam crouching over the box, turning over the decorations, bringing out much-loved objects: Victorian glass baubles, tiny carved wooden figures, glittering ropes of tinsel, and she recalled other trees and other Christmases, long past, and one in particular forty-five years ago. Hal and Kit had gone on to Devon at the beginning of the school holidays, she remembered, and she'd travelled from Bristol by train as soon as she'd finished work, arriving at The Keep late on Christmas Eve.

## Christmas 1965

When she comes into the hall, fetched from the station by Fox, they are all waiting for her. The tree, soaring up to the ceiling, is covered in lit candles, the only light apart from leaping flames in the great, granite fireplace. The tinsel and baubles shine and glitter, and tiny parcels, beautifully wrapped, hang from the stronger boughs. Holly and mistletoe, tied with scarlet ribbon, decorate the hall; mince pies and sherry are waiting on the table before the fire. She stands quite still, just inside the door, and stares in delight while the family smile at her pleasure.

'It's perfect,' she says at last and – as though she has released them from a spell – they surge forward to greet her, hugging and kissing her, making her welcome.

They gather about the fire, whilst Susanna and Mole crawl round the tree, feeling the presents piled beneath it and Hal, under the cover of conversation, kisses Fliss under the mistletoe whilst Kit watches them and smiles.

Later, Prue and Caroline, with the two girls and Hal and Theo, go to Midnight Mass. Caroline drives and Hal sits in the back with Fliss on his lap, whilst Prue and Kit squash in beside them. The old grey church is ablaze with candlelight and, when they come out, a cold white moon hangs in a starry sky. Their breath smokes in the freezing air and the frost crunches beneath their feet.

As the car pulls into the courtyard, the front door opens and the light from the hall streams down the steps and across the grass. Freddy stands waiting for them, tall and slim in her high-necked blouse and long velvet skirt, with a shawl about her shoulders.

'The children are in bed at last, stockings hung up,' she says, 'waiting for Father Christmas. Fox has made up the fire and Ellen has just brewed some hot coffee. Come in and get warm. And a very Happy Christmas to us all.'

They stand for a moment, listening to the Christmas bells ringing out across the quiet countryside, smiling at one another, and then they all go inside and close the door behind them.

'I can't believe we're really on our way,' Henrietta said, as they joined the M1 and headed to the North. 'And the traffic's not too bad, is it? Tomorrow would have been worse. Travelling on Christmas Eve would have been awful.'

'Susan seemed OK,' Jo said. 'Not as difficult as I thought she might be. Very matey, actually. Though with Maggie and Roger there I suppose she couldn't really be much else. They're absolutely thrilled. It was great to see them.'

Henrietta made a little face. 'She's got a soft spot for you, and it's difficult for her to be really negative when your family has known hers for such a long time, but she still gets very depressed and when we're on our own she does this boring preachy thing and tells me I need to be really sure and stuff like that. It's getting me down a bit, but thank God that the new nanny can start immediately after Christmas.

She's so nice and the children like her a lot. I think it will be fine.'

'It was lucky for us that Susan found someone so quickly. But can she afford to stay on in the house?'

Henrietta shrugged. 'There have been mutterings about Maggie and Roger selling the cottage and moving in on the top floor so that they can buy Iain out.'

Jo made a doubtful face. 'I heard that too. Would that be wise? Poor old Roger would certainly miss his sailing, and what about the dogs and the ponies?'

'Well, it wouldn't be easy, but all I'm saying is that it's under discussion. To be honest, I shall be glad to be out of it. I know that makes me sound a real cow but there's nothing I can do, and now that we're engaged it's changed the relationship between me and Susan somehow so that I don't feel that I'm being much comfort to her. I can't really settle back to it all and I don't like being so far away from you. It was just so nice having our own space. And I miss the dogs terribly, especially Tacker. He was just so sweet.'

'It's odd, isn't it, how life goes in cycles,' said Jo. 'Suddenly, out of the blue, something happens and everything changes.'

She nodded. 'It's a bit like you and your mum, isn't it? I'm glad that went OK.'

'I was a bit nervous,' he admitted. 'I thought there might be a touch of the old emotional drama once we were all on our own again but she was fine. She seems more balanced, calmer. I'm so glad she's decided to stay on for a bit with Penelope and Philip. They're such good friends and it gives everyone a breathing space.'

'And I think your present for her is a brilliant idea.'

'Well, it was Fliss's idea, really, but once we'd talked about it I knew she was right. I just hope she'll see the point of it.'

'Of course she will. I had the same problem about what to get for my mum. I think that she'll be really thrilled with the mobile, don't you? Hers is so old and out of date. It was so sweet of Fliss and Hal to invite her for Christmas Day. I'm glad she won't be on her own. So what have you bought for me, then?'

Jo pulled into the outside lane and put his foot down on the accelerator, remembering his conversation with Maggie a few weeks previously.

'It's just a thought, Jo,' she'd said, 'but I can see that there might be big changes coming up for us all, and poor Tacker misses Henrietta dreadfully. I know of someone who will take the ponies if it comes to it but the prospect of three dogs in London is a bit too much for me. What d'you think? Could you manage

457

Tacker, the two of you, in your gatehouse? He can be an early wedding present.'

He'd said 'yes' and arranged for Tacker to arrive the day after he and Henrietta got back to The Keep. She was watching him now, and he smiled.

'I've got you a small token of my esteem,' he said teasingly, 'but your real present will be waiting for you when we go home.'

'Home,' she said happily. 'Oh, Jo, won't it be fun?'

'That was a text from Henrietta,' Cordelia said, putting down her phone and picking up her glass. 'They've arrived safely at their hotel and everything is utterly wonderful. Let joy be unconfined.'

Angus slipped his arm around her. 'I'm sorry that we shan't be together for Christmas Day,' he said, not for the first time, 'but the boys thought it was such a great idea to take a house in Cornwall so that all the family could be together for the holiday that I didn't have the heart to refuse.'

'Of course not,' she said quickly, 'and I think it's important for you all to be together. I told you, I shall be very happy at The Keep, and after all, we'll be going to Pete and Julia at Trescairn for New Year together. That'll be great fun.'

He nodded and she felt relieved: it seemed that

they'd both entered into a tacit agreement that they should continue their relationship just the way it was. Cordelia had described to him her ideas for the new novel, and hinted at how hard she'd be working, and he'd told her about plans he'd made with Pete for an extended sailing trip in the Med next summer. Neither implied that their present living arrangements should change; both made it clear that they were extremely happy in each other's company.

'I told Henrietta that you and I were going to Trescairn for New Year,' she said, 'which was rather courageous of me, and she said, "Have a great time." Such a relief.'

'That's good,' he said. 'I can see that she'll need time to adjust to me being around but if she can accept our relationship it will be a miracle. I hope I'll get an invitation to the wedding.'

'Of course you will,' she said firmly. 'And meantime we'll play it by ear. Just as long as we can all keep playing happy families, that's all I care about.'

He chuckled, holding her closer. 'Don't you mean Cluedo?' he asked. 'Colonel Mustard and Mrs Peacock, in the bedroom, with the bottle.' He raised his glass. 'Happy Christmas, Dilly.'

\*     \*     \*

Fliss drove home alone from Midnight Mass. At least Susanna and Gus had been at church; she'd been so pleased to see them. At the last moment Hal had decided not to go; he would take Prue and Sam to the morning service, he'd said, whilst she and Susanna were organizing the lunch and waiting for Cordelia to arrive. Fliss had been surprised at his decision but she hadn't argued; he'd behaved as though there were some hidden agenda and she guessed that it might be to do with her present: perhaps it was a joint present from the three of them, Sam, Prue and Hal, and they wanted time together to sort it out. Anyway, she'd been slightly anxious at leaving Prue and Sam on their own together, the youngest and the eldest, although she wouldn't have wanted them to suspect such a thing. They were both very independent, and very capable. It was simply her mother-hen tendencies that made her worry about them.

As she drove through the archway she was struck by the oddness of seeing the gatehouse in darkness, though the lights shone out cheerfully from the hall. She put the car away and crossed the courtyard, climbed the steps and opened the door. To her surprise Prue was still up, sitting by the fire, and Hal was standing as if he'd just got to his feet, and was waiting for her. Sam was there too; obviously he'd had special dispensation to stay up late. He beamed at her – looking heartbreakingly like Mole – and she saw that all three of them were watching her in an oddly expectant way, with a kind of suppressed excitement. Puzzled, she shut the door, glancing round to see what it might be that they were so clearly hoping she would notice. From the corner of her eye she saw a figure step out from the shadows just behind her; she turned sharply with a little cry of alarm and Jamie said, 'Hi, Mum. Surprise! Happy Christmas,' and held out his arms to her.

Maria couldn't sleep. She looked at the bedside clock: twenty past twelve. It was Christmas Day; her first without Adam. Quickly she pulled on her dressing gown, slid her feet into her sheepskin slippers and went into the kitchen. Through the archway, in the sitting room, she'd put the tiny, pretty tree, standing it in a corner on a small, solid table. Its coloured lights comforted her on dark winter mornings and beneath its decorated branches she'd made a little pile of her presents. She was glad to be here; glad and grateful. Later she'd have Christmas lunch with Pen and Philip and one or two friends, all very civilized, and tomorrow she would be giving her own little party; her first since Adam had died. So many firsts . . . including telling Cordelia about Ed's disaster and having to sell the house. During the weekend of Hal's birthday party she and Cordelia had talked about it again, easily and calmly, divesting it of its nightmare proportions and giving her new confidence and a wonderful sense of release, so that soon – she knew the moment was not too far away now – soon, she'd be able to tell Pen the truth . . .

As the kettle boiled and she made some camomile tea she looked through the archway at the tree and the gaily packed parcels. Ed's was a flat oblong shape – probably a scarf, thought Maria, rather sadly, chosen by Rebecca – and Prue had rather given the game away with her big box of chocolates by writing 'Don't eat them all at once' on the greeting tag. Hal and Fliss's offering was of an alcoholic shape, though there was another small parcel with their names on the card. It was sweet of them to remember her, that's what mattered, but this year only one was of vital importance to her: Jolyon's large box-shaped present fascinated her.

'Be careful with it,' he'd warned her as they'd put it under the tree. 'It's very fragile,' and he'd looked at her, an intent, serious look so that she still wondered exactly what he'd meant. She'd promised she would take care of it and he'd given her a hug; a real hug, just like his schoolboy hugs, and she'd returned it joyfully, thankfully. She'd taken great trouble over her present for him. It had to be something special, something that showed him that she was trying to change, and regretted how she'd behaved to him in the past. Nothing seemed to meet this requirement. Then one morning, quite suddenly, she'd known what it should be. She'd found the little leather box in her large jewellery box and taken it out and opened it: a pair of delicately chased gold cufflinks, old and very valuable. They'd belonged to her grandfather – her mother's father – and once, many years ago, Ed and Jolyon had argued about who should have them.

'I'm the eldest,' Jolyon had said, 'they should be mine,' and Ed had protested, and then she'd taken the cufflinks and put them away, saying that they were both too young to wear cufflinks, and Jolyon had watched her with an expression of bitterness on his face. He'd known that Ed was her favourite and that secretly she'd wanted Ed to have them.

She'd found some plain gold paper and wrapped up the cufflinks in their little leather box and had given them to Jolyon, praying that when he opened them he would remember and understand, and would accept them in the new spirit in which she was offering them.

Now, she carried her mug of tea across to the tree and put it on the low table, and kneeled down to look at the box Jolyon had given her. She knew what he'd written on the card; she'd already looked, longing for it to be a special message. It said, 'Happy Christmas, Mum, love Jo', and there were two kisses. At least he'd written the word 'Mum' and she knew that even this was a small but crucial step. Gently she lifted the box out from amongst the other presents: it was Christmas morning, and she would open it now. Her heartbeat quickened. Would it be some mindless offering, quickly chosen, hastily wrapped? Or had he really thought about it; about her?

With trembling fingers she removed the card and put it on the table beside her mug, then she tore the paper away. The box was an ordinary, plain, used cardboard box, sealed with Sellotape. Maria ripped the sticky tape off and opened the two flaps. The box was full of bubble wrap and she put both her hands in so as to ease out the contents. It was a solid, rounded object, though not particularly heavy, and she set it down on the rug and pulled the bubble wrap apart so as to reveal it. As the wrapping fell away she sat back on her heels in amazement, gazing at the pretty colours; her fingers lightly touched the delicate patterns, tracing the cracks. Tears slipped down her cheeks and her heart brimmed with grateful joy. It was the ginger jar.